Five Tales

By

John Galsworthy

Life calls the tune—we dance

London
William Heinemann

LONDON: WILLIAM HEINEMANN, 1918.

To

ANDRÉ CHEVRILLON

Contents

THE FIRST AND THE LAST

I

"So the last shall be first, and the first last."—HOLY
WRIT.

IT was a dark room at that hour of six in the evening,
when just the single oil reading-lamp under its green
shade let fall a dapple of light over the Turkey carpet ;
over the covers of books taken out of the book-shelves,
and the open pages of the one selected ; over the deep
blue and gold of the coffee service on the little old
stool with its Oriental embroidery. Very dark in the
winter, with drawn curtains, many rows of leather-bound
volumes, oak-panelled walls and ceiling. So large, too,
that the lighted spot before the fire where he sat was
just an oasis. But that was what Keith Darrant liked,
after his day's work—the hard early morning study of
his " cases," the fret and strain of the day in court ;
it was his rest, these two hours before dinner, with
books, coffee, a pipe, and sometimes a nap. In red
Turkish slippers and his old brown velvet coat, he was
well suited to that framing of glow and darkness. A
painter would have seized avidly on his clear-cut,
yellowish face, with its black eyebrows twisting up
over eyes—grey or brown, one could hardly tell, and
its dark grizzling hair still plentiful, in spite of those
daily hours of wig. He seldom thought of his work
while he sat there, throwing off with practised ease the
strain of that long attention to the multiple threads
of argument and evidence to be disentangled—
work profoundly interesting, as a rule, to his clear

B 2

intellect, trained to almost instinctive rejection of all but the essential, to selection of what was legally vital out of the mass of confused tactical and human detail presented to his scrutiny; yet sometimes tedious and wearing. As for instance to-day, when he had suspected his client of perjury, and was almost convinced that he must throw up his brief. He had disliked the weak-looking, white-faced fellow from the first, and his nervous, shifty answers, his prominent startled eyes—a type too common in these days of canting tolerations and weak humanitarianism; no good, no good!

Of the three books he had taken down, a volume of Voltaire—curious fascination that Frenchman had, for all his destructive irony!—a volume of Burton's travels, and Stevenson's " New Arabian Nights," he had pitched upon the last. He felt, that evening, the want of something sedative, a desire to rest from thought of any kind. The court had been crowded, stuffy; the air, as he walked home, soft, sou'-westerly, charged with coming moisture, no quality of vigour in it; he felt relaxed, tired, even nervy, and for once the loneliness of his house seemed strange and comfortless.

Lowering the lamp, he turned his face towards the fire. Perhaps he would get a sleep before that boring dinner at the Tellasson's. He wished it were vacation, and Maisie back from school. A widower for many years, he had lost the habit of a woman about him; yet to-night he had a positive yearning for the society of his little daughter, with her quick ways, and bright, dark eyes. Curious what perpetual need of a woman some men had! His brother Laurence—wasted—all through women—atrophy of will power! A man on the edge of things; living from hand to mouth; his

gifts all down at heel! One would have thought the
Scottish strain might have saved him; and yet, when
a Scotsman did begin to go downhill, who could go
faster? Curious that their mother's blood should have
worked so differently in her two sons. He himself
had always felt he owed all his success to it.

His thoughts went off at a tangent to a certain issue
troubling his legal conscience. He had not wavered
in the usual assumption of omniscience, but he was by
no means sure that he had given right advice. Well!
Without that power to decide and hold to decision in
spite of misgiving, one would never have been fit for
one's position at the Bar, never have been fit for anything. The longer he lived, the more certain he
became of the prime necessity of virile and decisive
action in all the affairs of life. A word and a blow—
and the blow first! Doubts, hesitations, sentiment—
the muling and puking of this twilight age——! And
there welled up on his handsome face a smile that was
almost devilish—the tricks of firelight are so many!
It faded again in sheer drowsiness; he slept. . . .

He woke with a start, having a feeling of something
out beyond the light, and without turning his head
said: "What's that?" There came a sound as if
somebody had caught his breath. He turned up the
lamp.

"Who's there?"

A voice over by the door answered:

"Only I—Larry."

Something in the tone, or perhaps just being startled
out of sleep like this, made him shiver. He said:

"I was asleep. Come in!"

It was noticeable that he did not get up, or even turn
his head, now that he knew who it was, but waited,

his half-closed eyes fixed on the fire, for his brother to come forward. A visit from Laurence was not an unmixed blessing. He could hear him breathing, and became conscious of a scent of whisky. Why could not the fellow at least abstain when he was coming here ! It was so childish, so lacking in any sense of proportion or of decency ! And he said sharply :

" Well, Larry, what is it ? "

It was always something. He often wondered at the strength of that sense of trusteeship, which kept him still tolerant of the troubles, amenable to the petitions of this brother of his ; or was it just " blood " feeling, a Highland sense of loyalty to kith and kin ; an old-time quality which judgment and half his instincts told him was weakness, but which, in spite of all, bound him to the distressful fellow ? Was he drunk now, that he kept lurking out there by the door ? And he said less sharply :

" Why don't you come and sit down ? "

He was coming now, avoiding the light, skirting along the walls just beyond the radiance of the lamp, his feet and legs to the waist brightly lighted, but his face disintegrated in shadow, like the face of a dark ghost.

" Are you ill, man ? "

Still no answer, save a shake of that head, and the passing up of a hand, out of the light, to the ghostly forehead under the dishevelled hair. The scent of whisky was stronger now ; and Keith thought :

' He really is drunk. Nice thing for the new butler to see ! If he can't behave——'

The figure against the wall heaved a sigh—so truly from an overburdened heart that Keith was conscious with a certain dismay of not having yet fathomed the

cause of this uncanny silence. He got up, and, back
to the fire, said with a brutality born of nerves rather
than design :

" What is it, man ? Have you committed a murder,
that you stand there dumb as a fish ? "

For a second no answer at all, not even of breathing ;
then, just the whisper :

" Yes."

The sense of unreality which so helps one at moments
of disaster enabled Keith to say vigorously :

" By Jove ! You *have* been drinking ! "

But it passed at once into deadly apprehension.

" What do you mean ? Come here, where I can see
you. What's the matter with you, Larry ? "

With a sudden lurch and dive, his brother left the
shelter of the shadow, and sank into a chair in the
circle of light. And another long, broken sigh escaped
him.

" There's nothing the matter with me, Keith ! It's
true ! "

Keith stepped quickly forward, and stared down
into his brother's face ; and instantly he saw that it
was true. No one could have simulated the look in
those eyes—of horrified wonder, as if they would never
again get on terms with the face to which they belonged.
To see them squeezed the heart—only real misery
could look like that. Then that sudden pity became
angry bewilderment.

" What in God's name is this nonsense ? "

But it was significant that he lowered his voice ;
went over to the door, too, to see if it were shut.
Laurence had drawn his chair forward, huddling over
the fire—a thin figure, a worn, high-cheekboned face
with deep-sunk blue eyes, and wavy hair all ruffled

a face that still had a certain beauty.   Putting a hand on that lean shoulder, Keith said :

" Come, Larry ! Pull yourself together, and drop exaggeration."

" It's true, I tell you ; I've killed a man."

The noisy violence of that outburst acted like a *douche*. What was the fellow about—shouting out such words ! But suddenly Laurence lifted his hands and wrung them.   The gesture was so utterly painful that it drew a quiver from Keith's face.

" Why did you come here," he said, " and tell *me* this ? "

Larry's face was really unearthly sometimes, such strange gleams passed up on to it !

" Whom else should I tell ? I came to know what I'm to do, Keith ? Give myself up, or what ? "

At that sudden introduction of the practical Keith felt his heart twitch.   Was it then as real as all that ? But he said, very quietly :

" Just tell me—How did it come about, this—affair ? "

That question linked the dark, gruesome, fantastic nightmare on to actuality.

" When did it happen ? "

" Last night."

In Larry's face there was—there had always been—something childishly truthful. He would never stand a chance in court ! And Keith said :

" How ? Where ? You'd better tell me quietly from the beginning. Drink this coffee ; it'll clear your head."

Laurence took the little blue cup and drained it.

" Yes," he said.   " It's like this, Keith.   There's a girl I've known for some months now——"

Women! And Keith said between his teeth:
" Well ? "

" Her father was a Pole who died over here when
she was sixteen, and left her all alone. A man called
Walenn, a mongrel American, living in the same house,
married her, or pretended to—she's very pretty,
Keith—and left her with a baby six months old, and
another coming. That one died, and she did nearly.
Then she starved till another fellow took her on. She
lived with him two years; then Walenn turned up
again, and made her go back to him. The brute used
to beat her black and blue, all for nothing. Then he
left her again. When I met her she'd lost her elder
child, too, and was taking anybody who came along."

He suddenly looked up into Keith's face.

" But I've never met a sweeter woman, nor a truer,
that I swear. Woman! She's only twenty now! When
I went to her last night, that brute—that Walenn—had
found her out again; and when he came for me, swag-
gering and bullying—Look! "—he touched a dark mark
on his forehead—" I took his throat in my hands, and
when I let go——"

" Yes ? "

" Dead. I never knew till afterwards that she was
hanging on to him behind."

Again he made that gesture—wringing his hands.

In a hard dry voice Keith said:

" What did you do then ? "

" We sat by—by—it a long time. Then I carried
it on my back down the street, round a corner to an
archway."

" How far ? "

" About fifty yards."

" Was anyone—did anyone see ? "

" No."

" What time ? "

" Three."

" And then ? "

" Went back to her."

" Why—in Heaven's name ? "

" She was lonely and afraid ; so was I, Keith.'

" Where is this place ? "

" Forty-two, Borrow Street, Soho."

" And the archway ? "

" Corner of Glove Lane."

" Good God ! Why—I saw it in the paper ! "

And seizing the journal that lay on his bureau, Keith read again that paragraph : " The body of a man was found this morning under an archway in Glove Lane, Soho. From marks about the throat grave suspicions of foul play are entertained. The body had apparently been robbed, and nothing was discovered leading to identification."

It was real earnest, then. Murder ! His own brother ! He faced round and said :

" You saw this in the paper, and dreamed it. Understand—you dreamed it ! "

The wistful answer came :

" If only I had, Keith—if only I had ! "

In his turn, Keith very nearly wrung his hands.

" Did you take anything from the—body ? "

" This dropped while we were struggling."

It was an empty envelope with a South American post-mark addressed : " Patrick Walenn, Simon's Hotel, Farrier Street, London." Again with that twitching in his heart, Keith said :

" Put it in the fire."

Then suddenly he stooped to pluck it out. By that

command—he had—identified himself with this—
this—— But he did not pluck it out. It blackened,
writhed, and vanished. And once more he said:

"What in God's name made you come here and tell
me?"

"You know about these things. I didn't mean to
kill him. I love the girl. What shall I do, Keith?"

Simple! How simple! To ask what he was to do!
It was like Larry! And he said:

"You were not seen, you think?"

"It's a dark street. There was no one about."

"When did you leave this girl the second time?"

"About seven o'clock."

"Where did you go?"

"To my rooms."

"In Fitzroy Street?"

"Yes."

"Did anyone see you come in?"

"No."

"What have you done since?"

"Sat there."

"Not been out?"

"No."

"Not seen the girl?"

"No."

"You don't know, then, what she's done since?"

"No."

"Would she give you away?"

"Never."

"Would she give herself away—hysteria?"

"No."

"Who knows of your relations with her?"

"No one."

"No one?"

" I don't know who should, Keith."

" Did anyone see you going in last night, when you first went to her ? "

" No. She lives on the ground floor. I've got keys."

" Give them to me. What else have you that connects you with her ? "

" Nothing."

" In your rooms ? "

" No."

" No photographs. No letters ? "

" No."

" Be careful."

" Nothing."

" No one saw you going back to her the second time ? "

" No."

" No one saw you leave her in the morning ? "

" No."

" You were fortunate. Sit down again, man. I must think."

Think ! Think out this accursed thing—so beyond all thought, and all belief. But he could not think. Not a coherent thought would come. And he began again :

" Was it his first reappearance with her ? "

" Yes."

" She told you so ? "

" Yes."

" How did he find out where she was ? "

" I don't know."

" How drunk were you ? "

" I was not drunk."

" How much had you drunk ? "

" About two bottles of claret—nothing."

" You say you didn't mean to kill him ? "

" No—God knows ! "

" That's something. What made you choose the arch ? "

" It was the first dark place."

" Did his face look as if he had been strangled ? "

" Don't ! "

" Did it ? "

" Yes."

" Very disfigured ? "

" Yes."

" Did you look to see if his clothes were marked ? "

" No."

" Why not ? "

" Why not ? My God ! If you had done it—— ! "

" You say he was disfigured.   Would he be recognisable ? "

" I don't know."

" When she lived with him last—where was that ? "

" I don't know for certain.   Pimlico, I think."

" Not Soho ? "

" No."

" How long has she been at the Soho place ? "

" Nearly a year."

" Always the same rooms ? "

" Yes."

" Is there anyone living in that house or street who would be likely to know her as his wife ? "

" I don't think so."

" What was he ? "

" I should think he was a professional ' bully.' "

" I see.   Spending most of his time abroad, then ? "

" Yes."

" Do you know if he was known to the police ? "

" I haven't heard of it."

" Now, listen, Larry. When you leave here go straight home, and don't go out till I come to you, to-morrow morning. Promise that ! "

" I promise."

" I've got a dinner engagement. I'll think this out. Don't drink. Don't talk ! Pull yourself together."

" Don't keep me longer than you can help, Keith ! "

That white face, those eyes, that shaking hand ! With a twinge of pity in the midst of all the turbulence of his revolt, and fear, and disgust, Keith put his hand on his brother's shoulder, and said :

" Courage ! "

And suddenly he thought : ' My God ! Courage ! I shall want it all myself ! '

II

LAURENCE DARRANT, leaving his brother's house in the Adelphi, walked northwards, rapidly, slowly, rapidly again. For, if there are men who by force of will do one thing only at a time, there are men who from lack of will do now one thing, now another, with equal intensity. To such natures, to be gripped by the Nemesis which attends the lack of self-control is no reason for being more self-controlled. Rather does it foster their pet feeling : " What matter ? To-morrow we die ! " The effort of will required to go to Keith had relieved, exhausted and exasperated him. In accordance with those three feelings was the progress of his walk. He started from the door with the fixed resolve to go home and stay there quietly till Keith

came. He was in Keith's hands, Keith would know
what was to be done. But he had not gone three
hundred yards before he felt so utterly weary, body
and soul, that if he had but had a pistol in his pocket
he would have shot himself in the street. Not even
the thought of the girl—this young unfortunate with
her strange devotion, who had kept him straight these
last five months, who had roused in him a depth of
feeling he had never known before—would have
availed against that sudden black dejection. Why
go on—a waif at the mercy of his own nature, a straw
blown here and there by every gust which rose in him ?
Why not have done with it for ever, and take it out
in sleep ?

He was approaching the fatal street, where he and
the girl, that early morning, had spent the hours
clutched together, trying in the refuge of love to
forget for a moment their horror and fear. Should he
go in ? He had promised Keith not to. Why had he
promised ? He caught sight of himself in a chemist's
lighted window. Miserable, shadowy brute ! And he
remembered suddenly a dog he had picked up once
in the streets of Pera, a black-and-white creature—
different to the other dogs, not one of their breed, a
pariah of pariahs, who had strayed there somehow.
He had taken it home to the house where he was
staying, contrary to all custom of the country ; had
got fond of it ; had shot it himself, sooner than leave
it behind again to the mercies of its own kind in the
streets. Twelve years ago ! And those sleeve-links
made of little Turkish coins he had brought back for
the girl at the hairdresser's in Chancery Lane where
he used to get shaved—pretty creature, like a wild rose.
He had asked of her a kiss for payment. What queer

emotion when she put her face forward to his lips—a sort of passionate tenderness and shame, at the softness and warmth of that flushed cheek, at her beauty and trustful gratitude. She would soon have given herself to him—that one! He had never gone there again! And to this day he did not know why he had abstained; to this day did not know whether he were glad or sorry not to have plucked that rose. He must surely have been very different then! Queer business, life—queer, queer business!—to go through it never knowing what you would do next. Ah! to be like Keith, steady, buttoned-up in success; a brass pot, a pillar of society! Once, as a boy, he had been within an ace of killing Keith, for sneering at him. Once in Southern Italy he had been near killing a driver who was flogging his horse. And now, that dark-faced, swinish bully who had ruined the girl he had grown to love—he had done it! Killed him! Killed a man!

He who did not want to hurt a fly. The chemist's window comforted him with the sudden thought that he had at home that which made him safe, in case they should arrest him. He would never again go out without some of those little white tablets sewn into the lining of his coat. Restful, even exhilarating thought! They said a man should not take his own life. Let *them* taste horror—those glib citizens! Let them live as that girl had lived, as millions lived all the world over, under their canting dogmas! A man might rather even take his life than watch their cursed inhumanities.

He went into the chemist's for a bromide; and, while the man was mixing it, stood resting one foot like a tired horse. The "life" he had squeezed out of that fellow! After all, a billion living creatures gave up life each day, had it squeezed out of th m, mostly. And perhaps not one a day deserved de 1th so much as that loathly fellow. Life ! a breath —a flame ! Nothing ! Why, then, this icy clutching at his heart ?

The chemist brought the draught.

" Not sleeping, sir ? "

" No."

The man's eyes seemed to say : " Yes ! Burning the candle at both ends—I know ! " Odd life, a chemist's ; pills and powders all day long, to hold the machinery of men together ! Devilish odd trade !

In going out he caught the reflection of his face in a mirror ; it seemed too good altogether for a man who had committed murder. There was a sort of brightness underneath, an amiability lurking about its shadows ; how—how could it be the face of a man who had done what he had done ? His head felt lighter now, his feet lighter ; he walked rapidly again.

Curious feeling of relief and oppression all at once ! Frightful—to long for company, for talk, for distraction ; and—to be afraid of it ! The girl—the girl and Keith were now the only persons who would not give him that feeling of dread. And, of those two—Keith was not—— ! Who could consort with one who was never wrong, a successful, righteous fellow ; a chap built so that he knew nothing about himself, wanted to know nothing, a chap all solid actions. To be a quicksand swallowing up one's own resolutions was bad enough ! But to be like Keith—all will-power, marching along, treading down his own feelings and weaknesses !—No ! One could not make a comrade of a man like Keith, even if he were one's brother ? The only creature in all the world was the girl. She

alo: e knew and felt what he was feeling ; would put
up with him and love him whatever he did, or was done
to h'm. He stopped and took shelter in a doorway, to
ligh: a cigarette.

He had suddenly a fearful wish to pass the archway
where he had placed the body ; a fearful wish that had
no sense, no end in view, no anything ; just an insensate
craving to see the dark place again. He crossed
Borrow Street to the little lane. There was only one
person visible, a man on the far side with his shoulders
hunched against the wind ; a short, dark figure which
crossed and came towards him in the flickering lamplight. What a face ! Yellow, ravaged, clothed almost
to the eyes in a stubbly greyish growth of beard, with
blackish teeth, and haunting bloodshot eyes. And
what a figure of rags—one shoulder higher than the
other, one leg a little lame, and thin ! A surge of feeling
came up in Laurence for this creature, more unfortunate
than himself. There were lower depths than his !

"Well, brother," he said, "*you* don't look too
prosperous ! "

The smile which gleamed out on the man's face
seemed as unlikely as a smile on a scarecrow.

"Prosperity doesn't come my way," he said in a
rusty voice. "I'm a failure—always been a failure.
And yet—you wouldn't think it, would you ?—I was
a minister of religion once."

Laurence held out a shilling. But the man shook his
head.

"Keep your money," he said. "I've got more
than you to-day, I daresay. But thank you for taking
a little interest. That's worth more than money to a
man that's down."

"You're right."

" Yes," the rusty voice went on ; " I'd as soon die as go on living as I do. And now I've lost my self-respect. Often wondered how long a starving man could go without losing his self-respect. Not so very long. You take my word for that." And without the slightest change in the monotony of that creaking voice he added :

" Did you read of the murder ?   Just here.   I've been looking at the place."

The words : " So have I ! " leaped up to Laurence's lips ; he choked them down with a sort of terror.

" I wish you better luck," he said.   " Good-night ! " and hurried away. A sort of ghastly laughter was forcing its way up in his throat. Was everyone talking of the murder he had committed ? Even the very scarecrows ?

III

THERE are some natures so constituted that, due to be hung at ten o'clock, they will play chess at eight. Such men invariably rise. They make especially good bishops, editors, judges, impresarios, Prime ministers, money-lenders, and generals ; in fact, fill with exceptional credit any position of power over their fellow-men. They have spiritual cold storage, in which are preserved their nervous systems. In such men there is little or none of that fluid sense and continuity of feeling known under those vague terms, speculation, poetry, philosophy. Men of facts and of decision, switching imagination on and off at will, subordinating sentiment to reason . . . one does not think of them when watching wind ripple over cornfields, or swallows flying.

C 2

Keith Darrant had need for being of that breed during his dinner at the Tellassons. It was just eleven when he issued from the big house in Portland Place and refrained from taking a cab. He wanted to walk that he might better think. What crude and wanton irony there was in his situation ! To have been made father-confessor of a murderer, he—well on towards a judgeship ! With his contempt for the kind of weakness which landed men in such abysses, he felt it all so sordid, so " impossible," that he could hardly bring his mind to bear on it at all. And yet he must, because of two powerful instincts—self-preservation and blood-loyalty.

The wind had still the sapping softness of the afternoon, but rain had held off so far. It was warm, and he unbuttoned his fur overcoat. The nature of his thoughts deepened the dark austerity of his face, whose thin, well-cut lips were always pressing together, as if, by meeting, to dispose of each thought as it came up. He moved along the crowded pavements glumly. That air of festive conspiracy which drops with the darkness on to lighted streets, galled him. He turned off on a darker route.

This ghastly business ! Convinced of its reality, he yet could not see it. The thing existed in his mind, not as a picture, but as a piece of irrefutable evidence. Larry had not meant to do it, of course. But it was murder, all the same. Men like Larry—weak, impulsive, sentimental, introspective creatures—did they ever mean what they did ? This man, this Walenn, was, by all accounts, better dead than alive ; no need to waste a thought on him ! But, crime—the ugliness— Justice unsatisfied ! Crime concealed—and his own share in the concealment ! And yet—brother to

brother! Surely no one could demand action from him!
It was only a question of what he was going to advise
Larry to do. To keep silent, and disappear? Had that
a chance of success? Perhaps—if the answers to his
questions had been correct. But this girl! Suppose
the dead man's relationship to her were ferreted out,
could she be relied on not to endanger Larry? These
women were all the same, unstable as water, emotional,
shiftless—pests of society. Then, too, a crime un-
tracked, dogging all his brother's after life; a secret
following him wherever he might vanish to; hanging
over him, watching for some drunken moment, to slip
out of his lips. It was bad to think of. A clean breast
of it? But his heart twitched within him. " Brother
of Mr. Keith Darrant, the well-known King's Counsel"
—visiting a woman of the town, strangling with his
bare hands the woman's husband! No intention to
murder, but—a dead man! A dead man carried out
of the house, laid under a dark archway! Provocation!
Recommended to mercy—penal servitude for life!
Was that the advice he was going to give Larry to-
morrow morning?

And he had a sudden vision of shaven men with
clay-coloured features, run, as it were, to seed, as he
had seen them once in Pentonville, when he had gone
there to visit a prisoner. Larry! Whom, as a baby
creature, he had watched straddling; whom, as a
little fellow, he had fagged; whom he had seen through
scrapes at college; to whom he had lent money time
and again, and time and again admonished in his
courses. Larry! Five years younger than himself;
and committed to his charge by their mother when
she died. To become for life one of those men with
faces like diseased plants; with no hair but a bushy

stubble ; with arrows marked on their yellow clothes !
Larry ! One of those men herded like sheep ; at the
beck and call of common men ! A gentleman, his own
brother, to live that slave's life, to be ordered here and
there, year after year, day in, day out. Something
snapped within him. He could not give that advice.
Impossible ! But if not, he must make sure of his
ground, must verify, must know. This Glove Lane—
this archway ? It would not be far from where he was
that very moment. He looked for someone of whom
to make enquiry. A policeman was standing at the
corner, his stolid face illumined by a lamp ; capable
and watchful—an excellent officer, no doubt ; but,
turning his head away, Keith passed him without a
word. Strange to feel that cold, uneasy feeling in
presence of the law ! A grim little driving home of what
it all meant ! Then, suddenly, he saw that the turning
to his left was Borrow Street itself. He walked up one
side, crossed over, and returned. He passed Number
Forty-two, a small house with business names printed
on the lifeless windows of the first and second floors ;
with dark curtained windows on the ground floor, or
was there just a slink of light in one corner ? Which
way had Larry turned ? Which way under that grisly
burden ? Fifty paces of this squalid street—narrow,
and dark, and empty, thank heaven ! Glove Lane !
Here it was ! A tiny runlet of a street. And here——— ! ·
He had run right on to the arch, a brick bridge con-
necting two portions of a warehouse, and dark indeed.
" That's right; gov'nor ! That's the place ! " He
needed all his self-control to turn leisurely to the
speaker. " 'Ere's where they found the body—very
spot—leanin' up 'ere. They ain't got 'im yet. Lytest
—me lord ! "

It was a ragged boy holding out a dilapidated yellowish journal. His lynx eyes peered up from under lanky wisps of hair, and his voice had the proprietary note of one making " a corner " in his news. Keith took the paper and gave him twopence. He even found a sort of comfort in the young ghoul's hanging about there ; it meant that others besides himself had come morbidly to look. By the dim lamplight he read : " Glove Lane garrotting mystery. Nothing has yet been discovered of the murdered man's identity ; from the cut of his clothes he is supposed to be a foreigner." The boy had vanished, and Keith saw the figure of a policeman coming slowly down this gutter of a street. A second's hesitation, and he stood firm. Nothing obviously could have brought him here save this " mystery," and he stayed quietly staring at the arch. The policeman moved up abreast. Keith saw that he was the one whom he had passed just now. He noted the cold offensive question die out of the man's eyes when they caught the gleam of white shirt-front under the opened fur collar. And holding up the paper, he said :

" Is this where the man was found ? "

" Yes, sir."

" Still a mystery, I see ? "

" Well, we can't always go by the papers. But I don't fancy they do know much about it, yet."

" Dark spot. Do fellows sleep under here ? "

The policeman nodded. " There's not an arch in London where we don't get 'em sometimes."

" Nothing found on him—I think I read ? "

" Not a copper. Pockets inside out. There's some funny characters about this quarter. Greeks, Hitalians —all sorts."

Queer sensation this, of being glad of a policeman's confidential tone !

" Well, good-night ! "

" Good-night, sir. Good-night ! "

He looked back from Borrow Street. The policeman was still standing there holding up his lantern, so that its light fell into the archway, as if trying to read its secret.

Now that he had seen this dark, deserted spot, the chances seemed to him much better. " Pockets inside out ! " Either Larry had had presence of mind to do a very clever thing, or someone had been at the body before the police found it. That was the more likely. A dead backwater of a place ! At three o'clock—loneliest of all hours—Larry's five minutes' grim excursion to and fro might well have passed unseen ! Now, it all depended on the girl ; on whether Laurence had been seen coming to her or going away ; on whether, if the man's relationship to her were discovered, she could be relied on to say nothing. There was not a soul in Borrow Street now ; hardly even a lighted window ; and he took one of those rather desperate decisions only possible to men daily accustomed to the instant taking of responsibility. He would go to her, and see for himself. He came to the door of Forty-two, obviously one of those which are only shut at night, and tried the larger key. It fitted, and he was in a gas-lighted passage, with an oil-clothed floor, and a single door to his left. He stood there undecided. She must be made to understand that he knew everything. She must not be told more than that he was a friend of Larry's. She must not be frightened, yet must be forced to give her very soul away. A hostile witness—not to be treated as hostile—

a matter for delicate handling ! But his knock was not answered.

` Should he give up this nerve-racking, bizarre effort to come at a basis of judgment ; go away, and just tell Laurence that he could not advise him ? And then— what ? Something *must* be done. He knocked again. Still no answer. And with that impatience of being thwarted, natural to him, and fostered to the full by the conditions of his life, he tried the other key. It worked, and he opened the door. Inside all was dark, but a voice from some way off, with a sort of breathless relief in its foreign tones, said :

"Oh! then it's you, Larry! Why did you knock? I was so frightened. Turn up the light, dear. Come in!"

Feeling by the door for a switch in the pitch blackness he was conscious of arms round his neck, a warm thinly clad body pressed to his own ; then withdrawn as quickly, with a gasp, and the most awful terror-stricken whisper :

"Oh! Who is it ?"

With a glacial shiver down his own spine, Keith answered :

"A friend of Laurence. Don't be frightened!"

There was such silence that he could hear a clock ticking, and the sound of his own hand passing over the surface of the wall, trying to find the switch. He found it, and in the light which leaped up he saw, stiffened against a dark curtain evidently screening off a bedroom, a girl standing, holding a long black coat together at her throat, so that her face with its pale brown hair, short and square-cut and curling up underneath, had an uncanny look of being detached from any body. Her face was so alabaster pale that the staring, startled eyes, dark blue or brown, and the faint rose of the parted lips, were like colour stainings on a white mask ; and it had a strange delicacy, truth, and pathos, such as only suffering brings. Though not susceptible to æsthetic emotion, Keith was curiously affected. He said gently :

" You needn't be afraid. I haven't come to do you harm—quite the contrary. May I sit down and talk ? " And, holding up the keys, he added : " Laurence wouldn't have given me these, would he, if he hadn't trusted me ? "

Still she did not move, and he had the impression that he was looking at a spirit—a spirit startled out of its flesh. Nor at the moment did it seem in the least strange that he should conceive such an odd thought. He stared round the room—clean and tawdry, with its tarnished gilt mirror, marble-topped side-table, and plush-covered sofa. Twenty years and more since he had been in such a place. And he said :

" Won't you sit down ? I'm sorry to have startled you."

But still she did not move, whispering :

" Who are you, please ? "

And, moved suddenly beyond the realm of caution by the terror in that whisper, he answered :

" Larry's brother."

She uttered a little sigh of relief which went to Keith's heart, and, still holding the dark coat together at her throat, came forward and sat down on the sofa. He could see that her feet, thrust into slippers, were bare ; with her short hair, and those candid startled eyes, she looked like a tall child. He drew up a chair and said :

" You must forgive me coming at such an hour ; he's told me, you see."

He expected her to flinch and gasp; but she only clasped her hands together on her knees, and said :

" Yes ? "

Then horror and discomfort rose up in him, afresh.

" An awful business ! "

Her whisper echoed him :

" Yes, oh ! yes ! Awful—it is awful ! "

And suddenly realising that the man must have fallen dead just where he was sitting, Keith became stock silent, staring at the floor.

" Yes," she whispered ; " just there. I see him now always falling ! "

How she said that ! With what a strange gentle despair ! In this girl of evil life, who had brought on them this tragedy, what was it which moved him to a sort of unwilling compassion ?

" You look very young," he said.

" I am twenty."

" And you are fond of—my brother ? "

" I would die for him."

Impossible to mistake the tone of her voice, or the look in her eyes, true deep Slav eyes ; dark brown, not blue as he had thought at first.   It was a very pretty face—either her life had not eaten into it yet, or the suffering of these last hours had purged away those marks ; or perhaps this devotion of hers to Larry. He felt strangely at sea, sitting there with this child of twenty ; he, over forty, a man of the world, professionally used to every side of human nature.   But he said, stammering a little :

" I—I have come to see how far you can save him. Listen, and just answer the questions I put to you."

She raised her hands, squeezed them together, and murmured :

" Oh ! I will answer anything."

" This man, then—your—your husband—was he a bad man ? "

" A dreadful man."

" Before he came here last night, how long since you saw him ? "

" Eighteen months."

" Where did you live when you saw him last ? "

" In Pimlico."

" Does anybody about here know you as Mrs. Walenn ? "

" No. When I came here, after my little girl died, I came to live a bad life. Nobody knows me at all. I am quite alone."

" If they discover who he was, they will look for his wife ? "

" I do not know. He did not let people think I was married to him. I was very young ; he treated many, I think, like me."

" Do you think he was known to the police ? "

She shook her head. " He was very clever."

" What is your name now ? "

" Wanda Livinska."

" Were you known by that name before you were married ? "

" Wanda is my Christian name. Livinska—I just call myself."

" I see ; since you came here."

" Yes."

" Did my brother ever see this man before last night ? "

" Never."

" You had told him about his treatment of you ? "

" Yes.   And that man first went for him."

" I saw the mark.   Do you think anyone saw my brother come to you ? "

" I do not know.   He says not."

" Can you tell if anyone saw him carrying the—the thing away ? "

" No one in this street—I was looking."

" Nor coming back ? "

" No one."

" Nor going out in the morning ? "

" I do not think it."

" Have you a servant ? "

" Only a woman who comes at nine in the morning for an hour."

" Does she know Larry ? "

" No."

" Friends, acquaintances ? "

" No ; I am very quiet.   And since I knew your brother, I see no one.   Nobody comes here but him for a long time now."

" How long ? "

" Five months."

" Have you been out to-day ? "

" No."

" What have you been doing ? "

" Crying."

It was said with a certain dreadful simplicity, and pressing her hands together, she went on :

" He is in danger, because of me.   I am so afraid for him."

Holding up his hand to check that emotion, he said :

" Look at me ! "

She fixed those dark eyes on him, and in her bare throat, from which the coat had fallen back, he could see her resolutely swallowing down her agitation.

" If the worst comes to the worst, and this man is traced to you, can you trust yourself not to give my brother away ? "

Her eyes shone. She got up and went to the fireplace :

" Look ! I have burned all the things he has given me—even his picture. Now I have nothing from him."

Keith, too, got up.

" Good ! One more question : Do the police know you, because—because of your life ? "

She shook her head, looking at him intently, with those mournfully true eyes. And he felt a sort of shame.

" I was obliged to ask. Do you know where he lives ? "

" Yes."

" You must not go there. And he must not come to you, here."

Her lips quivered ; but she bowed her head. Suddenly he found her quite close to him, speaking almost in a whisper :

" Please do not take him from me altogether. I will be so careful. I will not do anything to hurt him ; but if I cannot see him sometimes, I shall die. Please do not take him from me." And catching his hand between her own, she pressed it desperately. It was several seconds before Keith said :

" Leave that to me. I will see him. I shall arrange. You must leave that to me."

" But you will be kind ? "

He felt her lips kissing his hand.   And the soft moist touch sent a queer feeling through him, protective, yet just a little brutal, having in it a shiver of sensuality. He withdrew his hand.   And as if warned that she had been too pressing, she recoiled humbly.   But suddenly she turned, and stood absolutely rigid ; then almost inaudibly whispered : " Listen ! Someone out— out there ! " And darting past him she turned out the light.

Almost at once came a knock on the door.   He could feel—actually feel the terror of this girl beside him in the dark.   And he, too, felt terror.   Who could it be ? No one came but Larry, she had said.   Who else then could it be ?   Again came the knock, louder !   He felt the breath of her whisper on his cheek : " If it is Larry ! I must open."   He shrank back against the wall ; heard her open the door and say faintly : " Yes. Please ! Who ? "

Light painted a thin moving line on the wall opposite, and a voice which Keith recognised answered :

" All right, miss.   Your outer door's open here. You ought to keep it shut after dark."

God !   That policeman !   And it had been his own doing, not shutting the outer door behind him when he came in.   He heard her say timidly in her foreign voice : " Thank you, sir ! " the policeman's retreating steps, the outer door being shut, and felt her close to him again.   That something in her youth and strange prettiness which had touched and kept him gentle, no longer blunted the edge of his exasperation, now that he could not see her.   They were all the same, these women ; could not speak the truth !   And he said brusquely :

" You told me they didn't know you ! "

Her voice answered like a sigh :

" I did not think they did, sir. It is so long I was not out in the town, not since I had Larry."

The repulsion which all the time seethed deep in Keith welled up at those words. His brother—son of *his* mother, a gentleman—the property of this girl, bound to her, body and soul, by this unspeakable event ! But she had turned up the light. Had she some intuition that darkness was against her ? Yes, she *was* pretty with that soft face, colourless save for its lips and dark eyes, with that face somehow so touchingly, so unaccountably good, and like a child's.

" I am going now," he said. " Remember ! He mustn't come here ; you mustn't go to him. I shall see him to-morrow. If you are as fond of him as you say—take care, take care ! "

She sighed out, " Yes ! oh, yes ! " and Keith went to the door. She was standing with her back to the wall, and to follow him she only moved her head—that dove-like face with all its life in eyes which seemed saying : " Look into us ; nothing we hide ; all—all is there ! "

And he went out.

In the passage he paused before opening the outer door. He did not want to meet that policeman again ; the fellow's round should have taken him well out of the street by now, and turning the handle cautiously, he looked out. No one in sight. He stood a moment, wondering if he should turn to right or left, then briskly crossed the street. A voice to his right hand said :

" Good-night, sir."

There in the shadow of a doorway the policeman was standing. The fellow must have seen him coming

out ! Utterly unable to restrain a start, and muttering
" Good-night ! " Keith walked on rapidly.

He went full quarter of a mile before he lost that
startled and uneasy feeling in sardonic exasperation
that he, Keith Darrant, had been taken for a frequenter
of a lady of the town. The whole thing—the whole
thing !—a vile and disgusting business ! His very mind
felt dirty and breathless ; his spirit, drawn out of
sheath, had slowly to slide back before he could at all
focus and readjust his reasoning faculty. Certainly,
he had got the knowledge he wanted. There was
less danger than he thought. That girl's eyes ! No
mistaking her devotion. She would not give Larry
away. Yes ! Larry must clear out—South America—
the East—it did not matter. But he felt no relief.
The cheap, tawdry room had wrapped itself round
his fancy with its atmosphere of murky love, with the
feeling it inspired, of emotion caged within those
yellowish walls and the red stuff of its furniture. That
girl's face ! Devotion ; truth, too, and beauty, rare
and moving, in its setting of darkness and horror,
in that nest of vice and of disorder ! . . . The dark
archway ; the street arab, with his gleeful : " They
'ain't got 'im yet ! " ; the feel of those bare arms round
his neck ; that whisper of horror in the darkness ;
above all, again, again, her child face looking into his,
so truthful ! And suddenly he stood quite still in the
street. What in God's name was he about ? What
grotesque juggling amongst shadows, what strange
and ghastly eccentricity was all this ? The forces of
order and routine, all the actualities of his daily
life, marched on him at that moment, and swept
everything before them. It was a dream, a nightmare—not real ! It was ridiculous ! That he—*he*

should thus be bound up with things so black and
bizarre !

He had come by now to the Strand, that street down
which every day he moved to the Law Courts, to his
daily work ; his work so dignified and regular, so
irreproachable, and solid. No ! The thing was all a
monstrous nightmare ! It would go, if he fixed his mind
on the familiar objects around, read the names on
the shops, looked at the faces passing. Far down the
thoroughfare he caught the outline of the old church,
and beyond, the loom of the Law Courts themselves.
The bell of a fire-engine sounded, and the horses came
galloping by, with the shining metal, rattle of hoofs
and hoarse shouting. Here was a sensation, real and
harmless, dignified and customary ! A woman flaunting
round the corner looked up at him, and leered out :
" Good-night ! " Even that was customary, tolerable.
Two policemen passed, supporting between them a man
the worse for liquor, full of fight and expletives ; the
sight was soothing, an ordinary thing which brought
passing annoyance, interest, disgust. It had begun
to rain ; he felt it on his face with pleasure—an
actual thing, not eccentric, a thing which happened
every day !

He began to cross the street. Cabs were going at
furious speed now that the last omnibus had ceased
to run ; it distracted him to take this actual, ordinary
risk run so often every day. During that crossing of
the Strand, with the rain in his face and the cabs
shooting past, he regained for the first time his assur-
ance, shook off this unreal sense of being in the grip of
something, and walked resolutely to the corner of his
home turning. But passing into that darker stretch,
he again stood still. A policeman had also turned into

that street on the other side. Not—surely not——!
Absurd ! They were all alike to look at—those fellows !
Absurd ! He walked on sharply, and let himself into
his house. But on his way upstairs he could not for
the life of him help raising a corner of a curtain and
looking from the staircase window. The policeman
was marching solemnly, about twenty-five yards
away, paying apparently no attention to anything
whatever.

IV

KEITH woke at five o'clock, his usual hour, without
remembrance. But the grisly shadow started up
when he entered his study, where the lamp burned, and
the fire shone, and the coffee was set ready, just as
when yesterday afternoon Larry had stood out there
against the wall. For a moment he fought against
realisation ; then, drinking off his coffee, sat down
sullenly at the bureau to his customary three hours'
study of the day's cases.

Not one word of his brief could he take in. It was
all jumbled with murky images and apprehensions,
and for full half an hour he suffered mental paralysis.
Then the sheer necessity of knowing something of the
case which he had to open at half-past ten that morning
forced him to a concentration which never quite subdued
the *malaise* at the bottom of his heart. Nevertheless,
when he rose at half-past eight and went into the
bathroom, he had earned his grim satisfaction in this
victory of will-power. By half-past nine he must be
at Larry's. A boat left London for the Argentine
to-morrow. If Larry was to get away at once, money

D 2

must be arranged for. And then at breakfast he came on this paragraph in the paper :

"SOHO MURDER.

"Enquiry late last night established the fact that the Police have discovered the identity of the man found strangled yesterday morning under an archway in Glove Lane. An arrest has been made."

By good fortune he had finished eating, for the words made him feel physically sick. At this very minute Larry might be locked up, waiting to be charged— might even have been arrested before his own visit to the girl last night. If Larry were arrested, she must be implicated. What, then, would be his own position ? Idiot to go and look at that archway, to go and see the girl ! Had that policeman really followed him home ? Accessory after the fact ! Keith Darrant, King's Counsel, man of mark ! He forced himself by an effort, which had something of the heroic, to drop this panicky feeling. Panic never did good. He must face it, and see. He refused even to hurry, calmly collected the papers wanted for the day, and attended to a letter or two, before he set out in a taxi-cab to Fitzroy Street.

Waiting outside there in the grey morning for his ring to be answered, he looked the very picture of a man who knew his mind, a man of resolution. But it needed all his will-power to ask without tremor : " Mr. Darrant in ? " to hear without sign of any kind the answer : " He's not up yet, sir."

" Never mind ; I'll go in and see him. Mr. Keith Darrant."

On his way to Laurence's bedroom, in the midst of

utter relief, he had the self-possession to think : ' This arrest is the best thing that could have happened. It'll keep their noses on a wrong scent till Larry's got away. The girl must be sent off too, but not with him.' Panic had ended in quite hardening his resolution. He entered the bedroom with a feeling of disgust. The fellow was lying there, his bare arms crossed behind his tousled head, staring at the ceiling, and smoking one of many cigarettes whose ends littered a chair beside him, whose sickly reek tainted the air. That pale face, with its jutting cheek-bones and chin, its hollow cheeks and blue eyes far sunk back—what a wreck of goodness !

He looked up at Keith through the haze of smoke and said quietly : " Well, brother, what's the sentence ? ' Transportation for life, and then to be fined forty pounds ? ' "

The flippancy revolted Keith. It was Larry all over ! Last night horrified and humble, this morning, " Don't care " and feather-headed. He said sourly :

" Oh ! You can joke about it now ? "

Laurence turned his face to the wall.

" Must."

Fatalism ! How detestable were natures like that !

" I've been to see her," he said.

" You ? "

" Last night. She can be trusted."

Laurence laughed.

" That I told you."

" I had to see for myself. You must clear out at once, Larry. She can come out to you by the next boat ; but you can't go together. Have you any money ? "

" No."

" I can foot your expenses, and lend you a year's

income in advance. But it must be a clean cut ; after you get out there your whereabouts must only be known to me."

A long sigh answered him.

" You're very good to me, Keith ; you've always been very good. I don't know why."

Keith answered drily :

" Nor I. There's a boat to the Argentine to-morrow. You're in luck ; they've made an arrest. It's in the paper."

" What ? "

The cigarette end dropped, the thin pyjama'd figure writhed up and stood clutching at the bed-rail.

" What ? "

The disturbing thought flitted through Keith's brain : ' I was a fool. He takes it queerly ; what now ? '

Laurence passed his hand over his forehead, and sat down on the bed.

" I hadn't thought of that," he said : " It does me ! "

Keith stared. In his relief that the arrested man was not Laurence, this had not occurred to him. What folly !

" Why ? " he said quickly ; " an innocent man's in no danger. They always get the wrong man first. It's a piece of luck, that's all. It gives us time."

How often had he not seen that expression on Larry's face, wistful, questioning, as if trying to see the thing with his—Keith's—eyes, trying to submit to better judgment ? And he said, almost gently :

" Now, look here, Larry ; this is too serious to trifle with. Don't worry about that. Leave it to me. Just get ready to be off. I'll take your berth and make arrangements. Here's some money for kit.

I can come round between five and six, and let you
know. Pull yourself together, man. As soon as the
girl's joined you out there, you'd better get across to
Chile, the further the better. You must simply lose
yourself. I must go now, if I'm to get to the Bank
before I go down to the courts." And looking very
steadily at his brother, he added :

" Come ! You've got to think of me in this matter
as well as of yourself. No playing fast and loose with
the arrangements. Understand ? "

But still Larry gazed up at him with that wistful
questioning, and not till he had repeated, " Understand ? " did he receive " Yes " for answer.

Driving away, he thought : ' Queer fellow ! I don't
know him, shall never know him ! ' and at once
began to concentrate on the practical arrangements.
At his bank he drew out £400 ; but waiting for the
notes to be counted he suffered qualms. A clumsy
way of doing things ! If there had been more time !
The thought : ' Accessory after the fact ! ' now infected everything. Notes were traceable. No other way
of getting him away at once, though. One must take
lesser risks to avoid greater. From the bank he drove
to the office of the steamship line. He had told Larry
he would book his passage. But that would not do ! He
must only ask anonymously if there were accommoda-
tion. Having discovered that there were vacant
berths, he drove on to the Law Courts. If he could
have taken a morning off, he would have gone down
to the police court and seen them charge this man.
But even that was not too safe, with a face so well
known as his. What would come of this arrest ?
Nothing, surely ! The police always took somebody
up, to keep the public quiet. Then, suddenly, he had

again the feeling that it was all a nightmare ; Larry
had never done it ; the police had got the right man !
But instantly the memory of the girl's awe-stricken
face, her figure huddling on the sofa, her words : " I
see him always falling ! " came back.   God !. What a
business !

He felt he had never been more clear-headed and
forcible than that morning in court.   When he came
out for lunch he bought the most sensational of the
evening papers.   But it was yet too early for news,
and he had to go back into court no whit wiser con-
cerning the arrest.   When at last he threw off wig and
gown, and had got through a conference and other
necessary work, he went out to Chancery Lane, buying
a paper on the way.   Then he hailed a cab, and drove
once more to Fitzroy Street.

V

LAURENCE had remained sitting on his bed for many
minutes.   An innocent man in no danger ! Keith had
said it—the celebrated lawyer ! Could he rely on
that ? Go out 8,000 miles, he and the girl, and leave
a fellow-creature perhaps in mortal peril for an act
committed by himself ?

In the past night he had touched bottom, as he
thought ; become ready to face anything.   When
Keith came in he would without murmur have accepted
the advice : " Give yourself up ! " He was prepared
to pitch away the end of his life as he pitched from
him the fag-ends of his cigarettes.   And the long sigh
he had heaved, hearing of reprieve, had been only
half relief.   Then, with incredible swiftness there had

rushed through him a feeling of unutterable joy and hope. Clean away—into a new country, a new life! The girl and he! Out there he wouldn't care, would rejoice even to have squashed the life out of such a noisome beetle of a man. Out there! Under a new sun, where blood ran quicker than in this foggy land, and people took justice into their own hands. For it had been justice on that brute even though he had not meant to kill him. And then to hear of this arrest! They would be charging the man to-day. He could go and see the poor creature accused of the murder he himself had committed! And he laughed. Go and see how likely it was that they might hang a fellow-man in place of himself? He dressed, but too shaky to shave himself, went out to a barber's shop. While there he read the news which Keith had seen. In this paper the name of the arrested man was given: "John Evan, no address." To be brought up on the charge at Bow Street. Yes! He must go! Once, twice, three times he walked past the entrance of the court before at last he entered and screwed himself away among the tag and bobtail.

The court was crowded; and from the murmurs round he could tell that it was his particular case which had brought so many there. In a dazed way he watched charge after charge disposed of with lightning quickness. But were they never going to reach his business? And then suddenly he saw the little scarecrow man of last night advancing to the dock between two policemen, more ragged and miserable than ever by light of day, like some shaggy, wan, grey animal, surrounded by sleek hounds.

A sort of satisfied purr was rising all round; and with horror Laurence perceived that this—*this* was

the man accused of what he himself had done
—this queer, battered unfortunate to whom he had
shown a passing friendliness. Then all feeling
merged in the appalling interest of listening. The
evidence was very short. Testimony of the hotel-
keeper where Walenn had been staying, identifying
his body, and a snake-shaped ring he had been wearing
at dinner that evening. Testimony of a pawnbroker,
that this same ring was pawned with him the first thing
yesterday morning by the prisoner. Testimony of a
policeman that he had noticed the man Evan several
times in Glove Lane, and twice moved him on from
sleeping under that arch. Testimony of another
policeman that, when arrested at midnight, Evan had
said : " Yes ; I took the ring off his finger. I found
him there dead. . . . I know I oughtn't to have done
it. . . . I'm an educated man ; it was stupid to pawn
the ring. I found him with his pockets turned inside
out."

Fascinating and terrible to sit staring at the man in
whose place he should have been ; to wonder when
those small bright-grey bloodshot eyes would spy him
out, and how he would meet that glance. Like a
baited raccoon the little man stood, screwed back into
a corner, mournful, cynical, fierce, with his ridged,
obtuse yellow face, and his stubbly grey beard and
hair, and his eyes wandering now and again amongst
the crowd. But with all his might Laurence kept his
face unmoved. Then came the word " Remanded " ;
and, more like a baited beast than ever, the man was
led away.

Laurence sat on, a cold perspiration thick on his
forehead. Someone else, then, had come on the body
and turned the pockets inside out before John Evan

took the ring. A man such as Walenn would not be
out at night without money. Besides, if Evan had
found money on the body he would never have run
the risk of taking that ring. Yes, someone else had
come on the body first. It was for that one to come
forward, and prove that the ring was still on the
dead man's finger when he left him, and thus clear
Evan. He clung to that thought ; it seemed to
make him less responsible for the little man's position ; to remove him and his own deed one step
further back. If they found the person who had
taken the money, it would prove Evan's innocence.
He came out of the court in a sort of trance. And a
craving to get drunk attacked him. One could not
go on like this without the relief of some oblivion.
If he could only get drunk, keep drunk till this business
was decided and he knew whether he must give himself
up or no. He had now no fear at all of people suspecting
him ; only fear of himself—fear that he might go and
give himself up. Now he could see the girl ; the
danger from that was as nothing compared with the
danger from his own conscience. He had promised
Keith not to see her. Keith had been decent and
loyal to him—good old Keith ! But he would never
understand that this girl was now all he cared about
in life ; that he would rather be cut off from life itself
than be cut off from her. Instead of getting less and
less, she was getting more and more to him—experience
strange and thrilling ! Out of deep misery she had
grown happy—through him ; out of a sordid, shifting
life recovered coherence and bloom, through devotion
to him—*him*, of all people in the world ! It was a
miracle. She demanded nothing of him, adored him,
as no other woman ever had—it was this which had

anchored his drifting barque ; this—and her truthful,
mild intelligence, and that burning warmth of a woman,
who, long treated by men as but a sack of sex, now
loves at last.

And suddenly, mastering his craving to get drunk,
he made towards Soho. He had been a fool to give
those keys to Keith. She must have been frightened
by his visit ; and, perhaps, doubly miserable since,
knowing nothing, imagining everything ! Keith was
sure to have terrified her. Poor little thing !

Down the street where he had stolen in the dark
with the dead body on his back, he almost ran for the
cover of her house. The door was opened to him before
he knocked, her arms were round his neck, her lips
pressed to his. The fire was out, as if she had been
unable to remember to keep warm. A stool had been
drawn to the window, and there she had evidently
been sitting, like a bird in a cage, looking out into the
grey street. Though she had been told that he was
not to come, instinct had kept her there ; or the
pathetic, aching hope against hope which lovers never
part with.

Now that he was there, her first thoughts were for
his comfort. The fire was lighted. He must eat,
drink, smoke. There was never in her doings any of
the " I am doing this for you, but you ought to be
doing that for me " which belongs to so many marriages,
and *liaisons*. She was like a devoted slave, so in
love with the chains that she never knew she wore
them. And to Laurence, who had so little sense of
property, this only served to deepen tenderness, and
the hold she had on him. He had resolved not to
tell her of the new danger he ran from his own
conscience. But resolutions with him were but the

opposites of what was sure to come ; and at last
the words :

" They've arrested someone," escaped him.

From her face he knew she had grasped the
danger at once ; had divined it, perhaps, before he
spoke. But she only twined her arms round him and
kissed his lips. And he knew that she was begging
him to put his love for her above his conscience. Who
would ever have thought that he could feel as he did
to this girl who had been in the arms of many ! The
stained and suffering past of a loved woman awakens
in some men only chivalry ; in others, more respectable,
it rouses a tigerish itch, a rancorous jealousy of what
in the past was given to others. Sometimes it will
do both. When he had her in his arms he felt no
remorse for killing the coarse, handsome brute who had
ruined her. He savagely rejoiced in it. But when
she laid her head in the hollow of his shoulder, turning
to him her white face with the faint colour-staining
on the parted lips, the cheeks, the eyelids ; when her
dark, wide-apart, brown eyes gazed up in the happiness
of her abandonment—he felt only tenderness and
protection.

He left her at five o'clock, and had not gone two
streets' length before the memory of the little grey
vagabond, screwed back in the far corner of the dock
like a baited raccoon, of his dreary, creaking voice,
took possession of him again ; and a kind of savagery
mounted in his brain against a world where one could
be so tortured without having meant harm to anyone.

At the door of his lodgings Keith was getting out of
a cab. They went in together, but neither of them
sat down ; Keith standing with his back to the carefully
shut door, Laurence with his back to the table, as

if they knew there was a tug coming. And Keith said :

" There's room on that boat. Go down and book your berth before they shut. Here's the money ! "

" I'm going to stick it, Keith."

Keith stepped forward, and put a roll of notes on the table.

" Now look here, Larry. I've read the police court proceedings. There's nothing in that. Out of prison, or in prison for a few weeks, it's all the same to a night-bird of that sort. Dismiss it from your mind—there's not nearly enough evidence to convict. This gives you your chance. Take it like a man, and make a new life for yourself."

Laurence smiled ; but the smile had a touch of madness and a touch of malice. He took up the notes.

" Clear out, and save the honour of brother Keith. Put them back in your pocket, Keith, or I'll put them in the fire. Come, take them ! " And, crossing to the fire, he held them to the bars. " Take them, or in they go ! "

Keith took back the notes.

" I've still got some kind of honour, Keith ; if I clear out I shall have none, not the rag of any, left. It may be worth more to me than that—I can't tell yet—I can't tell."

There was a long silence before Keith answered.

" I tell you you're mistaken ; no jury will convict. If they did, a judge would never hang on it. A ghoul who can rob a dead body *ought* to be in prison. What he did is worse than what you did, if you come to that ! "

Laurence lifted his face.

" Judge not, brother," he said ; " the heart is a dark well."

Keith's yellowish face grew red and swollen, as though he were mastering the tickle of a bronchial cough.

" What are you going to do, then ? I suppose I may ask you not to be entirely oblivious of our name ; or is such a consideration unworthy of your honour ? "

Laurence bent his head. The gesture said more clearly than words : " Don't kick a man when he's down ! "

" I don't know what I'm going to do—nothing at present. I'm awfully sorry, Keith ; awfully sorry."

Keith looked at him, and without another word went out.

VI

To any, save philosophers, reputation may be threatened almost as much by disgrace to name and family as by the disgrace of self. Keith's instinct was always to deal actively with danger. But this blow, whether it fell on him by discovery or by confession, could not be countered. As blight falls on a rose from who knows where, the scandalous murk would light on him. No repulse possible ! Not even a wriggling from under ! Brother of a murderer hung or sent to penal servitude ! His daughter niece to a murderer ! His dead mother—a murderer's mother ! And to wait day after day, week after week, not knowing whether the blow would fall, was an extraordinarily atrocious penance, the injustice of which, to a man of rectitude, seemed daily the more monstrous.

The remand had produced evidence that the

murdered man had been drinking heavily on the night
of his death, and further evidence of the accused's
professional vagabondage and destitution; it was
shown, too, that for some time the archway in Glove
Lane had been his favourite night haunt. He had
been committed for trial in January. This time,
despite misgivings, Keith had attended the police
court. To his great relief Larry was not there. But
the policeman who had come up while he was looking
at the archway, and given him afterwards that scare
in the girl's rooms, was chief witness to the way the
accused man haunted Glove Lane. Though Keith
held his silk hat high, he still had the uncomfortable
feeling that the man had recognised him.

His conscience suffered few, if any, twinges for letting
this man rest under the shadow of the murder. He
genuinely believed that there was not evidence enough
to convict; nor was it in him to appreciate the
tortures of a vagabond shut up. The scamp deserved
what he had got, for robbing a dead body; and in
any case such a scarecrow was better off in prison than
sleeping out under archways in December. Sentiment
was foreign to Keith's character, and his justice that
of those who subordinate the fates of the weak and
shiftless to the needful paramountcy of the strong and
well established.

His daughter came back from school for the Christmas
holidays. It was hard to look up from her bright eyes
and rosy cheeks and see this shadow hanging above
his calm and ordered life, as in a glowing room one's
eye may catch an impending patch of darkness drawn
like a spider's web across a corner of the ceiling.

On the afternoon of Christmas Eve they went, by
her desire, to a church in Soho, where the Christmas

Oratorio was being given ; and coming away passed,
by chance of a wrong turning, down Borrow Street.
Ugh ! How that startled moment, when the girl had
pressed herself against him in the dark, and her
terror-stricken whisper : " Oh ! Who is it ? " leaped
out before him ! Always that business—that ghastly
business ! After the trial he would have another try
to get them both away.   And he thrust his arm within
his little daughter's, hurrying her on, out of this street
where shadows filled all the winter air.

But that evening when she had gone to bed he felt
uncontrollably restless.   He had not seen Larry for
weeks.   What was he about ? What desperations were
hatching in his disorderly brain ? Was he very
miserable ; had he perhaps sunk into a stupor of
debauchery ? And the old feeling of protectiveness
rose up in him ; a warmth born of long ago Christmas
Eves, when they had stockings hung out in the night
stuffed by a Santa Claus, whose hand never failed to tuck
them up, whose kiss was their nightly waft into sleep.

Stars were sparkling out there over the river ; the
sky frosty-clear, and black.   Bells had not begun to
ring as yet.   And obeying an obscure, deep impulse,
Keith wrapped himself once more into his fur coat,
pulled a motoring cap over his eyes, and sallied forth.

In the Strand he took a cab to Fitzroy Street.   There
was no light in Larry's windows, and on a card he
saw the words " To Let."   Gone ! Had he after all
cleared out for good ? But how—without money ?
And the girl ? Bells were ringing now in the silent
frostiness.   Christmas Eve ! And Keith thought :
' If only this wretched business were off my mind !
Monstrous that one should suffer for the faults of
others ! '

He took a route which led him past Borrow Street. Solitude brooded there, and he walked resolutely down on the far side, looking hard at the girl's window. There was a light. The curtains just failed to meet, so that a thin gleam shone through. He crossed; and after glancing swiftly up and down, deliberately peered in.

He only stood there perhaps twenty seconds, but visual records gleaned in a moment sometimes outlast the visions of hours and days. The electric light was not burning; but, in the centre of the room the girl was kneeling in her nightgown before a little table on which were four lighted candles. Her arms were crossed on her breast; the candle-light shone on her fair cropped hair, on the profile of cheek and chin, on her bowed white neck. For a moment he thought her alone; then behind her saw his brother in a sleeping suit, leaning against the wall, with arms crossed, watching. It was the expression on his face which burned the whole thing in, so that always afterwards he was able to see that little scene—such an expression as could never have been on the face of one even faintly conscious that he was watched by any living thing on earth. The whole of Larry's heart and feeling seemed to have come up out of him. Yearning, mockery, love, despair! The depth of his feeling for this girl, his stress of mind, fears, hopes; the flotsam good and evil of his soul, all transfigured there, exposed and unforgettable. The candle-light shone upward on to his face, twisted by the strangest smile; his eyes, darker and more wistful than mortal eyes should be, seemed to beseech and mock the white-clad girl, who, all unconscious, knelt without movement, like a carved figure of devotion. The words seemed coming from

his lips : " Pray for us ! Bravo ! Yes ! Pray for us ! "
And suddenly Keith saw her stretch out her arms, and
lift her face with a look of ecstasy, and Laurence
starting forward. What had she seen beyond the
candle flames ? It is the unexpected which invests
visions with poignancy. Nothing more strange could
Keith have seen in this nest of the murky and illicit.
But in sheer panic lest he might be caught thus spying
he drew back and hurried on.

So Larry was living there with her ! When the
moment came he could still find him.

Before going in, he stood full five minutes leaning
on the terrace parapet before his house, gazing at the
star-frosted sky, and the river cut by the trees into
black pools, oiled over by gleams from the Embankment
lamps. And, deep down, behind his mere thoughts,
he ached—somehow, somewhere ached. Beyond the
cage of all that he saw and heard and thought, he had
perceived something he could not reach. But the
night was cold, the bells silent, for it had struck twelve.
Entering his house, he stole upstairs.

VII

IF for Keith those six weeks before the Glove Lane
murder trial came on were fraught with uneasiness and
gloom, they were for Laurence almost the happiest
since his youth. From the moment when he left his
rooms and went to the girl's to live, a kind of peace
and exaltation took possession of him. Not by any
effort of will did he throw off the nightmare hanging
over him. Nor was he drugged by love. He was in
a sort of spiritual catalepsy. In face of fate too

E 2

powerful for his will, his turmoil, anxiety, and even
restlessness had ceased ; his life floated in the ether
of " what must come, will." Out of this catalepsy,
his spirit sometimes fell headlong into black waters.
In one such whirlpool he was struggling on the night
of Christmas Eve. When the girl rose from her knees
he asked her :

" What did you see ? "

Pressing close to him, she drew him down on to the
floor before the fire ; and they sat, knees drawn up,
hands clasped, like two children trying to see over the
edge of the world.

" It was the Virgin I saw. She stood against the
wall and smiled. We shall be happy soon."

" When we die, Wanda," he said, suddenly, " let it
be together. We shall keep each other warm, out
there."

Huddling to him she whispered : " Yes, oh, yes !
If you die, I could not go on living."

It was this utter dependence on him, the feeling that
he had rescued something, which gave him sense of
anchorage. That, and his buried life in the retreat
of these two rooms. Just for an hour in the morning,
from nine to ten, the charwoman would come, but not
another soul all day. They never went out together.
He would stay in bed late, while Wanda bought
what they needed for the day's meals ; lying on his
back, hands clasped behind his head, recalling her face,
the movements of her slim, rounded, supple figure,
robing itself before his eyes ; feeling again the kiss she
had left on his lips, the gleam of her soft eyes, so
strangely dark in so fair a face. In a sort of trance
he would lie, till she came back. Then get up to
breakfast about noon off things which she had cooked,

drinking coffee.   In the afternoon he would go out
alone and walk for hours, anywhere, so long as it was
East.   To the East there was always suffering to be
seen, always that which soothed him with the feeling
that he and his troubles were only a tiny part of
trouble ;   that while so many other sorrowing and
shadowy creatures lived he was not cut off.   To go
West was to encourage dejection.   In the West all was
like Keith, successful, immaculate, ordered, resolute.
He would come back tired out, and sit watching her
cook their little dinner.   The evenings were given up
to love.   Queer trance of an existence, which both were
afraid to break.   No sign from her of wanting those
excitements which girls who have lived her life, even for
a few months, are supposed to need.   She never asked
him to take her anywhere ;   never, in word, deed,
look, seemed anything but almost rapturously content.
And yet he knew, and she knew, that they were only
waiting to see whether Fate would turn her thumb
down on them.   In these days he did not drink.   Out of
his quarter's money, when it came in, he had paid his
debts—their expenses were very small.   He never
went to see Keith, never wrote to him, hardly thought
of him.   And from those dread apparitions—Walenn
lying with the breath choked out of him, and the little
grey, driven animal in the dock—he hid, as only a man
can who must hide or be destroyed.   But daily he
bought a newspaper, and feverishly, furtively scanned
its columns.

VIII

COMING out of the Law Courts on the afternoon of
January 28th, at the triumphant end of a desperately

fought will case, Keith saw on a poster the words :
" Glove Lane Murder : Trial and Verdict " ; and with
a rush of dismay he thought : " Good God ! I never
looked at the paper this morning ! " The elation which
had filled him a second before, the absorption he had
felt for two days now in the case so hardly won, seemed
suddenly quite sickeningly trivial. What on earth had
he been doing to forget that horrible business even for
an instant ? He stood quite still on the crowded pave-
ment, unable, really unable, to buy a paper. But his
face was like a piece of iron when he did step forward
and hold his penny out. There it was in the Stop
Press ! " Glove Lane Murder. The jury returned a
verdict of Guilty. Sentence of death was passed."

His first sensation was simple irritation. How had
they come to commit such an imbecility ? Monstrous !
The evidence——! Then the futility of even reading the
report, of even considering how they had come to record
such a verdict struck him with savage suddenness.
There it was, and nothing he could do or say would
alter it ; no condemnation of this idiotic verdict
would help reverse it. The situation was desperate,
indeed ! That five minutes' walk from the Law Courts
to his chambers was the longest he had ever taken.

Men of decided character little know beforehand
what they will do in certain contingencies. For the
imaginations of decided people do not endow mere
contingencies with sufficient actuality. Keith had
never really settled what he was going to do if this
man were condemned. Often in those past weeks he
had said to himself : " Of course, if they bring him in
guilty, that's another thing ! " But, now that they
had, he was beset by exactly the same old arguments
and feelings, the same instincts of loyalty and protection

towards Laurence and himself, intensified by the
fearful imminence of the danger. And yet, here was
this man about to be hung for a thing he had not done !
Nothing could get over that ! But then he was such a
worthless vagabond, a ghoul who had robbed a dead
body. If Larry were condemned in his stead, would
there be any less miscarriage of justice ? To strangle a
brute who had struck you, by the accident of keeping
your hands on his throat a few seconds too long, was
there any more guilt in that—was there even as much,
as in deliberate theft from a dead man ? Reverence
for order, for justice, and established fact, will often
march shoulder to shoulder with Jesuitry in natures
to whom success is vital.

In the narrow stone passage leading to his staircase,
a friend had called out : " Bravo, Darrant ! That was
a squeak ! Congratulations ! " And with a bitter little
smile Keith thought : ' Congratulations ! I ! '

At the first possible moment he hurried back to the
Strand, and hailing a cab, he told the man to put him
down at a turning near to Borrow Street.

It was the girl who opened to his knock. Startled,
clasping her hands, she looked strange to Keith in her
black skirt and blouse of some soft velvety stuff the
colour of faded roses. Her round, rather long throat
was bare ; and Keith noticed fretfully that she wore
gold earrings. Her eyes, so pitch dark against her
white face, and the short fair hair, which curled into her
neck, seemed both to search and to plead.

" My brother ? "

" He is not in, sir, yet."

" Do you know where he is ? "

" No."

" He is living with you here now ? "

" Yes."

" Are you still as fond of him as ever, then ? "

With a movement, as though she despaired of words,
she clasped her hands over her heart.   And he said :

" I see."

He had the same strange feeling as on his first visit
to her, and when through the chink in the curtains he
had watched her kneeling—of pity mingled with some
faint sexual emotion.   And crossing to the fire he
asked :

" May I wait for him ? "

" Oh !   Please !   Will you sit down ? "

But Keith shook his head.   And with a catch in her
breath, she said :

" You will not take him from me.   I should die."

He turned round on her sharply.

" *I* don't want him taken from you.   I want to
help you keep him.   Are you ready to go away, at any
time ? "

" Yes.   Oh, yes ! "

" And he ? "

She answered almost in a whisper :

" Yes ; but there is that poor man."

" That poor man is a graveyard thief ; a hyena ; a
ghoul—not worth consideration."   And the rasp in his
own voice surprised him.

" Ah ! " she sighed.   " But I am sorry for him.
Perhaps he was hungry.   I have been hungry—you do
things then that you would not.   And perhaps he has
no one to love ; if you have no one to love you can be
very bad.   I think of him often—in prison."

Between   his   teeth   Keith   muttered :   " And
Laurence ? "

" We do never speak of it, we are afraid."

" He's not told you, then, about the trial ? "

Her eyes dilated.

" The trial ! Oh ! He was strange last night. This morning, too, he got up early. Is it—is it over ? "

" Yes."

" What has come ? "

" Guilty."

For a moment Keith thought she was going to faint. She had closed her eyes, and swayed so that he took a step, and put his hands on her arms.

" Listen ! " he said. " Help me ; don't let Laurence out of your sight. We must have time. I must see what they intend to do. They can't be going to hang this man. I must have time, I tell you. You must prevent his giving himself up."

She had opened her eyes at his words, and now stood stone-still, staring in his face, while he still held her arms, gripping into her soft flesh through the velvety sleeves.

" Do you understand ? "

" Yes—but if he has already ! "

Keith felt the shiver which ran through her. And the thought rushed into his mind : ' My God ! Suppose the police come round while I'm here ! ' He let go her arms. If Larry had indeed gone to them—no reason for himself to be involved more than he must be anyway ! If that policeman who had seen him here the night after the murder should find him here again just after the verdict ! He said almost fiercely :

" Can I trust you not to let Larry out of your sight ? Quick ! Answer ! "

Clasping her hands to her breast, she answered humbly :

" I will try."

He could not afford to be affected, and still more brusquely said :

" If he hasn't already done this, watch him like a lynx ! Don't let him go out without you. I'll come to-morrow morning early. You're a Catholic, aren't you ? Swear to me that you won't let him do anything till he's seen me again."

She did not answer, looking past him at the door ; and Keith heard a key in the latch. There was Laurence himself, holding in his hand a great bunch of pink lilies and white narcissi. His face was pale and haggard. He said quietly :

" Hallo, Keith ! "

The girl had not moved, her eyes were fastened on Larry's face ; and Keith, looking from one to the other, knew that he had never had more need for wariness.

" Have you seen ? " he said.

Laurence nodded. His expression, as a rule so tell-tale of his emotions, baffled Keith utterly.

" Well ? "

" I've been expecting it."

" The thing can't stand—that's certain. But I must have time to look into the report. I must have time to see what I can do. D'you understand me, Larry— I must have time." He knew he was talking at random. The only thing really was to get them clean away at once out of reach of confession ; but he dared not say so.

" Promise me that you'll do nothing, that you won't go out even till I've seen you to-morrow morning."

Again Laurence nodded. And Keith looked at the girl. Would she, could she, see that he did not break that promise ? Her eyes were still fixed immovably

on Larry's face.   And with the feeling that he could
get no further, Keith turned to go.

" Promise me," he said.

Laurence answered : " I promise."

He was smiling.   Keith could make nothing of
that smile, nor of the expression in the girl's eyes.   And
saying : " I have your promise, I rely on it ! " he
went.

IX

To keep from any woman who loves, knowledge of
her lover's mood, is as hard as to keep music from
moving the heart.   But when that woman has lived
in suffering, and for the first time knows the comfort
of love, then let the lover try as he may to disguise
his heart—no use ! Yet by virtue of subtler abnegation
she will often succeed in keeping it from him that she
knows.   For the nature of a man, no matter how
unstable and outcast, is to be lost in his own resolves,
and unconscious that his heart is being read.

When Keith was gone the girl made no outcry,
asked no questions, managed that Larry should not
suspect her intuition ; all that evening she acted as
if she knew of nothing preparing within him, and
through him, within herself.

His words, caresses, the very zest with which he
helped her to prepare the feast, the flowers he had
brought, the wine he made her drink, the avoidance
of any word which could spoil their happiness, all—all
told her.   He was too inexorably gay and loving.
Not for her—to whom every word and every kiss had
uncannily the desperate value of a last word and kiss—
not for her to deprive herself of these by any sign or

gesture which might betray her prescience. Poor soul—
she took all, and would have taken more, a hundredfold.
She did not want to drink the wine he kept tilting into
her glass, but, with the pathetic acceptance learned
by women who have lived her life, she did not refuse.
She had never refused him anything. So much had
been required of her by the detestable, that anything
required by the loved one was but an honour.

Laurence drank deeply; but he had never felt
clearer, never seen things more vividly. The wine
gave him what he wanted, an edge on these few hours
of pleasure, an exaltation of energy. It dulled his
sense of pity, too. It was pity he was afraid of—for
himself, and for this girl. An itch for beauty possessed
him—to make even this poor tawdry room look
beautiful, with firelight and candlelight, dark amber
wine in the glasses, tall pink lilies spilling their saffron,
exuding their hot perfume—an itch that she and even
himself might look their best. And, with a weight
as of lead on her heart, she managed that for him,
letting him strew her with flowers and crush them
together with herself. Not even music was lacking to
their feast. Someone was playing a pianola across
the street, and the sound, very faint, came stealing
when they were silent—swelling, sinking, festive,
mournful; having a far-off life of its own, like the
flickering fire-flames before which they lay embraced,
or the lilies delicate between the candles. Listening
to that music, tracing with his finger the tiny veins
on her breast, he lay like one recovering from a swoon.
No parting. None! But sleep, as the firelight sleeps
when flames die; as music sleeps on its deserted
strings!

And the girl watched him.

It was nearly ten when he bade her go to bed. And
after she had gone obedient into the bedroom, he
brought ink and paper down by the fire. It was strange
to himself that he—the drifter, the unstable, the
good-for-nothing—did not falter. One would have
thought, when it came to the point, he would fail
himself. A sort of rage bore him forward. If he
lived on, and confessed, they would shut him up,
take from him the one thing he loved, cut him off from
her ; sand up his only well in the desert. Curse
them ! And he wrote, cross-legged in firelight which
mellowed the white sheets of paper ; while, against the
dark curtain, the girl, in her nightdress, unconscious of
the cold, stood watching.

A man, when he drowns, remembers his past.
Like the lost poet he had " gone with the wind." Now
it was for him to be true in his fashion. Not really so
very strange that he did not falter. A man may falter
for weeks and weeks, consciously, subconsciously, even
in his dreams, till there comes that moment when the
only thing impossible is to go on faltering. The black
cap, the little driven grey man looking up at it with a
sort of wonder—faltering had ceased !

He had finished now, and was but staring into the
fire.

> " No more, no more, the moon is dead,
>   And all the people in it ;
> The poppy maidens strew the bed,
>   We'll come in half a minute."

Why did doggerel start up in the mind like that ?
Wanda ! The weed flower—become so rare—he would
not be parted from her ! The fire, the candles, and
the fire—no more the flame and flicker !

And, by the dark curtain, the girl watched.

X

KEITH went, not home, but to his club ; and in the
room devoted to the reception of guests, empty at this
hour, he sat down and read the report of the trial.
The fools had made out a case that looked black enough.
And for a long time, on the thick soft carpet which let
out no sound of footfall, he paced up and down,
thinking. He might see the defending counsel, might
surely do that as an expert who thought there had been
miscarriage of justice. They must appeal ; a petition
too might be started in the last event. The thing
could—must be put right yet, if only Larry and that
girl did nothing !

He had no appetite, but the custom of dining is too
strong. And while he ate, he glanced with irritation
at his fellow-members. They looked so at their ease.
Unjust ! Unjust—that this black cloud should hang
over one as blameless as any of them ! Friends, con-
noisseurs of such things—a judge among them—came
specially to his table to express their admiration of
his conduct of that will case. To-night he had real
excuse for pride, but he felt none. Yet, in this well-
warmed quietly glowing room, filled with decorously
eating, decorously talking men, he gained insensibly
some comfort. This surely was reality ; that shadowy
business out there was like the drear sound of a wind
one must and did keep out—like the poverty and
grime which had no real existence for the secure
and prosperous. He drank champagne. It helped to
fortify reality, to make shadows seem more shadowy.
And down in the smoking-room he sat before the fire,
in one of those chairs which embalm after-dinner dreams.

He had earned rest. He grew sleepy there, and at
eleven o'clock rose to go home. But when he had once
passed down the shallow marble steps, out through the
revolving door which let in no draughts, he was visited
by fear, as if he had drawn it in with the breath of
the January wind. Larry's face ; and the girl watching
it ! Why had she watched like that ? Larry's smile ;
and the flowers in his hand ? Buying flowers at such a
moment ! The girl was his slave—whatever he told
her, she would do. But she would never be able to
stop him. At this very moment he might be rushing
to give himself up !

His hand, thrust deep into the pocket of his fur coat,
came in contact suddenly with something cold. The
keys Larry had given him all that time ago. There
they had lain forgotten ever since. The chance touch
decided him. He turned off towards Borrow Street,
walking at full speed. He could but go again and see.
He would sleep better if he knew that he had left no
stone unturned. At the corner of that dismal street
he had to wait for solitude before he made for the house
which he now loathed with such deadly loathing. He
opened the outer door and shut it to behind him. He
would not make that mistake a second time. The same
dim gaslight in the passage, the same smell of oilcloth !
He knocked, but no one came. Perhaps they had gone
to bed. Again and again he knocked, then opened
the door, stepped in, and closed it carefully. Candles
lighted, the fire burning ; cushions thrown on the floor
in front of it and strewn with flowers ! The table, too,
covered with flowers and with the remnants of a meal.
Through the half-drawn curtain he could see that the
inner room was also lighted. Had they gone out,
leaving everything like this ? Gone out ! To do—

what ? His heart beat sickeningly. Bottles ! Larry
had been drinking !

Had it really come ? Must he go back home with this
murk on him ; knowing that his brother was a confessed and branded murderer ? He went quickly to the
half-drawn curtains and looked in. In the corner
against the wall he saw a bed, and those two in it,
asleep. And he recoiled in sheer amazement and relief.
Asleep ! Asleep with curtains undrawn, lights left on ?
Asleep through all his knocking ! They must both be
drunk. The blood rushed up in his neck, and he stood
shivering. Asleep ! And, suddenly, rushing forward
again, he called out : " Larry ! " beating on the wood-
work loudly. With a gasp he went towards the bed,
and cried again : " Larry ! " No answer ! No movement ! Seizing his brother's shoulder, he shook it
violently. It felt cold. They were lying in each
other's arms, breast to breast, lips to lips, their faces
white in the electric light shining above the dressing-
table by the foot of the bed. And such a shudder shook
Keith that he had to grasp the brass rail above their
heads. Then he bent down, and wetting his finger,
placed it close to their joined lips. A swoon ? No two
could ever swoon so utterly as that ; not even a
drunken sleep could be so fast. His wet finger felt not
the faintest stir of air, nor was there any movement
in the pulses of their hands. No breath ! No life !
The eyes of the girl were closed. How strangely
innocent she looked ! Larry's open eyes seemed to be
gazing at her shut eyes ; but Keith saw that they were
sightless. With a sort of sob he drew down the lids.
Then, by an impulse that he could never have explained,
he laid a hand on his brother's head, and a hand on the
girl's fair hair. The clothes had fallen down a little

from her bare shoulder ; he pulled them up, as if to keep her warm, and caught the glint of metal ; a tiny gilt crucifix no longer than a thumbnail, on a thread of steel chain, had slipped down from her breast into the hollow of the arm which lay round Larry's neck. Keith buried it beneath the clothes. Then for the first time he noticed an envelope pinned to the coverlet ; and, bending down, read : " Please give this at once to the police.—LAURENCE DARRANT." Snatching, he thrust it into his pocket. And, like elastic stretched beyond its uttermost, his reason, will, faculties of calculation and resolve snapped to within him. He thought with incredible swiftness : ' I must know nothing of this. I must go ! ' And almost before he knew that he had moved, he was out again in the street.

He could never have told of what he thought while he was walking home. He did not really come to himself till he was in his study. There, with a trembling hand, he poured himself out whisky and drank it off. If he had not chanced to go there, the charwoman would have found them when she came in the morning, and given that envelope to the police ! He took it out. He had a right—a right to know what was in it ! He broke it open.

" I, Laurence Darrant, about to die by my own hand, declare that this is a solemn and true confession. I committed what is known as the Glove Lane Murder on the night of November the 27th last in the following way "—on and on to the last words—" We didn't want to die ; but we could not bear separation, and I couldn't face letting an innocent man be hung for me. I do not see any other way. I beg that there may be no *post-mortem* on our bodies. The stuff we have taken is some of that which will be found on the dressing-table. Please bury us together.

"LAURENCE DARRANT.

"*January the 28th*, about ten o'clock p.m."

Full five minutes Keith stood with those sheets of paper in his hand, while the clock ticked, the wind moaned a little in the trees outside, the flames licked the logs with the quiet click and ruffle of their intense far-away life down there on the hearth. Then he roused himself, and sat down to read the whole again.

There it was, just as Larry had told it to him—nothing left out, very clear ; even to the addresses of people who could identify the girl as having once been Walenn's wife or mistress. It would convince. Yes ! It would convince.

The sheets dropped from his hand. Very slowly he was grasping the appalling fact that on the floor beside his chair lay the life or death of yet another man ; that by taking this confession he had taken into his own hands the fate of the vagabond lying under sentence of death ; that he could not give him back his life without incurring the smirch of this disgrace, without even endangering himself. If he let this confession reach the authorities, he could never escape the gravest suspicion that he had known of the whole affair during these two months. He would have to attend the inquest, and be recognised by that policeman as having come to the archway to see where the body had lain, as having visited the girl the very evening after the murder. Who would believe in the mere coincidence of such visits on the part of the murderer's brother. But apart from that suspicion, the fearful scandal which so sensational an affair must make would mar his

career, his life, his little daughter's life ! Larry's suicide
with this poor girl would make sensation enough as it
was ; but nothing to that other.   Such a death had its
romance ; involved him in no way save as a mourner,
could perhaps even be hushed up ! The other—nothing
could hush that up, nothing prevent its ringing to the
house-tops. He got up from his chair in sheer agitation,
and for many minutes roamed up and down the room,
unable to get his mind to bear on the issue at all.
Images kept starting up before him.   The face of the
man who handed him wig and gown each morning,
puffy and curious, with a sort of leer on it that he had
never noticed before ; his young daughter's face, with
lifted eyebrows, mouth drooping, eyes troubled ; the
tiny gilt crucifix glinting in the hollow of the dead
girl's arm ; the sightless look in Larry's unclosed eyes ;
'even his own thumb and finger pulling the lids down.
And then he saw a street and endless people passing,
turning to stare at him.   And, stopping in his tramp,
he said aloud : " Let them go to hell ! Seven days'
wonder ! " Was he not trustee to that confession !
Trustee !   After all he had done nothing to be ashamed
of, even if he had kept knowledge dark.   A brother !
Who could blame him ? And he picked up those sheets
of paper.   But then, like a great murky hand, the
scandal spread itself about him ; its coarse malignant
voice seemed shouting : " Paiper ! . . . Paiper ! . . .
Glove Lane Murder ! . . . Suicide and confession of
brother of well-known K.C. . . . Well-known K.C.'s
brother . . . Murder and suicide . . . Paiper ! " Was
he to let loose that flood of foulness ? Was he, who had
done nothing, to smirch his own little daughter's life ;
to smirch his dead brother, their dead mother—himself, his own valuable, important future ? And all

F 2

for a rat, a sewer rat ! Let him hang, let the fellow hang if he must ! And that was not certain. Appeal ! Petition ! He might—he should be saved ! To have got thus far, and then, by his own action, topple himself down !

With a sudden darting movement he thrust the confession in among the burning coals. And a smile licked at the folds in his dark face, like those flames licking the sheets of paper, till they writhed and blackened. With the toe of his boot he dispersed their scorched and crumbling wafer. Stamp them in ! Stamp in that man's life ! Burnt ! No more doubts, no more of this gnawing fear ! Burnt ? A man—an innocent—sewer rat ! Poison ! Recoiling from the fire he grasped his forehead. It was burning hot and seemed to be going round.

Well, it was done ! Only fools without will or purpose regretted. And suddenly he laughed. So Larry had died for nothing ! Nothing ! He had no will, no purpose, and he was dead ! He and that girl might now have been living, loving each other in the warm night, away at the other end of the world, instead of lying dead in the cold night here ! Fools and weaklings regretted, suffered from conscience and remorse. A man trod firmly, held to his purpose, no matter what !

He went to the window and drew back the curtain. What—what was that ? A gibbet in the air, a body hanging ? Ah ! Only the trees—the dark trees— the winter skeleton trees ! But, recoiling, he returned to his armchair and sat down before the fire. Yes ! It had been shining like that, the lamp turned low, his chair drawn up, when Larry came in that afternoon two months ago. Bah ! He had never come at all !

It was a nightmare. He had been asleep. How
his head burned! And leaping up, he looked at the
calendar on his bureau. "January the 28th!" No
dream! No dream! His face hardened and darkened.
On! Not like Larry! On!

1914.

A STOIC

I

I §

"Aequam memento rebus in arduis
Servare mentem."—HORACE.

IN the City of Liverpool, on a January day of 1905,
the Board-room of 'The Island Navigation Company'
rested, as it were, after the labours of the afternoon.
The long table was still littered with the ink, pens,
blotting-paper, and abandoned documents of six
persons—a deserted battlefield of the brain. And,
lonely, in his chairman's seat at the top end old
Sylvanus Heythorp sat, with closed eyes, still and
heavy as an image. One puffy, feeble hand, whose
fingers quivered, rested on the arm of his chair;
the thick white hair on his massive head glistened
in the light from a green-shaded lamp. He was not
asleep, for every now and then his sanguine cheeks
filled, and a sound, half sigh, half grunt, escaped his
thick lips between a white moustache and the tiny tuft
of white hairs above his cleft chin. Sunk in the chair,
that square thick trunk of a body in short black-
braided coat seemed divested of all neck.

Young Gilbert Farney, secretary of the 'Island
Navigation Company,' entering his hushed Board-room,
stepped briskly to the table, gathered some papers,
and stood looking at his chairman. Not more than
thirty-five, with the bright hues of the optimist in his
hair, beard, cheeks, and eyes, he had a nose and lips
which curled ironically. For, in his view, he *was* the

Company; and its Board did but exist to chequer his importance. Five days in the week for seven hours a day he wrote, and thought, and wove the threads of its business, and this lot came down once a week for two or three hours, and taught their grandmother to suck eggs. But watching that red-cheeked, white-haired, somnolent figure, his smile was not so contemptuous as might have been expected. For after all, the chairman was a wonderful old boy! A man of go and insight could not but respect him. Eighty! Half paralysed, over head and ears in debt, having gone the pace all his life—or so they said!—till at last that mine in Ecuador had done for him—before the secretary's day, of course, but he had heard of it. The old chap had bought it up on spec'—" *de l'audace, toujours de l'audace*," as he was so fond of saying—paid for it half in cash and half in promises, and then—the thing had turned out empty, and left him with £20,000 worth of the old shares unredeemed. The old boy had weathered it out without a bankruptcy so far. Indomitable old buffer; and never fussy like the rest of them! Young Farney, though a secretary, was capable of attachment; and his eyes expressed a pitying affection. The Board meeting had been long and " snadgy "—a final settling of that Pillin business. Rum go the chairman forcing it on them like this! And with quiet satisfaction the secretary thought : ' And he never would have got it through if I hadn't made up my mind that it really is good business ! " For to expand the company was to expand himself. Still, to buy four ships with the freight market so depressed was a bit startling, and there would be opposition at the general meeting. Never mind! He and the chairman could put it through—

put it through. And suddenly he saw the old man looking at him.

Only from those eyes could one appreciate the strength of life yet flowing underground in that well-nigh helpless carcase—deep-coloured little blue wells, tiny jovial round windows.

A sigh travelled up through layers of flesh, and he said almost inaudibly :

" Have they come, Mr. Farney ? "

" Yes, sir. I've put them in the transfer office ; said you'd be with them in a minute ; but I wasn't going to wake you."

" Haven't been asleep. Help me up."

Grasping the edge of the table with his trembling hands, the old man pulled, and, the secretary heaving behind, attained his feet. He stood about five feet ten, and weighed fully fourteen stone ; not corpulent, but very thick all through ; his round and massive head alone would have outweighed a baby. With eyes shut, he seemed to be trying to get the better of his own weight, then he moved with the slowness of a barnacle towards the door. The secretary, watching him, thought : ' Marvellous old chap ! How he gets about by himself is a miracle ! And he can't retire, they say—lives on his fees ! '

But the chairman was through the green baize door. At his tortoise gait he traversed the inner office, where the youthful clerks suspended their figuring—to grin behind his back—and entered the transfer office, where eight gentlemen were sitting. Seven rose, and one did not. Old Heythorp raised a saluting hand to the level of his chest and moving to a chair with arms, lowered himself into it.

" Well, gentlemen ? "

One of the eight gentlemen got up again.

" Mr. Heythorp, we've appointed Mr. Brownbee to voice our views. Mr. Brownbee ! " And down he sat.

Mr. Brownbee rose—a stoutish man some seventy years of age, with little grey side whiskers, and one of those utterly steady faces only to be seen in England, faces which convey the sense of business from father to son for generations ; faces which make wars, and passion, and free thought seem equally incredible ; faces which inspire confidence, and awaken in one a desire to get up and leave the room. Mr. Brownbee rose, and said in a suave voice :

" Mr. Heythorp, we here represent about £14,000. When we had the pleasure of meeting you last July, you will recollect that you held out a prospect of some more satisfactory arrangement by Christmas. We are now in January, and I am bound to say we none of us get younger."

From the depths of old Heythorp a preliminary rumble came travelling, reached the surface, and materialised :

" Don't know about you—I feel a boy."

The eight gentlemen looked at him. Was he going to try and put them off again ? Mr. Brownbee said with unruffled calm :

" I'm sure we're very glad to hear it. But to come to the point. We have felt, Mr. Heythorp, and I'm sure you won't think it unreasonable, that—er— bankruptcy would be the most satisfactory solution. We have waited a long time, and we want to know definitely where we stand ; for, to be quite frank, we don't see any prospect of improvement ; indeed, we fear the opposite."

" You think I'm going to join the majority."

This plumping out of what was at the back of their minds produced in Mr. Brownbee and his colleagues a sort of chemical disturbance. They coughed, moved their feet, and turned away their eyes, till the one who had not risen, a solicitor named Ventnor, said bluffly :

" Well, put it that way if you like."

Old Heythorp's little deep eyes twinkled.

" My grandfather lived to be a hundred ; my father ninety-six—both of them rips. I'm only eighty, gentlemen ; blameless life compared with theirs."

" Indeed," Mr. Brownbee said, " we hope you have many years of this life before you."

" More of this than of another." And a silence fell, till old Heythorp added : " You're getting a thousand a year out of my fees. Mistake to kill the goose that lays the golden eggs. I'll make it twelve hundred. If you force me to resign my directorships by bankruptcy, you won't get a rap, you know."

Mr. Brownbee cleared his throat :

" We think, Mr. Heythorp, you should make it at least fifteen hundred. In that case we might perhaps consider——"

Old Heythorp shook his head.

" We can hardly accept your assertion that we should get nothing in the event of bankruptcy. We fancy you greatly underrate the possibilities. Fifteen hundred a year is the least you can do for us."

" See you d——d first."

Another silence followed, then Ventnor, the solicitor, said irascibly :

" We know where we are, then."

Mr. Brownbee added almost nervously :

" Are we to understand that twelve hundred a year is your—your last word ? "

Old Heythorp nodded. "Come again this day month, and I'll see what I can do for you;" and he shut his eyes.

Round Mr. Brownbee six of the gentlemen gathered, speaking in low voices; Mr. Ventnor nursed a leg and glowered at old Heythorp, who sat with his eyes closed. Mr. Brownbee went over and conferred with Mr. Ventnor, then clearing his throat, he said:

"Well, sir, we have considered your proposal; we agree to accept it for the moment. We will come again, as you suggest, in a month's time. We hope that you will by then have seen your way to something more substantial, with a view to avoiding what we should all regret, but which I fear will otherwise become inevitable."

Old Heythorp nodded. The eight gentlemen took their hats, and went out one by one, Mr. Brownbee courteously bringing up the rear.

The old man, who could not get up without assistance, stayed musing in his chair. He had diddled 'em for the moment into giving him another month, and when that month was up—he would diddle 'em again! A month ought to make the Pillin business safe, with all that hung on it. That poor funkey chap Joe Pillin! A gurgling chuckle escaped his red lips. What a shadow the fellow had looked, trotting in that evening just a month ago, behind his valet's announcement: "Mr. Pillin, sir."

What a parchmenty, precise, threadpaper of a chap, with his bird's claw of a hand, and his muffled-up throat, and his quavery:

"How do you do, Sylvanus? I'm afraid you're not——"

"First rate. Sit down. Have some port."

" Port ! I never drink it.   Poison to me ! Poison ! "

" Do you good ! "

" Oh ! I know, that's what you always say.   You've
a monstrous constitution, Sylvanus.   If I drank port
and smoked cigars and sat up till one o'clock, I should
be in my grave to-morrow.   I'm not the man I was.
The fact is, I've come to see if you can help me.   I'm
getting old ; I'm growing nervous——"

" You always were as chickeny as an old hen, Joe."

" Well, my nature's not like yours.   To come to the
point, I want to sell my ships and retire.   I need rest.
Freights are very depressed.   I've got my family to
think of."

" Crack on, and go broke ; buck you up like anything ! "

" I'm quite serious, Sylvanus."

" Never knew you anything else, Joe."

A quavering cough, and out it had come :

" Now—in a word—won't your ' Island Navigation
Company ' buy my ships ? "

A pause, a twinkle, a puff of smoke.   " Make it
worth my while ! "   He had said it in jest ; and then,
in a flash, the idea had come to him.   Rosamund and
her youngsters !   What a chance to put something
between them and destitution when he had joined
the majority !   And so he said : " We don't want your
silly ships."

That claw of a hand waved in deprecation.   " They're
very good ships—doing quite well.   It's only my
wretched health.   If I were a strong man I shouldn't
dream——"

" What d'you want for 'em ? "   Good Lord ! how
he jumped if you asked him a plain question.   The
chap was as nervous as a guinea-fowl !

" Here are the figures—for the last four years. I think you'll agree that I couldn't ask less than seventy thousand."

Through the smoke of his cigar old Heythorp had digested those figures slowly, Joe Pillin feeling his teeth and sucking lozenges the while ; then he said :

" Sixty thousand ! And out of that you pay me ten per cent., if I get it through for you. Take it or leave it."

" My dear Sylvanus, that's almost—cynical."

" Too good a price—you'll never get it without me."

" But a—but a commission ! You could never disclose it ! "

" Arrange that all right. Think it over. Freights 'll go lower yet. Have some port."

" No, no ! Thank you. No ! So you think freights will go lower ? "

" Sure of it."

" Well, I'll be going. I'm sure I don't know. It's—it's—I must think."

" Think your hardest."

" Yes, yes. Good-bye. I can't imagine how you still go on smoking those things and drinking port."

" See you in your grave yet, Joe." What a feeble smile the poor fellow had ! Laugh—he couldn't ! And, alone again, he had browsed on and developed the idea which had come to him.

Though, to dwell in the heart of shipping, Sylvanus Heythorp had lived at Liverpool twenty years, he was from the Eastern Counties, of a family so old that it professed to despise the Conquest. Each of its generations occupied nearly twice as long as those of less tenacious men. Traditionally of Danish origin,

its men folk had as a rule bright reddish-brown hair,
red cheeks, large round heads, excellent teeth and
poor morals. They had done their best for the popula-
tion of any county in which they had settled ; their
offshoots swarmed. Born in the early twenties of the
nineteenth century, Sylvanus Heythorp, after an
education broken by escapades both at school and
college, had fetched up in that simple London of the
late forties, where claret, opera, and eight per cent.
for your money ruled a cheery roost. Made partner
in his shipping firm well before he was thirty, he had
sailed with a wet sheet and a flowing tide ; dancers,
claret, Cliquot, and piquet ; a cab with a tiger ; some
travel—all that delicious early-Victorian consciousness
of nothing save a golden time. It was all so full and
mellow that he was forty before he had his only love
affair of any depth—with the daughter of one of his
own clerks, a *liaison* so awkward as to necessitate a
sedulous concealment. The death of that girl, after
three years, leaving him a natural son, had been the
chief, perhaps the only real, grief of his life. Five
years later he married. What for ? God only knew !
as he was in the habit of remarking. His wife had
been a hard, worldly, well-connected woman, who
presented him with two unnatural children, a girl and a
boy, and grew harder, more worldly, less handsome,
in the process. The migration to Liverpool, which took
place when he was sixty and she forty-two, broke
what she still had of heart, but she lingered on twelve
years, finding solace in bridge, and being haughty
towards Liverpool. Old Heythorp saw her to her
rest without regret. He had felt no love for her
whatever, and practically none for her two children—
they were in his view colourless, pragmatical, very

G

unexpected characters. His son Ernest—in the
Admiralty—he thought a poor, careful stick. His
daughter Adela, an excellent manager, delighting in
spiritual conversation and the society of tame men,
rarely failed to show him that she considered him a
hopeless heathen. They saw as little as need be of
each other. She was provided for under that settlement he had made on her mother fifteen years ago,
well before the not altogether unexpected crisis in
his affairs. Very different was the feeling he had
bestowed on that son of his "under the rose."
The boy, who had always gone by his mother's
name of Larne, had on her death been sent to some
relations of hers in Ireland, and there brought up. He
had been called to the Dublin bar, and married,
young, a girl half Cornish and half Irish ; presently,
having cost old Heythorp in all a pretty penny, he had
died impecunious, leaving his fair Rosamund at thirty
with a girl of eight and a boy of five. She had not
spent six months of widowhood before coming over
from Dublin to claim the old man's guardianship.
A remarkably pretty woman, like a full-blown rose,
with greenish hazel eyes, she had turned up one
morning at the offices of ' The Island Navigation
Company,' accompanied by her two children—for
he had never divulged to them his private address.
And since then they had always been more or less on
his hands, occupying a small house in a suburb of
Liverpool. He visited them there, but never asked
them to the house in Sefton Park, which was in fact
his daughter's ; so that his proper family and friends
were unaware of their existence.

Rosamund Larne was one of those precarious ladies
who make uncertain incomes by writing full-bodied

storyettes. In the most dismal circumstances she
enjoyed a buoyancy bordering on the indecent, which
always amused old Heythorp's cynicism. But of his
grandchildren Phyllis and Jock (wild as colts) he had
become fond. And this chance of getting six thousand
pounds settled on them at a stroke had seemed to
him nothing but heaven-sent. As things were, if he
" went off "—as, of course, he might at any moment,
there wouldn't be a penny for them ; for he would
" cut up " a good fifteen thousand to the bad. He was
now giving them some three hundred a year out of his
fees ; and dead directors unfortuately earned no fees !
Six thousand pounds at four and a half per cent., settled
so that their mother couldn't " blue it," would give
them a certain two hundred and fifty pounds a year—
better than beggary. And the more he thought the
better he liked it, if only that shaky chap, Joe Pillin,
didn't shy off when he'd bitten his nails short
over it !

Four evenings later, the " shaky chap " had again
appeared at his house in Sefton Park.

" I've thought it over, Sylvanus. I don't like it."

" No ; but you'll do it."

" It's a sacrifice. Fifty-four thousand for four ships
—it means a considerable reduction in my income."

" It means security, my boy."

" Well, there is that ; but you know, I really can't
be party to a secret commission. If it came out,
think of my name and goodness knows what."

" It won't come out."

" Yes, yes, so you say, but——"

" All you've got to do's to execute a settlement on
some third parties that I'll name. I'm not going to
take a penny by it myself. Get your own lawyer to

draw it up and make him trustee. You can sign it
when the purchase has gone through. I'll trust you,
Joe. What stock have you got that gives four and a
half per cent. ? "

" Midland——"

" That'll do. You needn't sell."

" Yes, but who *are* these people ? "

" Woman and her children I want to do a good turn
to." What a face the fellow had made ! " Afraid of
being connected with a woman, Joe ? "

" Yes, you may laugh—I *am* afraid of being connected with someone else's woman. I don't like it—
I don't like it at all. I've not led your life, Sylvanus."

" Lucky for you ; you'd have been dead long ago.
Tell your lawyer it's an old flame of yours—you old
dog ! "

" Yes, there it is at once, you see. I might be
subject to blackmail."

" Tell him to keep it dark, and just pay over the
income, quarterly. They'll think I'm their benefactor,
and so I am."

" I don't like it, Sylvanus—I don't like it."

" Then leave it, and be hanged to you. Have a
cigar ! "

" You know I never smoke. Is there no other
way ? "

" Yes. Sell stock in London, bank the proceeds
there, and bring me six thousand pounds in notes.
I'll hold 'em till after the general meeting. If the
thing doesn't go through, I'll hand 'em back to you."

" No ; I like that even less."

" Rather I trusted *you*, eh ! "

" No, not at all, Sylvanus, not at all. But it's all
playing round the law."

" There's no law to prevent you doing what you like
with your money. What I do's nothing to you. And
mind you, I'm taking nothing from it—not a mag.
You assist the widowed and the fatherless—just your
line, Joe ! "

" What a fellow you are, Sylvanus ; you don't seem
capable of taking anything seriously."

" Care killed the cat ! "

Left alone after this second interview he had thought :
" The beggar'll jump."

And the beggar *had*. That settlement was drawn
and only awaited signature. The Board to-day had
decided on the purchase ; and all that remained was
to get it ratified at the general meeting. Let him but
get that over, and this provision for his grandchildren
made, and he would snap his fingers at Brownbee and
his crew—the canting humbugs ! " Hope you have
many years of this life before you ! " As if they cared
for anything but his money—*their* money rather !
And becoming conscious of the length of his reverie,
he grasped the arms of his chair, heaved at his own
bulk, in an effort to rise, growing redder and redder
in face and neck. It was one of the hundred things
his doctor had told him not to do for fear of apoplexy !
Humbug ! Why didn't Farney or one of those young
fellows come and help him up ? To call out was
undignified. But was he to sit there all night ? Three
times he failed, and after each failure sat motionless
again, crimson and exhausted ; the fourth time he
succeeded, and slowly made for the office. Passing
through, he stopped and said in his extinct voice :

" You young gentlemen had forgotten me."

" Mr. Farney said you didn't wish to be disturbed,
sir."

" Very good of him.   Give me my hat and coat."

" Yes, sir."

" Thank you.   What time is it ? "

" Six o'clock, sir."

" Tell Mr. Farney to come and see me to-morrow at noon, about my speech for the general meeting."

" Yes, sir."

" Good-night to you."

" Good-night, sir."

At his tortoise gait he passed between the office stools to the door, opened it feebly, and slowly vanished.

Shutting the door behind him, a clerk said :

" Poor old chairman !   He's on his last ! "

Another answered :

" Gosh !   He's a tough old hulk.   He'll go down fightin'."

2 §

Issuing from the offices of ' The Island Navigation Company,' Sylvanus Heythorp moved towards the corner whence he always took tram to Sefton Park. The crowded street had all that prosperous air of catching or missing something which characterises the town where London and New York and Dublin meet.   Old Heythorp had to cross to the far side, and he sallied forth without regard to traffic.   That snail-like passage had in it a touch of the sublime ; the old man seemed saying : " Knock me down and be d——d to you—I'm not going to hurry."   His life was saved perhaps ten times a day by the British character at large, compounded of phlegm and a liking to take something under its protection.   The tram conductors on that line were especially used to him, never failing to catch him under the arms and heave him like a sack of coals,

while with trembling hands he pulled hard at the rail
and strap.

" All right, sir ? "

" Thank you."

He moved into the body of the tram, where somebody
would always get up from kindness and the fear that
he might sit down on them ; and there he stayed
motionless, his little eyes tight closed. With his red
face, tuft of white hairs above his square cleft block
of shaven chin, and his big high-crowned bowler hat,
which yet seemed too petty for his head with its
thick hair—he looked like some kind of an idol dug
up and decked out in gear a size too small.

One of those voices of young men from public schools
and exchanges where things are bought and sold, said :

" How de do, Mr. Heythorp ? "

Old Heythorp opened his eyes. That sleek cub,
Joe Pillin's son ! What a young pup—with his round
eyes, and his round cheeks, and his little moustache,
his fur coat, his spats, his diamond pin !

" How's your father ? " he said.

" Thanks, rather below par, worryin' about his
ships. Suppose you haven't any news for him, sir ? "

Old Heythorp nodded. The young man was one of
his pet abominations, embodying all the complacent,
little-headed mediocrity of this new generation ;
natty fellows all turned out of the same mould, sippers
and tasters, chaps without drive or capacity, without
even vices ; and he did not intend to gratify the
cub's curiosity.

" Come to my house," he said ; " I'll give you a
note for him."

" Tha—anks ; I'd like to cheer the old man up."

The old man ! Cheeky brat ! And closing his eyes

he relapsed into immobility. The tram wound and
ground its upward way, and he mused. When he was
that cub's age—twenty-eight or whatever it might
be—he had done most things ; been up Vesuvius,
driven four-in-hand, lost his last penny on the Derby
and won it back on the Oaks, known all the dancers
and operatic stars of the day, fought a duel with a
Yankee at Dieppe and winged him for saying through
his confounded nose that Old England was played out ;
been a controlling voice already in his shipping firm ;
drunk five other of the best men in London under the
table ; broken his neck steeplechasing ; shot a burglar
in the legs ; been nearly drowned, for a bet ; killed
snipe in Chelsea ; been to Court—but never again !
stared a ghost out of countenance ; and travelled
with a lady of Spain. If this young pup had done
the last, it would be all he had ; and yet, no doubt,
he would call himself a " spark."

The conductor touched his arm.

" 'Ere you are, sir."

" Thank you."

He lowered himself to the ground, and moved in the
bluish darkness towards the gate of his daughter's
house. Bob Pillin walked beside him, thinking :
' Poor old josser, he *is* gettin' a back number ! ' And
he said : " I should have thought you ought to drive,
sir. My old guv'nor would knock up at once if he went
about at night like this."

The answer rumbled out into the misty air :

" Your father's got no chest ; never had."

Bob Pillin gave vent to one of those fat cackles
which come so readily from a certain type of man ;
and old Heythorp thought : ' Laughing at his father !
Parrot ! '

They had reached the porch.

A woman with dark hair and a thin, straight face and figure was arranging some flowers in the hall. She turned and said :

"You really ought not to be so late, father ! It's wicked at this time of year. Who is it—oh ! Mr. Pillin, how do you do ? Have you had tea ? Won't you come to the drawing-room ; or do you want to see my father ? "

' Tha—anks ! I believe your father——" And he thought : ' By Jove ! the old chap *is* a caution ! ' For old Heythorp was crossing the hall without having paid the faintest attention to his daughter. Murmuring again :

" Tha—anks awfully ; he wants to give me something," he followed. Miss Heythorp was not his style at all ; he had a kind of dread of that thin woman who looked as if she could never be unbuttoned. They said she was a great churchgoer and all that sort of thing.

In his sanctum old Heythorp had moved to his writing-table, and was evidently anxious to sit down.

" Shall I give you a hand, sir ? "

Receiving a shake of the head, Bob Pillin stood by the fire and watched. The old " sport " liked to paddle his own canoe. Fancy having to lower yourself into a chair like that ! When an old Johnny got to such a state it was really a mercy when he snuffed out, and made way for younger men. How his Companies could go on putting up with such a fossil for chairman was a marvel ! The fossil rumbled and said in that almost inaudible voice :

" I suppose you're beginning to look forward to your father's shoes ? "

Bob Pillin's mouth opened. The voice went on:

" Dibs and no responsibility. Tell him from me to
drink port—add five years to his life."

To this unwarranted attack Bob Pillin made no
answer save a laugh ; he perceived that a man-
servant had entered the room.

" A Mrs. Larne, sir. Will you see her ? "

At this announcement the old man seemed to try
and start ; then he nodded, and held out the note he
had written. Bob Pillin received it together with the
impression of a murmur which sounded like : " Scratch
a poll, Poll ! " and passing the fine figure of a woman
in a fur coat, who seemed to warm the air as she went
by, he was in the hall again before he perceived that
he had left his hat.

A young and pretty girl was standing on the bear-
skin before the fire, looking at him with round-eyed
innocence. He thought : ' This is better ; I mustn't
disturb them for my hat ' ; and approaching the fire,
said :

" Jolly cold, isn't it ? "

The girl smiled : " Yes—jolly."

He noticed that she had a large bunch of violets at
her breast, a lot of fair hair, a short straight nose, and
round blue-grey eyes very frank and open. " Er—— "
he said, " I've left my hat in there."

" What larks ! " And at her little clear laugh
something moved within Bob Pillin.

" You know this house well ? "

She shook her head. " But it's rather scrumny,
isn't it ? "

Bob Pillin, who had never yet thought so,
answered :

" Quite O.K."

The girl threw up her head to laugh again.
" O.K. ? What's that ? "

Bob Pillin saw her white round throat, and thought :
' She *is* a ripper ! ' And he said with a certain
desperation :

" My name's Pillin. Yours is Larne, isn't it ? Are
you a relation here ? "

" He's our Guardy. Isn't he a chook ? "

That rumbling whisper like " Scratch a poll, Poll ! "
recurring to Bob Pillin, he said with reservation :

" You know him better than I do."

" Oh ! Aren't you his grandson, or something ? "

Bob Pillin did not cross himself.

" Lord ! No ! My dad's an old friend of his ; that's
all."

" Is your dad like him ? "

" Not much."

" What a pity ! It would have been lovely if they'd
been Tweedles."

Bob Pillin thought : ' This bit is something new.
I wonder what her Christian name is.' And he said :

" What did your godfather and godmothers in your
baptism—— ? "

The girl laughed ; she seemed to laugh at everything.

" Phyllis."

Could he say : " Is my only joy " ? Better keep it !
But—for what ? He wouldn't see her again if he didn't
look out ! And he said :

" I live at the last house in the park—the red one.
D'you know it ? Where do you ? "

" Oh ! a long way—23, Millicent Villas. It's a
poky little house. I hate it. We have awful larks,
though."

" Who are we ? "

" Mother, and myself, and Jock—he's an awful
boy. You can't conceive what an awful boy he is.
He's got nearly red hair ; I think he'll be just like
Guardy when he gets old. He's *awful!* "

Bob Pillin murmured :

" I should like to see him."

" Would you ? I'll ask mother if you can. You
won't want to again ; he goes off all the time like a
squib." She threw back her head, and again Bob
Pillin felt a little giddy. He collected himself, and
drawled :

" Are you going in to see your Guardy ? "

" No. Mother's got something special to say.
We've never been here before, you see. Isn't he fun,
though ? "

" Fun ! "

" I think he's the greatest lark ; but he's awfully
nice to me. Jock calls him the last of the Stoic'uns."

A voice called from old Heythorp's den :

" Phyllis ! " It had a particular ring, that voice,
as if coming from beautifully formed red lips, of which
the lower one must curve the least bit over ; it had,
too, a caressing vitality, and a kind of warm falsity.

The girl threw a laughing look back over her shoulder,
and vanished through the door into the room.

Bob Pillin remained with his back to the fire and his
puppy round eyes fixed on the air that her figure had
last occupied. He was experiencing a sensation never
felt before. Those travels with a lady of Spain,
charitably conceded him by old Heythorp, had so far
satisfied the emotional side of this young man ; they
had stopped short at Brighton and Scarborough, and
been preserved from even the slightest intrusion of
love. A calculated and hygienic career had caused

no anxiety either to himself or his father ; and this sudden swoop of something more than admiration gave him an uncomfortable choky feeling just above his high round collar, and in the temples a sort of buzzing—those first symptoms of chivalry. A man of the world does not, however, succumb without a struggle ; and if his hat had not been out of reach, who knows whether he would not have left the house hurriedly, saying to himself : " No, no, my boy ; Millicent Villas is hardly your form, when your intentions are honourable " ? For somehow that round and laughing face, bob of glistening hair, those wide-opened grey eyes refused to awaken the beginnings of other intentions—such is the effect of youth and innocence on even the steadiest young men. With a kind of moral stammer, he was thinking : ' Can I—dare I offer to see them to their tram ? Couldn't I even nip out and get the car round and send them home in it ? No, I might miss them—better stick it out here ! What a jolly laugh ! What a tipping face—strawberries and cream, hay, and all that ! Millicent Villas ! ' And he wrote it on his cuff.

The door was opening ; he heard that warm vibrating voice : " Come along, Phyllis ! "—the girl's voice and laugh so high and fresh : " Right-o ! Coming ! " And with, perhaps, the first real tremor he had ever known, he crossed to the front door. All the more chivalrous to escort them to the tram without a hat ! And suddenly he heard : " I've got your hat, young man ! " And her mother's voice, warm, and simulating shock : " Phyllis, you awful gairl ! Did you ever see such an awful gairl, Mr. ——"

" Pillin, Mother."

And then—he did not quite know how—insulated
from the January air by laughter and the scent of fur
and violets, he was between them walking to their
tram. It was like an experience out of the " Arabian
Nights," or something of that sort, an intoxication
which made one say one was going their way, though
one would have to come all the way back in the same
beastly tram. Nothing so warming had ever happened
to him as sitting between them on that drive, so that
he forgot the note in his pocket, and his desire to
relieve the anxiety of the " old man," his father. At
the tram's terminus they all got out. There issued a
purr of invitation to come and see them some time ;
a clear : " Jock'll love to see you ! " A low laugh :
" You awful gairl ! " And a flash of cunning zigzagged
across his brain, so that, taking off his hat, he said :
" Thanks awfully ; rather ! " putting his foot back on
the step of the tram. Thus did he delicately expose
the depths of his chivalry !
" Oh ! you *said* you were going our way ! What
one-ers you do tell ! Oh ! " The words were as music ;
the sight of those eyes growing rounder the most
perfect he had ever seen ; and Mrs. Larne's low laugh,
so warm yet so preoccupied, and the tips of the girl's
fingers waving back above her head. He heaved a
sigh, and knew no more till he was seated at his club
before a bottle of champagne. Home ! Not he ! He
wished to drink and dream. " The old man " would
get his news all right to-morrow !

§ 3

The words : " A Mrs. Larne to see you, sir," had
been of a nature to astonish weaker nerves. Wha

had brought her here ? She knew she mustn't come ! Old Heythorp had watched her entrance with cynical amusement. The way she whiffed herself at that young pup in passing, the way her eyes slid round ! He had a very just appreciation of his son's widow ; and a smile settled deep between his chin tuft and his moustache. She lifted his hand, kissed it, pressed it to her splendid bust, and said :

. " So here I am at last, you see. Aren't you surprised ? "

Old Heythorp shook his head.

" I really had to come and see you, Guardy ; we haven't had a sight of you for such an age. And in this awful weather ! How are you, dear old Guardy ? "

" Never better." And, watching her green-grey eyes, he added : " Haven't a penny for you ! "

Her face did not fall ; she gave her feather-laugh.

" How dreadful of you to think I came for that ! But I *am* in an awful fix, Guardy."

" Never knew you not to be."

" Just let me tell you, dear ; it'll be some relief. I'm having the most terrible time."

She sank into a low chair, disengaging an overpowering scent of violets, while melancholy struggled to subdue her face and body.

" The most awful fix. I expect to be sold up any moment. We may be on the streets to-morrow. I daren't tell the children ; they're so happy, poor darlings. I shall be obliged to take Jock away from school. And Phyllis will have to stop her piano and dancing ; it's an absolute crisis. And all due to those Midland Syndicate people. I've been counting on at least two hundred for my new story, and the wretches have refused it."

With a tiny handkerchief she removed one tear from the corner of one eye. " It *is* hard, Guardy ; I worked my brain silly over that story."

From old Heythorp came a mutter which sounded suspiciously like : " Rats ! "

Heaving a sigh, which conveyed nothing but the generosity of her breathing apparatus, Mrs. Larne went on :

" You couldn't, I suppose, let me have just one hundred ? "

" Not a bob."

She sighed again, her eyes slid round the room ; then in 'her warm voice she murmured :

" Guardy, you *were* my dear Philip's father, weren't you ? I've never said anything ; but *of course* you were. He was so like you, and so is Jock."

Nothing moved in old Heythorp's face. No pagan image consulted with flowers and song and sacrifice could have returned less answer. Her dear Philip ! She had led him the devil of a life, or he was a Dutchman ! And what the deuce made her suddenly trot out the skeleton like this ? But Mrs. Larne's eyes were still wandering.

" What a lovely house ! You know, I think you ought to help me, Guardy. Just imagine if your grandchildren were thrown out into the street ! "

The old man grinned. He was not going to deny his relationship—it was her look-out, not his. But neither was he going to let her rush him.

" And they will be ; you *couldn't* look on and see it. Do come to my rescue this once. You really might do something for them."

With a rumbling sigh he answered :

" Wait. Can't give you a penny now. Poor as a church mouse."

" Oh ! Guardy ! "

" Fact."

Mrs. Larne heaved one of her most buoyant sighs. She certainly did not believe him.

" Well ! " she said ; " you'll be sorry when we come round one night and sing for pennies under your window. Wouldn't you like to see Phyllis ? I left her in the hall. She's growing such a sweet gairl. Guardy—just fifty ! "

" Not a rap."

Mrs. Larne threw up her hands. " Well ! You'll repent it. I'm at my last gasp." She sighed profoundly, and the perfume of violets escaped in a cloud. Then, getting up, she went to the door and called : " Phyllis ! "

When the girl entered old Heythorp felt the nearest approach to a flutter of the heart for many years. She had put her hair up ! She was like a spring day in January ; such a relief from that scented humbug, her mother. Pleasant the touch of her lips on his forehead, the sound of her clear voice, the sight of her slim movements, the feeling that she did him credit—clean-run stock, she and that young scamp Jock—better than the holy woman, his daughter, Adela, would produce if anyone were ever fool enough to marry her, or that pragmatical fellow, his son Ernest.

And when they were gone he reflected with added zest on the six thousand pounds he was getting for them out of Joe Pillin and his ships. He would have to pitch it strong in his speech at the general meeting. With freights so low, there was bound to be opposition.

No dash nowadays; nothing but flabby caution! They were a scrim-shanking lot on the Board—he had had to pull them round one by one—the deuce of a tug getting this thing through! And yet, the business was sound enough. Those ships would earn money, properly handled—good money!

His valet, coming in to prepare him for dinner, found him asleep. He had for the old man as much admiration as may be felt for one who cannot put his own trousers on. He would say to the housemaid Molly: "He's a game old blighter—must have been a rare one in his day. Cocks his hat at you, now, I see!" To which the girl, an Irish one and pretty, would reply: "Well, an' sure I don't mind, if it gives um a pleasure. 'Tis better annyway than the sad eye I get from herself."

At dinner, old Heythorp always sat at one end of the rosewood table and his daughter at the other. It was the eminent moment of the day. With napkin tucked high into his waistcoat, he gave himself to the meal with passion. His palate was undimmed, his digestion unimpaired. He could still eat as much as two men, and drink more than one. And while he savoured each mouthful he never spoke if he could help it. The holy woman had nothing to say that he cared to hear, and he nothing to say that she cared to listen to. She had a horror, too, of what she called "the pleasures of the table"—those lusts of the flesh! She was always longing to dock his grub, he knew. Would see her further first! What other pleasures were there at his age? Let her wait till *she* was eighty. But she never would be; too thin and holy!

This evening however, with the advent of the partridge she *did* speak.

" Who were your visitors, Father ? "

Trust her for nosing anything out ! Fixing his little
blue eyes on her, he mumbled with a very full mouth :
" Ladies."

" So I saw ; what ladies ? "

He had a longing to say : " Part of one of my
families under the rose." As a fact it was the best
part of the only one, but the temptation to multiply
exceedingly was almost overpowering. He checked himself, however, and went on eating partridge, his secret
irritation crimsoning his cheeks ; and he watched
her eyes, those cold precise and round grey eyes, noting
it, and knew she was thinking : ' He eats too much.'

She said : " Sorry I'm not considered fit to be told.
You ought not to be drinking hock."

Old Heythorp took up the long green glass, drained
it, and repressing fumes and emotion went on with his
partridge. His daughter pursed her lips, took a sip
of water, and said :

" I know their name is Larne, but it conveyed
nothing to me ; perhaps it's just as well."

The old man, mastering a spasm, said with a grin :

" My daughter-in-law and my granddaughter."

" What ! Ernest married—Oh ! nonsense ! "

He chuckled, and shook his head.

" Then do you mean to say, Father, that you were
married before you married my mother ? "

" No."

The expression on her face was as good as a play !

She said with a sort of disgust : " Not married ! I
see. I suppose those people are hanging round your
neck, then ; no wonder you're always in difficulties.
Are there any more of them ? "

Again the old man suppressed that spasm, and the

veins in his neck and forehead swelled alarmingly.
If he had spoken he would infallibly have choked.
He ceased eating, and putting his hands on the table
tried to raise himself. He could not, and subsiding
in his chair sat glaring at the stiff, quiet figure of his
daughter.

" Don't be silly, Father, and make a scene before
Meller. Finish your dinner."

He did not answer. He was not going to sit there
to be dragooned and insulted! His helplessness had
never so weighed on him before. It was like a revelation. A log—that had to put up with anything! A
log! And, waiting for his valet to return, he cunningly
took up his fork.

In that saintly voice of hers she said :

" I suppose you don't realise that it's a shock to me.
I don't know what Ernest will think——"

" Ernest be d——d."

" I do wish, Father, you wouldn't swear."

Old Heythorp's rage found vent in a sort of rumble.
How the devil had he gone on all these years in the same
house with that woman, dining with her day after day!
But the servant had come back now, and putting down
his fork he said :

" Help me up ! "

The man paused, thunderstruck, with the *soufflé*
balanced. To leave dinner unfinished—it was a
portent !

" Help me up ! "

" Mr. Heythorp's not very well, Meller ; take his
other arm."

The old man shook off her hand.

" I'm very well. Help me up. Dine in my own
room in future."

Raised to his feet, he walked slowly out ; but in his sanctum he did not sit down, obsessed by this first overwhelming realisation of his helplessness. He stood swaying a little, holding on to the table, till the servant, having finished serving dinner, brought in his port.

" Are you waiting to sit down, sir ? "

He shook his head. Hang it, he could do that for himself, anyway. He must think of something to fortify his position against that woman ! And he said :

" Send me Molly ! "

" Yes, sir." The man put down the port and went. Old Heythorp filled his glass, drank, and filled again. He took a cigar from the box and lighted it. The girl came in, a grey-eyed, dark-haired damsel, and stood with her hands folded, her head a little to one side, her lips a little parted. The old man said :

" You're a human being."

" I would hope so, sirr."

" I'm going to ask you something as a human being— not a servant—see ? "

" No, sirr ; but I will be glad to do annything you like."

" Then put your nose in here every now and then, to see if I want anything. Meller goes out sometimes. Don't say anything ; just put your nose in."

" Oh ! an' I will ; 'tis a pleasure 'twill be to do ut."

He nodded, and when she had gone lowered himself into his chair with a sense of appeasement. Pretty girl ! Comfort to see a pretty face—not a pale, peeky thing like Adela's. His anger burned up anew. So she counted on his helplessness, had begun to count on that, had she ? She should see that there was life in the old dog yet ! And his sacrifice of the uneaten *soufflé,* the still less eaten mushrooms, the peppermint sweet with which he usually concluded dinner, seemed to consecrate that purpose. They all thought he was a hulk, without a shot left in the locker ! He had seen a couple of them at the Board that afternoon shrugging at each other, as though saying : " Look at him ! " And young Farney pitying him. Pity, forsooth ! And that coarse-grained solicitor chap at the creditors' meeting curling his lip as much as to say : " One foot in the grave ! " He had seen the clerks dowsing the glim of their grins ; and that young pup Bob Pillin screwing up his supercilious mug over his dog-collar. He knew that scented humbug Rosamund was getting scared that he'd drop off before she'd squeezed him dry. And his valet was always looking him up and down queerly. As to that holy woman——! Not quite so fast ! Not quite so fast ! And filling his glass for the fourth time, he slowly sucked down the dark red fluid, with the " old boots " flavour which his soul loved, and, drawing deep at his cigar, closed his eyes.

II

1 §

THE room in the hotel where the general meetings of
'The Island Navigation Company' were held was
nearly full when the secretary came through the door
which as yet divided the shareholders from their
directors. Having surveyed their empty chairs, their
ink and papers, and nodded to a shareholder or two, he
stood, watch in hand, contemplating the congregation.
A thicker attendance than he had ever seen! Due, no
doubt, to the lower dividend, and this Pillin business.
And his tongue curled. For if he had a natural
contempt for his Board, with the exception of the
chairman, he had a still more natural contempt for his
shareholders. Amusing spectacle, when you came to
think of it, a general meeting! Unique! Eighty or a
hundred men, and five women, assembled through
sheer devotion to their money. Was any other
function in the world so single-hearted. Church was
nothing to it—so many motives were mingled there
with devotion to one's soul. A well-educated young
man—reader of Anatole France, and other writers—he
enjoyed ironic speculation. What earthly good did
they think they got by coming here? Half-past two!
He put his watch back into his pocket, and passed
into the board-room.

There, the fumes of lunch and of a short preliminary
meeting made cosy the February atmosphere. By the
fire four directors were conversing rather restlessly
the fifth was combing his beard; the chairman sat

with eyes closed and red lips moving rhythmically in the sucking of a lozenge, the slips of his speech ready in his hand. The secretary said in his cheerful voice: " Time, sir."

Old Heythorp swallowed, lifted his arms, rose with help, and walked through to his place at the centre of the table. The five directors followed. And, standing at the chairman's right, the secretary read the minutes, forming the words precisely with his curling tongue. Then, assisting the chairman to his feet, he watched those rows of faces, and thought: ' Mistake to let them see he can't get up without help. He ought to have let me read his speech—I wrote it.'

The chairman began to speak:

" It is my duty and my pleasure, ladies and gentlemen, for the nineteenth consecutive year to present to you the directors' report and the accounts for the past twelve months. You will all have had special notice of a measure of policy on which your Board has decided, and to which you will be asked to-day to give your adherence—to that I shall come at the end of my remarks . . ."

" Excuse me, sir ; we can't hear a word down here."

' Ah ! ' thought the secretary, ' I was expecting that.'

The chairman went on, undisturbed. But several shareholders now rose, and the same speaker said testily : " We might as well go home. If the chairman's got no voice, can't somebody read for him ? "

The chairman took a sip of water, and resumed. Almost all in the last six rows were now on their feet, and amid a hubbub of murmurs the chairman held out to the secretary the slips of his speech, and fell heavily back into his chair.

The secretary re-read from the beginning; and as each sentence fell from his tongue, he thought: 'How good that is!' 'That's very clear!' 'A neat touch!' 'This is getting them.' It seemed to him a pity they could not know it was all his composition. When at last he came to the Pillin sale he paused for a second.

"I come now to the measure of policy to which I made allusion at the beginning of my speech. Your Board has decided to expand your enterprise by purchasing the entire fleet of Pillin & Co., Ltd. By this transaction we become the owners of the four steamships *Smyrna*, *Damascus*, *Tyre*, and *Sidon*, vessels in prime condition with a total freight-carrying capacity of fifteen thousand tons, at the low inclusive price of sixty thousand pounds. Gentlemen, "*Vestigia nulla retrorsum!*"—it was the chairman's phrase, his bit of the speech, and the secretary did it more than justice. "Times are bad, but your Board is emphatically of the opinion that they are touching bottom; and this, in their view, is the psychological moment for a forward stroke. They confidently recommend your adoption of their policy and the ratification of this purchase, which they believe will, in the not far distant future, substantially increase the profits of the Company." The secretary sat down with reluctance. The speech should have continued with a number of appealing sentences which he had carefully prepared, but the chairman had cut them out with the simple comment: "They ought to be glad of the chance." It was, in his view, an error.

The director who had combed his beard now rose— a man of presence, who might be trusted to say nothing long and suavely. While he was speaking the secretary

was busy noting whence opposition was likely to come.
The majority were sitting owl-like—a good sign ; but
some dozen were studying their copies of the report,
and three at least were making notes—Westgate, for
instance, who wanted to get on the Board, and was
sure to make himself unpleasant—the time-honoured
method of vinegar ; and Batterson, who also desired
to come on, and might be trusted to support the
Board—the time-honoured method of oil ; while, if
one knew anything of human nature, the fellow who
had complained that he might as well go home would
have something uncomfortable to say. The director
finished his remarks, combed his beard with his fingers,
and sat down.

A momentary pause ensued. Then Messieurs
Westgate and Batterson rose together. Seeing the
chairman nod towards the latter, the secretary thought :
' Mistake ! He should have humoured Westgate by
giving him precedence.' But that was the worst of
the old man, he had no notion of the *suaviter in modo !*
Mr. Batterson—thus unchained—" would like, if he
might be so allowed, to congratulate the Board on
having piloted their ship so smoothly through the
troublous waters of the past year. With their worthy
chairman still at the helm, he had no doubt that in
spite of the still low—he would not say falling—
barometer, and the—er—unseasonable climacteric,
they might rely on weathering the—er—he would
not say storm. He would confess that the present
dividend of four per cent. was not one which satisfied
every aspiration (Hear, hear !), but speaking for himself, and he hoped for others "—and here Mr. Batterson
looked round—" he recognised that in all the circumstances it was as much as they had the right—er—

to expect. By following the bold but to *his* mind prudent development which the Board proposed to make, he thought that they might reasonably, if not sanguinely, anticipate a more golden future." (" No, no ! ") " A shareholder said, ' No, no ! ' That might seem to indicate a certain lack of confidence in the special proposal before the meeting." (" Yes ! ") " From that lack of confidence he would like at once to dissociate himself. Their chairman, a man of foresight and acumen, and valour proved on many a field and—er—sea, would not have committed himself to this policy without good reason. In his opinion they. were in safe hands, and he was glad to register his support of the measure proposed. The chairman had well said in his speech : ' *Vestigia nulla retrorsum !* ' Shareholders would agree with him that there could be no better motto for Englishmen. Ahem ! "

Mr. Batterson sat down. And Mr. Westgate rose : " He wanted "—he said—" to know more, much more, about this proposition, which to his mind was of a very dubious wisdom " . . . ' Ah ! ' thought the secretary, ' I told the old boy he must tell them more ' . . . " To whom, for instance, had the proposal first been made ? To him !—the chairman said. Good ! But why were Pillins selling, if freights were to go up, as they were told ? "

" Matter of opinion."

" Quite so ; and in his opinion they were going lower, and Pillins were right to sell. It followed that they were wrong to buy. (" Hear, hear ! " " No, no ! ") " Pillins' were shrewd people. What did the chairman say ? Nerves ! Did he mean to tell them that this sale was the result of nerves ? "

The chairman nodded.

"That appeared to him a somewhat fantastic theory; but he would leave that and confine himself to asking the grounds on which the chairman based his confidence; in fact, what it was which was actuating the Board in pressing on them at such a time what he had no hesitation in stigmatising as a rash proposal. In a word, he wanted light as well as leading in this matter."

Mr. Westgate sat down.

What would the chairman do now? The situation was distinctly awkward—seeing his helplessness and the lukewarmness of the Board behind him. And the secretary felt more strongly than ever the absurdity of his being an underling, he who in a few well-chosen words could so easily have twisted the meeting round his thumb. Suddenly he heard the long, rumbling sigh which preluded the chairman's speeches.

"Has any other gentleman anything to say before I move the adoption of the report?"

Phew! That would put their backs up. Yes, sure enough it had brought that fellow, who had said he might as well go home, to his feet! Now for something nasty!

"Mr. Westgate requires answering. I don't like this business. I don't impute anything to anybody; but it looks to me as if there were something behind it which the shareholders ought to be told. Not only that; but, to speak frankly, I'm not satisfied to be ridden over roughshod in this fashion by one who, whatever he may have been in the past, is obviously not now in the prime of his faculties."

With a gasp the secretary thought: 'I knew that was a plain-spoken man!'

He heard again the rumbling beside him. The chairman had gone crimson, his mouth was pursed, his little eyes were very blue.

"Help me up," he said.

The secretary helped him, and waited, rather breathless.

The chairman took a sip of water, and his voice, unexpectedly loud, broke an ominous hush.

"Never been so insulted in my life. My best services have been at your disposal for nineteen years; you know what measure of success this Company has attained. I am the oldest man here, and my experience of shipping is, I hope, a little greater than that of the two gentlemen who spoke last. I have done my best for you, ladies and gentlemen, and we shall see whether you are going to endorse an indictment of my judgment and of my honour, if I am to take the last speaker seriously. This purchase is for your good. 'There is a tide in the affairs of men '—and I for one am not content, never have been, to stagnate. If that is what you want, however, by all means give your support to these gentlemen and have done with it. I tell you freights will go up before the end of the year; the purchase is a sound one, more than a sound one—I, at any rate, stand or fall by it. Refuse to ratify it, if you like; if you do, I shall resign."

He sank back into his seat. The secretary, stealing a glance, thought with a sort of enthusiasm: 'Bravo! Who'd have thought he could rally his voice like that? A good touch, too, that about his honour! I believe he's knocked them. It's still dicky, though, if that fellow at the back gets up again; the old chap can't work that stop a second time.' Ah! here was 'old Apple-pie' on his hind legs. That was all right!

" I do not hesitate to say that I am an old friend of the chairman ; we are, many of us, old friends of the chairman, and it has been painful to me, and I doubt not to others, to hear an attack made on him. If he is old in body, he is young in mental vigour and courage. I wish we were all as young. We ought to stand by him ; I say, we ought to stand by him." ("Hear, hear ! Hear, hear ! ") And the secretary thought : ' That's done it ! ' And he felt a sudden odd emotion, watching the chairman bobbing his body, like a wooden toy, at old Appleby ; and old Appleby bobbing back. Then, seeing a shareholder close to the door get up, thought : ' Who's that ? I know his face—Ah ! yes ; Ventnor, the solicitor—he's one of the chairman's creditors that are coming again this afternoon. What now ? '

" I can't agree that we ought to let sentiment interfere with our judgment in this matter. The question is simply : How are our pockets going to be affected ? I came here with some misgivings, but the attitude of the chairman has been such as to remove them ; and I shall support the proposition." The secretary thought : ' That's all right—only, he said it rather queerly—rather queerly.'

Then, after a long silence, the chairman, without rising, said :

" I move the adoption of the report and accounts."

" I second that."

" Those in favour signify the same in the usual way. Contrary ? Carried." The secretary noted the dissentients, six in number, and that Mr. Westgate did not vote.

A quarter of an hour later he stood in the body of the emptying room supplying names to one of the gentle-

men of the Press.   The passionless fellow said : " Hay-
thorp, with an ' a ' ;   oh ! an ' e ' ;   he seems an old
man.   Thank you.   I may have the slips ?   Would
you like to see a proof ?   With an ' a ' you said—oh !
an ' e.'   Good afternoon ! " And the secretary thought:
' Those fellows, what *does* go on inside them ? Fancy
not knowing the old chairman by now ! ' . . .

2 §

Back in the proper office of ' The Island Navigation
Company ' old Heythorp sat smoking a cigar and
smiling like a purring cat.   He was dreaming a little
of his triumph, sifting with his old brain, still subtle,
the wheat from the chaff of the demurrers : Westgate—
nothing in that—professional discontent till they
silenced him with a place on the board—but not while
he held the reins !   That chap at the back—an ill-
conditioned fellow ! " Something behind ! " Suspicious
brute !   There *was* something—but—hang it ! they
might think themselves lucky to get four ships at that
price, and all due to him ! It was on the last speaker
that his mind dwelt with a doubt.   That fellow
Ventnor, to whom he owed money—there had been
something just a little queer about his tone—as much
as to say, " I smell a rat."   Well ! one would see that
at the creditors' meeting in half an hour."
  " Mr. Pillin, sir."
  " Show him in ! "
  In a fur coat which seemed to extinguish his thin
form, Joe Pillin entered.   It was snowing, and the cold
had nipped and yellowed his meagre face between its
slight grey whiskering.   He said thinly :

" How are you, Sylvanus ? Aren't you perished in this cold ? "

" Warm as a toast. Sit down. Take off your coat."

" Oh ! I should be lost without it. You must have a fire inside you. So—so it's gone through ? "

Old Heythorp nodded ; and Joe Pillin, wandering like a spirit, scrutinised the shut door. He came back to the table, and said in a low voice :

" It's a great sacrifice."

Old Heythorp smiled.

" Have you signed the deed poll ? "

Producing a parchment from his pocket Joe Pillin unfolded it with caution to disclose his signature, and said :

" I don't like it—it's irrevocable."

A chuckle escaped old Heythorp.

" As death."

Joe Pillin's voice passed up into the treble clef.

" I can't bear irrevocable things. I consider you stampeded me, playing on my nerves."

Examining the signatures old Heythorp murmured :

" Tell your lawyer to lock it up. He must think you a sad dog, Joe."

" Ah ! Suppose on my death it comes to the know-ledge of my wife ! "

" She won't be able to make it hotter for you than you'll be already."

Joe Pillin replaced the deed within his coat, emitting a queer thin noise. He simply could not bear joking on such subjects.

" Well," he said, " you've got your way ; you always do. Who is this Mrs. Larne ? You oughtn't to keep me in the dark. It seems my boy met her at your house. You told me she didn't come there."

Old Heythorp said with relish :

" Her husband was my son by a woman I was fond of before I married ; her children are my grandchildren. You've provided for them. Best thing you ever did."

" I don't know—I don't know. I'm sorry you told me. It makes it all the more doubtful. As soon as the transfer's complete, I shall get away abroad. This cold's killing me. I wish you'd give me your recipe for keeping warm."

" Get a new inside."

Joe Pillin regarded his old friend with a sort of yearning. " And yet," he said, " I suppose, with your full-blooded habit, your life hangs by a thread, doesn't it ? "

" A stout one, my boy ! "

" Well, good-bye, Sylvanus. You're a Job's comforter ; I must be getting home." He put on his hat, and, lost in his fur coat, passed out into the corridor. On the stairs he met a man who said :

" How do you do, Mr. Pillin ? I know your son. Been seeing the chairman ? I see your sale's gone through all right. I hope that'll do us some good, but I suppose you think the other way ? "

Peering at him from under his hat, Joe Pillin said :

" Mr. Ventnor, I think ? Thank you ! It's very cold, isn't it ? " And, with that cautious remark, he passed on down.

Alone again, old Heythorp thought : ' By George ! What a wavering, quavering, threadpaper of a fellow ! What misery life must be to a chap like that ! He walks in fear—he wallows in it. Poor devil ! ' And a curious feeling swelled his heart, of elation, of lightness such as he had not known for years. Those two young things were safe now from penury—safe !

After dealing with those infernal creditors of his he would go round and have a look at the children. With a hundred and twenty a year the boy could go into the Army—best place for a young scamp like that. The girl would go off like hot cakes, of course, but she needn't take the first calf that came along. As for their mother, she must look after herself; nothing under two thousand a year would keep *her* out of debt. But trust her for wheedling and bluffing her way out of any scrape! Watching his cigar-smoke curl and disperse he was conscious of the strain he had been under these last six weeks, aware suddenly of how greatly he had baulked at thought of to-day's general meeting. Yes! It might have turned out nasty. He knew well enough the forces on the Board, and off, who would be only too glad to shelve him. If he were shelved here his other two Companies would be sure to follow suit, and bang would go every penny of his income—he would be a pauper dependant on that holy woman. Well! Safe now for another year if he could stave off these sharks once more. It might be a harder job this time, but he was in luck—in luck, and it must hold. And taking a luxurious pull at his cigar, he rang the hand-bell.

"Bring 'em in here, Mr. Farney. And let me have a cup of China tea as strong as you can make it."

"Yes, sir. Will you see the proof of the press report, or will you leave it to me?"

"To you."

"Yes, sir. It was a good meeting, wasn't it?"

Old Heythorp nodded.

"Wonderful how your voice came back just at the right moment. I was afraid things were going to be difficult. The insult did it, I think. It was a monstrous thing to say. I could have punched his head."

Again old Heythorp nodded ; and, looking into the secretary's fine blue eyes, he repeated : " Bring 'em in."

The lonely minute before the entrance of his creditors passed in the thought : ' So that's how it struck him ! Short shrift I should get if it came out.'

The gentlemen, who numbered ten this time, bowed to their debtor, evidently wondering why the deuce they troubled to be polite to an old man who kept them out of their money. Then, the secretary reappearing with a cup of China tea, they watched while their debtor drank it. The feat was tremulous. Would he get through without spilling it all down his front, or choking ? To those unaccustomed to his private life it was slightly miraculous. He put the cup down empty, tremblingly removed some yellow drops from the little white tuft below his lip, relit his cigar, and said :

" No use beating about the bush, gentlemen ; I can offer you fourteen hundred a year so long as I live and hold my directorships, and not a penny more. If you can't accept that, you must make me bankrupt and get about sixpence in the pound. My qualifying shares will fetch a couple of thousand at market price. I own nothing else. The house I live in, and everything in it, barring my clothes, my wine, and my cigars, belong to my daughter under a settlement fifteen years old. My solicitors and bankers will give you every information. That's the position in a nutshell."

In spite of business habits the surprise of the ten gentlemen was only partially concealed. A man who owed them so much would naturally say he owned nothing, but would he refer them to his solicitors and bankers unless he were telling the truth? Then Mr. Ventnor said :

" Will you submit your pass books ? "

" No, but I'll authorise my bankers to give you a full statement of my receipts for the last five years— longer, if you like."

The strategic stroke of placing the ten gentlemen round the Board table had made it impossible for them to consult freely without being overheard, but the low-voiced transference of thought travelling round was summed up at last by Mr. Brownbee.

" We think, Mr. Heythorp, that your fees and dividends should enable you to set aside for us a larger sum. Sixteen hundred, in fact, is what we think you should give us yearly. Representing, as we do, sixteen thousand pounds, the prospect is not cheering, but we hope you have some good years before you yet. We understand your income to be two thousand pounds."

Old Heythorp shook his head. " Nineteen hundred and thirty pounds in a good year. Must eat and drink ; must have a man to look after me—not as active as I was. Can't do on less than five hundred pounds. Fourteen hundred's all I can give you, gentlemen ; it's an advance of two hundred pounds. That's my last word."

The silence was broken by Mr. Ventnor.

" And it's my last word that I'm not satisfied. If these other gentlemen accept your proposition I shall be forced to consider what I can do on my own account."

The old man stared at him, and answered:

" Oh ! you will, sir ; we shall see."

The others had risen and were gathered in a knot at the end of the table ; old Heythorp and Mr. Ventnor alone remained seated. The old man's lower lip projected till the white hairs below stood out like bristles. 'You ugly dog,' he was thinking, 'you think you've got something up your sleeve. Well, do your worst!' The "ugly dog" rose abruptly and joined the others. And old Heythorp closed his eyes, sitting perfectly still, with his cigar, which had gone out, sticking up between his teeth. Mr. Brownbee, turning to voice the decision come to, cleared his throat.

"Mr. Heythorp," he said, "if your bankers and solicitors bear out your statements, we shall accept your offer *faute de mieux*, in consideration of your ——" but meeting the old man's eyes, which said so very plainly: "Blow your consideration!" he ended with a stammer: "Perhaps you will kindly furnish us with the authorisation you spoke of?"

Old Heythorp nodded, and Mr. Brownbee, with a little bow, clasped his hat to his breast and moved towards the door. The nine gentlemen followed. Mr. Ventnor, bringing up the rear, turned and looked back. But the old man's eyes were already closed again.

The moment his creditors were gone, old Heythorp sounded the hand-bell.

"Help me up, Mr. Farney. That Ventnor—what's his holding?"

"Quite small. Only ten shares, I think."

"Ah! What time is it?"

"Quarter to four, sir."

"Get me a taxi."

After visiting his bank and his solicitors, he struggled once more into his cab and caused it to be driven towards Millicent Villas. A kind of sleepy triumph permeated his whole being, bumped and shaken by the

cab's rapid progress. So ! He was free of those sharks
now so long as he could hold on to his Companies ;
and he would still have a hundred a year or more to
spare for Rosamund and her youngsters. He could
live on four hundred, or even three-fifty, without losing
his independence, for there would be no standing life
in that holy woman's house unless he could pay his own
scot ! A good day's work ! The best for many a long
month !

The cab stopped before the villa.

3 §

There are rooms which refuse to give away their
owners, and rooms which seem to say : " They really
are like this." Of such was Rosamund Larne's—a sort
of permanent confession, seeming to remark to anyone
who entered : " Her taste ? Well, you can see—
cheerful and exuberant ; her habits—yes, she sits here
all the morning in a dressing-gown, smoking cigarettes
and dropping ink ; kindly observe my carpet. Notice
the piano—it has a look of coming and going, according
to the exchequer. This very deep-cushioned sofa is
permanent, however ; the water-colours on the walls
are safe, too—they're by herself. Mark the scent of
mimosa—she likes flowers, and likes them strong.
No clock, of course. Examine the bureau—she is
obviously always ringing for ' the drumstick,' and
saying : ' Where's this, Ellen, and where's that ?
You naughty gairl, you've been tidying.' Cast an
eye on that pile of manuscript—she has evidently a
genius for composition ; it flows off her pen—like
Shakespeare, she never blots a line. See how she's had
the electric light put in, instead of that horrid gas ;

but try and turn either of them on—you can't ; last
quarter isn't paid, of course ; and she uses an oil lamp,
you can tell that by the ceiling. The dog over there,
who will not answer to the name of 'Carmen,' a
Pekinese spaniel like a little Djin, all prominent eyes
rolling their blacks, and no nose between—yes, Carmen
looks as if she didn't know what was coming next ;
she's right—it's a pet-and-slap-again life ! Consider,
too, the fittings of the tea-tray, rather soiled, though
not quite tin, but I say unto you that no millionaire's
in all its glory ever had a liqueur bottle on it."

When old Heythorp entered this room, which
extended from back to front of the little house, preceded
by the announcement " Mr. Æsop," it was resonant
with a very clatter-bodandigo of noises, from Phyllis
playing the Machiche ; from the boy Jock on the
hearthrug, emitting at short intervals the most piercing
notes from an ocarina ; from Mrs. Larne on the sofa,
talking with her trailing volubility to Bob Pillin ; from
Bob Pillin muttering : " Ye—es ! Qui—ite ! Ye—es ! "
and gazing at Phyllis over his collar. And, on the
window-sill, as far as she could get from all this noise,
the little dog Carmen was rolling her eyes. At sight
of their visitor Jock blew one rending screech, and
bolting behind the sofa, placed his chin on its top, so
that nothing but his round pink unmoving face was
visible ; and the dog Carmen tried to climb the blind
cord.

Encircled from behind by the arms of Phyllis, and
preceded by the gracious perfumed bulk of Mrs. Larne,
old Heythorp was escorted to the sofa. It was low,
and when he had plumped down on to it, the boy Jock
emitted a hollow groan. Bob Pillin was the first to
break the silence.

"How are you, sir? I hope it's gone through."

Old Heythorp nodded. His eyes were fixed on the liqueur, and Mrs. Larne murmured:

"Guardy, you *must* try our new liqueur. Jock, you awful boy, get up and bring Guardy a glass."

The boy Jock approached the tea-table, took up a glass, put it to his eye and filled it rapidly.

"You horrible boy, you could see that glass has been used."

In a high round voice rather like an angel's, Jock answered:

"All right, mother; I'll get rid of it," and rapidly swallowing the yellow liquor, took up another glass.

Mrs. Larne laughed.

"What *am* I to do with him?"

A loud shriek prevented a response. Phyllis, who had taken her brother by the ear to lead him to the door, let him go to clasp her injured self. Bob Pillin went hastening towards her; and following the young man with her chin, Mrs. Larne said, smiling:

"Aren't those children awful? He's such a nice fellow. We like him so much, Guardy."

The old man grinned. So she was making up to that young pup! Rosamund Larne, watching him, murmured:

"Oh! Guardy, you're as bad as Jock. He takes after you terribly. Look at the shape of his head. Jock, come here!" The innocent boy approached; with his girlish complexion, his flowery blue eyes, his perfect mouth, he stood before his mother like a large cherub. And suddenly he blew his ocarina in a dreadful manner. Mrs. Larne launched a box at his ears, and receiving the wind of it he fell prone.

" That's the way he behaves. Be off with you, you awful boy. I want to talk to Guardy."

. The boy withdrew on his stomach, and sat against the wall cross-legged, fixing his innocent round eyes on old Heythorp. Mrs. Larne sighed.

" Things are worse and worse, Guardy. I'm at my wits' end to tide over this quarter. You wouldn't advance me a hundred on my new story ? I'm sure to get two for it in the end."

The old man shook his head.

" I've done something for you and the children," he said. " You'll get notice of it in a day or two ; ask no questions."

" Oh ! Guardy ! Oh ! you dear ! " And her gaze rested on Bob Pillin, leaning over the piano, where Phyllis again sat.

Old Heythorp snorted. " What are you cultivating that young gaby for ? She mustn't be grabbed up by any fool who comes along."

Mrs. Larne murmured at once :

" Of course, the dear gairl is *much* too young. Phyllis, come and talk to Guardy ! "

When the girl was installed beside him on the sofa, and he had felt that little thrill of warmth the proximity of youth can bring, he said :

" Been a good girl ? "

She shook her head.

" Can't, when Jock's not at school. Mother can't pay for him this term."

Hearing his name, the boy Jock blew his ocarina till Mrs. Larne drove him from the room, and Phyllis went on :

" He's more awful than anything you can think of. Was my dad at all like him, Guardy ? Mother's always so mysterious about him. I suppose you knew him well."

Old Heythorp, incapable of confusion, answered stolidly :

" Not very."

" Who was his father ? I don't believe even mother knows."

" Man about town in my day."

" Oh ! your day must have been jolly. Did you wear peg-top trousers, and dundreary's ? "

Old Heythorp nodded.

" What larks ! And I suppose you had lots of adventures with opera dancers and gambling. The young men are all so good now." Her eyes rested on Bob Pillin. " That young man's a perfect stick of goodness."

Old Heythorp grunted.

" You wouldn't know how good he was," Phyllis went on musingly, " unless you'd sat next him in a tunnel. The other day he had his waist squeezed and he simply sat still and did nothing. And then when the tunnel ended, it was Jock after all, not me. His face was—Oh ! ah ! ha ! ha ! Ah ! ha !" She threw back her head, displaying all her white, round throat. Then edging near, she whispered :

" He likes to pretend, of course, that he's fearfully lively. He's promised to take mother and me to the theatre and supper afterwards. Won't it be scrummy ! Only, I haven't anything to go in."

Old Heythorp said : " What d'you want ? Irish poplin ? "

Her mouth opened wide : " Oh ! Guardy ! Soft white satin ! "

" How many yards 'll go round you ? "

" I should think about twelve. We could make it ourselves. You *are* a chook ! "

A scent of hair, like hay, enveloped him, her lips bobbed against his nose, and there came a feeling in his heart as when he rolled the first sip of a special wine against his palate. This little house was a rumty-too affair, her mother was a humbug, the boy a cheeky young rascal, but there was a warmth here he never felt in that big house which had been his wife's and was now his holy daughter's. And once more he rejoiced at his day's work, and the success of his breach of trust, which put some little ground beneath these young feet, in a hard and unscrupulous world. Phyllis whispered in his ear :

" Guardy, do look ; he *will* stare at me like that. Isn't it awful—like a boiled rabbit ? "

Bob Pillin, attentive to Mrs. Larne, was gazing with all his might over her shoulder at the girl. The young man was moonstruck, that was clear ! There was something almost touching in the stare of those puppy dog's eyes. And he thought : ' Young beggar—wish I were his age ! ' The utter injustice of having an old and helpless body, when your desire for enjoyment was as great as ever ! They said a man was as old as he felt ! Fools ! A man was as old as his legs and arms, and not a day younger. He heard the girl beside him utter a discomfortable sound, and saw her face cloud as if tears were not far off ; she jumped up, and going to the window, lifted the little dog and buried her face in its brown and white fur. Old Heythorp thought : ' She sees that her humbugging mother is using her as a decoy.' But she had come back, and the little dog, rolling its eyes horribly at the strange figure on the sofa, in a desperate effort to escape succeeded in reaching her shoulder, where it stayed perched like a cat, held by one paw and trying to back away into space. Old Heythorp said abruptly :

" Are you very fond of your mother ? "

" Of course I am, Guardy. I adore her."

" H'm ! Listen to me. When you come of age or marry, you'll have a hundred and twenty a year of your own that you can't get rid of. Don't ever be persuaded into doing what you don't want. And remember : Your mother's a sieve, no good giving her money ; keep what you'll get for yourself—it's only a pittance, and you'll want it all—every penny."

Phyllis's eyes had opened very wide ; so that he wondered if she had taken in his words.

" Oh ! Isn't money horrible, Guardy ? "

" The want of it."

" No, it's beastly altogether. If only we were like birds. Or if one could put out a plate overnight, and have just enough in the morning to use during the day."

Old Heythorp sighed.

" There's only one thing in life that matters—independence. Lose that, and you lose everything. That's the value of money. Help me up."

Phyllis stretched out her hands, and the little dog, running down her back, resumed its perch on the window-sill, close to the blind cord.

Once on his feet, old Heythorp said :

" Give me a kiss. You'll have your satin to-morrow."

Then looking at Bob Pillin, he remarked :

" Going my way ? I'll give you a lift."

The young man, giving Phyllis one appealing look, answered dully : " Tha-anks ! " and they went out together to the taxi. In that draughtless vehicle they sat, full of who knows what contempt of age for youth,

and youth for age ; the old man resenting this young
pup's aspiration to his granddaughter ; the young
man annoyed that this old image had dragged him
away before he wished to go. Old Heythorp said
at last :

" Well ? "

Thus expected to say something, Bob Pillin muttered :

" Glad your meetin' went off well, sir. You scored
a triumph I should think."

" Why ? "

" Oh ! I don't know. I thought you had a good
bit of opposition to contend with."

Old Heythorp looked at him.

" Your grandmother ! " he said ; then, with his
habitual instinct of attack, added : " You make the
most of your opportunities, I see."

At this rude assault Bob Pillin's red-cheeked face
assumed a certain dignity. " I don't know what you
mean, sir. Mrs. Larne is very kind to me."

" No doubt. But don't try to pick the flowers."

Thoroughly upset, Bob Pillin preserved a dogged
silence. This fortnight, since he had first met Phyllis
in old Heythorp's hall, had been the most singular of
his existence up to now. He would never have believed
that a fellow could be so quickly and completely
bowled, could succumb without a kick, without even
wanting to kick. To one with his philosophy of having
a good time and never committing himself too far,
it was in the nature of " a fair knock-out," and yet
so pleasurable, except for the wear and tear about
one's chances. If only he knew how far the old boy
really counted in the matter ! To say : " My intentions
are strictly honourable " would be old-fashioned ;

besides—the old fellow might have no right to hear
it. They called him Guardy, but without knowing
more he did not want to admit the old curmudgeon's
right to interfere.

" Are you a relation of theirs, sir ? "

Old Heythorp nodded.

Bob Pillin went on with desperation :

" I should like to know what your objection to me is."

The old man turned his head as far as he was able ;
a grim smile bristled the hairs about his lips, and
twinkled in his eyes. What did he object to ? Why—
everything ! Object to ! That sleek head, those
puppy-dog eyes, fattish red cheeks, high collars, pearl
pin, spats, and drawl—pah ! the imbecility, the smug-
ness of his mug ; no go, no devil in any of his sort,
in any of these fish-veined, coddled-up young bloods,
nothing but playing for safety ! And he wheezed out :

" Milk and water masquerading as port wine."

Bob Pillin frowned.

It was almost too much for the composure even of
a man of the world. That this paralytic old fellow
should express contempt for his virility was really
the last thing in jests. Luckily he could not take it
seriously. But suddenly he thought : ' What if he
really has the power to stop my going there, and means
to turn them against me ! ' And his heart quailed.

" Awfully sorry, sir," he said, " if you don't think
I'm wild enough. Anything I can do for you in that
line——"

The old man grunted ; and realising that he had
been quite witty, Bob Pillin went on :

" I know I'm not in debt, no entanglements, got a
decent income, pretty good expectations and all that ;
but I can soon put that all right if I'm not fit without."

It was perhaps his first attempt at irony, and he could not help thinking how good it was.

But old Heythorp preserved a deadly silence. He looked like a stuffed man, a regular Aunt Sally sitting there, with the fixed red in his cheeks, his stivered hair, square block of a body, and no neck that you could see —only wanting the pipe in his mouth! Could there really be danger from such an old fool? The idol spoke:

" I'll give you a word of advice. Don't hang round there, or you'll burn your fingers. Remember me to your father. Good-night! "

The taxi had stopped before the house in Sefton Park. An insensate impulse to remain seated and argue the point fought in Bob Pillin with an impulse to leap out, shake his fist in at the window, and walk off. He merely said, however:

" Thanks for the lift. Good-night! " And, getting out deliberately, he walked off.

Old Heythorp, waiting for the driver to help him up, thought:

' Fatter, but no more guts than his father! '

In his sanctum he sank at once into his chair. It was wonderfully still there every day at this hour; just the click of the coals, just the faintest ruffle from the wind in the trees of the park. And it was cosily warm, only the fire lightening the darkness. A drowsy beatitude pervaded the old man. A good day's work! A triumph—that young pup had said. Yes! Something of a triumph! He had held on, and won. And dinner to look forward to, yet. A nap—a nap! And soon, rhythmic, soft, sonorous, his breathing rose, with now and then that pathetic twitching of the old who dream.

III

1 §

WHEN Bob Pillin emerged from the little front garden
of 23, Millicent Villas ten days later, his sentiments
were ravelled, and he could not get hold of an end to
pull straight the stuff of his mind.

He had found Mrs. Larne and Phyllis in the sitting-
room, and Phyllis had been crying; he was sure she
had been crying; and that memory still infected the
sentiments evoked by later happenings. Old Heythorp
had said: " You'll burn your fingers." The process
had begun. Having sent her daughter away on a
pretext really a bit too thin, Mrs. Larne had installed
him beside her scented bulk on the sofa, and poured
into his ear such a tale of monetary woe and entangle-
ment, such a mass of present difficulties and rosy
prospects, that his brain still whirled, and only one
thing emerged clearly—that she wanted fifty pounds,
which she would repay him on quarter-day; for their
Guardy had made a settlement by which, until the dear
children came of age, she would have sixty pounds
every quarter. It was only a question of a few weeks;
he might ask Messrs. Scriven and Coles; they would
tell him the security was quite safe. He certainly
might ask Messrs. Scriven and Coles—they happened
to be his father's solicitors; but it hardly seemed to
touch the point. Bob Pillin had a certain shrewd
caution, and the point was whether he was going to
begin to lend money to a woman who, he could see,
might borrow up to seventy times seven on the strength

of his infatuation for her daughter. That was rather too strong ! Yet, if he didn't—she might take a sudden dislike to him, and where would he be then ? Besides, would not a loan make his position stronger ? And then —such is the effect of love even on the younger genera- tion—that thought seemed to him unworthy. If he lent at all, it should be from chivalry—ulterior motives might go hang ! And the memory of the tear-marks on Phyllis's pretty pale-pink cheeks ; and her petulantly mournful : " Oh ! young man, isn't money beastly ! " scraped his heart, and ravished his judgment. All the same, fifty pounds was fifty pounds, and goodness knew how much more ; and what did he know of Mrs. Larne, after all, except that she was a relative of old Heythorp's and wrote stories—told them too, if he was not mistaken. Perhaps it would be better to see Scrivens.' But again that absurd nobility assaulted him. Phyllis ! Phyllis ! Besides, were not settlements always drawn so that they refused to form security for anything ? Thus, hampered and troubled, he hailed a cab. He was dining with the Ventnors on the Cheshire side, and would be late if he didn't get home sharp to dress.

Driving, white-tied and waistcoated, in his father's car, he thought with a certain contumely of the younger Ventnor girl, whom he had been wont to consider pretty before he knew Phyllis. And seated next her at dinner, he quite enjoyed his new sense of superiority to her charms, and the ease with which he could chaff and be agreeable. And all the time he suffered from the suppressed longing which scarcely ever left him now, to think and talk of Phyllis. Ventnor's fizz was good and plentiful, his old Madeira absolutely first chop, and the only other man present a teetotal curate, who with-

drew with the ladies to talk his parish shop.   Favoured
by these circumstances, and the perception that
Ventnor was an agreeable fellow, Bob Pillin yielded to
his secret itch to get near the subject of his affections.

" Do you happen," he said airily, " to know a
Mrs. Larne—relative of old Heythorp's—rather a
handsome woman—she writes stories."

Mr. Ventnor shook his head.   A closer scrutiny than
Bob Pillin's would have seen that he also moved his
ears.

" Of old Heythorp's ? Didn't know he had any,
except his daughter, and that son of his in the
Admiralty."

Bob Pillin felt the glow of his secret hobby
spreading within him.

" She is, though—lives rather out of town ; got a son
and daughter.   I thought you might know her stories—
clever woman."

Mr. Ventnor smiled.

" Ah ! " he said enigmatically, " these lady novelists !
Does she make any money by them ? "

Bob Pillin knew that to make money by writing
meant success, but that not to make money by writing
was artistic, and implied that you had private means,
which perhaps was even more distinguished.   And he
said :

" Oh ! she has private means, I know."

Mr. Ventnor reached for the Madeira.

" So she's a relative of old Heythorp's," he said.
" He's a very old friend of your father's.   He ought to
go bankrupt, you know."

To Bob Pillin, glowing with passion and Madeira,
the idea of bankruptcy seemed discreditable in connection with a relative of Phyllis.   Besides, the old

boy was far from that ! Had he not just made this settlement on Mrs. Larne ? And he said :

" I think you're mistaken. That's of the past."

Mr. Ventnor smiled.

" Will you bet ? " he said.

Bob Pillin also smiled. " I should be bettin' on a certainty."

Mr. Ventnor passed his hand over his whiskered face. " Don't you believe it ; he hasn't a mag to his name. Fill your glass."

Bob Pillin said, with a certain resentment :

" Well, I happen to know he's just made a settlement of five or six thousand pounds. Don't know if you call that being bankrupt."

" What ! On this Mrs. Larne ? "

Confused, uncertain whether he had said something derogatory or indiscreet, or something which added distinction to Phyllis, Bob Pillin hesitated, then gave a nod.

Mr. Ventnor rose and extended his short legs before the fire.

" No, my boy," he said. " No ! "

Unaccustomed to flat contradiction, Bob Pillin reddened.

" I'll bet you a tenner. Ask Scrivens'."

Mr. Ventnor ejaculated :

" Scrivens'—but they're not——" then, staring rather hard, he added : " I won't bet. You may be right. Scrivens' are your father's solicitors too, aren't they ? Always been sorry he didn't come to me. Shall we join the ladies ? " And to the drawing-room he preceded a young man more uncertain in his mind than on his feet. . . .

Charles Ventnor was not one to let you see that

more was going on within than met the eye. But there
was a good deal going on that evening, and after his
conversation with young Bob he had occasion more
than once to turn away and rub his hands together.
When, after that second creditors' meeting, he had
walked down the stairway which led to the offices of
' The Island Navigation Company,' he had been deep
in thought. Short, squarely built, rather stout, with
moustache and large mutton-chop whiskers of a red-
brown, and a faint floridity in face and dress, he
impressed at first sight only by a certain truly British
vulgarity. One felt that here was a hail-fellow-well-
met man who liked lunch and dinner, went to Scarborough for his summer holidays, sat on his wife, took
his daughters out in a boat and was never sick. One
felt that he went to church every Sunday morning,
looked upwards as he moved through life, disliked the
unsuccessful, and expanded with his second glass of
wine. But then a clear look into his well-clothed face
and red-brown eyes would give the feeling : ' There's
something fulvous here ; he might be a bit too foxy.'
A third look brought the thought : ' He's certainly a
bully.' He was not a large creditor of old Heythorp.
With interest on the original, he calculated his claim at
three hundred pounds—unredeemed shares in that old
Ecuador mine. But he had waited for his money eight
years, and could never imagine how it came about that
he had been induced to wait so long. There had been,
of course, for one who liked " big pots," a certain
glamour about the personality of old Heythorp, still
a bit of a swell in shipping circles, and a bit of an
aristocrat in Liverpool. But during the last year
Charles Ventnor had realised that the old chap's star
had definitely set—when that happens, of course,

there is no more glamour, and the time has come to get your money. Weakness in oneself and others is despicable ! Besides, he had food for thought, and descending the stairs he chewed it. He smelt a rat—creatures for which both by nature and profession he had a nose. Through Bob Pillin, on whom he sometimes dwelt in connection with his younger daughter, he knew that old Pillin and old Heythorp had been friends for thirty years and more. That, to an astute mind, suggested something behind this sale. The thought had already occurred to him when he read his copy of the report. A commission would be a breach of trust, of course, but there were ways of doing things ; the old chap was devilish hard pressed, and human nature was human nature ! His lawyerish mind habitually put two and two together. The old fellow had deliberately appointed to meet his creditors again just after the general meeting which would decide the purchase—had said he might do something for them then. Had that no significance ?

In these circumstances Charles Ventnor had come to the meeting with eyes wide open and mouth tight closed. And he had watched. It was certainly remarkable that such an old and feeble man, with no neck at all, who looked indeed as if he might go off with apoplexy any moment, should actually say that he " stood or fell " by this purchase, knowing that if he fell he would be a beggar. Why should the old chap be so keen on getting it through ? It would do him personally no good, unless—Exactly ! He had left the meeting, therefore, secretly confident that old Heythorp had got something out of this transaction which would enable him to make a substantial proposal to his creditors. So that when the old man had

declared that he was going to make none, something
had turned sour in his heart, and he had said to himself : " All right, you old rascal ! You don't know
C. V." The cavalier manner of that beggarly old rip,
the defiant look of his deep little eyes, had put a polish
on the rancour of one who prided himself on letting
no man get the better of him. All that evening, seated
on one side of the fire, while Mrs. Ventnor sat on the
other, and the younger daughter played Gounod's
Serenade on the violin—he cogitated. And now and
again he smiled, but not too much. He did not see
his way as yet, but had little doubt that before long
he would. It would not be hard to knock that chipped
old idol off his perch. There was already a healthy
feeling among the shareholders that he was past work
and should be scrapped. The old chap should find
that Charles V. was not to be defied ; that when he
got his teeth into a thing, he did not let it go. By
hook or crook he would have the old man off his
Boards, or his debt out of him as the price of leaving
him alone. His life or his money—and the old fellow
should determine which. With the memory of that
defiance fresh within him, he almost hoped it might
come to be the first, and turning to Mrs. Ventnor, he
said abruptly :

" Have a little dinner Friday week, and ask young
Pillin and the curate." He specified the curate, a
teetotaller, because he had two daughters, and males
and females must be paired, but he intended to pack
him off after dinner to the drawing-room to discuss
parish matters while he and Bob Pillin sat over their
wine. What he expected to get out of the young man
he did not as yet know.

On the day of the dinner, before departing for the

office, he had gone to his cellar. Would three bottles
of Perrier Jouet do the trick, or must he add one of
the old Madeira ? He decided to be on the safe side.
A bottle or so of champagne went very little way with
him personally, and young Pillin might be another.

The Madeira having done its work by turning the
conversation into such an admirable channel, he had
cut it short for fear young Pillin might drink the lot
or get wind of the rat. And when his guests were
gone, and his family had retired, he stood staring into
the fire, putting together the pieces of the puzzle.
Five or six thousand pounds—six would be ten per cent.
on sixty ! Exactly ! Scrivens'—young Pillin had
said ! But Crow & Donkin, not Scriven & Coles, were
old Heythorp's solicitors. What could that mean,
save that the old man wanted to cover the tracks of
a secret commission, and had handled the matter
through solicitors who did not know the state of his
affairs ! But why Pillin's solicitors ? With this sale
just going through, it must look deuced fishy to them
too. Was it all a mare's nest, after all ? In such
circumstances he himself would have taken the matter
to a London firm who knew nothing of anybody.
Puzzled, therefore, and rather disheartened, feeling
too that touch of liver which was wont to follow his
old Madeira, he went up to bed and woke his wife to
ask her why the dickens they couldn't always have
soup like that !

Next day he continued to brood over his puzzle, and
no fresh light came ; but having a matter on which
his firm and Scrivens' were in touch, he decided to go
over in person, and see if he could surprise something
out of them. Feeling, from experience, that any really
delicate matter would only be entrusted to the most

responsible member of the firm, he had asked to see
Scriven himself, and just as he had taken his hat to
go, he said casually :

"By the way, you do some business for old
Mr. Heythorp, don't you ? "

Scriven, raising his eyebrows a little, murmured :
"Er—no," in exactly the tone Mr. Ventnor himself
used when he wished to imply that though he didn't
as a fact do business, he probably soon would. He
knew therefore that the answer was a true one. And
nonplussed, he hazarded :

"Oh ! I thought you did, in regard to a Mrs.
Larne."

This time he had certainly drawn blood of sorts, for
down came Scriven's eyebrows, and he said :

"Mrs. Larne—we know a Mrs. Larne, but not in
that connection. Why ? "

"Oh ! Young Pillin told me——"

"Young Pillin ? Why it's his—— ! " A little pause,
and then : "Old Mr. Heythorp's solicitors are Crow
& Donkin, I believe."

Mr. Ventnor held out his hand. "Yes, yes," he
said ; "good-bye. Glad to have got that matter
settled up," and out he went, and down the street,
important, smiling. By George ! He had got it !
"It's his father "—Scriven had been going to say.
What a plant ! Exactly ! Oh ! neat ! Old Pillin had
made the settlement direct ; and the solicitors were in
the dark ; that disposed of his difficulty about *them*.
No money had passed between old Pillin and old
Heythorp—not a penny. Oh ! neat ! But not neat
enough for Charles Ventnor, who had that nose for
rats. Then his smile died, and with a little chill he
perceived that it was all based on supposition—not

quite good enough to go on ! What then ? Somehow
he must see this Mrs. Larne, or better—old Pillin
himself. The point to ascertain was whether she had
any connection of her own with Pillin. Clearly young
Pillin didn't know of it ; for according to him, old
Heythorp had made the settlement. By Jove ! That
old rascal was deep—all the more satisfaction in proving
that he was not as deep as C. V. To unmask the old
cheat was already beginning to seem in the nature of a
public service. But on what pretext could he visit
Pillin ? A subscription to the Windeatt almshouses !
That would put him into a chatty mood, if he took care
not to press the request to the actual point of getting
a subscription. And he caused himself to be driven
to the Pillin residence in Sefton Park. Ushered into
a room on the ground floor, heated in American fashion,
Mr. Ventnor unbuttoned his coat. A man of sanguine
constitution, he found this hot-house atmosphere a
little trying. And having sympathetically obtained
Joe Pillin's reluctant refusal—Quite so ! One could not
indefinitely extend one's subscriptions even for the best
of causes !—he said gently :

"By the way, you know Mrs. Larne, don't
you ? "

The effect of that simple shot surpassed his highest
hopes. Joe Pillin's face, never highly coloured, turned
a sort of grey ; he opened his thin lips, shut them
quickly, as birds do, and something seemed to pass
with difficulty down his scraggy throat. The hollows,
which nerve exhaustion delves in the cheeks of men
whose cheek-bones are not high, increased alarmingly.
For a moment he looked deathly ; then, moistening
his lips, he said :

" Larne—Larne ? No, I don't seem——"

Mr. Ventnor, who had taken care to be drawing on his gloves, murmured :

" Oh ! I thought—your son knows her ; a relation of old Heythorp's," and he looked up.

Joe Pillin had his handkerchief to his mouth ; he coughed feebly, then with more and more vigour :

" I'm in very poor health," he said, at last. " I'm getting abroad at once. This cold's killing me. What name did you say ? " And he remained with his handkerchief against his teeth.

Mr. Ventnor repeated :

" Larne. Writes stories."

Joe Pillin muttered into his handkerchief :

" Ah ! H'm ! No—I—no ! My son knows all sorts of people. I shall have to try Mentone. Are you going ? Good-bye ! Good-bye ! I'm sorry ; ah ! ha ! My cough—ah ! ha h'h'm ! Very distressing. Ye—hes ! My cough—ah ! ha h'h'm ! Most distressing. Ye—hes ! "

Out in the drive Mr. Ventnor took a deep breath of the frosty air. Not much doubt now ! The two names had worked like charms. This weakly old fellow would make a pretty witness, would simply crumple under cross-examination. What a contrast to that hoary old sinner Heythorp, whose brazenness nothing could affect. The rat was as large as life ! And the only point was, how to make the best use of it. Then—for his experience was wide—the possibility dawned on him, that after all, this Mrs. Larne might only have been old Pillin's mistress—or be his natural daughter, or have some other blackmailing hold on him. Any such connection would account for his agitation, for his denying her, for his son's ignorance. Only it wouldn't account for young Pillin's saying that old Heythorp

had made the settlement. He could only have got
that from the woman herself. Still, to make absolutely
sure, he had better try and see her. But how ? It
would never do to ask Bob Pillin for an introduction,
after this interview with his father. He would have
to go on his own and chance it ! Wrote stories did she ?
Perhaps a newspaper would know her address ; or
the Directory would give it—not a common name !
And, hot on the scent, he drove to a post office. Yes,
there it was, right enough ! " Larne, Mrs. R.—23,
Millicent Villas." And thinking to himself : ' No
time like the present,' he turned in that direction.
The job was delicate. He must be careful not to do
anything which might compromise his power of making
public use of his knowledge. Yes—ticklish ! What
he did now must have a proper legal bottom. Still,
anyway you looked at it, he had a *right* to investigate
a fraud on him as a shareholder of ' The Island Navigation Company,' and a fraud on him as a creditor of
old Heythorp. Quite ! But suppose this Mrs. Larne
was really entangled with old Pillin, and the settlement
a mere reward of virtue. Well ! in that case there
would be no secret commission, nothing to make
public, and he would not be going further. So that,
in either event, he would be all right. Only—how to
introduce himself ? He might pretend he was a newspaper man wanting a story. No, that wouldn't do !
He must not represent that he was what he was not,
in case he had afterwards to justify his actions publicly,
always a difficult thing, if you were not careful ! At
that moment there came into his mind a question
Bob Pillin had asked the other night. " By the way,
you can't borrow on a settlement, can you ? Isn't
there generally some clause against it ? " Had this

woman been trying to borrow from him on that settlement ? But at this moment he reached the house, and
got out of his cab still undecided as to how he was
going to work the oracle. Impudence, constitutional
and professional, sustained him in saying to the little
maid :

" Mrs. Larne at home ? Say Mr. Charles Ventnor,
will you ? "

His quick brown eyes took in the apparel of the
passage which served for hall—the deep blue paper on
the walls, lilac-patterned curtains over the doors, the
well-known print of a nude young woman looking over
her shoulder, and he thought : ' H'm ! Distinctly
tasty ! ' They noted, too, a small brown-and-white
dog cowering in terror at the very end of the passage,
and he murmured affably : " Fluffy ! Come here,
Fluffy ! " till Carmen's teeth chattered in her head.

" Will you come in, sir ? "

Mr. Ventnor ran his hand over his whiskers, and,
entering a room, was impressed at once by its air of
domesticity. On a sofa a handsome woman and a
pretty young girl were surrounded by sewing apparatus
and some white material. The girl looked up, but the
elder lady rose.

Mr. Ventnor said easily :

" You know my young friend, Mr. Robert Pillin,
I think."

The lady, whose bulk and bloom struck him to
the point of admiration, murmured in a full, sweet
drawl :

" Oh ! Ye—es. Are you from Messrs. Scrivens' ? "

With the swift reflection : ' As I thought ! '
Mr. Ventnor answered :

" Er—not exactly. I *am* a solicitor though ; came

just to ask about a certain settlement that Mr. Pillin tells me you're entitled under."

" Phyllis dear ! "

Seeing the girl about to rise from underneath the white stuff, Mr. Ventnor said quickly :

" Pray don't disturb yourself—just a formality ! " It had struck him at once that the lady would have to speak the truth in the presence of this third party, and he went on : " Quite recent, I think. This'll be your first interest—on six thousand pounds ? Is that right ? " And at the limpid assent of that rich, sweet voice, he thought : ' Fine woman ; what eyes ! '

" Thank you ; that's quite enough. I can go to Scrivens' for any detail. Nice young fellow, Bob Pillin, isn't he ? " He saw the girl's chin tilt, and Mrs. Larne's full mouth curling in a smile.

" Delightful young man ; we're very fond of him."

And he proceeded :

" I'm quite an old friend of his ; have you known him long ? "

" Oh ! no. How long, Phyllis, since we met him at Guardy's ? About a month. But he's so unaffected —quite at home with us. A *nice* fellow."

Mr. Ventnor murmured :

" Very different from his father, isn't he ? "

" Is he ? We don't know his father ; he's a ship-owner, I think."

Mr. Ventnor rubbed his hands : " Ye—es," he said, " just giving up—a warm man. Young Pillin's a lucky fellow—only son. So you met him at old Mr. Heythorp's. I know him too—relation of yours, I believe."

" Our dear Guardy—such a wonderful man."

Mr. Ventnor echoed: "Wonderful—regular old Roman."

"Oh! but he's so *kind!*" Mrs. Larne lifted the white stuff: "Look what he's given this naughty gairl!"

Mr. Ventnor murmured: "Charming! Charming! Bob Pillin said, I think, that Mr. Heythorp was your settlor."

One of those little clouds which visit the brows of women who have owed money in their time passed swiftly athwart Mrs. Larne's eyes. For a moment they seemed saying: "Don't you want to know too much?" Then they slid from under it.

"Won't you sit down?" she said. "You must forgive our being at work."

Mr. Ventnor, who had need of sorting his impressions, shook his head.

"Thank you; I must be getting on. Then Messrs. Scriven can—a mere formality! Good-bye! Good-bye, Miss Larne. I'm sure the dress will be most becoming."

And with memories of a too clear look from the girl's eyes, of a warm firm pressure from the woman's hand, Mr. Ventnor backed towards the door and passed away just in time to avoid hearing in two voices:

"What a nice lawyer!"

"What a horrid man!"

Back in his cab, he continued to rub his hands. No, she *didn't* know old Pillin! That was certain; not from her words, but from her face. She wanted to know him, or about him, anyway. She was trying to hook young Bob for that sprig of a girl—it was as clear as mud. H'm! it would astonish his young friend to hear that he had called. Well, let it! And a curious mixture of emotions beset Mr. Ventnor. He saw the whole thing now so plain, and really could not refrain from a certain admiration. The law had been properly diddled! There was nothing to prevent a man from settling money on a woman he had never seen ; and so old Pillin's settlement could probably not be upset. But old Heythorp could. It was neat, though, oh! neat! And that was a fine woman— remarkably! He had a sort of feeling that if only the settlement had been in danger, it might have been worth while to have made a bargain—a woman like that could have made it worth while! And he believed her quite capable of entertaining the proposition! Her eye! Pity—quite a pity! Mrs. Ventnor was not a wife who satisfied every aspiration. But alas! the settlement *was* safe. This baulking of the sentiment of love, whipped up, if anything, the longing for justice in Mr. Ventnor. That old chap should feel his teeth now. As a piece of investigation it was not so bad—not so bad at all! He had had a bit of luck, of course,—no, not luck,—just that knack of doing the right thing at the right moment which marks a real genius for affairs.

But getting into his train to return to Mrs. Ventnor, he thought : ' A woman like that would have been —— ! ' And he sighed.

2 §

With a neatly written cheque for fifty pounds in his pocket Bob Pillin turned in at 23, Millicent Villas on the afternoon after Mr. Ventnor's visit. Chivalry had won the day. And he rang the bell with an elation which astonished him, for he knew he was doing a soft thing.

"Mrs. Larne is out, sir; Miss Phyllis is at home."
His heart leaped.

"Oh—h! I'm sorry. I wonder if she'd see me?"
The little maid answered:

"I think she's been washin' 'er 'air, sir, but it may
be dry be now. I'll see."

Bob Pillin stood stock still beneath the young
woman on the wall. He could scarcely breathe. If
her hair were not dry—how awful! Suddenly he heard
floating down a clear but smothered: "Oh! Gefooz-
leme!" and other words which he could not catch.
The little maid came running down.

"Miss Phyllis says, sir, she'll be with you in a
jiffy. And I was to tell you that Master Jock is
loose, sir."

Bob Pillin answered "Tha—anks," and passed
into the drawing-room. He went to the bureau, took
an envelope, enclosed the cheque, and addressing it:
"Mrs. Larne," replaced it in his pocket. Then he
crossed over to the mirror. Never till this last month
had he really doubted his own face; but now he
wanted for it things he had never wanted. It had
too much flesh and colour. It did not reflect his
passion. It was a handicap. With the narrow white
piping round his waistcoat opening, and a buttonhole
of tuberoses, he had tried to repair its deficiencies.
But do what he would, he was never easy about himself
nowadays, never up to that pitch which could make
him confident in her presence. And until this month
to lack confidence had never been his wont. A clear,
high, mocking voice said:

"Oh—h! Conceited young man!"

And spinning round he saw Phyllis in the doorway.
Her light-brown hair was fluffed out on her shoulders,

so that he felt a kind of fainting-sweet sensation, and murmured inarticulately :

" Oh ! I say—how jolly ! "

" Lawks ! It's awful ! Have you come to see mother ? "

Balanced between fear and daring, conscious of a scent of hay and verbena and camomile, Bob Pillin stammered :

" Ye—es. I—I'm glad she's not in, though."

Her laugh seemed to him terribly unfeeling.

" Oh ! oh ! Don't be foolish. Sit down. Isn't washing one's head awful ? "

Bob Pillin answered feebly :

" Of course, I haven't much experience."

Her mouth opened.

" Oh ! You *are*—aren't you ? "

And he thought desperately : ' Dare I—oughtn't I —couldn't I somehow take her hand or put my arm round her, or something ? ' Instead, he sat very rigid at his end of the sofa, while she sat lax and lissom at the other, and one of those crises of paralysis which beset would-be lovers fixed him to the soul.

Sometimes during this last month memories of a past existence, when chaff and even kisses came readily to the lips, and girls were fair game, would make him think : ' Is she really such an innocent ? Doesn't she really want me to kiss her ? ' Alas ! such intrusions lasted but a moment before a blast of awe and chivalry withered them, and a strange and tragic delicacy—like nothing he had ever known—resumed its sway. And suddenly he heard her say :

" Why do you know such awful men ? "

" What ? I don't know any *awful* men."

"Oh yes, you do; one came here yesterday; he had whiskers, and he was awful."

"Whiskers?" His soul revolted in disclaimer. "I believe I only know one man with whiskers—a lawyer."

"Yes—that was him; a perfectly horrid man. Mother didn't mind him, but *I* thought he was a beast."

"Ventnor! Came here? How d'you mean?"

"He did; about some business of yours, too." Her face had clouded over. Bob Pillin had of late been harassed by the still-born beginning of a poem:

> "I rode upon my way and saw
> A maid who watched me from the door."

It never grew longer, and was prompted by the feeling that her face was like an April day. The cloud which came on it now was like an April cloud, as if a bright shower of rain must follow. Brushing aside the two distressful lines, he said:

"Look here, Miss Larne—Phyllis—look here!"

"All right, I'm looking!"

"What does it mean—how did he come? What did he say?"

She shook her head, and her hair quivered; the scent of camomile, verbena, hay was wafted; then looking at her lap, she muttered:

"I wish you wouldn't—I wish mother wouldn't—I hate it. Oh! Money! Beastly—beastly!" and a tearful sigh shivered itself into Bob Pillin's reddening ears.

"I say—don't! And do tell me, because——"

"Oh! you *know*."

" I don't—I don't know anything at all. I never——"

Phyllis looked up at him. " Don't tell fibs ; you know mother's borrowing money from you, and it's hateful ! "

A desire to lie roundly, a sense of the cheque in his pocket, a feeling of injustice, the emotion of pity, and a confused and black astonishment about Ventnor, caused Bob Pillin to stammer :

" Well, I'm d——d ! " and to miss the look which Phyllis gave him through her lashes—a look saying :

" Ah ! that's better ! "

" I *am* d——d ! Look here ! D'you mean to say that Ventnor came here about my lending money ? I never said a word to him——"

" There you see—you *are* lending ! "

He clutched his hair.

" We've got to have this out," he added.

" Not by the roots ! Oh ! you do look funny. I've never seen you with your hair untidy. Oh ! oh ! "

Bob Pillin rose and paced the room. In the midst of his emotion he could not help seeing himself sidelong in the mirror ; and on pretext of holding his head in both his hands, tried earnestly to restore his hair. Then coming to a halt he said :

" Suppose I *am* lending money to your mother, what does it matter ? It's only till quarter-day. Anybody might want money."

Phyllis did not raise her face.

" Why are you lending it ? "

" Because—because—why shouldn't I ? " and diving suddenly, he seized her hands.

She wrenched them free ; and with the emotion of despair, Bob Pillin took out the envelope.

"If you like," he said, "I'll tear this up. I don't want to lend it, if you don't want me to ; but I thought —I thought——" It was for her alone he had been going to lend this money !

Phyllis murmured through her hair :

"Yes ! You thought that *I*—that's what's so hateful ! "

Apprehension pierced his mind.

"Oh ! I never—I swear I never——"

"Yes, you did ; you thought I wanted you to lend it."

She jumped up, and brushed past him into the window.

So she thought she was being used as a decoy ! That was awful—especially since it was true. He knew well enough that Mrs. Larne was working his admiration for her daughter for all that it was worth. And he said with simple fervour :

"What rot ! " It produced no effect, and at his wits end, he almost shouted : "Look, Phyllis ! If you don't want me to—here goes ! " Phyllis turned. Tearing the envelope across he threw the bits into the fire. "There it is," he said.

Her eyes grew round ; she said in an awed voice : "Oh ! "

In a sort of agony of honesty he said :

"It was only a cheque. Now you've got your way."

Staring at the fire she answered slowly :

"I expect you'd better go before mother comes."

Bob Pillin's mouth fell ajar ; he secretly agreed, but the idea of sacrificing a moment alone with her was intolerable, and he said hardily :

"No, I shall stick it ! "

Phyllis sneezed.

" My hair isn't a bit dry," and she sat down on the
fender with her back to the fire.

A certain spirituality had come into Bob Pillin's
face. If only he could get that wheeze off : " Phyllis
is my only joy ! " or even : " Phyllis—do you
—won't you—mayn't I ? " But nothing came—
nothing.

And suddenly she said :

" Oh ! don't breathe so loud ; it's awful ! "

" Breathe ? I wasn't ! "

" You were ; just like Carmen when she's dreaming."

He had walked three steps towards the door, before
he thought : ' What does it matter ? I can stand
anything from her ' ; and walked the three steps back
again.

She said softly :

" Poor young man ! "

He answered gloomily :

" I suppose you realise that this may be the last
time you'll see me ? "

" Why ? I thought you were going to take us to the
theatre."

" I don't know whether your mother will—
after——"

Phyllis gave a little clear laugh.

" You don't know mother. Nothing makes any
difference to her."

And Bob Pillin muttered :

" I see." He did not, but it was of no consequence.
Then the thought of Ventnor again ousted all others.
What on earth—how on earth ! He searched his mind
for what he could possibly have said the other night.
Surely he had not asked him to do anything ; certainly
not given him their address. There was something very

odd about it that had jolly well got to be cleared up !
And he said :

"Are you sure the name of that Johnny who came
here yesterday was Ventnor ? "

Phyllis nodded.

"And he was short, and had whiskers ? "

"Yes ; red, and red eyes."

He murmured reluctantly :

"It must be him. Jolly good cheek ; I simply can't
understand. I shall go and see him. How on earth
did he know your address ? "

"I expect you gave it him."

"I did not. I won't have you thinking me a squirt."

Phyllis jumped up. "Oh ! Lawks ! Here's
mother ! " Mrs. Larne was coming up the garden.
Bob Pillin made for the door. "Good-bye," he said ;
"I'm going." But Mrs. Larne was already in the
hall. Enveloping him in fur and her rich personality,
she drew him with her into the drawing-room, where
the back window was open and Phyllis gone.

"I hope," she said, "those naughty children have
been making you comfortable. That nice lawyer of
yours came yesterday. He seemed quite satisfied."

Very red above his collar, Bob Pillin stammered :

"I never told him to ; he isn't my lawyer. I don't
know what it means."

Mrs. Larne smiled. "My dear boy, it's all right.
You needn't be so squeamish. I want it to be quite
on a business footing."

Restraining a fearful inclination to blurt out :
"It's not going to be on any footing ! " Bob Pillin
mumbled : "I must go ; I'm late."

"And when will you be able——— ? "

"Oh ! I'll—I'll send—I'll write. Good-bye ! " And

suddenly he found that Mrs. Larne had him by the
lapel of his coat. The scent of violets and fur was
overpowering, and the thought flashed through him :
' I believe she only wanted to take money off old
Joseph in the Bible. I can't leave my coat in her
hands ! What shall I do ? '

Mrs. Larne was murmuring :

" It would be *so* sweet of you if you could manage
it to-day " ; and her hand slid over his chest. " Oh !
You *have* brought your cheque-book—what a nice
boy ! "

Bob Pillin took it out in desperation, and, sitting
down at the bureau, wrote the identical cheque he
had torn and burned. A warm kiss lighted on his
eyebrow, his head was pressed for a moment to a furry
bosom ; a hand took the cheque ; a voice said : " How
delightful ! " and a sigh immersed him in a bath of
perfume. Backing to the door, he gasped :

" Don't mention it ; and—and *don't tell Phyllis,
please.* Good-bye ! "

Once through the garden gate, he thought : ' By
gum ! I've done it now. That Phyllis should know
about it at all ! That beast Ventnor ! '

His face grew almost grim. He would go and see
what that meant, anyway !

3 §

Mr. Ventnor had not left his office when his young
friend's card was brought to him. Tempted for a
moment to deny his own presence, he thought : ' No !
What's the good ? Bound to see him some time ! '
If he had not exactly courage, he had that peculiar
blend of self-confidence and insensibility which must

needs distinguish those who follow the law ; nor did he ever forget that he was in the right.

" Show him in ! " he said.

He would be quite bland, but young Pillin might whistle for an explanation ; he was still tormented, too, by the memory of rich curves and moving lips, and the possibilities of better acquaintanceship.

While shaking the young man's hand his quick and fulvous eye detected at once the discomposure behind that mask of cheek and collar, and relapsing into one of those swivel chairs which give one an advantage over men more statically seated, he said :

" You look pretty bobbish. Anything I can do for you ? "

Bob Pillin, in the fixed chair of the consultor, nursed his bowler on his knee.

" Well, yes, there is. I've just been to see Mrs. Larne."

Mr. Ventnor did not flinch.

" Ah ! Nice woman ; pretty daughter, too ! " And into those words he put a certain meaning. He never waited to be bullied. Bob Pillin felt the pressure of his blood increasing.

" Look here, Ventnor," he said, " I want an explanation."

" What of ? "

" Why, of your going there, and using my name, and God knows what."

Mr. Ventnor gave his chair two little twiddles before he said :

" Well, you won't get it."

Bob Pillin remained for a moment taken aback ; then he muttered resolutely :

" It's not the conduct of a gentleman."

Every man has his illusions, and no man likes them disturbed. The gingery tint underlying Mr. Ventnor's colouring overlaid it ; even the whites of his eyes grew red.

" Oh ! " he said ; " indeed ! You mind your own business, will you ? "

" It is my business—very much so. You made use of my name, and I don't choose——"

" The devil you don't ! Now, I tell you what——" Mr. Ventnor leaned forward—" you'd better hold your tongue, and not exasperate me. I'm a good-tempered man, but I won't stand your impudence."

Clenching his bowler hat, and only kept in his seat by that sense of something behind, Bob Pillin ejaculated :

" Impudence ! That's good—after what you did ! Look here, why did you ? It's so extraordinary ! "

Mr. Ventnor answered :

" Oh ! is it ? You wait a bit, my friend ! "

Still more moved by the mystery of this affair, Bob Pillin could only mutter :

" I never gave you their address ; we were only talking about old Heythorp."

And at the smile which spread between Mr. Ventnor's whiskers, he jumped up, crying :

" It's not the thing, and you're not going to put me off. I insist on an explanation."

Mr. Ventnor leaned back, crossing his stout legs, joining the tips of his thick fingers. In this attitude he was always self-possessed.

" You do—do you ? "

" Yes. You must have had some reason."

Mr. Ventnor gazed up at him.

" I'll give you a piece of advice, young cock, and

charge you nothing for it, too : Ask no questions, and
you'll be told no lies. And here's another : Go away
before you forget yourself again."

The natural stolidity of Bob Pillin's face was only
just proof against this speech. He said thickly :

" If you go there again and use my name, I'll—
Well, it's lucky for you you're not my age. Anyway
I'll relieve you of my acquaintanceship in future.
Good-evening ! " and he went to the door. Mr. Ventnor
had risen.

" Very well," he said loudly. " Good riddance ! You
wait and see which boot the leg is on ! "

But Bob Pillin was gone, leaving the lawyer with a
very red face, a very angry heart, and a vague sense
of disorder in his speech. Not only Bob Pillin, but his
tender aspirations had all left him ; he no longer
dallied with the memory of Mrs. Larne, but like a man
and a Briton thought only of how to get his own back,
and punish evildoers. The atrocious words of his
young friend, " It's not the conduct of a gentleman,"
festered in the heart of one who was made gentle not
merely by nature but by Act of Parliament, and he
registered a solemn vow to wipe the insult out, if not
with blood, with verjuice. It was his duty, and they
should d——d well see him do it !

IV

1 §

SYLVANUS HEYTHORP seldom went to bed before
one or rose before eleven. The latter habit alone
kept his valet from handing in the resignation which
the former habit prompted almost every night.

Propped on his pillows in a crimson dressing-gown,
and freshly shaved, he looked more Roman than he
ever did, except in his bath. Having disposed of
coffee, he was wont to read his letters, and *The Morning
Post,* for he had always been a Tory, and could not
stomach paying a halfpenny for his news. Not that
there were many letters—when a man has reached the
age of eighty, who should write to him, except to ask
for money ?

It was Valentine's Day. Through his bedroom
window he could see the trees of the park, where the
birds were in song, though he could not hear them.
He had never been interested in Nature—full-blooded
men with short necks seldom are.

This morning indeed there *were* two letters, and he
opened that which smelt of something. Inside was a
thing like a Christmas card, save that the naked babe
had in his hands a bow and arrow, and words coming
out of his mouth : " To be your Valentine." There
was also a little pink note with one blue forget-me-not
printed at the top. It ran :

"DEAREST GUARDY,—I'm sorry this is such a
mangy little valentine ; I couldn't go out to get it

because I've got a beastly cold, so I asked Jock, and
the pig bought this. The satin is simply scrumptious.
If you don't come and see me in it some time soon, I
shall come and show it to you. I wish I had a moustache, because my top lip feels just like a matchbox,
but it's rather ripping having breakfast in bed.
Mr. Pillin's taking us to the theatre the day after
to-morrow evening. Isn't it nummy! I'm going to
have rum and honey for my cold.

" Good-bye,

" Your PHYLLIS."

So this that quivered in his thick fingers, too insensitive to feel it, was a valentine for *him!* Forty years
ago that young thing's grandmother had given him
his last. It made him out a very old chap! Forty
years ago! Had that been himself living then? And
himself, who, as a youth came on the town in 'forty-
five? Not a thought, not a feeling the same! They
said you changed your body every seven years. The
mind with it, too, perhaps! Well, he had come to the
last of his bodies, now! And that holy woman had
been urging him to take it to Bath, with her face as
long as a tea-tray, and some gammon from that doctor
of his. Too full a habit—dock his port—no alcohol—
might go off in a coma any night! Knock off—not he!
Rather die any day than turn teetotaller! When a
man had nothing left in life except his dinner, his bottle,
his cigar, and the dreams they gave him—these doctors
forsooth must want to cut them off! No, no! *Carpe
diem!* while you lived, get something out of it. And
now that he had made all the provision he could for
those youngsters, his life was no good to anyone but
himself; and the sooner he went off the better, if he
ceased to enjoy what there was left, or lost the power

to say : " I'll do this and that, and you be jiggered ! "
Keep a stiff lip until you crashed, and then go clean !
He sounded the bell beside him twice—for Molly, not
his man.   And when the girl came in, and stood, pretty
in her print frock, her fluffy over-fine dark hair escaping
from under her cap, he gazed at her in silence.

" Yes, sirr ? "

" Want to look at you, that's all."

" Oh ! an' I'm not tidy, sirr."

" Never mind.   Had your valentine ? "

" No, sirr ; who would send me one, then ? "

" Haven't you a young man ? "

" Well, I might.   But he's over in my country."

" What d'you think of this ? "

He held out the little boy.

The girl took the card and scrutinised it reverently ;
she said in a detached voice :

" Indeed, an' ut's pretty, too."

" Would you like it ? "

" Oh ! if 'tis not taking ut from you."

Old Heythorp shook his head, and pointed to the
dressing-table.

" Over there—you'll find a sovereign.   Little present
for a good girl."

She uttered a deep sigh.   " Oh ! sirr, ut's too much ;
'tis kingly."

" Go on ; take it."

She took it, and came back, her hands clasping the
sovereign and the valentine, in an attitude as of
prayer.

The old man's gaze rested on her with satisfaction.

" I like pretty faces—can't bear sour ones.   Tell
Meller to get my bath ready."

When she had gone he took up the other letter—

some lawyer's writing, and opening it with the usual
difficulty, read :

" February 13th, 1905.

" SIR,—Certain facts having come to my knowledge,
I deem it my duty to call a special meeting of the
shareholders of ' The Island Navigation Coy.,' to
consider circumstances in connection with the purchase
of Mr. Joseph Pillin's fleet. And I give you notice
that at this meeting your conduct will be called in .
question.

" I am, Sir,
" Yours faithfully,
" CHARLES VENTNOR.

" SYLVANUS HEYTHORP, Esq."

Having read this missive, old Heythorp remained
some minutes without stirring. Ventnor ! That
solicitor chap who had made himself unpleasant at the
creditors' meetings !

There are men whom a really bad bit of news at
once stampedes out of all power of coherent thought
and action, and men who at first simply do not take
it in. Old Heythorp took it in fast enough ; coming
from a lawyer it was about as nasty as it could be.
But, at once, with stoic wariness his old brain began
casting round. What did this fellow really know ?
And what exactly could he do ? One thing was
certain ; even if he knew everything, he couldn't upset
that settlement. The youngsters were all right. The
old man grasped the fact that only his own position
was at stake. But this was enough in all conscience ; a
name which had been before the public fifty odd years
—income, independence, more perhaps. It would take
little, seeing his age and feebleness, to make his Companies throw him over. But what had the fellow

got hold of ? How decide whether or no to take notice ; to let him do his worst, or try and get into touch with him ? And what was the fellow's motive ? He held ten shares ! That would never make a man take all this trouble, and over a purchase which was really first-rate business for the Company. Yes ! His conscience was quite clean. He had not betrayed his Company—on the contrary, had done it a good turn, got them four sound ships at a low price— against much opposition. That he might have done the Company a better turn, and got the ships at fifty-four thousand, did not trouble him—the six thousand was a deuced sight better employed ; and he had not pocketed a penny piece himself ! But the fellow's motive ? Spite ? Looked like it. Spite, because he had been disappointed of his money, and defied into the bargain ! H'm ! If that were so, he might still be got to blow cold again. His eyes lighted on the pink note with the blue forget-me-not. It marked as it were the high-water mark of what was left to him of life ; and this other letter in his hand— by Jove !—low-water mark ! And with a deep and rumbling sigh he thought : 'No, I'm not going to be beaten by this fellow.'

" Your bath is ready, sir."

Crumpling the two letters into the pocket of his dressing-gown, he said :

" Help me up ; and telephone to Mr. Farney to be good enough to come round." . . .

An hour later, when the secretary entered, his chairman was sitting by the fire perusing the articles of association. And, waiting for him to look up, watching the articles shaking in that thick, feeble hand, the secretary had one of those moments of philosophy not too frequent with his kind. Some said the only happy time of life was when you had no passions, nothing to hope and live for. But did you really ever reach such a stage ? The old chairman, for instance, still had his passion for getting his own way, still had his prestige, and set a lot of store by it ! And he said :

" Good morning, sir ; I hope you're all right in this east wind. The purchase is completed."

" Best thing the company ever did. Have you heard from a shareholder called Ventnor. You know the man I mean ? "

" No, sir. I haven't."

" Well ! You may get a letter that'll make you open your eyes. An impudent scoundrel ! Just write at my dictation."

" *February 14th,* 1905.

" CHARLES VENTNOR, Esq.

" SIR,—I have your letter of yesterday's date, the contents of which I am at a loss to understand. My solicitors will be instructed to take the necessary measures."

" Phew ! What's all this about ? " the secretary thought.

" Yours truly . . . I'll sign."

And the shaky letters closed the page :

" SYLVANUS HEYTHORP."

" Post that as you go."

" Anything else I can do for you, sir ? "

" Nothing, except to let me know if you hear from this fellow."

When the secretary had gone the old man thought : ' So ! The ruffian hasn't called the meeting yet.

That'll bring him round here fast enough if it's his money he wants—blackmailing scoundrel ! '

" Mr. Pillin, sir ; and will you wait lunch, or will you have it in the dining-room ? "

" In the dining-room."

At sight of that death's-head of a fellow, old Heythorp felt a sort of pity. He looked bad enough already— and this news would make him look worse. Joe Pillin glanced round at the two closed doors.

" How are you, Sylvanus ? I'm very poorly." He came closer, and lowered his voice : " Why did you get me to make that settlement ? I must have been mad. I've had a man called Ventnor—I didn't like his manner. He asked me if I knew a Mrs. Larne."

" Ha ! What did you say ? "

" What could I say ? I *don't* know her. But why did he ask ? "

" Smells a rat."

Joe Pillin grasped the edge of the table with both hands.

" Oh ! " he murmured. " Oh ! don't say that ! "

Old Heythorp held out to him the crumpled letter.

When he had read it Joe Pillin sat down abruptly before the fire.

" Pull yourself together, Joe ; they can't touch you, and they can't upset either the purchase or the settlement. They can upset me, that's all."

Joe Pillin answered, with trembling lips :

" How you can sit there, and look the same as ever ! Are you sure they can't touch me ? "

Old Heythorp nodded grimly.

" They talk of an Act, but they haven't passed it yet. They might prove a breach of trust against me.

F.T   M

But I'll diddle them. Keep your pecker up, and get off abroad."

"Yes, yes. I must. I'm very bad. I was going to-morrow. But I don't know, I'm sure, with this hanging over me. My son knowing her makes it worse. He picks up with everybody. He knows this man Ventnor too. And I daren't say anything to Bob. What are you thinking of, Sylvanus? You look very funny?"

Old Heythorp seemed to rouse himself from a sort of coma.

"I want my lunch," he said. "Will you stop and have some?"

Joe Pillin stammered out:

"Lunch! I don't know when I shall eat again. What are you going to do, Sylvanus?"

"Bluff the beggar out of it."

"But suppose you can't?"

"Buy him off. He's one of my creditors."

Joe Pillin stared at him afresh. "You always had such nerve," he said yearningly. "Do you ever wake up between two and four? I do—and everything's black."

"Put a good stiff nightcap on, my boy, before going to bed."

"Yes; I sometimes wish I was less temperate. But I couldn't stand it. I'm told your doctor forbids you alcohol."

"He does. That's why I drink it."

Joe Pillin, brooding over the fire, said: "This meeting—d'you think they mean to have it? D'you think this man really knows? If my name gets into the newspapers——" but encountering his old friend's deep little eyes, he stopped. "So you advise me to get off to-morrow, then?"

Old Heythorp nodded.

" Your lunch is served, sir."

Joe Pillin started violently, and rose.

" Well, good-bye, Sylvanus—good-bye ! I don't
suppose I shall be back till the summer, if I ever come
back ! " He sank his voice : " I shall rely on you.
You won't let them, will you ? "

Old Heythorp lifted his hand, and Joe Pillin put into
that swollen shaking paw his pale and spindly fingers.
" I wish I had your pluck," he said sadly. " Good-bye,
Sylvanus," and turning, he passed out.

Old Heythorp thought : ' Poor shaky chap. All to
pieces at the first shot ! ' And, going to his lunch,
ate more heavily than usual.

2 §

Mr. Ventnor, on reaching his office and opening his
letters, found, as he had anticipated, one from " that
old rascal." Its contents excited in him the need to
know his own mind. Fortunately this was not compli-
cated by a sense of dignity—he only had to consider
the position with an eye on not being made to *look* a
fool. The point was simply whether he set more store
by his money than by his desire for—er—justice. If
not, he had merely to convene the special meeting, and
lay before it the plain fact that Mr. Joseph Pillin, selling
his ships for sixty thousand pounds, had just made a
settlement of six thousand pounds on a lady whom he
did not know, a daughter, ward, or what-not—of the
purchasing company's chairman, who had said, more-
over, at the general meeting, that he stood or fell by the
transaction ; he had merely to do this, and demand
that an explanation be required from the old man of

such a startling coincidence. Convinced that no explanation would hold water, he felt sure that his action would be at once followed by the collapse, if nothing more, of that old image, and the infliction of a nasty slur on old Pillin and his hopeful son. On the other hand, three hundred pounds was money ; and, if old Heythorp were to say to him : " What do you want to make this fuss for—here's what I owe you ! " could a man of business and the world let his sense of justice— however he might itch to have it satisfied—stand in the way of what was after all also his sense of justice ?— for this money had been owing to him for the deuce of a long time. In this dilemma, the words : " My solicitors will be instructed " were of notable service in helping him to form a decision, for he had a certain dislike of other solicitors, and an intimate knowledge of the law of libel and slander ; if by any remote chance there should be a slip between the cup and the lip, Charles Ventnor might be in the soup—a position which he deprecated both by nature and profession. High thinking, therefore, decided him at last to answer thus :

" February 15th, 1905.

" SIR,—I have received your note. I think it may be fair, before taking further steps in this matter, to ask you for a personal explanation of the circumstances to which I alluded. I therefore propose with your permission to call on you at your private residence at five o'clock to-morrow afternoon.

" Yours faithfully,
" CHARLES VENTNOR.

" SYLVANUS HEYTHORP, Esq."

Having sent this missive, and arranged in his mind the damning, if circumstantial, evidence he had accumulated, he awaited the hour with confidence, for his nature was not lacking in the cock-surety of a Briton. All the same, he dressed himself particularly well that morning, putting on a blue and white striped waistcoat which, with a cream-coloured tie, set off his fulvous whiskers and full blue eyes ; and he lunched, if anything, more fully than his wont, eating a stronger cheese and taking a glass of special Club ale. He took care to be late, too, to show the old fellow that his coming at all was in the nature of an act of grace. A strong scent of hyacinths greeted him in the hall ; and Mr. Ventnor, who was an amateur of flowers, stopped to put his nose into a fine bloom and think uncontrollably of Mrs. Larne. Pity ! The things one had to give up in life—fine women—one thing and another. Pity ! The thought inspired in him a timely anger ; and he followed the servant, intending to stand no nonsense from this paralytic old rascal.

The room he entered was lighted by a bright fire, and a single electric lamp with an orange shade on a table covered by a black satin cloth. There were heavily gleaming oil paintings on the walls, a heavy old brass chandelier without candles, heavy dark red curtains, and an indefinable scent of burnt acorns, coffee, cigars, and old man. He became conscious of a candescent spot on the far side of the hearth, where the light fell on old Heythorp's thick white hair.

" Mr. Ventnor, sir."

The candescent spot moved. A voice said : " Sit down."

Mr. Ventnor sat in an armchair on the opposite side of the fire ; and, finding a kind of somnolence creeping over him, pinched himself. He wanted all his wits about him.

The old man was speaking in that extinct voice of his, and Mr. Ventnor said rather pettishly :

" Beg pardon, I don't get you."

Old Heythorp's voice swelled with sudden force :

" Your letters are Greek to me."

" Oh ! indeed, I think we can soon make them into plain English ! "

" Sooner the better."

Mr. Ventnor passed through a moment of indecision. Should he lay his cards on the table ? It was not his habit, and the proceeding was sometimes attended with risk. The knowledge, however, that he could always take them up again, seeing there was no third person here to testify that he had laid them down, decided him, and he said :

" Well, Mr. Heythorp, the long and short of the matter is this : Our friend Mr. Pillin paid you a commission of ten per cent. on the sale of his ships. Oh ! yes. He settled the money, not on you, but on your relative Mrs. Larne and her children. This, as you know, is a breach of trust on your part."

The old man's voice : " Where did you get hold of that cock-and-bull story ? " brought him to his feet before the fire.

" It won't do, Mr. Heythorp. My witnesses are Mr. Pillin, Mrs. Larne, and Mr. Scriven."

" What have you come here for, then—blackmail ? "

Mr. Ventnor straightened his waistcoat ; a rush of conscious virtue had dyed his face.

" Oh ! you take that tone," he said, " do you ? You think you can ride roughshod over everything ? Well, you're very much mistaken. I advise you to keep a civil tongue and consider your position, or I'll

make a beggar of you. I'm not sure this isn't a case
for a prosecution ! "

" Gammon ! "

The choler in Charles Ventnor kept him silent for
a moment ; then he burst out :

" Neither gammon nor spinach. You owe me
three hundred pounds, you've owed it me for years,
and you have the impudence to take this attitude with
me, have you ? Now, I never bluster ; I say what I
mean. You just listen to me. Either you pay me
what you owe me at once, or I call this meeting and
make what I know public. You'll very soon find
out where you are. And a good thing, too, for a
more unscrupulous—unscrupulous——" he paused for
breath.

Occupied with his own emotion, he had not observed
the change in old Heythorp's face. The imperial
on that lower lip was bristling, the crimson of those
cheeks had spread to the roots of his white hair.
He grasped the arms of his chair, trying to rise ; his
swollen hands trembled ; a little saliva escaped one
corner of his lips. And the words came out as if
shaken by his teeth :

" So—so—you—you bully me ! "

Conscious that the interview had suddenly passed
from the phase of negotiation, Mr. Ventnor looked
hard at his opponent. He saw nothing but a decrepit,
passionate, crimson-faced old man at bay, and all the
instincts of one with everything on his side boiled up
in him. The miserable old turkey-cock—the apoplectic
image ! And he said :

" And you'll do no good for yourself by getting in
a passion. At your age, and in your condition, I
recommend a little prudence. Now just take my terms

quietly, or you know what'll happen. I'm not to be intimidated by any of your airs." And seeing that the old man's rage was such that he simply could not speak, he took the opportunity of going on : " I don't care two straws which you do—I'm out to show you who's master. If you think in your dotage you can domineer any longer—well, you'll find two can play at that game. Come, now, which are you going to do ? "

The old man had sunk back in his chair, and only his little deep-blue eyes seemed living. Then he moved one hand, and Mr. Ventnor saw that he was fumbling to reach the button of an electric bell at the end of a cord. ' I'll show him,' he thought, and stepping forward, he put it out of reach.

Thus frustrated, the old man remained motionless, staring up. The word " blackmail " resumed its buzzing in Mr. Ventnor's ears. The impudence—the consummate impudence of it from this fraudulent old ruffian with one foot in bankruptcy and one foot in the grave, if not in the dock.

" Yes," he said, " it's never too late to learn ; and for once you've come up against someone a leetle bit too much for you. Haven't you now ? You'd better cry ' *Peccavi*.' "

Then, in the deathly silence of the room, the moral force of his position, and the collapse as it seemed of his opponent, awakening a faint compunction, he took a turn over the Turkey carpet to readjust his mind.

" You're an old man, and I don't want to be too hard on you. I'm only showing you that you can't play fast and loose as if you were God Almighty any louger. You've had your own way too many years. And now you can't have it, see ! " Then, as the old

man again moved forward in his chair, he added :
" Now, don't get in a passion again ; calm yourself,
because I warn you—this is your last chance. I'm a
man of my word ; and what I say, I do."

By a violent and unsuspected effort the old man
jerked himself up and reached the bell. Mr. Ventnor
heard it ring, and said sharply :

" Mind you, it's nothing to me which you do. I
came for your own good. Please yourself. Well ? "

He was answered by the click of the door and the
old man's husky voice :

" Show this hound out ! And then come back ! "

Mr. Ventnor had presence of mind enough not to
shake his fist. Muttering : " Very well, Mr. Heythorp ! Ah ! *Very* well ! " he moved with dignity
to the door. The careful shepherding of the servant
renewed the fire of his anger. Hound ! He had been
called a hound !

3 §

After seeing Mr. Ventnor off the premises the man
Meller returned to his master, whose face looked very
odd—" all patchy-like," as he put it in the servants'
hall, as though the blood driven to his head had mottled
for good the snowy whiteness of the forehead. He
received the unexpected order :

" Get me a hot bath ready, and put some pine stuff
in it."

When the old man was seated there, the valet
asked :

" How long shall I give you, sir ? "

" Twenty minutes."

" Very good, sir."

Lying in that steaming brown fragrant liquid, old
Heythorp heaved a stertorous sigh. By losing his
temper with that ill-conditioned cur he had cooked
his goose. It was done to a turn ; and he was a ruined
man. If only—oh ! if only he could have seized the
fellow by the neck and pitched him out of the room !
To have lived to be so spoken to ; to have been unable
to lift hand or foot, hardly even his voice—he would
sooner have been dead ! Yes—sooner have been dead !
A dumb and measureless commotion was still at work
in the recesses of that thick old body, silver-brown in
the dark water, whose steam he drew deep into his
wheezing lungs, as though for spiritual relief. To be
beaten by a cur like that ! To have that common cad
of a pettifogging lawyer drag him down and kick him
about ; tumble a name which had stood high, in the
dust ! The fellow had the power to make him a by-
word and a beggar ! It was incredible ! But it was a
fact. And to-morrow he would begin to do it—
perhaps had begun already. His tree had come
down with a crash ! Eighty years — eighty good
years ! He regretted none of them—regretted nothing ;
least of all this breach of trust which had provided for
his grandchildren—one of the best things he had ever
done. The fellow was a cowardly hound, too ! The
way he had snatched the bell-pull out of his reach—
despicable cur ! And a chap like that was to put "paid"
to the account of Sylvanus Heythorp, to " scratch "
him out of life—so near the end of everything, the very
end ! His hand raised above the surface fell back on
his stomach through the dark water, and a bubble or
two rose. Not so fast—not so fast ! He had but to
slip down a foot, let the water close over his head, and
" Good-bye " to Master Ventnor's triumph ! Dead

men could not be kicked off the Boards of Companies.
Dead men could not be beggared, deprived of their
independence. He smiled and stirred a little in the
bath till the water reached the white hairs on his lower
lip. It smelt nice ! And he took a long sniff. He had
had a good life, a good life ! And with the thought that
he had it in his power at any moment to put Master
Ventnor's nose out of joint—to beat the beggar after
all, a sense of assuagement and well-being crept over
him. His blood ran more evenly again. He closed
his eyes. They talked about an after-life—people like
that holy woman. Gammon ! You went to sleep—a
long sleep ; no dreams. A nap after dinner ! Dinner !
His tongue sought his palate ! Yes ! he could eat a good
dinner ! That dog hadn't put him off his stroke ! The
best dinner he had ever eaten was the one he gave to
Jack Herring, Chichester, Thornworthy, Nick Treffry
and Jolyon Forsyte at Pole's. Good Lord ! In 'sixty—
yes—'sixty-five ? Just before he fell in love with
Alice Larne—ten years before he came to Liverpool.
That *was* a dinner ! Cost twenty-four pounds for the
six of them—and Forsyte an absurdly moderate fellow.
Only Nick Treffry and himself had been three-bottle
men ! Dead ! Every jack man of them. And suddenly
he thought : ' My name's a good one—I was never
down before—never beaten ! '

A voice above the steam said :

" The twenty minutes is up, sir."

" All right ; I'll get out. Evening clothes."

And Meller, taking out dress suit and shirt, thought :
' Now, what does the old bloomer want dressin' up
again for ; why can't he go to bed and have his dinner
there ? When a man's like a baby, the cradle's the
place for him.' . . .

An hour later, at the scene of his encounter with Mr. Ventnor, where the table was already laid for dinner, old Heythorp stood and gazed. The curtains had been drawn back, the window thrown open to air the room, and he could see out there the shapes of the dark trees and a sky grape-coloured, in the mild, moist night. It smelt good. A sensuous feeling stirred in him, warm from his bath, clothed from head to foot in fresh garments. Deuce of a time since he had dined in full fig! He would have liked a woman dining opposite—but not that holy woman; no, by George!— would have liked to see light falling on a woman's shoulders once again, and a pair of bright eyes! He crossed, snail-like, towards the fire. There that bullying fellow had stood with his back to it—confound his impudence!—as if the place belonged to him. And suddenly he had a vision of his three secretaries' faces— especially young Farney's—as they would look, when the pack got him by the throat and pulled him down. His co-directors, too! Old Heythorp! How are the mighty fallen! And that hound jubilant!

His valet passed across the room to shut the window and draw the curtains. This chap too! The day he could no longer pay his wages, and had lost the power to say " Shan't want your services any more "—when he could no longer even pay his doctor for doing his best to kill him off! Power, interest, independence, all—gone! To be dressed and undressed, given pap, like a baby in arms, served as they chose to serve him, and wished out of the way—broken, dishonoured! By money alone an old man had his being! Meat, drink, movement, breath! When all his money was gone the holy woman would let him know it fast enough. They would all let him know it; or if they didn't, it

would be out of pity ! He had never been pitied yet—
thank God ! And he said :

" Get me up a bottle of Perrier Jouet. What's the
menu ? "

" Germane soup, sir ; filly de sole ; sweetbread ;
cutlet soubees, rum souffly."

" Tell her to give me a *hors d'œuvre*, and put on a
savoury."

" Yes, sir."

When the man had gone, he thought : ' I should
have liked an oyster—too late now ! ' and going over
to his bureau, he fumblingly pulled out the top drawer.
There was little in it—just a few papers, business papers
on his Companies, and a schedule of his debts ; not
even a copy of his will—he had not made one, nothing
to leave ! Letters he had never kept. Half a dozen
bills, a few receipts, and the little pink note with the
blue forget-me-not. That was the lot ! An old tree
gives up bearing leaves, and its roots dry up, before it
comes down in a wind ; an old man's world slowly falls
away from him till he stands alone in the night.
Looking at the pink note, he thought : ' Suppose I'd
married Alice—a man never had a better mistress ! '
He fumbled the drawer to ; but still he strayed feebly
about the room, with a curious shrinking from sitting
down, legacy from the quarter of an hour he had been
compelled to sit while that hound worried at his throat.
He was opposite one of the pictures now. It gleamed,
dark and oily, limning a Scots Grey who had mounted
a wounded Russian on his horse, and was bringing him
back prisoner from the Balaclava charge. A very old
friend—bought in 'fifty-nine. It had hung in his
chambers in the Albany—hung with him ever since.
With whom would it hang when he was gone ? For

that holy woman would scrap it, to a certainty, and
stick up some Crucifixion or other, some new-fangled
high art thing ! She could even do that now if she liked
—for she owned it, owned every mortal stick in the
room, to the very glass he would drink his champagne
from ; all made over under the settlement fifteen years
ago, before his last big gamble went wrong. " *De
l'audace, toujours de l'audace !* " The gamble which
had brought him down till his throat at last was at the
mercy of a bullying hound. The pitcher and the well !
At the mercy——! The sound of a popping cork dragged
him from reverie. He moved to his seat, back to the
window, and sat down to his dinner. By George !
They had got him an oyster ! And he said :

" I've forgotten my teeth ! "

While the man was gone for them, he swallowed the
oysters, methodically touching them one by one with
cayenne, Chili vinegar, and lemon. Ummm ! Not
quite what they used to be at Pym's in the best days,
but not bad—not bad ! Then seeing the little blue
bowl lying before him, he looked up and said :

" My compliments to cook on the oysters. Give me
the champagne." And he lifted his trembling teeth.
Thank God, he could still put 'em in for himself ! The
creaming goldenish fluid from the napkined bottle
slowly reached the brim of his glass, which had a hollow
stem ; raising it to his lips, very red between the white
hairs above and below, he drank with a gurgling noise,
and put the glass down—empty. Nectar ! And just
cold enough !

" I frapped it the least bit, sir."

" Quite right. What's that smell of flowers ? "

" It's from those 'yacinths on the sideboard, sir.
They come from Mrs. Larne, this afternoon."

" Put 'em on the table. Where's my daughter ? "

" She's had dinner, sir ; goin' to a ball, I think."

" A ball ! "

" Charity ball, I fancy, sir."

" Ummm ! Give me a touch of the old sherry with the soup."

" Yes, sir. I shall have to open a bottle."

" Very well, then, do ! "

On his way to the cellar the man confided to Molly, who was carrying the soup :

" The Gov'nor's going it to-night ! What he'll be like to-morrow I dunno."

The girl answered softly :

" Poor old man, let um have his pleasure." And, in the hall, with the soup tureen against her bosom, she hummed above the steam, and thought of the ribbons on her new chemises, bought out of the sovereign he had given her.

And old Heythorp, digesting his oysters, snuffed the scent of the hyacinths, and thought of the St. Germain, his favourite soup. It wouldn't be first-rate, at this time of year—should be made with little young home-grown peas. Paris was the place for it. Ah ! The French were the fellows for eating, and—looking things in the face ! Not hypocrites—not ashamed of their reason or their senses !

The soup came in. He sipped it, bending forward as far as he could, his napkin tucked in over his shirt-front like a bib. He got the bouquet of that sherry to a T—his sense of smell was very keen to-night ; rare old stuff it was—more than a year since he had tasted it—but no one drank sherry nowadays, hadn't the constitution for it ! The fish came up, and went down ; and with the sweetbread he took his second glass of

champagne. Always the best, that second glass—the
stomach well warmed, and the palate not yet dulled.
Umm ! So that fellow thought he had him beaten, did
he ? And he said suddenly :

" The fur coat in the wardrobe, I've no use for it.
You can take it away to-night."

With tempered gratitude the valet answered :

" Thank you, sir ; much obliged, I'm sure." So the
old buffer had found out there was moth in it !

" Have I worried you much ? "

" No, sir ; not at all, sir—that is, no more than
reason."

" Afraid I have. Very sorry—can't help it. You'll
find that, when you get like me."

" Yes, sir ; I've always admired your pluck, sir."

" Um ! Very good of you to say so."

" Always think of you keepin' the flag flyin', sir."

Old Heythorp bent his body from the waist.

" Much obliged to you."

" Not at all, sir. Cook's done a little spinach in
cream with the soubees."

" Ah ! Tell her from me it's a capital dinner, so far."

" Thank you, sir."

Alone again, old Heythorp sat unmoving, his brain
just narcotically touched. " The flag flyin'—the flag
flyin' ! " He raised his glass and sucked. He had an
appetite now, and finished the three cutlets, and all
the sauce and spinach. Pity ! he could have managed
a snipe—fresh shot ! A desire to delay, to lengthen
dinner, was strong upon him ; there were but the
soufflé and the savoury to come. He would have
enjoyed, too, someone to talk to. He had always been
fond of good company—been good company himself,
or so they said—not that he had had a chance of late.

Even at the Boards they avoided talking to him, he had
noticed for a long time. Well! that wouldn't trouble
him again—he had sat through his last Board, no
doubt. They shouldn't kick him off, though; he
wouldn't give them that pleasure—had seen the
beggars hankering after his chairman's shoes too long.
The *soufflé* was before him now, and lifting his glass, he
said :

" Fill up."

" These are the special glasses, sir ; only four to the
bottle."

" Fill up."

The servant filled, screwing up his mouth.

Old Heythorp drank, and put the glass down empty
with a sigh. He had been faithful to his principles,
finished the bottle before touching the sweet—a good
bottle—of a good brand! And now for the *soufflé!*
Delicious, flipped down with the old sherry! So that
holy woman was going to a ball, was she! How deuced
funny! Who would dance with a dry stick like that,
all eaten up with a piety which was just sexual disappointment ? Ah! yes, lots of women like that—had
often noticed 'em—pitied 'em too, until you had to do
with them and they made you as unhappy as themselves, and were tyrants into the bargain. And he
asked :

" What's the savoury ? "

" Cheese remmykin, sir."

His favourite.

" I'll have my port with it—the 'sixty-eight."

The man stood gazing with evident stupefaction. He
had not expected this. The old man's face was very
flushed, but that might be the bath. He said feebly :

" Are you sure you ought, sir ? "

"No, but I'm going to."

"Would you mind if I spoke to Miss Heythorp, sir?"

"If you do, you can leave my service."

"Well, sir, I don't accept the responsibility."

"Who asked you to?"

"No, sir."

"Well, get it, then; and don't be an ass."

"Yes, sir." If the old man were not humoured he
would have a fit, perhaps!

And the old man sat quietly staring at the hyacinths.
He felt happy, his whole being lined and warmed and
drowsed—and there was more to come! What had the
holy folk to give you compared with the comfort of a
good dinner? Could they make you dream, and see
life rosy for a little? No, they could only give you
promissory notes which never would be cashed. A man
had nothing but his pluck—they only tried to under-
mine it, and make him squeal for help. He could see
his precious doctor throwing up his hands: "Port
after a bottle of champagne—you'll die of it!" And
a very good death too—none better. A sound
broke the silence of the closed-up room. Music? His
daughter playing the piano overhead. Singing too!
What a trickle of a voice! Jenny Lind! The Swedish
nightingale—he had never missed the nights when she
was singing—Jenny Lind!

"It's very hot, sir. Shall I take it out of the case?"

Ah! The ramequin!

"Touch of butter, and the cayenne!"

"Yes, sir."

He ate it slowly, savouring each mouthful; had
never tasted a better. With cheese—port! He drank
one glass, and said:

"Help me to my chair."

And settled there before the fire with decanter and glass and hand-bell on the little low table by his side, he murmured :

" Bring coffee, and my cigar, in twenty minutes."

To-night he would do justice to his wine, not smoking till he had finished. As old Horace said :

" Aequam memento rebus in arduis
Servare mentem."

And, raising his glass, he sipped slowly, spilling a drop or two, shutting his eyes.

The faint silvery squealing of the holy woman in the room above, the scent of hyacinths, the drowse of the fire, on which a cedar log had just been laid, the feeling of the port soaking down into the crannies of his being, made up a momentary Paradise. Then the music stopped ; and no sound rose but the tiny groans of the log trying to resist the fire. Dreamily he thought : ' Life wears you out—wears you out. Logs on a fire ! ' And he filled his glass again. That fellow had been careless ; there were dregs at the bottom of the decanter and he had got down to them ! Then, as the last drop from his tilted glass trickled into the white hairs on his chin, he heard the coffee tray put down, and taking his cigar he put it to his ear, rolling it in his thick fingers. In prime condition ! And drawing a first whiff, he said :

" Open that bottle of the old brandy in the sideboard."

" Brandy, sir ? I really daren't, sir."

" Are you my servant or not ? "

" Yes, sir, but——"

A minute of silence, then the man went hastily to the sideboard, took out the bottle, and drew the cork. The tide of crimson in the old man's face had frightened him.

" Leave it there."

The unfortunate valet placed the bottle on the little table. ' I'll have to tell her,' he thought ; ' but if I take away the port decanter and the glass, it won't look so bad.' And, carrying them, he left the room.

Slowly the old man drank his coffee, and the liqueur of brandy. The whole gamut ! And watching his cigar-smoke wreathing blue in the orange glow, he smiled. The last night to call his soul his own, the last night of his independence. Send in his resignations to-morrow—not wait to be kicked off ! Not give that fellow a chance !

A voice which seemed to come from far off, said :

" Father ! You're drinking brandy ! How *can* you— you know it's simple poison to you ! " A figure in white, scarcely actual, loomed up close. He took the bottle to fill up his liqueur glass, in defiance ; but a hand in a long white glove, with another dangling from its wrist, pulled it away, shook it at him, and replaced it in the sideboard. And, just as when Mr. Ventnor stood there accusing him, a swelling and churning in his throat prevented him from speech ; his lips moved, but only a little froth came forth.

His daughter had approached again. She stood quite close, in white satin, thin-faced, sallow, with eyebrows raised, and her dark hair frizzed—yes ! frizzed—the holy woman ! With all his might he tried to say : " So you bully me, do you—you bully me *to-night !* " but only the word " so " and a sort of whispering came forth. He heard her speaking. " It's no good your getting angry, father. After champagne —it's wicked ! " Then her form receded in a sort of rustling white mist ; she was gone ; and he heard the sputtering and growling of her taxi, bearing her to the ball. So! She tyrannised and bullied, even before she had him at her mercy, did she? She should see! Anger had brightened his eyes; the room came clear again. And slowly raising himself he sounded the bell twice, for the girl, not for that fellow Meller, who was in the plot. As soon as her pretty black and white-aproned figure stood before him, he said:

"Help me up!"

Twice her soft pulling was not enough, and he sank back. The third time he struggled to his feet.

"Thank you; that'll do." Then, waiting till she was gone, he crossed the room, fumbled open the sideboard door, and took out the bottle. Reaching over the polished oak, he grasped a sherry glass; and holding the bottle with both hands, tipped the liquor into it, put it to his lips and sucked. Drop by drop it passed over his palate—mild, very old, old as himself, coloured like sunlight, fragrant. To the last drop he drank it, then hugging the bottle to his shirt-front, he moved snail-like to his chair, and fell back into its depths. For some minutes he remained there motionless, the bottle clasped to his chest, thinking: 'This is not the attitude of a gentleman. I must put it down on the table—on the table;' but a thick cloud was between him and everything. It was with his hands he would have to put the bottle on the table! But he could not find his hands, could not feel them. His mind see-sawed in strophe and antistrophe: "You can't move!"—"I will move!" "You're beaten"—"I'm not beat." "Give up"—"I won't." That struggle to find his hands seemed to last for ever—h *must* find them! After that—go down—all standing—after that! Everything round him was red. Then the red cloud cleared just a little, and he could hear the

clock—" tick—tick—tick " ; a faint sensation spread
from his shoulders down to his wrists, down his palms ;
and yes—he could feel the bottle ! He redoubled his
struggle to get forward in his chair ; to get forward and
put the bottle down. It was not dignified like this !
One arm he could move now ; but could not grip the
bottle nearly tight enough to put it down. Working
his whole body forward, inch by inch, he shifted himself
up in the chair till he could lean sideways, and the
bottle, slipping down his chest, dropped slanting to the
edge of the low stool-table. Then with all his might
he screwed his trunk and arms an inch further, and the
bottle stood. He had done it—done it ! His lips
twitched into a smile ; his body sagged back to its
old position. He had done it ! And he closed his
eyes. . . .

At half-past eleven the girl Molly, opening the door,
looked at him and said softly : " Sirr ! there's some
ladies, and a gentleman ! " But he did not answer.
And, still holding the door, she whispered out into the
hall :

" He's asleep, miss."

A voice whispered back :

" Oh ! Just let me go in, I won't wake him unless
he does. But I do want to show him my dress."

The girl moved aside ; and on tiptoe Phyllis passed
in. She walked to where, between the lamp-glow and
the fire-glow, she was lighted up. White satin—her
first low-cut dress—the flush of her first supper party—
a gardenia at her breast, another in her fingers ! Oh !
what a pity he was asleep ! How red he looked ! How
funnily old men breathed ! And mysteriously, as a
child might, she whispered :

" Guardy ! "

No answer ! And pouting, she stood twiddling the gardenia. Then suddenly she thought : ' I'll put it in his buttonhole ! When he wakes up and sees it, how he'll jump ! '

And stealing close, she bent and slipped it in. Two faces looked at her from round the door ; she heard Bob Pillin's smothered chuckle ; her mother's rich and feathery laugh. Oh ! How red his forehead was ! She touched it with her lips ; skipped back, twirled round, danced silently a second, blew a kiss, and like quicksilver was gone.

And the whispering, the chuckling, and one little outpealing laugh rose in the hall.

But the old man slept. Nor until Meller came at his usual hour of half-past twelve, was it known that he would never wake.

1916.

THE APPLE TREE

"The Apple-tree, the singing and the gold."
MURRAY'S "HIPPOLYTUS OF EURIPIDES."

ON their silver-wedding day Ashurst and his wife were motoring along the outskirts of the moor, intending to crown the festival by stopping the night at Torquay, where they had first met. This was the idea of Stella Ashurst, whose character contained a streak of sentiment. If she had long lost the blue-eyed, flower-like charm, the cool slim purity of face and form, the apple-blossom colouring, which had so swiftly and so oddly affected Ashurst twenty-six years ago, she was still at forty-three a comely and faithful companion, whose cheeks were faintly mottled, and whose grey-blue eyes had acquired a certain fullness.

It was she who had stopped the car where the common rose steeply to the left, and a narrow strip of larch and beech, with here and there a pine, stretched out to the right, towards the valley between the road and the first long high hill of the full moor. She was looking for a place where they might lunch, for Ashurst never looked for anything ; and this, between the golden furze and the feathery green larches smelling of lemons in the last sun of April—this, with a view into the deep valley and up to the long moor heights, seemed fitting to the decisive nature of one who sketched in water-colours, and loved romantic spots. Grasping her paint box, she got out.

"Won't this do, Frank ? "

Ashurst, rather like a bearded Schiller, grey in the

wings, tall, long-legged, with large remote grey eyes
which sometimes filled with meaning and became almost
beautiful, with nose a little to one side, and bearded
lips just open — Ashurst, forty-eight, and silent,
grasped the luncheon basket, and got out too.

" Oh ! Look, Frank ! A grave ! "

By the side of the road, where the track from the top
of the common crossed it at right angles and ran through
a gate past the narrow wood, was a thin mound of turf,
six feet by one, with a moorstone to the west, and on
it someone had thrown a blackthorn spray and a
handful of bluebells. Ashurst looked, and the poet in
him moved. At cross-roads—a suicide's grave ! Poor
mortals with their superstitions ! Whoever lay there,
though, had the best of it—no clammy sepulchre
among other hideous graves carved with futilities—
just a rough stone, the wide sky, and wayside blessings !
And, without comment, for he had learned not to be a
philosopher in the bosom of his family, he strode away
up on to the common, dropped the luncheon basket
under a wall, spread a rug for his wife to sit on—she
would turn up from her sketching when she was
hungry—and took from his pocket Murray's translation
of the " Hippolytus." He had soon finished reading
of " The Cyprian " and her revenge, and looked at the
sky instead. And watching the white clouds so bright
against the intense blue, Ashurst, on his silver-wedding
day, longed for—he knew not what. Mal-adjusted to
life—man's organism ! One's mode of life might be
high and scrupulous, but there was always an under-
current of greediness, a hankering, and sense of waste.
Did women have it too ? Who could tell ? And yet,
men who gave vent to their appetites for novelty, their
riotous longings for new adventures, new risks new

pleasures, these suffered, no doubt, from the reverse side of starvation, from surfeit. No getting out of it— a mal-adjusted animal, civilised man ! There could be no garden of his choosing, of " the Apple-tree, the singing, and the gold," in the words of that lovely Greek chorus, no achievable elysium in life, or lasting haven of happiness for any man with a sense of beauty —nothing which could compare with the captured loveliness in a work of art, set down for ever, so that to look on it or read was always to have the same precious sense of exaltation and restful inebriety. Life no doubt had moments with that quality of beauty, of unbidden flying rapture, but the trouble was, they lasted no longer than the span of a cloud's flight over the sun ; impossible to keep them with you, as Art caught beauty and held it fast. They were as fleeting as one of the glimmering or golden visions one had of the soul in nature, glimpses of its remote and brooding spirit. Here, with the sun hot on his face, a cuckoo calling from a thorn tree, and in the air the honey savour of gorse—here among the little fronds of the young fern, the starry blackthorn, while the bright clouds drifted by high above the hills and dreamy valleys—here and now was such a glimpse. But in a moment it would pass—as the face of Pan, which looks round the corner of a rock, vanishes at your stare. And suddenly he sat up. Surely there was something familiar about this view, this bit of common, that ribbon of road, the old wall behind him. While they were driving he had not been taking notice— never did; thinking of far things or of nothing—but now he saw ! Twenty-six years ago, just at this time of year, from the farmhouse within half a mile of this very spot he had started for that day in Torquay whence

it might be said he had never returned. And a sudden
ache beset his heart ; he had stumbled on just one of
those past moments in his life, whose beauty and
rapture he had failed to arrest, whose wings had
fluttered away into the unknown ; he had stumbled
on a buried memory, a wild sweet time, swiftly choked
and ended. And, turning on his face, he rested his
chin on his hands, and stared at the short grass where
the little blue milkwort was growing. . . .

And this is what he remembered.

1 §

On the first of May, after their last year together at
college, Frank Ashurst and his friend Robert Garton
were on a tramp. They had walked that day from
Brent, intending to make Chagford, but Ashurst's
football knee had given out, and according to their
map they had still some seven miles to go. They
were sitting on a bank beside the road, where a track
crossed alongside a wood, resting the knee and talking
of the universe, as young men will. Both were over
six feet, and as thin as rails ; Ashurst pale, idealistic,
full of absence; Garton queer, round-the-corner,
knotted, curly, like some primeval beast. Both had
a literary bent ; neither wore a hat. Ashurst's hair
was smooth, pale, wavy, and had a way of rising on
either side of his brow, as if always being flung back ;
Garton's was a kind of dark unfathomed mop. They
had not met a soul for miles.

" My dear fellow," Garton was saying, " pity's only
an effect of self-consciousness ; it's a disease of the
last five thousand years. The world was happier
without."

Ashurst, following the clouds with his eyes, answered :
" It's the pearl in the oyster, anyway."
" My dear chap, all our modern unhappiness comes
from pity.   Look at animals, and Red Indians, limited
to feeling their own occasional misfortunes ; then look
at ourselves—never free from feeling the toothaches
of others.   Let's get back to feeling for nobody, and
have a better time."
" You'll never practise that."
Garton pensively stirred the hotch-potch of his hair.
" To attain full growth, one mustn't be squeamish.
To starve oneself emotionally's a mistake.   All emotion
is to the good—enriches life."
" Yes, and when it runs up against chivalry ? "
" Ah ! That's so English ! If you speak of emotion
the English always think you want something physical,
and are shocked.   They're afraid of passion, but not
of lust—oh, no !—so long as they can keep it secret."
Ashurst did not answer ; he had plucked a blue
floweret, and was twiddling it against the sky.   A
cuckoo began calling from a thorn-tree.   The sky,
the flowers, the songs of birds ! Robert was talking
through his hat ! And he said :
" Well, let's go on, and find some farm where we can
put up."   In uttering those words, he was conscious
of a girl coming down from the common just above
them.   She was outlined against the sky, carrying a
basket, and you could see that sky through the crook
of her arm.   And Ashurst, who saw beauty without
wondering how it could advantage him, thought :
' How pretty ! '   The wind, blowing her dark frieze ˎ
skirt against her legs, lifted her battered peacock
tam-o'-shanter ; her greyish blouse was worn and old,
her shoes were split, her little hands rough and red,

her neck browned, Her dark hair waved untidy across
her broad forehead, her face was short, her upper lip
short, showing a glint of teeth, her brows were straight
and dark, her lashes long and dark, her nose straight ;
but her grey eyes were the wonder—as dewy as if
opened for the first time that day. She looked at
Ashurst—perhaps he struck her as strange, limping
along without a hat, with his large eyes on her, and his
hair flung back. He could not take off what was not
on his head, but put up his hand in a salute, and said :

" Can you tell us if there's a farm near here where we
could stay the night ? I've gone lame."

" There's only our farm near, sir." She spoke
without shyness, in a pretty soft crisp voice.

" And where is that ? "

" Down here, sir."

" Would you put us up ? "

" Oh ! I think we would."

" Will you show us the way ? "

" Yes, sir."

He limped on, silent, and Garton took up the
catechism.

" Are you a Devonshire girl ? "

" No, sir."

" What then ? "

" From Wales."

" Ah ! I *thought* you were a Celt ; so it's not your
farm ? "

" My aunt's, sir."

" And your uncle's ? "

" He is dead."

" Who farms it, then ? "

" My aunt, and my three cousins."

" But your uncle was a Devonshire man ? "

" Yes, sir."

" Have you lived here long ? "

" Seven years."

" And how d'you like it after Wales ? "

" I don't know, sir."

" I suppose you don't remember ? "

" Oh, yes ! But it is different."

" I believe you ! "

Ashurst broke in suddenly :

" How old are you ? "

" Seventeen, sir."

" And what's your name ? "

" Megan David."

" This is Robert Garton, and I am Frank Ashurst. We wanted to get on to Chagford."

" It is a pity your leg is hurting you."

Ashurst smiled, and when he smiled his face was rather beautiful.

Descending past the narrow wood, they came on the farm suddenly—a long, low, stone-built dwelling with casement windows, in a farmyard where pigs and fowls and an old mare were straying. A short steep-up grass hill behind was crowned with a few Scotch firs, and in front, an old orchard of apple trees, just breaking into flower, stretched down to a stream and a long wild meadow. A little boy with oblique dark eyes was shepherding a pig, and by the house door stood a woman, who came towards them. The girl said :

" It is Mrs. Narracombe, my aunt."

" Mrs. Narracombe, my aunt," had a quick, dark eye, like a mother wild-duck's, and something of the same snaky turn about her neck.

" We met your niece on the road," said Ashurst ;

" she thought you might perhaps put us up for the night."

Mrs. Narracombe, taking them in from head to heel, answered :

" Well, I can, if you don't mind one room. Megan, get the spare room ready, and a bowl of cream. You'll be wanting tea, I suppose."

Passing through a sort of porch made by two yew trees and some flowering-currant bushes, the girl disappeared into the house, her peacock tam-o'-shanter bright athwart that rosy-pink and the dark green of the yews.

" Will you come into the parlour and rest your leg ? You'll be from college, perhaps ? "

" We were, but we've gone down now."

Mrs. Narracombe nodded sagely.

The parlour, brick-floored, with bare table and shiny chairs and sofa stuffed with horsehair, seemed never to have been used, it was so terribly clean. Ashurst sat down at once on the sofa, holding his lame knee between his hands, and Mrs. Narracombe gazed at him. He was the only son of a late professor of chemistry, but people found a certain lordliness in one who was often so sublimely unconscious of them.

" Is there a stream where we could bathe ? "

" There's the strame at the bottom of the orchard, but sittin' down you'll not be covered ! "

" How deep ? "

" Well, 'tis about a foot and a half, maybe."

" Oh ! That'll do fine. Which way ? "

" Down the lane, through the second gate on the right, an' the pool's by the big apple tree that stands by itself. There's trout there, if you can tickle them."

" They're more likely to tickle us ! "

Mrs. Narracombe smiled. "There'll be the tea ready when you come back."

The pool, formed by the damming of a rock, had a sandy bottom; and the big apple tree, lowest in the orchard, grew so close that its boughs almost over-hung the water; it was in leaf, and all but in flower—its crimson buds just bursting. There was not room for more than one at a time in that narrow bath, and Ashurst waited his turn, rubbing his knee and gazing at the wild meadow, all rocks and thorn trees and field flowers, with a grove of beeches beyond, raised up on a flat mound. Every bough was swinging in the wind, every spring bird calling, and a slanting sunlight dappled the grass. He thought of Theocritus, and the river Cherwell, of the moon, and the maiden with the dewy eyes; of so many things that he seemed to think of nothing; and he felt absurdly happy.

2 §

During a late and sumptuous tea with eggs to it, cream and jam, and thin, fresh cakes touched with saffron, Garton descanted on the Celts. It was about the period of the Celtic awakening, and the discovery that there was Celtic blood about this family had excited one who believed that he was a Celt himself. Sprawling on a horsehair chair, with a hand-made cigarette dribbling from the corner of his curly lips, he had been plunging his cold pin-points of eyes into Ashurst's and praising the refinement of the Welsh. To come out of Wales into England was like the change from china to earthenware! Frank, as a d——d Englishman, had not of course perceived the exquisite refinement and emotional capacity of that Welsh girl! And, delicately stirring in the dark mat of his still wet hair, he explained how exactly she illustrated the writings of the Welsh bard Morgan-ap-Something in the twelfth century.

Ashurst, full length on the horsehair sofa, and jutting far beyond its end, smoked a deeply-coloured pipe, and did not listen, thinking of the girl's face when she brought in a relay of cakes. It had been exactly like looking at a flower, or some other pretty sight in Nature—till, with a funny little shiver, she had lowered her glance and gone out, quiet as a mouse.

" Let's go to the kitchen," said Garton, " and see some more of her."

The kitchen was a white-washed room with rafters, to which were attached smoked hams ; there were flower-pots on the window-sill, and guns hanging on nails, queer mugs, china and pewter, and portraits of Queen Victoria. A long, narrow table of plain wood was set with bowls and spoons, under a string of high-hung onions ; two sheep-dogs and three cats lay here and there. On one side of the recessed fire-place sat two small boys, idle, and good as gold ; on the other sat a stout, light-eyed, red-faced youth with hair and lashes the colour of the tow he was running through the barrel of a gun ; between them Mrs. Narracombe dreamily stirred some savoury-scented stew in a large pot. Two other youths, oblique-eyed, dark-haired, rather sly-faced, like the two little boys, were talking together and lolling against the wall ; and a short, elderly, clean-shaven man in corduroys, seated in the window, was conning a battered journal. The girl Megan seemed the only active creature— drawing cider and passing with the jugs from cask to table. Seeing them thus about to eat, Garton said :

" Ah ! If you'll let us, we'll come back when supper's over," and without waiting for an answer they withdrew again to the parlour. But the colour in the kitchen, the warmth, the scents, and all those faces, heightened the bleakness of their shiny room, and they resumed their seats moodily.

" Regular gipsy type, those boys. There was only one Saxon—the fellow cleaning the gun. That girl is a very subtle study psychologically."

Ashurst's lips twitched. Garton seemed to him an ass just then. Subtle study ! She was a wild flower. A creature it did you good to look at. Study !

Garton went on :

" Emotionally she would be wonderful. She wants awakening."

" Are you going to awaken her ? "

Garton looked at him and smiled. " How coarse and English you are ! " that curly smile seemed saying.

And Ashurst puffed his pipe. Awaken her ! This fool had the best opinion of himself ! He threw up the window and leaned out. Dusk had gathered thick. The farm buildings and the wheel-house were all dim and bluish, the apple trees but a blurred wilderness ; the air smelled of wood-smoke from the kitchen fire. One bird going to bed later than the others was uttering a half-hearted twitter, as though surprised at the darkness. From the stable came the snuffle and stamp of a feeding horse. And away over there was the loom of the moor, and away and away the shy stars which had not as yet full light, pricking white through the deep blue heavens. A quavering owl hooted. Ashurst drew a deep breath. What a night to wander out in ! A padding of unshod hoofs came up the lane, and

three dim, dark shapes passed—ponies on an evening
march. Their heads, black and fuzzy, showed above
the gate. At the tap of his pipe, and a shower of little
sparks, they shied round and scampered. A bat went
fluttering past, uttering its almost inaudible " chip,
chip." Ashurst held out his hand ; on the upturned
palm he could feel the dew. Suddenly from overhead
he heard little burring boys' voices, little thumps of
boots thrown down, and another voice, crisp and
soft—the girl's, putting them to bed, no doubt ;
and nine clear words : " No, Rick, you can't have the
cat in bed " ; then came a skirmish of giggles and
gurgles, a soft slap, a laugh so low and pretty that it
made him shiver a little. A blowing sound, and the
glim of the candle which was fingering the dusk above,
went out ; silence reigned. Ashurst withdrew into
the room and sat down ; his knee pained him, and
his soul felt gloomy.

" You go to the kitchen," he said ; " I'm going to
bed."

3 §

For Ashurst the wheel of slumber was wont to turn
noiseless and slick and swift, but though he seemed
sunk in sleep when his companion came up, he was
really wide awake ; and long after Garton, smothered
in the other bed of that low-roofed room, was worship-
ping darkness with his upturned nose, he heard the
owls. Barring the discomfort of his knee, it was not
unpleasant—the cares of life did not loom large in
night watches for this young man. In fact he had
none ; just enrolled a barrister, with literary aspirations, the world before him, no father or mother, and
four hundred a year of his own. Did it matter where

he went, what he did, or when he did it ? His bed, too, was hard, and this preserved him from fever. He lay, sniffing the scent of the night which drifted into the low room through the open casement close to his head. Except for a definite irritation with his friend, natural when you have tramped with a man for three days, Ashurst's memories and visions that sleepless night were kindly and wistful and exciting. One vision, specially clear and unreasonable, for he had not even been conscious of noting it, was the face of the youth cleaning the gun ; its intent, stolid, yet startled uplook at the kitchen doorway, quickly shifted to the girl carrying the cider jug. This red, blue-eyed, light-lashed, tow-haired face stuck as firmly in his memory as the girl's own face, so dewy and simple. But at last, in the square of darkness through the uncurtained casement, he saw day coming, and heard one hoarse and sleepy caw. Then followed silence, dead as ever, till the song of a blackbird, not properly awake, adventured into the hush. And, from staring at the framed brightening light, Ashurst fell asleep.

Next day his knee was badly swollen ; the walking tour was obviously over. Garton, due back in London on the morrow, departed at midday with an ironical smile which left a scar of irritation—healed the moment his loping figure vanished round the corner of the steep lane. All day Ashurst rested his knee, in a green-painted wooden chair on the patch of grass by the yew-tree porch, where the sunlight distilled the scent of stocks and gillyflowers, and a ghost of scent from the flowering-currant bushes. Beatifically he smoked, dreamed, watched.

A farm in spring is all birth—young things coming out of bud and shell, and human beings watching over the process with faint excitement, feeding and tending what has been born. So still the young man sat, that a mother-goose, with stately cross-footed waddle, brought her six yellow-necked grey-backed goslings to strop their little beaks against the grass blades at his feet. Now and again Mrs. Narracombe or the girl Megan would come and ask if he wanted anything, and he would smile and say: "Nothing, thanks. It's splendid here." Towards tea-time they came out together, bearing a long poultice of some dark stuff in a bowl, and after a long and solemn scrutiny of his swollen knee, bound it on. When they were gone, he thought of the girl's soft "Oh!"—of her pitying eyes, and the little wrinkle in her brow. And again he felt that unreasoning irritation against his departed friend, who had talked such rot about her. When she brought out his tea, he said:

"How did you like my friend, Megan?"

She forced down her upper lip, as if afraid that to smile was not polite. "He was a funny gentleman; he made us laugh. I think he is very clever."

"What did he say to make you laugh?"

"He said I was a daughter of the bards. What are they?"

"Welsh poets, who lived hundreds of years ago."

"Why am I their daughter, please?"

"He meant that you were the sort of girl they sang about."

She wrinkled her brows. "I think he likes to joke. Am I?"

"Would you believe me, if I told you?"

"Oh, yes!"

"Well, I think he was right."

She smiled.

And Ashurst thought : ' You *are* a pretty thing ! '

" He said, too, that Joe was a Saxon type. What would that be ? "

" Which is Joe ? With the blue eyes and red face ? "

" Yes. My uncle's nephew."

" Not your cousin, then ? "

" No."

" Well, he meant that Joe was like the men who came over to England about fourteen hundred years ago, and conquered it."

" Oh ! I know about them ; but is he ? "

" Garton's crazy about that sort of thing ; but I must say Joe does look a bit Early Saxon."

" Yes."

That " Yes " tickled Ashurst. It was so crisp and graceful, so conclusive, and politely acquiescent in what was evidently Greek to her.

" He said that all the other boys were regular gipsies. He should not have said that. My aunt laughed, but she didn't like it, of course, and my cousins were angry. Uncle was a farmer—farmers are not gipsies. It is wrong to hurt people."

Ashurst wanted to take her hand and give it a squeeze, but he only answered :

" Quite right, Megan. By the way, I heard you putting the little ones to bed last night."

She flushed a little. " Please to drink your tea—it is getting cold. Shall I get you some fresh ? "

" Do you ever have time to do anything for yourself ? "

" Oh ! Yes."

" I've been watching, but I haven't seen it yet."

She wrinkled her brows in a puzzled frown, and her colour deepened.

When she was gone, Ashurst thought : ' Did she
think I was chaffing her ? I wouldn't for the world ! '
He was at that age when to some men " Beauty's a
flower," as the poet says, and inspires in them the
thoughts of chivalry. Never very conscious of his
surroundings, it was some time before he was aware
that the youth whom Garton had called " a Saxon
type " was standing outside the stable door ; and a
fine bit of colour he made in his soiled brown velvet-
cords, muddy gaiters, and blue shirt ; red-armed,
red-faced, the sun turning his hair from tow to flax ;
immovably stolid, persistent, unsmiling he stood.
Then, seeing Ashurst looking at him, he crossed the
yard at that gait of the young countryman always
ashamed not to be slow and heavy-dwelling on each
leg, and disappeared round the end of the house towards
the kitchen entrance. A chill came over Ashurst's
mood. Clods ? With all the good will in the world,
how impossible to get on terms with them. And yet—
see that girl ! Her shoes were split, her hands rough ;
but—what was it ? Was it really her Celtic blood, as
Garton had said ?—she was a lady born, a jewel, though
probably she could do no more than just read and write !

The elderly, clean-shaven man he had seen last night
in the kitchen had come into the yard with a dog,
driving the cows to their milking. Ashurst saw that
he was lame.

" You've got some good ones there ! "

The lame man's face brightened. He had the upward
look in his eyes which prolonged suffering often brings.

" Yeas ; they'm praaper buties ; gude milkers tu."

" I bet they are."

" 'Ope as yure leg's better, zurr."

" Thank you, it's getting on."

The lame man touched his own: "I know what 'tes, meself; 'tes a main worritin' thing, the knee. I've a—'ad mine bad this ten year."

Ashurst made the sound of sympathy which comes so readily from those who have an independent income, and the lame man smiled again.

"Mustn't complain, though—they mighty near 'ad it off."

"Ho!"

"Yeas; an' compared with what 'twas, 'tes almost so gude as nu."

"They've put a bandage of splendid stuff on mine."

"The maid she picks et. She'm a gude maid wi' the flowers. There's folks zeem to know the healin' in things. My mother was a rare one for that. 'Ope as yu'll zune be better, zurr. Goo ahn, therr!"

Ashurst smiled. "Wi' the flowers!" A flower herself!

That evening, after his supper of cold duck, junket, and cider, the girl came in.

"Please, auntie says—will you try a piece of our Mayday cake?"

"If I may come to the kitchen for it."

"Oh, yes! You'll be missing your friend."

"Not I. But are you sure no one minds?"

"Who would mind? We shall be very pleased."

Ashurst rose too suddenly for his stiff knee, staggered, and subsided. The girl gave a little gasp, and held out her hands. Ashurst took them, small, rough, brown; checked his impulse to put them to his lips, and let her pull him up. She came close beside him, offering her shoulder. And leaning on her he walked across the room. That shoulder seemed quite the pleasantest thing he had ever touched. But he had presence of mind enough to catch his stick out of the rack, and withdraw his hand before arriving at the kitchen.

That night he slept like a top, and woke with his knee of almost normal size. He again spent the morning in his chair on the grass patch, scribbling down verses ; but in the afternoon he wandered about with the two little boys Nick and Rick. It was Saturday, so they were early home from school ; quick, shy, dark little rascals of seven and six, soon talkative, for Ashurst had a way with children. They had shown him all their methods of destroying life by four o'clock, except the tickling of trout ; and with breeches tucked up, lay on their stomachs over the trout stream, pretending they had this accomplishment also. They tickled nothing, of course, for their giggling and shouting scared every spotted thing away. Ashurst, on a rock at the edge of the beech clump, watched them, and listened to the cuckoos, till Nick, the elder and less persevering, came up and stood beside him.

" The gipsy bogle zets on that stone," he said.

" What gipsy bogle ? "

" Dunno ; never zeen 'e. Megan zays 'e zets there ; an' old Jim zeed 'e once. 'E was zettin' there naight afore our pony kicked-in father's 'ead. 'E plays the viddle."

" What tune does he play ? "

" Dunno."

" What's he like ? "

" 'E's black. Old Jim zays 'e's all over 'air. 'E's a praaper bogle. 'E don' come only at naight." The little boy's oblique dark eyes slid round. " D'yu think 'e might want to take me away ? Megan's feared of 'e."

" Has she seen him ? "

" No. She's not afeared o' yu."

" I should think not. Why should she be ? "

" She zays a prayer for yu."

" How do you know that, you little rascal ? "

" When I was asleep, she said : ' God bless us all, an' Mr. Ashes.' I yeard 'er whisperin'."

" You're a little ruffian to tell what you hear when you're not meant to hear it ! "

The little boy was silent. Then he said aggressively :

" I can skin rabbits. Megan, she can't bear skinnin' 'em. I like blood."

" Oh ! you do ; you little monster ! "

" What's that ? "

" A creature that likes hurting others."

The little boy scowled. " They'm only dead rabbits, what us eats."

" Quite right, Nick. I beg your pardon."

" I can skin frogs, tu."

But Ashurst had become absent. " God bless us all, and Mr. Ashes ! " And puzzled by that sudden inaccessibility, Nick ran back to the stream, where the giggling and shouts again uprose at once.

When Megan brought his tea, he said :

" What's the gipsy bogle, Megan ? "

She looked up, startled.

" He brings bad things."

" Surely you don't believe in ghosts ? "

" I hope I will never see him."

" Of course you won't. There aren't such things. What old Jim saw was a pony."

" No ! There are bogles in the rocks ; they are the men who lived long ago."

" They aren't gipsies, anyway ; those old men were dead long before gipsies came."

She said simply : " They are all bad."

" Why ? If there are any, they're only wild, like
the rabbits. The flowers aren't bad for being wild ;
the thorn trees were never planted—and you don't
mind them. I shall go down at night and look for
your bogle, and have a talk with him."

" Oh, no ! Oh, no ! "

" Oh, yes ! I shall go and sit on his rock."

She clasped her hands together : " Oh, please ! "

" Why ! What does it matter if anything happens to
me ? "

She did not answer ; and in a sort of pet he added :

" Well, I daresay I shan't see him, because I suppose
I must be off soon."

" Soon ? "

" Your aunt won't want to keep me here."

" Oh, yes ! We always let lodgings in summer."

Fixing his eyes on her face, he asked :

" Would you like me to stay ? "

" Yes."

" I'm going to say a prayer for *you* to-night ! "

She flushed crimson, frowned, and went out of the
room. He sat, cursing himself, till his tea was stewed.
It was as if he had hacked with his thick boots at a
clump of bluebells. Why had he said such a silly
thing ? Was he just a towny college ass like Robert
Garton, as far from understanding this girl ?

4 §

Ashurst spent the next week confirming the restora-
tion of his leg, by exploration of the country within
easy reach. Spring was a revelation to him this year.
In a kind of intoxication he would watch the pink-

white buds of some backward beech tree sprayed up
in the sunlight against the deep blue sky, or the trunks
and limbs of the few Scotch firs, tawny in violent
light, or again, on the moor, the gale-bent larches
which had such a look of life when the wind streamed
in their young green, above the rusty black under-
boughs. Or he would lie on the banks, gazing at the
clusters of dog-violets, or up in the dead bracken,
fingering the pink, transparent buds of the dewberry,
while the cuckoos called and yaffles laughed, or a
lark, from very high, dripped its beads of song. It
was certainly different from any spring he had ever
known, for spring was within him, not without. In
the daytime he hardly saw the family ; and when
Megan brought in his meals she always seemed too
busy in the house or among the young things in the
yard to stay talking long. But in the evenings he
installed himself in the window seat in the kitchen,
smoking and chatting with the lame man Jim, or
Mrs. Narracombe, while the girl sewed, or moved
about, clearing the supper things away. And sometimes, with the sensation a cat must feel when it
purrs, he would become conscious that Megan's eyes—
those dew-grey eyes—were fixed on him with a sort
of lingering soft look which was strangely flattering.

It was on Sunday week in the evening, when he
was lying in the orchard listening to a blackbird and
composing a love poem, that he heard the gate swing
to, and saw the girl come running among the trees,
with the red-cheeked, stolid Joe in swift pursuit.
About twenty yards away the chase ended, and the
two stood fronting each other, not noticing the stranger
in the grass—the boy pressing on, the girl fending him
off. Ashurst could see her face, angry, disturbed ;

and the youth's—who would have thought that red-faced yokel could look so distraught ! And painfully affected by that sight, he jumped up. They saw him then. Megan dropped her hands, and shrunk behind a tree-trunk ; the boy gave an angry grunt, rushed at the bank, scrambled over and vanished. Ashurst went slowly up to her. She was standing quite still, biting her lip—very pretty, with her fine, dark hair blown loose about her face, and her eyes cast down.

" I beg your pardon," he said.

She gave him one upward look, from eyes much dilated ; then, catching her breath, turned away. Ashurst followed.

" Megan ! "

But she went on ; and taking hold of her arm, he turned her gently round to him.

" Stop and speak to me."

" Why do you beg my pardon ? It is not to me you should do that."

" Well, then, to Joe."

" How dare he come after me ? "

" In love with you, I suppose."

She stamped her foot.

Ashurst uttered a short laugh. " Would you like me to punch his head ? "

She cried with sudden passion :

" You laugh at me—you laugh at us ! "

He caught hold of her hands, but she shrank back, till her passionate little face and loose dark hair were caught among the pink clusters of the apple blossom. Ashurst raised one of her imprisoned hands and put his lips to it. He felt how chivalrous he was, and superior to that clod Joe—just brushing that small, rough hand with his mouth ! Her shrinking ceased suddenly; she seemed to tremble towards him. A sweet warmth overtook Ashurst from top to toe. This slim maiden, so simple and fine and pretty, was pleased, then, at the touch of his lips! And, yielding to a swift impulse, he put his arms round her, pressed her to him, and kissed her forehead. Then he was frightened—she went so pale, closing her eyes, so that the long, dark lashes lay on her pale cheeks; her hands, too, lay inert at her sides. The touch of her breast sent a shiver through him. "Megan!" he sighed out, and let her go. In the utter silence a blackbird shouted. Then the girl seized his hand, put it to her cheek, her heart, her lips, kissed it passionately, and fled away among the mossy trunks of the apple trees, till they hid her from him.

Ashurst sat down on a twisted old tree growing almost along the ground, and, all throbbing and bewildered, gazed vacantly at the blossom which had crowned her hair—those pink buds with one white open apple star. What had he done? How had he let himself be thus stampeded by beauty—pity—or—just the spring! He felt curiously happy, all the same; happy and triumphant, with shivers running through his limbs, and a vague alarm. This was the beginning of—what? The midges bit him, the dancing gnats tried to fly into his mouth, and all the spring around him seemed to grow more lovely and alive; the songs of the cuckoos and the blackbirds, the laughter of the yaffles, the level-slanting sunlight, the apple blossom which had crowned her head——! He got up from the old trunk and strode out of the orchard, wanting space, an open sky, to get on terms with these new sensations. He made for the moor, and from an ash tree in the hedge a magpie flew out to herald him.

Of man—at any age from five years on—who can
say he has never been in love? Ashurst had loved
his partners at his dancing class; loved his nursery
governess; girls in school-holidays; perhaps never
been quite out of love, cherishing always some more
or less remote admiration. But this was different, not
remote at all. Quite a new sensation; terribly delightful, bringing a sense of completed manhood. To be
holding in his fingers such a wild flower, to be able
to put it to his lips, and feel it tremble with delight
against them! What intoxication, and—embarrass-
ment! What to do with it—how meet her next time?
His first caress had been cool, pitiful; but the next
could not be, now that, by her burning little kiss on his
hand, by her pressure of it to her heart, he knew that
she loved him. Some natures are coarsened by love
bestowed on them; others, like Ashurst's, are swayed
and drawn, warmed and softened, almost exalted, by
what they feel to be a sort of miracle.

And up there among the tors he was torn between
the passionate desire to revel in this new sensation of
spring fulfilled within him, and a vague but very real
uneasiness. At one moment he gave himself up
completely to his pride at having captured this pretty,
trustful, dewy-eyed thing! At the next he thought
with factitious solemnity: 'Yes, my boy! But
look out what you're doing! You know what comes
of it!'

Dusk dropped down without his noticing—dusk on
the carved, Assyrian-looking masses of the rocks.
And the voice of Nature said: "This is a new world
for you!" As when a man gets up at four o'clock and
goes out into a summer morning, and beasts, birds,
trees stare at him as if all had been made new.

He stayed up there for hours, till it grew cold, then groped his way down the stones and heather roots to the road, back into the lane, and came again past the wild meadow to the orchard. There he struck a match and looked at his watch. Nearly twelve! It was black and unstirring in there now, very different from the lingering, bird-befriended brightness of six hours ago! And suddenly he saw this idyll of his with the eyes of the outer world—had mental vision of Mrs. Narracombe's snake-like neck turned, her quick dark glance taking it all in, her shrewd face hardening; saw the gipsy-like cousins coarsely mocking and distrustful; Joe stolid and furious; only the lame man, Jim, with the suffering eyes, seemed tolerable to his mind. And the village pub! —the gossiping matrons he passed on his walks; and then—his own friends—Robert Garton's smile when he went off that morning ten days ago; so ironical and knowing! Disgusting! For a minute he literally hated this earthy, cynical world to which one belonged, willy-nilly. The gate where he was leaning grew grey. a sort of shimmer passed before him and spread into the bluish darkness. The moon! He could just see it over the bank behind; red, nearly round—a strange moon! And turning away, he went up the lane which smelled of the night and cow-dung and young leaves. In the straw-yard he could see the dark shapes of cattle, broken by the pale sickles of their horns, like so many thin moons, fallen ends-up. He unlatched the farm gate stealthily. All was dark in the house. Muffling his footsteps, he gained the porch, and, blotted against one of the yew trees, looked up at Megan's window. It was open. Was she sleeping, or lying awake perhaps, disturbed—unhappy at his absence?

An owl hooted while he stood there peering up, and the sound seemed to fill the whole night, so quiet was all else, save for the never-ending murmur of the stream running below the orchard. The cuckoos by day, and now the owls—how wonderfully they voiced this troubled ecstasy within him! And suddenly he saw her at her window, looking out. He moved a little from the yew tree, and whispered: "Megan!" She drew back, vanished, reappeared, leaning far down. He stole forward on the grass patch, hit his shin against the green-painted chair, and held his breath at the sound. The pale blur of her stretched-down arm and face did not stir; he moved the chair, and noiselessly mounted it. By stretching up his arm he could just reach. Her hand held the huge key of the front door, and he clasped that burning hand with the cold key in it. He could just see her face, the glint of teeth between her lips, her tumbled hair. She was still dressed—poor child, sitting up for him, no doubt! "Pretty Megan!" Her hot, roughened fingers clung to his; her face had a strange, lost look. To have been able to reach it—even with his hand! The owl hooted, a scent of sweetbriar crept into his nostrils. Then one of the farm dogs barked; her grasp relaxed, she shrank back.

"Good-night, Megan!"

"Good-night, sir!" She was gone! With a sigh he dropped back to earth, and sitting on that chair, took off his boots. Nothing for it but to creep in and go to bed; yet for a long while he sat unmoving, his feet chilly in the dew, drunk on the memory of her lost, half-smiling face, and the clinging grip of her burning fingers, pressing the cold key into his hand.

5 §

He awoke feeling as if he had eaten heavily overnight, instead of having eaten nothing. And far off, unreal, seemed yesterday's romance! Yet it was a golden morning. Full spring had burst at last—in one night the "goldie-cups," as the little boys called them, seemed to have made the field their own, and from his window he could see apple blossom covering the orchard as with a rose and white quilt. He went down almost dreading to see Megan; and yet, when not she but Mrs. Narracombe brought in his breakfast, he felt vexed and disappointed. The woman's quick eye and snaky neck seemed to have a new alacrity this morning. Had she noticed?

"So you an' the moon went walkin' last night, Mr. Ashurst! Did ye have your supper anywheres?"

Ashurst shook his head.

"We kept it for you, but I suppose you was too busy in your brain to think o' such a thing as that?"

Was she mocking him, in that voice of hers, which still kept some Welsh crispness against the invading burr of the West Country? If she knew! And at that moment he thought: 'No, no; I'll clear out. I won't put myself in such a beastly false position.'

But, after breakfast, the longing to see Megan began and increased with every minute, together with fear lest something should have been said to her which had spoiled everything. Sinister that she had not appeared, not given him even a glimpse of her! And the love poem, whose manufacture had been so important and, absorbing yesterday afternoon under the apple trees, now seemed so paltry that he tore it up and rolled it into pipe spills. What had he known of love, till she seized his hand and kissed it! And now—what did he not know? But to write of it seemed mere insipidity! He went up to his bedroom to get a book, and his heart began to beat violently, for she was in there making the bed. He stood in the doorway watching; and suddenly, with turbulent joy, he saw her stoop and kiss his pillow, just at the hollow made by his head last night. How let her know he had seen that, pretty act of devotion? And yet, if she heard him stealing away, it would be even worse. She took the pillow up, holding it as if reluctant to shake out the impress of his cheek, dropped it, and turned round.

"Megan!"

She put her hands up to her cheeks, but her eyes seemed to look right into him. He had never before realised the depth and purity and touching faithfulness in those dew-bright eyes, and he stammered:

"It was sweet of you to wait up for me last night."

She still said nothing, and he stammered on:

"I was wandering about on the moor; it was such a jolly night. I—I've just come up for a book."

Then, the kiss he had seen her give the pillow afflicted him with sudden headiness, and he went up to her. Touching her eyes with his lips, he thought with queer excitement: 'I've done it! Yesterday all was sudden —anyhow; but now—I've done it!' The girl let her forehead rest against his lips, which moved downwards till they reached hers. That first real lover's kiss—strange, wonderful, still almost innocent—in which heart did it make the most disturbance?

"Come to the big apple tree to-night, after they've gone to bed. Megan—promise!"

She whispered back: "I promise."

Then, scared at her white face, scared at everything,

he let her go, and went downstairs again. Yes! he
had done it now! Accepted her love, declared his
own! He went out to the green chair as devoid of
a book as ever; and there he sat staring vacantly
before him, triumphant and remorseful, while under
his nose and behind his back the work of the farm
went on. How long he had been sitting in that curious
state of vacancy he had no notion when he saw Joe
standing a little behind him to the right. The youth
had evidently come from hard work in the fields, and
stood shifting his feet, breathing loudly, his face
coloured like a setting sun, and his arms, below the
rolled-up sleeves of his blue shirt, showing the hue and
furry sheen of ripe peaches. His red lips were open,
his blue eyes with their flaxen lashes stared fixedly
at Ashurst, who said ironically:

" Well, Joe, anything 1 can do for you? "

" Yeas."

" What, then? "

" Yu can goo away from yere. Us don' want yu."

Ashurst's face, never too humble, assumed its most
lordly look.

" Very good of you, but, do you know, I prefer the
others should speak for themselves."

The youth moved a pace or two nearer, and the
scent of his honest heat afflicted Ashurst's nostrils.

" What d'yu stay yere for? "

" Because it pleases me."

" Twon't please yu when I've bashed yure lead
in! "

" Indeed! When would you like to begin that? "

Joe answered only with the loudness of his breathing,
but his eyes looked like those of a young and angry
bull. Then a sort of spasm seemed to convulse his face

" Megan don' want yu."

A rush of jealousy, of contempt, and anger with this thick, loud-breathing rustic got the better of Ashurst's self-possession ; he jumped up, and pushed back his chair.

" You can go to the devil ! "

And as he said those simple words, he saw Megan in the doorway with a tiny brown spaniel puppy in her arms. She came up to him quickly.

" Its eyes are blue ! " she said.

Joe turned away ; the back of his neck was literally crimson.

Ashurst put his finger to the mouth of the tiny brown bull-frog of a creature in her arms. How cosy it looked against her !

" It's fond of you already. Ah ! Megan, everything is fond of *you*."

" What was Joe saying to you, please ? "

" Telling me to go away, because you didn't want me here."

She stamped her foot ; then looked up at Ashurst. At that adoring look he felt his nerves quiver, just as if he had seen a moth scorching its wings.

" To-night ! " he said. " Don't forget ! "

" No." And smothering her face against the puppy's little fat, brown body, she slipped back into the house.

Ashurst wandered down the lane. And at the gate of the wild meadow he came on the lame man and his cows.

" Beautiful day, Jim ! "

" Ah ! 'Tes brave weather for the grass. The ashes be later than th' oaks this year. ' When th' oak before th' ash——' "

Ashurst said idly : " Where were you standing when you saw the gipsy bogle, Jim ? "

" It might be under that big apple tree, as you might say."

" And you really do think it was there ? ".

The lame man answered cautiously :

" I shouldn't like to say rightly that 't *was* there. 'Twas in my mind as 'twas there."

" What do you make of it ? "

The lame man lowered his voice.

" They du zay old master, Mist' Narracombe, come o' gipsy stock. But that's tellin'. They'm a wonderful people, yu know, for claimin' their own. Maybe they knu 'e was goin', an' sent this feller along for company. That's what I've a-thought about it."

" What was he like ? "

" 'E 'ad 'air all over 'is face, an' goin' like this, he was, zame as if 'e 'ad a viddle. They zay there's no such thing as bogles, but I've a-zeen the 'air on this dog standin' up of a dark naight, when I couldn' zee nothin', meself."

" Was there a moon ? "

" Yeas, very near full, but 'twas on'y just risen, gold-like be'ind them trees."

" And you think a ghost means trouble, do you ? "

The lame man pushed his hat up ; his aspiring eyes looked at Ashurst more earnestly than ever.

" 'Tes not for me to zay that—but 'tes they bein' so unrestin'-like. There's things us don' understand, that's zartin, for zure. There's people that zee things, tu, an' others that don' never zee nothin'. Now, our Joe—yu might putt anything under 'is eyes an' 'e'd never zee it ; and them other boys, tu, they'm rattlin' fellers. But yu take an' putt our Megan where

there's suthin', she'll zee it, an' more tu, or I'm
mistaken."

"She's sensitive, that's why."

"What's that?"

"I mean, she feels everything."

"Ah! She'm very lovin'-'earted."

Ashurst, who felt colour coming into his cheeks, held
out his tobacco pouch.

"Have a fill, Jim?"

"Thank 'ee, sir. She'm one in an 'underd, I think."

"I expect so," said Ashurst shortly, and folding up
his pouch, walked on.

"Lovin'-'earted!" Yes! And what was he doing?
What were his intentions—as they say—towards this
loving-hearted girl? The thought dogged him, wandering through fields bright with buttercups, where the
little red calves were feeding, and the swallows flying
high. Yes, the oaks were before the ashes, brown-gold
already; every tree in different stage and hue. The
cuckoos and a thousand birds were singing; the little
streams were very bright. The ancients believed in a
golden age, in the garden of the Hesperides! . . . A
queen wasp settled on his sleeve. Each queen wasp
killed meant two thousand fewer wasps to thieve the
apples which would grow from that blossom in the
orchard; but who, with love in his heart, could kill
anything on a day like this? He entered a field where
a young red bull was feeding. It seemed to Ashurst
that he looked like Joe. But the young bull took no
notice of this visitor, a little drunk himself, perhaps,
on the singing and the glamour of the golden pasture
under his short legs. Ashurst crossed out unchal-
lenged to the hillside above the stream. From that
slope a tor mounted to its crown of rocks. The

ground there was covered with a mist of bluebells, and
nearly a score of crab-apple trees were in full bloom.
He threw himself down on the grass. The change from
the buttercup glory and oak-goldened glamour of the
fields to this ethereal beauty under the grey tor filled
him with a sort of wonder ; nothing the same, save the
sound of running water and the songs of the cuckoos.
He lay there a long time, watching the sunlight wheel
till the crab-trees threw shadows over the bluebells,
his only companions a few wild bees. He was not quite
sane, thinking of that morning's kiss, and of to-night
under the apple tree. In such a spot as this, fauns
and dryads surely lived ; nymphs, white as the crab-
apple blossom, retired within those trees ; fauns, brown
as the dead bracken, with pointed ears, lay in wait for
them. The cuckoos were still calling when he
woke, there was the sound of running water ; but
the sun had couched behind the tor, the hillside
was cool, and some rabbits had come out. 'To-
night !' he thought. Just as from the earth
everything was pushing up, unfolding under the
soft insistent fingers of an unseen hand, so were
his heart and senses being pushed, unfolded. He
got up and broke off a spray from a crab-apple tree.
The buds were like Megan—shell-like, rose-pink, wild,
and fresh ; and so, too, the opening flowers, white,
and wild, and touching. He put the spray into his
coat. And all the rush of the spring within him escaped
in a triumphant sigh. But the rabbits scurried away.

6 §

It was nearly eleven that night when Ashurst put
down the pocket " Odyssey " which for half an hour

he had held in his hands without reading, and slipped through the yard down to the orchard. The moon had just risen, very golden, over the hill, and like a bright, powerful, watching spirit peered through the bars of an ash tree's half-naked boughs. In among the apple trees it was still dark, and he stood making sure of his direction, feeling the rough grass with his feet. A black mass close behind him stirred with a heavy grunting sound, and three large pigs settled down again close to each other, under the wall. He listened. There was no wind, but the stream's burbling whispering chuckle had gained twice its daytime strength. One bird, he could not tell what, cried " Pip—pip," " Pip—pip," with perfect monotony ; he could hear a night-jar spinning very far off ; an owl hooting. Ashurst moved a step or two, and again halted, aware of a dim living whiteness all round his head. On the dark unstirring trees innumerable flowers and buds all soft and blurred were being bewitched to life by the creeping moonlight. He had the oddest feeling of actual companionship, as if a million white moths or spirits had floated in and settled between dark sky and darker ground, and were opening and shutting their wings on a level with his eyes. In the bewildering, still, scentless beauty of that moment he almost lost memory of why he had come to the orchard. The flying glamour which had clothed the earth all day had not gone now that night had fallen, but only changed into this new form. He moved on through the thicket of stems and boughs covered with that live powdering whiteness, till he reached the big apple tree. No mistaking that, even in the dark ; nearly twice the height and size of any other, and leaning out towards the open meadow and the stream. Under its thick branches he stood still again, to listen. The same sounds exactly, and a faint grunting from the sleepy pigs. He put his hands on the dry, almost warm tree trunk, whose rough mossy surface gave forth a peaty scent at his touch. Would she come—would she? And among these quivering, haunted, moon-witched trees he was seized with doubts of everything! All was unearthly here, fit for no earthly lovers; fit only for god and goddess, faun and nymph—not for him and this little country girl. Would it not be almost a relief if she did not come? But all the time he was listening. And still that unknown bird went " Pip—pip," " Pip—pip," and there rose the busy chatter of the little trout stream, whereon the moon was flinging glances through the bars of her tree-prison. The blossom on a level with his eyes seemed to grow more living every moment, seemed with its mysterious white beauty more and more a part of his suspense. He plucked a fragment and held it close—three blossoms. Sacrilege to pluck fruit-tree blossom—soft, sacred, young blossom—and throw it away! Then suddenly he heard the gate close, the pigs stirring again and grunting; and leaning against the trunk, he pressed his hands to its mossy sides behind him, and held his breath. She might have been a spirit threading the trees, for all the noise she made! Then he saw her quite close—her dark form part of a little tree, her white face part of its blossom; so still, and peering towards him. He whispered: " Megan! " and held out his hands. She ran forward, straight to his breast. When he felt her heart beating against him, Ashurst knew to the full the sensations of chivalry and passion. Because she was not of his world, because she was so simple and young and headlong, adoring and defenceless, how

could he be other than her protector, in the dark!
Because she was all simple, loving nature and beauty,
as much a part of this spring night as was the living
blossom, how should he not take all that she would
give him—how not fulfil the spring in her heart and
his! And torn between these two emotions he clasped
her close, and kissed her hair. How long they stood
there without speaking he knew not. The stream went
on chattering, the owls hooting, the moon kept stealing
up and growing whiter; the blossom all round them
and above brightened in suspense of living beauty.
Their lips had sought each other's, and they did not
speak. The moment speech began all would be unreal!
Spring has no speech, nothing but rustling and whispering. Spring has so much more than speech in its
unfolding flowers and leaves, and the coursing of its
streams, and in its sweet restless seeking! And sometimes spring will come alive, and, like a mysterious
Presence stand, encircling lovers with its arms, laying
on them the fingers of enchantment, so that, standing
lips to lips, they forget everything but just a kiss.
While her heart beat against him, and her lips quivered
on his, Ashurst felt nothing but simple rapture—
Destiny meant her for his arms, Love could not be
flouted! But when their lips parted for breath, division
began again at once. Only, passion now was so much
the stronger, and he sighed:

"Oh! Megan! Why did you come?"

She looked up, hurt, amazed.

"Sir, you asked me to."

"Don't call me 'sir,' my pretty sweet."

"What should I be callin' you?"

"Frank."

"I could not. Oh, no!"

" But you love me—don't you ? "

" I could not help lovin' you. I want to be with you—that's all."

" All ! "

So faint that he hardly heard, she whispered :

" I shall die if I can't be with you."

Ashurst took a mighty breath.

" Come and be with me, then ! ''

" Oh ! '

Intoxicated by the awe and rapture in that " Oh! " he went on, whispering :

" We'll go to London. I'll show you the world. And I *will* take care of you, I promise, Megan. I won't be a brute to you ! "

" If I can be with you—that is all."

He stroked her hair, and whispered on :

" To-morrow I'll go to Torquay and get some money, and get you some clothes that won't be noticed, and then we'll steal away. And when we get to London, soon perhaps, if you love me well enough, we'll be married."

He could feel her hair shiver with the shake of her head.

" Oh, no ! I could not. I only want to be with you ! "

Drunk on his own chivalry, Ashurst went on murmuring :

" It's I who am not good enough for you. Oh ! Megan, when did you begin to love me ? "

" When I saw you in the road, and you looked at me. The first night I loved you ; but I never thought you would want me."

She slipped down suddenly to her knees, trying to kiss his feet.

A shiver of horror went through Ashurst; he lifted her up bodily and held her fast—too upset to speak.

She whispered: " Why won't you let me ? "

" It's I who will kiss your feet ! "

Her smile brought tears into his eyes. The whiteness of her moonlit face so close to his, the faint pink of her opened lips, had the living unearthly beauty of the apple blossom.

And then, suddenly, her eyes widened and stared past him painfully; she writhed out of his arms, and whispered: " Look ! "

Ashurst saw nothing but the brightened stream, the furze faintly gilded, the beech trees glistening, and behind them all the wide loom of the moonlit hill. Behind him came her frozen whisper: " The gipsy bogle ! "

" Where ? "

" There—by the stone—under the trees ! "

Exasperated, he leaped the stream, and strode towards the beech clump. Prank of the moonlight ! Nothing ! In and out of the boulders and thorn trees, muttering and cursing, yet with a kind of terror, he rushed and stumbled. Absurd ! Silly ! Then he went back to the apple tree. But she was gone; he could hear a rustle, the grunting of the pigs, the sound of a gate closing. Instead of her, only this old apple tree ! He flung his arms round the trunk. What a substitute for her soft body; the rough moss against his face— what a substitute for her soft cheek; only the scent, as of the woods, a little the same ! And above him, and around, the blossoms, more living, more moonlit than ever, seemed to glow and breathe.

7 §

Descending from the train at Torquay station, Ashurst wandered uncertainly along the front, for he did not know this particular queen of English watering places. Having little sense of what he had on, he was quite unconscious of being remarkable among its inhabitants, and strode along in his rough Norfolk jacket, dusty boots, and battered hat, without observing that people gazed at him rather blankly. He was seeking a branch of his London bank, and having found one, found also the first obstacle to his mood. Did he know anyone in Torquay? No. In that case, if he would wire to his bank in London, they would be happy to oblige him on receipt of the reply. That suspicious breath from the matter-of-fact world somewhat tarnished the brightness of his visions. But he sent the telegram.

Nearly opposite to the post office he saw a shop full of ladies' garments, and examined the window with strange sensations. To have to undertake the clothing of his rustic love was more than a little disturbing. He went in. A young woman came forward; she had blue eyes and a faintly puzzled forehead. Ashurst stared at her in silence.

" Yes, sir ? "

" I want a dress for a young lady."

The young woman smiled. Ashurst frowned—the peculiarity of his request struck him with sudden force.

The young woman added hastily:

" What style would you like—something modish ? "

" No. Simple."

" What figure would the young lady be ? "

" I don't know ; about two inches shorter than you, I should say."

" Could you give me her waist measurement ? "

Megan's waist !

" Oh ! anything usual ! "

" Quite ! "

While she was gone he stood disconsolately eyeing the models in the window, and suddenly it seemed to him incredible that Megan—his Megan—could ever be dressed save in the rough tweed skirt, coarse blouse, and tam-o'-shanter cap he was wont to see her in. The young woman had come back with several dresses in her arms, and Ashurst eyed her laying them against her own modish figure. There was one whose colour he liked, a dove-grey, but to imagine Megan clothed in it was beyond him. The young woman went away, and brought some more. But on Ashurst there had now come a feeling of paralysis. How choose? She would want a hat too, and shoes, and gloves ; and, suppose, when he had got them all, they commonised her, as Sunday clothes always commonised village folk ! Why should she not travel as she was ? Ah ! but conspicuousness would matter ; this was a serious elopement. And, staring at the young woman, he thought : ' I wonder if she guesses, and thinks me a blackguard ? '

" Do you mind putting aside that grey one for me ? " he said desperately at last. " I can't decide now ; I'll come in again this afternoon."

The young woman sighed.

" Oh ! certainly. It's a very tasteful costume. I don't think you'll get anything that will suit your purpose better."

" I expect not," Ashurst murmured, and went out.

Freed again from the suspicious matter-of-factness of the world, he took a long breath, and went back to visions. In fancy he saw the trustful, pretty creature who was going to join her life to his ; saw himself and her stealing forth at night, walking over the moor under the moon, he with his arm round her, and carrying her new garments, till, in some far-off wood, when dawn was coming, she would slip off her old things and put on these, and an early train at a distant station would bear them away on their honeymoon journey, till London swallowed them up, and the dreams of love came true.

" Frank Ashurst ! Haven't seen you since Rugby, old chap ! "

Ashurst's frown dissolved ; the face, close to his own, was blue-eyed, suffused with sun—one of those faces where sun from within and without join in a sort of lustre. And he answered :

" Phil Halliday, by Jove ! "

" What are you doing here ? "

" Oh ! nothing. Just looking round, and getting some money. I'm staying on the moor."

" Are you lunching anywhere ? Come and lunch with us ; I'm here with my young sisters. They've had measles."

Hooked in by that friendly arm Ashurst went along, up a hill, down a hill, away out of the town, while the voice of Halliday, redolent of optimism as his face was of sun, explained how " in this mouldy place the only decent things were the bathing and boating," and so on, till presently they came to a crescent of houses a little above and back from the sea, and into the centre one—an hotel—made their way.

Q .

" Come up to my room and have a wash. Lunch'll
be ready in a jiffy."

Ashurst contemplated his visage in a looking-glass.
After his farmhouse bedroom, the comb and one spare
shirt *régime* of the last fortnight, this room littered
with clothes and brushes was a sort of Capua ; and
he thought : ' Queer—one doesn't realise——' But
what—he did not quite know.

When he followed Halliday into the sitting-room
for lunch, three faces, very fair and blue-eyed, were
turned suddenly at the words : " This is Frank Ashurst
—my young sisters."

Two were indeed young, about eleven and ten. The
third was perhaps seventeen, tall and fair-haired too,
with pink-and-white cheeks just touched by the sun,
and eyebrows, rather darker than the hair, running
a little upwards from her nose to their outer points.
The voices of all three were like Halliday's, high and
cheerful ; they stood up straight, shook hands with
a quick movement, looked at Ashurst critically, away
again at once, and began to talk of what they were
going to do in the afternoon. A regular Diana and
attendant nymphs ! After the farm this crisp, slangy,
eager talk, this cool, clean, off-hand refinement, was
queer at first, and then so natural that what he had
come from became suddenly remote. The names of
the two little ones seemed to be Sabina and Freda ;
of the eldest, Stella.

Presently the one called Sabina turned to him and said :

"I say, will you come shrimping with us ?—it's
awful fun ! "

Surprised by this unexpected friendliness, Ashurst
murmured :

" I'm afraid I've got to get back this afternoon."

" Oh ! "

" Can't you put it off ? "

Ashurst turned to the new speaker, Stella, shook his head, and smiled. She was very pretty ! Sabina said regretfully : " You might ! " Then the talk switched off to caves and swimming.

" Can you swim far ? "

" About two miles."

" Oh ! "

" I say ! "

" How jolly ! "

The three pairs of blue eyes, fixed on him, made him conscious of his new importance. The sensation was agreeable. Halliday said :

" I say, you simply must stop and have a bathe. You'd better stay the night."

" Yes, do ! "

But again Ashurst smiled and shook his head. Then suddenly he found himself being catechised about his physical achievements. He had rowed—it seemed— in his college boat, played in his college football team, won his college mile ; and he rose from table a sort of hero. The two little girls insisted that he must see " their " cave, and they set forth chattering like magpies, Ashurst between them, Stella and her brother a little behind. In the cave, damp and darkish like any other cave, the great feature was a pool with possibility of creatures which might be caught and put into bottles. Sabina and Freda, who wore no stockings on their shapely brown legs, exhorted Ashurst to join them in the middle of it, and help sieve the water. He too was soon bootless and sockless. Time goes fast for one who has a sense of beauty, when there are pretty children in a pool and a young Diana on

the edge, to receive with wonder anything you can
catch! Ashurst never had much sense of time. It
was a shock when, pulling out his watch, he saw it was
well past three. No cashing his cheque to-day—the
bank would be closed before he could get there.
Watching his expression, the little girls cried out at
once :

"Hurrah! Now you'll have to stay!"

Ashurst did not answer. He was seeing again
Megan's face, when at breakfast time he had whispered :
"I'm going to Torquay, darling, to get everything ;
I shall be back this evening. If it's fine we can go
to-night. Be ready." He was seeing again how
she quivered and hung on his words. What would
she think? Then he pulled himself together, conscious
suddenly of the calm scrutiny of this other young
girl, so tall and fair and Diana-like, at the edge of the
pool, of her wondering blue eyes under those brows
which slanted up a little. If they knew what was in
his mind—if they knew that this very night he had
meant——! Well, there would be a little sound of disgust, and he would be alone in the cave. And with a
curious mixture of anger, chagrin, and shame, he put
his watch back into his pocket and said abruptly :

"Yes ; I'm dished for to-day."

"Hurrah! Now you can bathe with us."

It was impossible not to succumb a little to the
contentment of these pretty children, to the smile on
Stella's lips, to Halliday's "Ripping, old chap! I
can lend you things for the night!" But again a
spasm of longing and remorse throbbed through
Ashurst, and he said moodily :

"I must send a wire!"

The attractions of the pool palling, they went back

to the hotel. Ashurst sent his wire, addressing it to
Mrs. Narracombe : " Sorry, detained for the night,
back to-morrow." Surely Megan would understand
that he had too much to do ; and his heart grew lighter.
It was a lovely afternoon, warm, the sea calm and blue,
and swimming his great passion ; the favour of these
pretty children flattered him, the pleasure of looking
at them, at Stella, at Halliday's sunny face ; the slight
unreality, yet extreme naturalness of it all—as of a
last peep at normality before he took this plunge
with Megan ! He got his borrowed bathing dress, and
they all set forth. Halliday and he undressed behind
one rock, the three girls behind another. He was first
into the sea, and at once swam out with the bravado
of justifying his self-given reputation. When he
turned he could see Halliday swimming along shore,
and the girls flopping and dipping, and riding the
little waves, in the way he was accustomed to despise,
but now thought pretty and sensible, since it gave
him the distinction of the only deep-water fish. But
drawing near, he wondered if they would like him, a
stranger, to come into their splashing group ; he felt
shy, approaching that slim nymph. Then Sabina
summoned him to teach her to float, and between them
the little girls kept him so busy that he had no time
even to notice whether Stella was accustomed to his
presence, till suddenly he heard a startled sound from
her. She was standing submerged to the waist, leaning
a little forward, her slim white arms stretched out
and pointing, her wet face puckered by the sun and
an expression of fear.

" Look at Phil ! Is he all right ? Oh, look ! "

Ashurst saw at once that Phil was not all right. He
was splashing and struggling, out of his depth, perhaps

a hundred yards away ; suddenly he gave a cry, threw up his arms, and went down. Ashurst saw the girl launch herself towards him, and crying out: "Go back, Stella! Go back!" he dashed out. He had never swum so fast, and reached Halliday just as he was coming up a second time. It was a case of cramp, but to get him in was not difficult, for he did not struggle. The girl, who had stopped where Ashurst told her to, helped as soon as he was in his depth, and once on the beach they sat down one on each side of him to rub his limbs, while the little ones stood by with scared faces. Halliday was soon smiling. It was—he said—rotten of him, absolutely rotten! If Frank would give him an arm, he could get to his clothes all right now. Ashurst gave him the arm, and as he did so caught sight of Stella's face, wet and flushed and tearful, all broken up out of its calm ; and he thought : 'I called her Stella! Wonder if she minded ? '

While they were dressing, Halliday said quietly :

" You saved my life, old chap ! "

" Rot ! "

Clothed, but not quite in their right minds, they went up all together to the hotel and sat down to tea, except Halliday, who was lying down in his room. After some slices of bread and jam, Sabina said :

" I say, you know, you *are* a brick ! " And Freda chimed in :

" Rather ! "

Ashurst saw Stella looking down ; he got up in confusion, and went to the window. From there he heard Sabina mutter : " I say, let's swear blood bond. Where's your knife, Freda ? " and out of the corner of his eye could see each of them solemnly prick herself, squeeze out a drop of blood and dabble on a bit of paper. He turned and made for the door.

"Don't be a stoat! Come back!" His arms were seized; imprisoned between the little girls he was brought back to the table. On it lay a piece of paper with an effigy drawn in blood, and the three names Stella Halliday, Sabina Halliday, Freda Halliday— also in blood, running towards it like the rays of a star. Sabina said:

"That's you. We shall have to kiss you, you know."

And Freda echoed:

"Oh! Blow—Yes!"

Before Ashurst could escape, some wettish hair dangled against his face, something like a bite descended on his nose, he felt his left arm pinched, and other teeth softly searching his cheek. Then he was released, and Freda said:

"Now, Stella."

Ashurst, red and rigid, looked across the table at a red and rigid Stella. Sabina giggled; Freda cried:

"Buck up—it spoils everything!"

A queer, ashamed eagerness shot through Ashurst; then he said quietly:

"Shut up, you little demons!"

Again Sabina giggled.

"Well, then, she can kiss her hand, and you can put it against your nose. It *is* on one side!"

To his amazement the girl did kiss her hand and stretch it out. Solemnly he took that cool, slim hand and laid it to his cheek. The two little girls broke into clapping, and Freda said:

"Now, then, we shall have to save your life at any time; that's settled. Can I have another cup, Stella, not so beastly weak?"

Tea was resumed, and Ashurst, folding up the paper, put it in his pocket. The talk turned on the advantages of measles, tangerine oranges, honey in a spoon, no lessons, and so forth. Ashurst listened, silent, exchanging friendly looks with Stella, whose face was again of its normal sun-touched pink and white. It was soothing to be so taken to the heart of this jolly family, fascinating to watch their faces. And after tea, while the two little girls pressed seaweed, he talked to Stella in the window seat and looked at her water-colour sketches. The whole thing was like a pleasurable dream; time and incident hung up, importance and reality suspended. To-morrow he would go back to Megan, with nothing of all this left save the paper with the blood of these children, in his pocket. Children! Stella was not quite that—as old as Megan! Her talk—quick, rather hard and shy, yet friendly—seemed to flourish on his silences, and about her there was something cool and virginal—a maiden in a bower. At dinner, to which Halliday, who had swallowed too much sea-water, did not come, Sabina said :

" I'm going to call you Frank."

Freda echoed :

" Frank, Frank, Franky."

Ashurst grinned and bowed.

" Every time Stella calls you Mr. Ashurst, she's got to pay a forfeit. It's ridiculous."

Ashurst looked at Stella, who grew slowly red. Sabina giggled ; Freda cried :

" She's ' smoking '—' smoking ! '—Yah ! "

Ashurst reached out to right and left, and grasped some fair hair in each hand.

" Look here," he said, " you two ! Leave Stella alone, or I'll tie you together ! "

Freda gurgled :

" Ouch ! You *are* a beast ! "

Sabina murmured cautiously :

" *You* call *her* Stella, you see ! "

" Why shouldn't I ? It's a jolly name ! "

" All right ; we give you leave to ! "

Ashurst released the hair. Stella ! What would she call him—after this ? But she called him nothing ; till at bedtime he said, deliberately :

" Good-night, Stella ! "

" Good-night, Mr.—— Good-night, Frank ! It *was* jolly of you, you know ! "

" Oh—that ! Bosh ! "

Her quick, straight handshake tightened suddenly, and as suddenly became slack.

Ashurst stood motionless in the empty sitting-room. Only last night, under the apple tree and the living blossom, he had held Megan to him, kissing her eyes and lips. And he gasped, swept by that rush of remembrance. To-night it should have begun—his life with her who only wanted to be with him ! And now, twenty-four hours and more must pass, because— of not looking at his watch ! Why had he made friends with this family of innocents just when he was saying good-bye to innocence, and all the rest of it ? ' But I mean to marry her,' he thought ; ' I told her so ! '

He took a candle, lighted it, and went to his bed- room, which was next to Halliday's. His friend's voice called, as he was passing :

" Is that you, old chap ? I say, come in."

He was sitting up in bed, smoking a pipe and reading.

" Sit down a bit."

Ashurst sat down by the open window.

" I've been thinking about this afternoon, you

know," said Halliday rather suddenly. "They say you go through all your past. I didn't. I suppose I wasn't far enough gone."

"What did you think of?"

Halliday was silent for a little, then said quietly:

"Well, I did think of one thing—rather odd—of a girl at Cambridge that I might have—you know; I was glad I hadn't got her on my mind. Anyhow, old chap, I owe it to you that I'm here; I should have been in the big dark by now. No more bed, or baccy; no more anything. I say, what d'you suppose happens to us?"

Ashurst murmured:

"Go out like flames, I expect."

"Phew!"

"We may flicker, and cling about a bit, perhaps."

"H'm! I think that's rather gloomy. I say, I hope my young sisters have been decent to you?"

"Awfully decent."

Halliday put his pipe down, crossed his hands behind his neck, and turned his face towards the window. "They're not bad kids!" he said.

Watching his friend, lying there, with that smile, and the candle-light on his face, Ashurst shuddered. Quite true! He might have been lying there with no smile, with all that sunny look gone out for ever! He might not have been lying there at all, but "sanded" at the bottom of the sea, waiting for resurrection on the—ninth day, was it? And that smile of Halliday's seemed to him suddenly something wonderful, as if in it were all the difference between life and death— the little flame—the all! He got up, and said softly:

"Well, you ought to sleep, I expect. Shall I blow out?"

Halliday caught his hand.

" I can't say it, you know ; but it must be rotten to be dead. Good-night, old boy ! "

Stirred and moved, Ashurst squeezed the hand, and went downstairs. The hall door was still open, and he passed out on to the lawn before the Crescent. The stars were bright in a very dark blue sky, and by their light some lilacs had that mysterious colour of flowers by night which no one can describe. Ashurst pressed his face against a spray ; and before his closed eyes Megan started up, with the tiny brown spaniel pup against her breast. " I thought of a girl that I might have—you know. I was glad I hadn't got her on my mind ! " He jerked his head away from the lilac, and began pacing up and down over the grass, a grey phantom coming to substance for a moment in the light from the lamp at either end. He was with her again under the living, breathing whiteness of the blossom, the stream chattering by, the moon glinting steel-blue on the bathing-pool ; back in the rapture of his kisses on her upturned face of innocence and humble passion, back in the suspense and beauty of that pagan night. He stood still once more in the shadow of the lilacs. Here the sea, not the stream, was Night's voice ; the sea with its sigh and rustle ; no little bird, no owl, no night-jar called or spun ; but a piano tinkled, and the white houses cut the sky with solid curve, and the scent from the lilacs filled the air. A window of the hotel, high up, was lighted ; he saw a shadow move across the blind. And most queer sensa ions stirred within him, a sort of churning, and twining, and turning of a single emotion on itself, as though spring and love, bewildered and confused, seeking the way, were baffled. This girl, who had

called him Frank, whose hand had given his that
sudden little clutch, this girl so cool and pure—what
would *she* think of such wild, unlawful loving ? He
sank down on the grass, sitting there cross-legged,
with his back to the house, motionless as some carved
Buddha.   Was he really going to break through
innocence, and steal ? Sniff the scent out of a wild
flower, and—perhaps—throw it away ? " Of a girl
at Cambridge that I might have—you know ! " He
put his hands to the grass, one on each side, palms
downwards, and pressed ; it was just warm still—the
grass, barely moist, soft and firm and friendly.
' What am I going to do ? ' he thought.   Perhaps
Megan was at her window, looking out at the blossom,
thinking of him !   Poor little Megan !   ' Why not ? '
he thought. ' I love her !   But do I—really love her ?
or do I only want her because she is so pretty, and
loves me ?   What am I going to do ? '   The piano
tinkled on, the stars winked ; and Ashurst gazed out
before him at the dark sea, as if spell-bound.   He got
up at last, cramped and rather chilly.   There was no
longer light in any window.   And he went in to bed.

8 §

Out of a deep and dreamless sleep he was awakened
by the sound of thumping on the door.   A shrill voice
called :
" Hi ! Breakfast's ready."
He jumped up.   Where was he—— ?   Ah !
He found them already eating marmalade, and sat
down in the empty place between Stella and Sabina,
who, after watching him a little, said :
" I say, do buck up ; we're going to start at half-past
nine."

" We're going to Berry Head, old chap ; you *must*
come ! "

Ashurst thought : ' Come ! Impossible. I shall
be getting things and going back.'   He looked at
Stella.   She said quickly :

" Do come ! "

Sabina chimed in :

" It'll be no fun without you."

Freda got up and stood behind his chair.

" You've got to come, or else I'll pull your hair ! "

Ashurst thought : ' Well—one day more—to think
it over ! One day more ! '   And he said :

" All right ! You needn't tweak my mane ! "

" Hurrah ! "

At the station he wrote a second telegram to the
farm, and then—tore it up ; he could not have explained why.   From Brixham they drove in a very
little wagonette.   There, squeezed between Sabina and
Freda, with his knees touching Stella's, they played
" Up, Jenkins " ; and the gloom he was feeling gave
way to frolic.   In this one day more to think it over,
he did not want to think !   They ran races, wrestled,
paddled—for to-day nobody wanted to bathe—they
sang catches, played games, and ate all they had
brought.   The little girls fell asleep against him on
the way back, and his knees still touched Stella's in
the narrow wagonette.   It seemed incredible that
thirty hours ago he had never set eyes on any of those
three flaxen heads.   In the train he talked to Stella
of poetry, discovering her favourites, and telling her
his own with a pleasing sense of superiority ;   till
suddenly she said, rather low :

" Phil says you don't believe in a future life, Frank.
I think that's dreadful."

Disconcerted, Ashurst muttered :

"I don't either believe or not believe—I simply don't know."

She said quickly :

"I couldn't bear that. What would be the use of living ? "

Watching the frown of those pretty oblique brows, Ashurst answered :

"I don't believe in believing things because one wants to."

"But why should one *wish* to live again, if one isn't going to ? "

And she looked full at him.

He did not want to hurt her, but an itch to dominate pushed him on to say :

"While one's alive one naturally wants to go on living for ever ; that's part of being alive. But it probably isn't anything more."

"Don't you believe in the Bible at all, then ? "

Ashurst thought : ' Now I shall really hurt her ! '

"I believe in the Sermon on the Mount, because it's beautiful and good for all time."

"But don't you believe Christ was divine ? "

He shook his head.

She turned her face quickly to the window, and there sprang into his mind Megan's prayer, repeated by little Nick : " God bless us all, and Mr. Ashes ! " Who else would ever say a prayer for him, like her who at this moment must be waiting—waiting to see him come down the lane ? And he thought suddenly : ' What a scoundrel I am ! '

All that evening this thought kept coming back ; but, as is not unusual, each time with less poignancy, till it seemed almost a matter of course to be a scoundrel.

And—strange !—he did not know whether he was a
scoundrel if he meant to go back to Megan, or if he
did not mean to go back to her.

They played cards till the children were sent off to
bed ; then Stella went to the piano. From over on
the window seat, where it was nearly dark, Ashurst
watched her between the candles—that fair head on
the long, white neck bending to the movement of her
hands. She played fluently, without much expression ;
but what a picture she made, the faint golden radiance,
a sort of angelic atmosphere—hovering about her !
Who could have passionate thoughts or wild desires
in the presence of that swaying, white-clothed girl
with the seraphic head ? She played a thing of
Schumann's, called " *Warum ?* " Then Halliday
brought out a flute, and the spell was broken. After
this they made Ashurst sing, Stella playing his accom-
paniments from a book of Schumann songs, till, in
the middle of " *Ich grolle nicht*," two small figures
clad in blue dressing-gowns crept in and tried to
conceal themselves beneath the piano. The evening
broke up in confusion, and what Sabina called " a
splendid rag."

That night Ashurst hardly slept at all. He was
thinking, only too hard, and tossed and turned. The
intense domestic intimacy of these last two days, the
strength of this Halliday atmosphere, seemed to ring
him round, and make the farm and Megan—even
Megan—seem unreal. Had he really made love to her—
really promised to take her away to live with him ?
He must have been bewitched by the spring, the night,
the apple blossom ! This May madness could but
destroy them both ! The notion that he was going
to make her his mistress—that simple child not yet

eighteen—now filled him with a sort of horror, even
while it still stung and whipped his blood. He muttered to himself : " It's awful, what I've done—
awful ! " And the sound of Schumann's music throbbed
and mingled with his fevered thoughts, and he saw
again Stella's cool, white, fair-haired figure and bending
neck, the queer, angelic radiance about her.   ' I must
have been—I must be—mad ! ' he thought. ' What
came into me ? Poor little Megan !   " God bless us
all, and Mr. Ashes ! "   " I want to be with you—only
to be with you ! " '   And burying his face in his pillow,
he smothered down a fit of sobbing. Not to go back
was awful ! To go back—more awful still !

Emotion, when you are young, and give real vent
to it, loses its power of torture. And he fell asleep,
thinking : ' What was it—a few kisses—all forgotten
in a month ! '

Next morning he got his cheque cashed, but avoided
the shop of the dove-grey dress like the plague ; and,
instead, bought himself some necessaries. He spent
the whole day in a queer mood, cherishing a kind of
sullenness against himself. Instead of the hankering
of the last two days, he felt nothing but a blank—all
passionate longing gone, as if quenched in that outburst
of tears. After tea Stella put a book down beside him,
and said shyly :

" Have you read that, Frank ? "

It was Farrar's " Life of Christ." Ashurst smiled.
Her anxiety about his beliefs seemed to him comic,
but touching. Infectious too, perhaps, for he began
to have an itch to justify himself, if not to convert
her. And in the evening, when the children and
Halliday were mending their shrimping nets, he said :

" At the back of orthodox religion, so far as I can

see, there's always the idea of reward—what you can get for being good ; a kind of begging for favours. I think it all starts in fear."

She was sitting on the sofa, making reefer knots with a bit of string. She looked up quickly :

" I think it's much deeper than that."

Ashurst felt again that wish to dominate.

" You think so," he said ; " but wanting the ' *quid pro quo* ' is about the deepest thing in all of us ! It's jolly hard to get to the bottom of it ! "

She wrinkled her brows in a puzzled frown.

" I don't think I understand."

He went on obstinately :

" Well, think, and see if the most religious people aren't those who feel that this life doesn't give them all they want. I believe in being good because to be good is good in itself."

" Then you do believe in being good ? "

How pretty she looked now—it was easy to be good with her ! And he nodded and said :

" I say, show me how to make that knot ! "

With her fingers touching his, in manœuvring of the bit of string, he felt soothed and happy. And when he went to bed he wilfully kept his thoughts on her, wrapping himself in her fair, cool sisterly radiance, as in some garment of protection.

Next day he found they had arranged to go by train to Totnes, and picnic at Berry Pomeroy Castle. Still in that resolute oblivion of the past, he took his place with them in the landau beside Halliday, back to the horses. And, then, along the sea front, nearly at the turning to the railway station, his heart almost leaped into his mouth. Megan—Megan herself !—was walking on the far pathway, in her old skirt and jacket and

her tam-o'-shanter, looking up into the faces of the
passers-by. Instinctively he threw his hand up for
cover, then made a feint of clearing dust out of his
eyes ; but between his fingers he could see her still,
moving, not with her free country step, but wavering,
lost-looking, pitiful—like some little dog which has
missed its master and does not know whether to run
on, to run back—where to run. How had she come
like this ?—what excuse had she found to get away ?—
what did she hope for ? But with every turn of the
wheels bearing him away from her, his heart revolted
and cried to him to stop them, to get out, and go to
her ! When the landau turned the corner to the
station he could stand it no more, and opening the
carriage door, muttered : " I've forgotten something !
Go on—don't wait for me ! I'll join you at the castle by
the next train ! " He jumped, stumbled, spun round,
recovered his balance, and walked forward, while the
carriage with the astonished Hallidays rolled on.

From the corner he could only just see Megan, a
long way ahead now. He ran a few steps, checked
himself, and dropped into a walk. With each step
nearer to her, further from the Hallidays, he walked
more and more slowly. How did it alter anything—
this sight of her ? How make the going to her, and
that which must come of it, less ugly ? For there was
no hiding it—since he had met the Hallidays he had
become gradually sure that he would not marry Megan.
It would only be a wild love-time, a troubled, remorseful,
difficult time—and then—well, then he would get tired,
just because she gave him everything, was so simple,
and so trustful, so dewy. And dew—wears off ! The
little spot of faded colour, her tam-o'-shanter cap,
wavered on far in front of him, as she looked up into

every face, and at the house windows. Had any man
ever such a cruel moment to go through ? Whatever
he did, he felt he would be a beast. And he uttered a
groan which made a nursemaid turn and stare. He saw
Megan stop and lean against the sea-wall, looking at
the sea ; and he too stopped. Quite likely she had
never seen the sea before, and even in her distress
could not resist that sight. ' Yes—she's seen nothing,'
he thought ; ' everything's before her. And just for
a few weeks' passion, 1 shall be cutting her life to
ribbons. I'd better go and hang myself rather than
do it ! ' And suddenly he seemed to see Stella's calm
eyes looking into his, the wave of fluffy hair on her
forehead stirred by the wind. Ah ! it would be madness, would mean giving up all that he respected, and
his own self-respect. He turned and walked quickly
back towards the station. But memory of that poor,
bewildered little figure, those anxious eyes searching
the passers-by, smote him too hard again, and once
more he turned towards the sea. The cap was no longer
visible ; that little spot of colour had vanished in the
stream of the noon promenaders. And impelled by
the passion of longing, the dearth which comes on one
when life seems to be whirling something out of reach,
he hurried forward. She was nowhere to be seen ; for
half an hour he looked for her ; then on the beach
flung himself face downward in the sand. To find her
again he knew he had only to go to the station
and wait till she returned from her fruitless quest, to
take her train home ; or to take train himself and go
back to the farm, so that she found him there when
she returned. But he lay inert in the sand, among
the indifferent groups of children with their spades
and buckets. Pity at her little figure wandering,

seeking, was well-nigh merged in the spring-running
of his blood; for it was all wild feeling now—the
chivalrous part, what there had been of it, was gone.
He wanted her again, wanted her kisses, her soft, little
body, her abandonment, all her quick, warm, pagan
emotion; wanted the wonderful feeling of that night
under the moonlit apple boughs; wanted it all with
a horrible intensity, as the faun wants the nymph.
The quick chatter of the little bright trout-stream,
the dazzle of the buttercups, the rocks of the old
" wild men "; the calling of the cuckoos and yaffles,
the hooting of the owls; and the red moon peeping
out of the velvet dark at the living whiteness of the
blossom; and her face just out of reach at the window,
lost in its love-look; and her heart against his, her
lips answering his, under the apple tree—all this
besieged him. Yet he lay inert. What was it which
struggled against pity and this feverish longing, and
kept him there paralysed in the warm sand? Three
flaxen heads—a fair face with friendly blue-grey eyes,
a slim hand pressing his, a quick voice speaking his
name—" So you do believe in being good? " Yes,
and a sort of atmosphere as of some old walled-in
English garden, with pinks, and cornflowers, and
roses, and scents of lavender and lilac—cool and fair,
untouched, almost holy—all that he had been brought
up to feel was clean and good. And suddenly he
thought: ' She might come along the front again and
see me! ' and he got up and made his way to the rock
at the far end of the beach. There, with the spray
lifting into his face, he could think more coolly. To
go back to the farm and love Megan out in the woods,
among the rocks, with everything around wild and
fitting—that, he knew, was impossible, utterly. To

transplant her to a great town, to keep, in some little
flat or rooms, one who belonged so wholly to Nature—
the poet in him shrank from it. His passion would be
a mere sensuous revel, soon gone ; in London, her very
simplicity, her lack of all intellectual quality, would
make her his secret plaything—nothing else.   The
longer he sat on the rock, with his feet dangling over
a greenish pool from which the sea was ebbing, the
more clearly he saw this ; but it was as if her arms
and all of her were slipping slowly, slowly down from
him, into the pool, to be carried away out to sea ; and
her face looking up, her lost face with beseeching eyes,
and dark, wet hair—possessed, haunted, tortured
him ! He got up at last, scaled the low rock-cliff,
and made his way down into a sheltered cove. Perhaps
in the sea he could get back his control—lose this
fever ! And stripping off his clothes, he swam out.
He wanted to tire himself so that nothing mattered,
and swam recklessly, fast and far ; then suddenly,
for no reason, felt afraid. Suppose he could not reach
shore again—suppose the current set him out—or he
got cramp, like Halliday ! He turned to swim in.
The red cliffs looked a long way off. If he were drowned
they would find his clothes. The Hallidays would
know ; but Megan perhaps never—they took no
newspaper at the farm. And Phil Halliday's words
came back to him again : " A girl at Cambridge I
might have—— Glad I hadn't got her on my mind ! "
And in that moment of unreasoning fear he vowed he
would not have her on his mind. Then his fear left
him ; he swam in easily enough, dried himself in the
sun, and put on his clothes. His heart felt sore, but
no longer ached ; his body cool and refreshed.

When one is as young as Ashurst, pity is not a violent

emotion. And, back in the Hallidays' sitting-room,
eating a ravenous tea, he felt much like a man recovered
from fever. Everything seemed new and clear ; the
tea, the buttered toast and jam tasted absurdly good ;
tobacco had never smelt so nice. And walking up
and down the empty room, he stopped here and there
to touch or look. He took up Stella's work-basket,
fingered the cotton reels and a gaily-coloured plait
of sewing silks, smelt at the little bag filled with wood-
roffe she kept among them. He sat down at the
piano, playing tunes with one finger, thinking : ' To-
night she'll play ; I shall watch her while she's playing ;
it does me good to watch her.' He took up the book,
which still lay where she had placed it beside him,
and tried to read. But Megan's little, sad figure began
to come back at once, and he got up and leaned in the
window, listening to the thrushes in the Crescent
gardens, gazing at the sea, dreamy and blue below
the trees. A servant came in and cleared the tea away,
and he still stood, inhaling the evening air, trying not
to think. Then he saw the Hallidays coming through
the gate of the Crescent, Stella a little in front of Phil
and the children, with their baskets, and instinctively
he drew back. His heart, too sore and discomfited,
shrank from this encounter, yet wanted its friendly
solace—bore a grudge against this influence, yet craved
its cool innocence, and the pleasure of watching
Stella's face. From against the wall behind the piano
he saw her come in and stand looking a little blank as
though disappointed ; then she saw him and smiled, a
swift, brilliant smile which warmed yet irritated Ashurst.

" You never came after us, Frank."

" No ; I found I couldn't."

" Look ! We picked such lovely late violets ! "

She held out a bunch. Ashurst put his nose to them, and there stirred within him vague longings, chilled instantly by a vision of Megan's anxious face lifted to the faces of the passers-by.

He said shortly : " How jolly ! " and turned away. He went up to his room, and, avoiding the children, who were coming up the stairs, threw himself on his bed, and lay there with his arms crossed over his face. Now that he felt the die really cast, and Megan given up, he hated himself, and almost hated the Hallidays and their atmosphere of healthy, happy English homes. Why should they have chanced here, to drive away first love—to show him that he was going to be no better than a common seducer ? What right had Stella, with her fair, shy beauty, to make him know for certain that he would never marry Megan ; and, tarnishing it all, bring him such bitterness of regretful longing and such pity ? Megan would be back by now, worn out by her miserable seeking—poor little thing!—expecting, perhaps, to find him there when she reached home. Ashurst bit at his sleeve, to stifle a groan of remorseful longing. He went to dinner glum and silent, and his mood threw a dinge even over the children. It was a melancholy, rather ill-tempered evening, for they were all tired ; several times he caught Stella looking at him with a hurt, puzzled expression, and this pleased his evil mood. He slept miserably ; got up quite early, and wandered out. He went down to the beach. Alone there with the serene, the blue, the sunlit sea, his heart relaxed a little. Conceited fool—to think that Megan would take it so hard ! In a week or two she would almost have forgotten ! And he—well, he would have the reward of virtue ! A good young man ! If

Stella knew, she would give him her blessing for resisting that devil she believed in; and he uttered a hard laugh. But slowly the peace and beauty of sea and sky, the flight of the lonely seagulls, made him feel ashamed. He bathed, and turned homewards.

In the Crescent gardens Stella herself was sitting on a camp stool, sketching. He stole up close behind. How fair and pretty she was, bent diligently, holding up her brush, measuring, wrinkling her brows.

He said gently :

" Sorry I was such a beast last night, Stella."

She turned round, startled, flushed very pink, and said in her quick way :

" It's all right. I knew there was something. Between friends it doesn't matter, does it ? "

Ashurst answered :

" Between friends—and we are, aren't we ? "

She looked up at him, nodded vehemently, and her upper teeth gleamed again in that swift, brilliant smile.

Three days later he went back to London, travelling with the Hallidays. He had not written to the farm. What was there he could say ?

On the last day of April in the following year he and Stella were married. . . .

Such were Ashurst's memories, sitting against the wall among the gorse, on his silver-wedding day. At this very spot, where he had laid out the lunch, Megan must have stood outlined against the sky when he had first caught sight of her. Of all queer coincidences ! And there moved in him a longing to go down and see again the farm and the orchard, and the meadow

of the gipsy bogle. It would not take long ; Stella
would be an hour yet, perhaps.

How well he remembered it all—the little crowning
group of pine trees, the steep-up grass hill behind ! He
paused at the farm gate. The low stone house, the
yew tree porch, the flowering currants—not changed
a bit ; even the old green chair was out there on the
grass under the window, where he had reached up to
her that night to take the key. Then he turned down
the lane, and stood leaning on the orchard gate—
grey skeleton of a gate, as then. A black pig even
was wandering in there among the trees. Was it true
that twenty-six years had passed, or had he dreamed
and awakened to find Megan waiting for him by the
big apple tree ? Unconsciously he put up his hand
to his grizzled beard and brought himself back to
reality. Opening the gate, he made his way down
through the docks and nettles till he came to the edge,
and the old apple tree itself. Unchanged ! A little
more of the grey-green lichen, a dead branch or two,
and for the rest it might have been only last night that
he had embraced that mossy trunk after Megan's flight
and inhaled its woody savour, while above his head
the moonlit blossom had seemed to breathe and live.
In that early spring a few buds were showing already ;
the blackbirds shouting their songs, a cuckoo calling,
the sunlight bright and warm. Incredibly the same—
the chattering trout-stream, the narrow pool he had
lain in every morning, splashing the water over his
flanks and chest ; and out there in the wild meadow
the beech clump and the stone where the gipsy bogle
was supposed to sit. And an ache for lost youth, a
hankering, a sense of wasted love and sweetness, gripped
Ashurst by the throat. Surely, on this earth of such

wild beauty, one was meant to hold rapture to one's heart, as this earth and sky held it ! And yet, one could not !

He went to the edge of the stream, and looking down at the little pool, thought : ' Youth and spring ! What has become of them all, I wonder ? ' And then, in sudden fear of having this memory jarred by human encounter, he went back to the lane, and pensively retraced his steps to the cross-roads.

Beside the car an old, grey-bearded labourer was leaning on a stick, talking to the chauffeur. He broke off at once, as though guilty of disrespect, and touching his hat, prepared to limp on down the lane.

Ashurst pointed to the narrow green mound. " Can you tell me what this is ? "

The old fellow stopped ; on his face had come a look as though he were thinking : ' You've come to the right shop, mister ! '

" 'Tes a grave," he said.

" But why out here ? "

The old man smiled. " That's a tale, as yu may say. An' not the first time as I've a-told et—there's plenty folks asks 'bout that bit o' turf. ' Maid's Grave ' us calls et, 'ereabouts."

Ashurst held out his pouch. " Have a fill ? "

The old man touched his hat again, and slowly filled an old clay pipe. His eyes, looking upward out of a mass of wrinkles and hair, were still quite bright.

" If yu don' mind, zurr, I'll zet down—my leg's 'urtin' a bit to-day." And he sat down on the mound of turf.

" There's always a vlower on this grave. An' 'tain't so very lonesome, neither ; brave lot o' folks goes by now, in they new motor cars an' things—not

as 'twas in th' old days. She've a got company up
'ere. 'Twas a poor soul killed 'erself."

"I see!" said Ashurst. "Cross-roads burial. I
didn't know that custom was kept up."

"Ah! but 'twas a main long time ago. Us 'ad a
parson as was very God-fearin' then. Let me see, I've
a 'ad my pension six year come Michaelmas, an' I
were just on fifty when t'appened. There's no one
livin' knows more about et than I du. She belonged
close 'ere ; same farm as where I used to work along
o' Mrs. Narracombe—'tes Nick Narracombe's now ;
I dus a bit for 'im still, odd times."

Ashurst, who was leaning against the gate, lighting
his pipe, left his curved hands before his face for long
after the flame of the match had gone out.

"Yes?" he said, and to himself his voice sounded
hoarse and queer.

"She was one in an 'underd, poor maid! I putts a
vlower 'ere every time I passes. Pretty maid an' gude
maid she was, though they wouldn't burry 'er up tu
th' church, nor where she wanted to be burried neither."
The old labourer paused, and put his hairy, twisted
hand flat down on the turf beside the bluebells.

"Yes?" said Ashurst.

"In a manner of speakin'," the old man went on.
"I think as 'twas a love-story—though there's no one
never knu for zartin. Yu can't tell what's in a maid's
'ead—but that's wot I think about it." He drew his
hand along the turf. "I was fond o' that maid—don'
know as there was anyone as wasn' fond of 'er. But
she was tu lovin'-'earted—that's where 'twas, I think."
He looked up. And Ashurst, whose lips were trembling
in the cover of his beard, murmured again : "Yes?"

"'Twas in the spring, 'bout now as 't might be, or

a little later—blossom time—an' we 'ad one o' they young college gentlemen stayin' at the farm—nice feller tu, with 'is 'ead in the air. I liked 'e very well, an' I never see nothin' between 'em, but to my thinkin' 'e turned the maid's fancy." The old man took the pipe out of his mouth, spat, and went on :

" Yu see, 'e went away sudden one day, an' never come back. They got 'is knapsack and bits o' things down there still. That's what stuck in my mind—'is never sendin' for 'em. 'Is name was Ashes, or some-then' like that."

" Yes ? " said Ashurst once more.

The old man licked his lips.

" 'Er never said nothin', but from that day 'er went kind of dazed lukin' ; didn' seem rightly therr at all. I never knu a 'uman creature so changed in me life— never. There was another young feller at the farm— Joe Biddaford 'is name wer', that was praaperly sweet on 'er, tu ; I guess 'e used to plague 'er wi' 'is atten- tions. She got to luke quite wild. I'd zee her some- times of an avenin' when I was bringin' up the calves ; ther' she'd stand in th' orchard, under the big apple tree, lukin' straight before 'er. ' Well,' I used t'think, ' I dunno what 'tes that's the matter wi' yu, but yu'm lukin' pitiful, that yu are.' "

The old man relit his pipe, and sucked at it reflec- tively.

" Yes ? " said Ashurst.

" I remembers one day I said to 'er : ' What's the matter, Megan ? '—'er name was Megan David, she come from Wales same as 'er aunt, ol' Missis Narra- combe. ' Yu'm frettin' about somethin', I says. ' No, Jim,' she says, ' I'm not frettin'.' ' Yes, yu are ! ' I says. ' No,' she says, and tu tears cam' rollin' out.

' Yu'm cryin'—what's that, then ? ' I says. She putts
'er 'and over 'er 'eart : ' It 'urts me,' she says ; ' but
'twill sune be better,' she says. ' But if anything shude
'appen to me, Jim, I wants to be burried under this
'ere apple tree.' I laughed. ' What's goin' to 'appen
to yu ? ' I says ; ' don't 'ee be fulish.' ' No,' she says,
' I won't be fulish.' Well, I know what maids are,
an' I never thought no more about et, till tu days
arter that, 'bout six in the avenin' I was comin' up wi'
the calves, when I see somethin' dark lyin' in the
strame, close to that big apple tree. I says to meself :
' Is that a pig—funny place for a pig to get to ! ' an'
I goes up to et, an' I see what 'twas."

The old man stopped ; his eyes, turned upward, had
a bright, suffering look.

" 'Twas the maid, in a little narrer pool ther' that's
made by the stoppin' of a rock—where I see the young
gentleman bathin' once or twice. 'Er was lyin' on 'er
face in the watter. There was a plant o' goldie-cups
growin' out o' the stone just above 'er 'ead. An'
when I come to luke at 'er face, 'twas luvly, butiful,
so calm's a baby's—wonderful butiful et was. When
the doctor saw 'er, 'e said : ' 'Er culdn' never a-done
it in that little bit o' watter ef' er 'adn't a-been in an
extarsy.' Ah ! an' judgin' from 'er face, that was just
'ow she was. Et made me cry praaper—butiful et
was ! 'Twas June then, but she'd a-found a little bit
of apple-blossom left over somewheres, and stuck et
in 'er 'air. That's why I thinks 'er must a-been in an
extarsy, to go to et gay, like that. Why ! there wasn't
more than a fute and a 'arf o' watter. But I tell 'ee
one thing—that meadder's 'arnted ; I knu et, an'
she knu et ; an' no one'll persuade me as 'tesn't. I
told 'em what she said to me 'bout bein' burried under

th' apple tree. But I think that turned 'em—made
et luke tu much 's ef she'd 'ad it in 'er mind deliberate ;
an' so they burried 'er up 'ere. Parson we 'ad then
was very particular, 'e was."

Again the old man drew his hand over the turf.

" 'Tes wonderful, et seems," he added slowly, " what
maids 'll du for love. She 'ad a lovin' 'eart ; I guess
'twas broken. But us never *knu* nothin' ! "

He looked up as if for approval of his story, but
Ashurst had walked past him as if he were not there.

Up on the top of the hill, beyond where he had
spread the lunch, over, out of sight, he lay down on
his face. So had his virtue been rewarded, and " the
Cyprian," goddess of love, taken her revenge ! And
before his eyes, dim with tears, came Megan's face
with the sprig of apple blossom in her dark, wet hair.
' What did I do that was wrong ? ' he thought.
' What *did* I do ? ' But he could not answer. Spring,
with its rush of passion, its flowers and song—the
spring in his heart and Megan's ! Was it just Love
seeking a victim ! The Greek was right, then—the
words of the " Hippolytus " as true to-day !

> "For mad is the heart of Love,
> And gold the gleam of his wing;
> And all to the spell thereof
> Bend when he makes his spring.
> All life that is wild and young
> In mountain and wave and stream
> All that of earth is sprung,
> Or breathes in the red sunbeam;
> Yea, and Mankind. O'er all a royal throne,
> Cyprian, Cyprian, is thine alone!"

The Greek was right ! Megan ! Poor little Megan—
coming over the hill ! Megan under the old apple
tree waiting and looking ! Megan dead, with beauty
printed on her ! . . .

A voice said :

" Oh, there you are ! Look ! "

Ashurst rose, took his wife's sketch, and stared at it in silence.

" Is the foreground right, Frank ? "

" Yes."

" But there's something wanting, isn't there ? "

Ashurst nodded. Wanting ? The Apple tree, the singing, and the gold !

And solemnly he put his lips to her forehead. It was his silver-wedding day.

1916.

THE JURYMAN

I.

"Don't you see, brother, I was reading yesterday the Gospel about Christ, the little Father; how He suffered, how He walked on the earth. I suppose you have heard about it?"

"Indeed, I have," replied Stepanuitch; "but we are people in darkness; we can't read."—TOLSTOI.

MR. HENRY BOSENGATE, of the London Stock Exchange, seated himself in his car that morning during the great war with a sense of injury. Major in a Volunteer Corps; member of all the local committees; lending this very car to the neighbouring hospital, at times even driving it himself for their benefit; subscribing to funds, so far as his diminished income permitted—he was conscious of being an asset to the country, and one whose time could not be wasted with impunity. To be summoned to sit on a jury at the local assizes, and not even the grand jury at that! It was in the nature of an outrage.

Strong and upright, with hazel eyes and dark eyebrows, pinkish-brown cheeks, a forehead white, well-shaped, and getting high, with greyish hair glossy and well-brushed, and a trim moustache, he might have been taken for that colonel of Volunteers which indeed he was in a fair way of becoming.

His wife had followed him out under the porch, and stood bracing her supple body clothed in lilac linen. Red rambler roses formed a sort of crown to her dark head; her ivory-coloured face had in it just a suggestion of the Japanese.

Mr. Bosengate spoke through the whirr of the engine:

"I don't expect to be late, dear. This business is

ridiculous. There oughtn't to *be* any crime in these
days."

His wife—her name was Kathleen—smiled. She
looked very pretty and cool, Mr. Bosengate thought. To
one bound on this dull and stuffy business everything
he owned seemed pleasant—the geranium beds beside
the gravel drive, his long, red-brick house mellowing
decorously in its creepers and ivy, the little clock-tower
over stables now converted to a garage, the dovecote,
masking at the other end the conservatory which
adjoined the billiard-room. Close to the red-brick
lodge his two children, Kate and Harry, ran out from
under the acacia trees, and waved to him, scrambling
bare-legged on to the low, red, ivy-covered wall which
guarded his domain of eleven acres. Mr. Bosengate
waved back, thinking : ' Jolly couple—by Jove, they
are ! ' Above their heads, through the trees, he could
see right away to some Downs, faint in the July heat
haze. And he thought : ' Pretty a spot as one could
have got, so close to Town ! '

Despite the war he had enjoyed these last two
years more than any of the ten since he built " Charmleigh " and settled down to semi-rural domesticity with
his young wife. There had been a certain piquancy,
a savour added to existence, by the country's peril,
and all the public service and sacrifice it demanded.
His chauffeur was gone, and one gardener did the work
of three. He enjoyed—positively enjoyed, his committee work ; even the serious decline of business and
increase of taxation had not much worried one continually conscious of the national crisis and his own
part therein. The country had wanted waking up,
wanted a lesson in effort and economy ; and the
feeling that he had not spared himself in these strenuous

times, had given a zest to those quiet pleasures of bed
and board which, at his age, even the most patriotic
could retain with a good conscience. He had denied
himself many things—new clothes, presents for Kathleen and the children, travel, and that pine-apple house
which he had been on the point of building when the
war broke out ; new wine, too, and cigars, and member-
ship of the two Clubs which he had never used in the
old days. The hours had seemed fuller and longer,
sleep better earned—wonderful, the things one could
do without when put to it ! He turned the car into the
high road, driving dreamily for he was in plenty of
time. The war was going pretty well now ; he was no
fool optimist, but now that conscription was in force,
one might reasonably hope for its end within a year.
Then there would be a boom, and one might let oneself
go a little. Visions of theatres and supper with his
wife at the Savoy afterwards, and cosy night drives
back into the sweet-smelling country behind your own
chauffeur once more teased a fancy which even now
did not soar beyond the confines of domestic pleasures.
He pictured his wife in new dresses by Jay—she was
fifteen years younger than himself, and "paid for
dressing" as they said. He had always delighted—as
men older than their wives will—in the admiration she
excited from others not privileged to enjoy her charms.
Her rather queer and ironical beauty, her cool irreproachable wifeliness, was a constant balm to him.
They would give dinner parties again, have their friends
down from town, and he would once more enjoy
sitting at the foot of the dinner table while Kathleen
sat at the head, with the light soft on her ivory
shoulders, behind flowers she had arranged in that
original way of hers, and fruit which he had grown in

his hot-houses ; once more he would take legitimate interest in the wine he offered to his guests—once more stock that Chinese cabinet wherein he kept cigars. Yes—there was a certain satisfaction in these days of privation, if only from the anticipation they created.

The sprinkling of villas had become continuous on either side of the high road ; and women going out to shop, tradesmen's boys delivering victuals, young men in khaki, began to abound. Now and then a limping or bandaged form would pass—some bit of human wreckage ; and Mr. Bosengate would think mechanically : ' Another of those poor devils ! Wonder if we've had his case before us ! '

Running his car into the best hotel garage of the little town, he made his way leisurely over to the court. It stood back from the market-place, and was already lapped by a sea of persons having, as in the outer ring at race meetings, an air of business at which one must not be caught out, together with a soaked or flushed appearance. Mr. Bosengate could not resist putting his handkerchief to his nose. He had carefully drenched it with lavender water, and to this fact owed, perhaps, his immunity from the post of foreman on the jury—for, say what you will about the English, they have a deep instinct for affairs.

He found himself second in the front row of the jury box, and through the odour of " Sanitas " gazed at the judge's face expressionless up there, for all the world like a bewigged bust. His fellows in the box had that appearance of falling between two classes characteristic of jurymen. Mr. Bosengate was not impressed. On one side of him the foreman sat, a prominent upholsterer, known in the town as " Gentleman Fox." His dark and beautifully brushed and oiled hair and moustache, his radiant linen, gold watch and chain, the white piping to his waistcoat, and a habit of never saying " Sir " had long marked him out from commoner men ; he undertook to bury people too, to save them trouble ; and was altogether superior. On the other side Mr. Bosengate had one of those men, who, except when they sit on juries, are never seen without a little brown bag, and the appearance of having been interrupted in a drink. Pale and shiny, with large loose eyes shifting from side to side, he had an underdone voice and uneasy flabby hands. Mr. Bosengate disliked sitting next to him. Beyond this commercial traveller sat a dark pale young man with spectacles ; beyond him again, a short old man with grey moustache, mutton chops, and innumerable wrinkles ; and the front row was completed by a chemist. The three immediately behind, Mr. Bosengate did not thoroughly master ; but the three at the end of the second row he learned in their order of an oldish man in a grey suit, given to winking ; an inanimate person with the mouth of a moustachioed cod-fish, over whose long bald crown three wisps of damp hair were carefully arranged ; and a dried, dapperish, clean-shorn man, whose mouth seemed terrified lest it should be surprised without a smile. Their first and second verdicts were recorded without the necessity for withdrawal, and Mr. Bosengate was already sleepy when the third case was called. The sight of khaki revived his drooping attention. But what a weedy-looking specimen ! This prisoner had a truly nerveless pitiable dejected air. If he had ever had a military bearing it had shrunk into him during his confinement. His ill-shaped brown tunic, whose little brass buttons seemed trying to keep smiling, struck Mr. Bosengate as ridiculously short, used though he was to such things. 'Absurd,' he thought—'Lumbago! Just where they ought to be covered!' Then the officer and gentleman stirred in him, and he added to himself : 'Still, there must be some distinction made!' The little soldier's visage had once perhaps been tanned, but was now the colour of dark dough ; his large brown eyes with white showing below the iris, as so often in the eyes of very nervous people—wandered from face to face, of judge, counsel, jury, and public. There were hollows in his cheeks, his dark hair looked damp ; around his neck he wore a bandage. The commercial traveller on Mr. Bosengate's left turned, and whispered : "*Felo de se!* My hat! what a guy!" Mr. Bosengate pretended not to hear—he could not bear that fellow !— and slowly wrote on a bit of paper : "Owen Lewis." Welsh! Well, he looked it—not at all an English face. Attempted suicide—not at all an English crime! Suicide implied surrender, a putting-up of hands to Fate—to say nothing of the religious aspect of the matter. And suicide in khaki seemed to Mr. Bosengate particularly abhorrent ; like turning tail in face of the enemy ; almost meriting the fate of a deserter. He looked at the prisoner, trying not to give way to this prejudice. And the prisoner seemed to look at him, though this, perhaps, was fancy.

The Counsel for the prosecution, a little, alert, grey, decided man, above military age, began detailing the circumstances of the crime. Mr. Bosengate, though not particularly sensitive to atmosphere, could perceive a sort of current running through the Court. It was as if jury and public were thinking rhythmically in obedience to the same unexpressed prejudice of which he himself was conscious. Even the Cæsar-like pale

face up there, presiding, seemed in its ironic serenity
responding to that current.

" Gentlemen of the jury, before I call my evidence,
I direct your attention to the bandage the accused is
still wearing. He gave himself this wound with his
Army razor, adding, if I may say so, insult to the injury
he was inflicting on his country. He pleads not guilty ;
and before the magistrates he said that absence from
his wife was preying on his mind ''—the advocate's
close lips widened—" Well, gentlemen, if such an
excuse is to weigh with us in these days, I'm sure I
don't know what's to happen to the Empire."   .

' No, by George ! ' thought Mr. Bosengate.

The evidence of the first witness, a room-mate who
had caught the prisoner's hand, and of the sergeant,
who had at once been summoned, was conclusive
and he began to cherish a hope that they would get
through without withdrawing, and he would be home
before five. But then a hitch occurred. The regimental doctor failed to respond when his name was
called ; and the judge having for the first time that
day showed himself capable of human emotion, inti-
mated that he would adjourn until the morrow.

Mr. Bosengate received the announcement with
equanimity. He would be home even earlier ! And
gathering up the sheets of paper he had scribbled on,
he put them in his pocket and got up. The would-
be suicide was being taken out of the court — a
shambling drab figure with shoulders hunched. What
good were men like that in these days ! What good !
The prisoner looked up. Mr. Bosengate encountered
in full the gaze of those large brown eyes, with the
white showing underneath. What a suffering, wretched,
pitiful face ! A man had no business to give you a look

like that! The prisoner passed on down the stairs,
and vanished. Mr. Bosengate went out and across the
market place to the garage of the hotel where he had
left his car. The sun shone fiercely and he thought :
' I must do some watering in the garden.' He brought
the car out, and was about to start the engine, when
someone passing, said : " Good evenin'. Seedy-
lookin' beggar that last prisoner, ain't he ? We don't
want men of that stamp." It was his neighbour on
the jury, the commercial traveller, in a straw hat, with
a little brown bag already in his hand and the froth
of an interrupted drink on his moustache. Answering
curtly : " Good evening ! " and thinking : ' Nor of
yours, my friend ! ' Mr. Bosengate started the car
with unnecessary clamour. But as if brought back to
life by the commercial traveller's remark, the prisoner's
figure seemed to speed along too, turning up at Mr.
Bosengate his pitifully unhappy eyes. Want of his
wife !—queer excuse that for trying to put it out of
his power ever to see her again ! Why ! Half a loaf,
even a slice, was better than no bread. Not many of
that neurotic type in the Army—thank Heaven ! The
lugubrious figure vanished, and Mr. Bosengate pictured
instead the form of his own wife bending over her
" Gloire de Dijon "'s in the rosery, where she generally
worked a little before tea now that they were short
of gardeners. He saw her, as often he had seen her,
raise herself and stand, head to one side, a gloved hand
on her slender hip, gazing as it were ironically from
under drooped lids at buds which did not come out fast
enough. And the word ' *Caline*,' for he was something
of a French scholar, shot through his mind : ' Kathleen—*Caline* ! ' If he found her there when he got in,
he would steal up on the grass and—ah ! but with great

care not to crease her dress or disturb her hair ! ' If only she weren't quite so self-contained,' he thought ; ' It's like a cat you can't get near, not really near ! '

The car, returning faster than it had come down that morning, had already passed the outskirt villas, and was breasting the hill to where, among fields and the old trees, Charmleigh lay apart from commoner life. Turning into his drive, Mr. Bosengate thought with a certain surprise : ' I wonder what she *does* think of ! I wonder ! ' He put his gloves and hat down in the outer hall and went into the lavatory, to dip his face in cool water and wash it with sweet-smelling soap— delicious revenge on the unclean atmosphere in which he had been stewing so many hours. He came out again into the hall dazed by soap and the mellowed light, and a voice from half-way up the stairs said : " Daddy ! Look ! " His little daughter was standing up there with one hand on the bannisters. She scrambled on to them and came sliding down, her frock up to her eyes, and her holland knickers to her middle. Mr. Bosengate said mildly :

" Well, that's elegant ! "

" Tea's in the summer-house. Mummy's waiting. Come on ! "

With her hand in his, Mr. Bosengate went on, through the drawing-room, long and cool, with sun-blinds down, through the billiard-room, high and cool, through the conservatory, green and sweet-smelling, out on to the terrace and the upper lawn. He had never felt such sheer exhilarated joy in his home surroundings, so cool, glistening and green under the July sun ; and he said :

" Well, Kit, what have you all been doing ? "

" I've fed my rabbits and Harry's ; and we've been

in the attic ; Harry got his leg through the sky-light.''

Mr. Bosengate drew in his breath with a hiss.

" It's all right, Daddy ; we got it out again, it's only grazed the skin. And we've been making swabs—I made seventeen, Mummy made thirty-three, and then she went to the hospital. Did you put many men in prison ? "

Mr. Bosengate cleared his throat. The question seemed to him untimely.

" Only two.''

" What's it like in prison, Daddy ? "

Mr. Bosengate, who had no more knowledge than his little daughter, replied in an absent voice :

" Not very nice.''

They were passing under a young oak tree, where the path wound round to the rosery and summer-house. Something shot down and clawed Mr. Bosengate's neck. His little daughter began to hop and suffocate with laughter.

" Oh, Daddy ! Aren't you caught ! I led you on purpose ! "

Looking up, Mr. Bosengate saw his small son lying along a low branch above him—like the leopard he was declaring himself to be (for fear of error), and thought blithely : ' What an active little chap it is ! '

" Let me drop on your shoulders, Daddy—like they do on the deer.''

" Oh, yes ! Do be a deer, Daddy ! "

Mr. Bosengate did not see being a deer ; his hair had just been brushed. But he entered the rosery buoyantly between his offspring. His wife was standing precisely as he had imagined her, in a pale blue frock open at the neck, with a narrow black band round the waist, and little accordion pleats below. She looked her coolest. Her smile, when she turned her head, hardly seemed to take Mr. Bosengate seriously enough. He placed his lips below one of her half-drooped eyelids. She even smelled of roses. His children began to dance round their mother, and Mr. Bosengate, firmly held between them, was also compelled to do this, until she said :

" When you've quite done, let's have tea ! "

It was not the greeting he had imagined coming along in the car. Earwigs were plentiful in the summer-house—used perhaps twice a year, but indispensable to every country residence—and Mr. Bosengate was not sorry for the excuse to get out again. Though all was so pleasant, he felt oddly restless, rather suffocated ; and lighting his pipe, began to move about among the roses, blowing tobacco at the greenfly ; in war-time one was never quite idle ! And suddenly he said :

" We're trying a wretched Tommy at the assizes."

His wife looked up from a rose.

" What for ? "

" Attempted suicide."

" Why did he ? "

" Can't stand the separation from his wife."

She looked at him, gave a low laugh, and said :

" Oh dear ! "

Mr. Bosengate was puzzled. Why did she laugh ? He looked round, saw that the children were gone, took his pipe from his mouth, and approached her.

" You look very pretty," he said. " Give me a kiss ! "

His wife bent her body forward from the waist, and pushed her lips out till they touched his moustache. Mr. Bosengate felt a sensation as if he had arisen from breakfast without having eaten marmalade. He mastered it, and said :

"That jury are a rum lot."

His wife's eyelids flickered. " I wish women sat on juries."

" Why ? "

" It would be an experience."

Not the first time she had used that curious expression ! Yet her life was far from dull, so far as he could see ; with the new interests created by the war, and the constant calls on her time made by the perfection of their home life, she had a useful and busy existence. Again the random thought passed through him : ' But she never tells me anything ! ' And suddenly that lugubrious khaki-clad figure started up among the rose bushes. "We've got a lot to be thankful for ! " he said abruptly. " I must go to work ! " His wife, raising one eyebrow, smiled. " And I to weep ! " Mr. Bosengate laughed—she had a pretty wit ! And stroking his comely moustache where it had been kissed, he moved out into the sunshine. All the evening, throughout his labours, not inconsiderable, for this jury business had put him behind time, he was afflicted by that restless pleasure in his surroundings ; would break off in mowing the lower lawn to look at the house through the trees ; would leave his study and committee papers, to cross into the drawing-room and sniff its dainty fragrance ; paid a special good-night visit to the children having supper in the schoolroom ; pottered in and out from his dressing room to admire his wife while she was changing for dinner ; dined with his mind perpetually on the next course ; talked volubly of the war ; and in the billiard room afterwards, smoking the pipe which had taken the place of his cigar, could not keep still, but roamed about, now in conservatory, now in the drawing-room, where his wife and the governess were still making swabs. It seemed to him that he could not have enough of anything. About eleven o'clock he strolled out—beautiful night, only just dark enough—under the new arrangement with Time—and went down to the little round fountain below the terrace. His wife was playing the piano. Mr. Bosengate looked at the water and the flat dark water-lily leaves which floated there ; looked up at the house, where only narrow chinks of light showed, because of the Lighting Order. The dreamy music drifted out ; there was a scent of heliotrope. He moved a few steps back, and sat in the children's swing under an old lime tree. Jolly—blissful—in the warm, bloomy dark ! Of all hours of the day, this before going to bed was perhaps the pleasantest. He saw the light go up in his wife's bedroom, unscreened for a full minute, and thought : ' Aha ! If I did my duty as a special, I should " strafe " her for that.' She came to the window, her figure lighted, hands up to the back of her head, so that her bare arms gleamed. Mr. Bosengate wafted her a kiss, knowing he could not be seen. ' Lucky chap ! ' he mused ; ' she's a great joy ! ' Up went her arm, down came the blind—the house was dark again. He drew a long breath. ' Another ten minutes,' he thought, ' then I'll go in and shut up. By Jove ! The limes are beginning to smell already ! ' And, the better to take in that acme of his well-being, he tilted the swing, lifted his feet from the ground, and swung himself toward the scented blossoms. He wanted to whelm his senses in their perfume, and closed his eyes. But instead of the domestic vision he expected, the face

of the little Welsh soldier, hare-eyed, shadowy, pinched
and dark and pitiful, started up with such disturbing
vividness that he opened his eyes again at once.
Curse ! The fellow almost haunted one ! Where would
he be now—poor little devil !—lying in his cell, thinking
—thinking of his wife ! Feeling suddenly morbid,
Mr. Bosengate arrested the swing and stood up.
Absurd !—all his well-being and mood of warm anticipation had deserted him ! ' A d——d world ! ' he
thought. ' Such a lot of misery ! Why should I have
to sit in judgment on that poor beggar, and condemn
him ? ' He moved up on to the terrace and walked
briskly, to rid himself of this disturbance before going
in. ' That commercial traveller chap,' he thought
' the rest of those fellows—they see nothing ! ' And,
abruptly turning up the three stone steps, he entered
the conservatory, locked it, passed into the billiard
room, and drank his barley water. One of the pictures
was hanging crooked ; he went up to put it straight.
Still life. Grapes and apples, and—lobsters ! They
struck him as odd for the first time. Why lobsters ?
The whole picture seemed dead and oily. He turned
off the light, and went upstairs, passed his wife's door,
into his own room, and undressed. Clothed in his
pyjamas he opened the door between the rooms. By
the light coming from his own he could see her dark
head on the pillow. Was she asleep ? No—not asleep,
certainly. The moment of fruition had come ; the
crowning of his pride and pleasure in his home. But he
continued to stand there. He had suddenly no pride,
no pleasure, no desire ; nothing but a sort of dull
resentment against everything. He turned back ;
shut the door, and slipping between the heavy curtains
and his open window, stood looking out at the night.

'Full of misery!' he thought. 'Full of d——d misery!'

II.

FILING into the jury box next morning, Mr. Bosengate collided slightly with a short juryman, whose square figure and square head of stiff yellow-red hair he had only vaguely noticed the day before. The man looked angry, and Mr. Bosengate thought: 'An ill-bred dog, that!'

He sat down quickly, and, to avoid further recognition of his fellows, gazed in front of him. His appearance on Saturdays was always military, by reason of the route march of his Volunteer Corps in the afternoon. Gentleman Fox, who belonged to the corps too, was also looking square; but that commercial traveller on his other side seemed more *louche*, and as if surprised in immorality, than ever; only the proximity of Gentleman Fox on the other side kept Mr. Bosengate from shrinking. Then he saw the prisoner being brought in, shadowy and dark behind the brightness of his buttons, and he experienced a sort of shock, this figure was so exactly that which had several times started up in his mind. Somehow he had expected a fresh sight of the fellow to dispel and disprove what had been haunting him, had expected to find him just an outside phenomenon, not, as it were, a part of his own life. And he gazed at the carven immobility of the judge's face, trying to steady himself, as a drunken man will, by looking at a light. The regimental doctor, unabashed by the judge's comment on his absence the day before, gave his evidence like a man who had better things to do, and the case for the prosecution was

T 2

forthwith rounded in by a little speech from counsel.
The matter—he said—was clear as daylight. Those
who wore His Majesty's uniform, charged with the
responsibility and privilege of defending their country,
were no more entitled to desert their regiments by
taking their own lives than they were entitled to desert
in any other way. He asked for a conviction. Mr.
Bosengate felt a sympathetic shuffle passing through
all feet; the judge was speaking:

" Prisoner, you can either go into the witness box
and make your statement on oath, in which case you
may be cross-examined on it; or you can make your
statement there from the dock, in which case you will
not be cross-examined. Which do you elect to do?"

" From here, my lord."

Seeing him now full face, and, as it might be, come
to life in the effort to convey his feelings, Mr. Bosengate
had suddenly a quite different impression of the fellow.
It was as if his khaki had fallen off, and he had stepped
out of his own shadow, a live and quivering creature.
His pinched clean-shaven face seemed to have an
irregular, wilder, hairier look, his large nervous brown
eyes darkened and glowed; he jerked his shoulders,
his arms, his whole body, like a man suddenly freed
from cramp or a suit of armour. He spoke, too,
in a quick, crisp, rather high voice, pinching his
consonants a little, sharpening his vowels, like a true
Welshman.

" My lord and misters the jury," he said: " I was
a hairdresser when the call came on me to join the
army. I had a little home and a wife. I never thought
what it would be like to be away from them, I surely
never did; and I'm ashamed to be speaking it out like
this—how it can squeeze and squeeze a man, how it

can prey on your mind, when you're nervous like I am.
'Tis not everyone that cares for his home—there's
lots o' them never wants to see their wives again. But
for me 'tis like being shut up in a cage, it is!" Mr.
Bosengate saw daylight between the skinny fingers of
the man's hand thrown out with a jerk. "I cannot
bear it shut up away from wife and home like what
you are in the army. So when I took my razor
that morning I was wild—an' I wouldn't be here
now but for that man catching my hand. There
was no reason in it, I'm willing to confess. It was
foolish; but wait till you get feeling like what I was,
and see how it draws you. Misters the jury, don't
send me back to prison; it is worse still there. If you
have wives you will know what it is like for lots of
us; only some is more nervous than others. I swear
to you, sirs, I could not help it——" Again the little
man flung out his hand, and his whole thin body shook.
Mr. Bosengate felt the same sensation as when he
drove his car over a dog—"Misters the jury, I
hope you may never in your lives feel as I've been
feeling."

The little man ceased, his eyes shrank back into
their sockets, his figure back into its mask of shadowy
brown and gleaming buttons, and Mr. Bosengate was
conscious that the judge was making a series of
remarks; and, very soon, of being seated at a mahogany
table in the jury's withdrawing room, hearing the voice
of the man with hair like an Irish terrier's saying:
"Didn't he talk through his hat, that little blighter!"
Conscious, too, of the commercial traveller, still on
his left—always on his left!—mopping his brow, and
muttering: "Phew! It's hot in there to-day!" while
an effluvium, as of an inside accustomed to whisky,

came from him. Then the man with the underlip and the three plastered wisps of hair said :

" Don't know why we withdrew, Mr. Foreman ! "

Mr. Bosengate looked round to where, at the head of the table, Gentleman Fox sat, in defensive gentility and the little white piping to his waistcoat. " I shall be happy to take the sense of the jury " ; he was saying blandly.

There was a short silence, then the chemist murmured :

" I should say he must have what they call claustrophobia."

" Clauster fiddlesticks ! The feller's a shirker, that's all. Missed his wife—pretty excuse ! Indecent, I call it ! "

The speaker was the little wire-haired man ; and emotion, deep and angry, stirred in Mr. Bosengate. That ill-bred little cur ! He gripped the edge of the table with both hands.

" I think it's d——d natural ! " he muttered. But almost before the words had left his lips he felt dismay. What had he said—he, nearly a colonel of volunteers— endorsing such a want of patriotism ! And hearing the commercial traveller murmuring : " 'Ear, 'ear ! " he reddened violently.

The wire-headed man said roughly :

" There's too many of these blighted shirkers, and too much pampering of them."

The turmoil in Mr. Bosengate increased ; he remarked in an icy voice :

" I agree to no verdict that'll send the man back to prison."

At this a real tremor seemed to go round the table, as if they all saw themselves sitting there through lunch time. Then the large grey-haired man given to winking, said :

" Oh ! Come, sir—after what the judge said ! Come, sir ! What do you say, Mr. Foreman ? "

Gentleman Fox—as who should say " This is excellent value, but I don't wish to press it on you ! "—answered :

" We are only concerned with the facts. Did he or did he not try to shorten his life ? "

" Of course he did—said so himself," Mr. Bosengate heard the wire-haired man snap out, and from the following murmur of assent he alone abstained. Guilty ! Well—yes ! There was no way out of admitting that, but his feelings revolted against handing " that poor little beggar " over to the tender mercy of his country's law. His whole soul rose in arms against agreeing with that ill-bred little cur, and the rest of this job-lot. He had an impulse to get up and walk out, saying : " Settle it your own way. Good-morning."

" It seems, sir," Gentleman Fox was saying, " that we're all agreed to guilty, except yourself. If you will allow me, I don't see how you can go behind what the prisoner himself admitted."

Thus brought up to the very guns, Mr. Bosengate, red in the face, thrust his hands deep into the side pocket of his tunic, and, staring straight before him, said :

" Very well ; on condition we recommend him to mercy."

" What do you say, gentlemen ; shall we recommend him to mercy ? "

" 'Ear, 'ear ! " burst from the commercial traveller, and from the chemist came the murmur :

" No harm in that."

" Well, I think there is. They shoot deserters at
the front, and we let this fellow off. I'd hang the cur."

Mr. Bosengate stared at that little wire-haired brute.
" Haven't you *any* feeling for others ? " he wanted to
say. " Can't you see that this poor devil suffers
tortures ? " But the sheer impossibility of doing this
before ten other men brought a slight sweat out on his
face and hands ; and in agitation he smote the table
a blow with his fist. The effect was instantaneous.
Everybody looked at the wire-haired man, as if saying :
" Yes, you've gone a bit too far there ! " The " little
brute " stood it for a moment, then muttered surlily :

" Well, commend 'im to mercy if you like ; I don't
care."

" That's right ; they never pay any attention to it,"
said the grey-haired man winking heartily. And
Mr. Bosengate filed back with the others into court.

But when from the jury box his eyes fell once more
on the hare-eyed figure in the dock, he had his worst
moment yet. Why should this poor wretch suffer so—
for no fault, no fault ; while he, and these others,
and that snapping counsel, and the Cæsar-like judge
up there, went off to their women and their homes,
blithe as bees, and probably never thought of him
again ? And suddenly he was conscious of the judge's
voice :

" You will go back to your regiment, and endeavour
to serve your country with better spirit. You may
thank the jury that you are not sent to prison, and your
good fortune that you were not at the front when you
tried to commit this cowardly act. You are lucky to
be alive."

A policeman pulled the little soldier by the arm ;

his drab figure with eyes fixed and lustreless, passed down and away. From his very soul Mr. Bosengate wanted to lean out and say : " Cheer up, cheer up ! *I* understand."

It was nearly ten o'clock that evening before he reached home, motoring back from the route march. His physical tiredness was abated, for he had partaken of a snack and a whisky and soda at the hotel ; but mentally he was in curious mood. His body felt appeased, his spirit hungry. To-night he had a yearning, not for his wife's kisses, but for her understanding. He wanted to go to her and say : ' I've learnt a lot to-day—found out things I never thought of. Life's a wonderful thing, Kate, a thing one can't live all to oneself ; a thing one shares with everybody, so that when another suffers, one suffers too. It's come to me that what one *has* doesn't matter a bit— it's what one does, and how one sympathises with other people. It came to me in the most extraordinary vivid way, when I was on that jury, watching that poor little rat of a soldier in his trap ; it's the first time I've ever felt—the—the spirit of Christ, you know. It's a wonderful thing, Kate—wonderful ! We haven't been close—really close, you and I, so that we each understand what the other is feeling. It's all in that, you know ; understanding—sympathy—it's priceless. When I saw that poor little devil taken down and sent back to his regiment to begin his sorrows all over again—wanting his wife, thinking and thinking of her just as you know I'd be thinking and wanting you, I felt what an awful outside sort of life we lead, never telling each other what we really think and feel, never being really close. I daresay that little chap and his wife keep nothing from each other—live each other's

lives. That's what *we* ought to do. Let's get to
feeling that what really matters is—understanding and
loving, and not only just saying it as we all do ; as
those fellows on the jury with me do, and even that
poor devil of a judge—what an awful life judging one's
fellow-creatures ! When I left that poor little Tommy
this morning, and ever since, I've longed to get back
here quietly to you and tell you about it, and make
a beginning. There's something wonderful in this,
and I want you to feel it as I do, because you mean such
a lot to me.'

This was what he wanted to say to his wife, not
touching, or kissing her, just looking into her eyes,
watching them soften and glow as they surely must,
catching the infection of his new ardour. And he felt
unsteady, fearfully unsteady with the desire to say it
all as it should be said : swiftly, quietly, with the truth
and fervour of his feeling.

The hall was not lit up, for daylight still lingered
under the new arrangement. He went towards the
drawing-room, but from the very door shied off to his
study and stood irresolute under the picture of a " Man
catching a flea " (Dutch school), which had come down
to him from his father. The governess would be in
there with his wife ! He must wait. Essential to go
straight to Kathleen and pour it all out, or he would
never do it. He felt as nervous as an undergraduate
going up for his *vivâ voce*. This thing was so big, so
astoundingly and unexpectedly important. He was
suddenly afraid of his wife, afraid of her coolness and
her grace, and that something Japanese about her—of
all those attributes he had been accustomed to admire
most ; afraid, as it were, of her attraction. He felt
young to-night, almost boyish ; would she see that he

was not really fifteen years older than herself, and she
not really a part of his collection, of all the admirable
appointments of his home ; but a companion spirit
to one who wanted a companion badly. In this
agitation of his soul he could keep still no more than
he could last night in the agitation of his senses ;
and he wandered into the dining-room. A dainty
supper was set out there, sandwiches, and cake, whisky
and the cigarettes—even an early peach. Mr. Bosengate looked at this peach with sorrow rather than
disgust. The perfection of it was of a piece with all
that had gone before this new and sudden feeling. Its
delicious bloom seemed to heighten his perception of
the hedge around him, that hedge of the things he so
enjoyed, carefully planted and tended these many
years. He passed it by uneaten, and went to the
window. Out there all was darkening, the fountain,
the lime tree, the flower-beds, and the fields below,
with the Jersey cows who would come to your call ;
darkening slowly, losing form, blurring into soft
blackness, vanishing, but there none the less—all
there—the hedge of his possessions. He heard the
door of the drawing-room open, the voices of his wife
and the governess in the hall, going up to bed. If only
they didn't look in here ! If only—— ! The voices
ceased. He was safe now—had but to follow in a few
minutes, to make sure of Kathleen alone. He turned
round and stared down the length of the dark dining-
room, over the rosewood table, to where in the mirror
above the sideboard at the far end, his figure bathed,
a stain, a mere blurred shadow ; he made his way down
to it along the table edge, and stood before himself
as close as he could get. His throat and the roof of
his mouth felt dry with nervousness ; he put out his

finger and touched his face in the glass. ' You're an
ass ! ' he thought. ' Pull yourself together, and get
it over. She will see ; of course she will ! ' He
swallowed, smoothed his moustache, and walked out.
Going up the stairs, his heart beat painfully ; but
he was in for it now, and marched straight into
her room.

Dressed only in a loose blue wrapper, she was
brushing her dark hair before the glass. Mr. Bosengate went up to her and stood there silent, looking
down. The words he had thought of were like a
swarm of bees buzzing in his head, yet not one would
fly from between his lips. His wife went on brushing
her hair under the light which shone on her polished
elbows. She looked up at him from beneath one lifted
eyebrow.

" Well, dear—tired ? "

With a sort of vehemence the single word " No "
passed out. A faint, a quizzical smile flitted over her
face ; she shrugged her shoulders ever so gently. That
gesture—he had seen it before ! And in desperate
desire to make her understand, he put his hand on her
lifted arm.

" Kathleen, stop—listen to me ! " His fingers
tightened in his agitation and eagerness to make his
great discovery known. But before he could get out
a word he became conscious of that cool round arm,
conscious of her eyes half-closed, sliding round at him,
of her half-smiling lips, of her neck under the wrapper.
And he stammered :

" I want—I must—Kathleen, I——"

She lifted her shoulders again in that little shrug.
" Yes—I know ; all right ! "

A wave of heat and shame, and of God-knows what

came over Mr. Bosengate; he fell on his knees and
pressed his forehead to her arm; and he was silent,
more silent than the grave. Nothing—nothing came
from him but two long sighs. Suddenly he felt her
hand stroke his cheek—compassionately, it seemed
to him. She made a little movement towards him;
her lips met his, and he remembered nothing but
that . . .

In his own room Mr. Bosengate sat at his wide-open
window, smoking a cigarette; there was no light.
Moths went past, the moon was creeping up. He sat
very calm, puffing the smoke out into the night air.
Curious thing—life! Curious world! Curious forces in
it—making one do the opposite of what one wished;
always—always making one do the opposite, it seemed!
The furtive light from that creeping moon was getting
hold of things down there, stealing in among the
boughs of the trees. 'There's something ironical,' he
thought, 'which walks about. Things don't come off
as you think they will. I meant, I tried—but one
doesn't change like that all of a sudden, it seems.
Fact, is, life's too big a thing for one! All the same, I'm
not the man I was yesterday—not quite!' He closed
his eyes, and in one of those flashes of vision which come
when the senses are at rest, he saw himself as it were
far down below—down on the floor of a street narrow
as a grave, high as a mountain, a deep dark slit of a
street—walking down there, a black midget of a fellow
among other black midgets—his wife, and the little
soldier, the judge, and those jury chaps—*fantoches*
straight up on their tiny feet, wandering down there in
that dark, infinitely tall, and narrow street. 'Too
much for one!' he thought; 'Too high for one—no
getting on top of it. We've got to be kind, and help

one another, and not expect too much, and not think too much. That's—all!' And, squeezing out his cigarette, he took six deep breaths of the night air, and got into bed.

1916.

INDIAN SUMMER OF A FORSYTE

"And summer's lease hath all too short a date."
SHAKESPEARE.

ON the last day of May in the early 'nineties, about
six o'clock of the evening, old Jolyon Forsyte sat under
the oak tree before the terrace of his house at Robin
Hill. He was waiting for the midges to bite him,
before abandoning the glory of the afternoon. His
thin brown hand, where blue veins stood out, held
the end of a cigar in its tapering, long-nailed fingers—
a pointed polished nail had survived with him from
those earlier Victorian days when to touch nothing,
even with the tips of the fingers, had been so distinguished. His domed forehead, great white moustache,
lean cheeks, and long lean jaw were covered from the
westering sunshine by an old brown Panama hat.
His legs were crossed ; in all his attitude was serenity
and a kind of elegance, as of an old man who every
morning put eau de Cologne upon his silk handkerchief.
At his feet lay a woolly black-and-white dog trying to
be a Pomeranian—the dog Balthasar between whom
and old Jolyon primal aversion had changed into
attachment with the years. Close to his chair was a
swing, and on the swing was seated one of Holly's
dolls—called ' Duffer Alice '—with her body fallen
over her legs and her doleful nose buried in a black
petticoat. She was never out of disgrace, so it did not
matter to her how she sat. Below the oak tree the
lawn dipped down a bank, stretched to the fernery,
and, beyond that refinement, became fields, dropping
to the pond, the coppice, and that prospect—' Fine,

remarkable '—at which Swithin Forsyte, from under
this very tree, had stared four years ago when he drove
down with Irene to look at the house. Old Jolyon had
heard of his brother's exploit—that drive which had
become quite celebrated on Forsyte 'Change.' Swithin !
And the fellow had gone and died, last November, at
the age of only seventy-nine, renewing the doubt
whether Forsytes could live for ever, which had first
arisen when Aunt Ann passed away. Died ! and left
only Jolyon and James, Roger and Nicholas and
Timothy—Julia and Hester ! And old Jolyon thought :
' Eighty-four ! I don't feel it—except when I get that
pain.'

His memory went searching. He had not felt his
age since he had bought his nephew Soames's ill-starred
house and settled into it here at Robin Hill nearly
three years ago. It was as if he had been getting
younger every spring, living in the country with his
son and his grandchildren—June, and the little ones
of the second marriage, Jolly and Holly ; living down
here out of the racket of London and the cackle of
Forsyte ' Change,' free of his Boards, in a delicious
atmosphere of no work and all play, with plenty of
occupation in the perfecting and mellowing of the house
and its twenty acres, and in ministering to the whims
of Holly and Jolly. All the knots and crankiness,
which had gathered in his heart during that long and
tragic business of June, Soames, Irene his wife, and
poor young Bosinney, had been smoothed out. Even
June had thrown off her melancholy at last—witness
this travel in Spain she was taking now with her father
and her step-mother. Curiously perfect peace was
left by their departure ; blissful, yet blank, because
his son was not there. Jo was never anything but a

comfort and a pleasure to him nowadays—an amiable chap ; but women, somehow—even the best—got a little on one's nerves, unless of course one admired them.

Far-off a cuckoo called ; a wood pigeon was cooing from the first elm tree in the field, and how the daisies and buttercups had sprung up after the last mowing ! The wind had got into the sou'-west, too—a delicious air, sappy ! He pushed his hat back and let the sun fall on his chin and cheek. Somehow, to-day, he wanted company—wanted a pretty face to look at. People treated the old as if they wanted nothing. And with the un-Forsytean philosophy which ever intruded on his soul, he thought : ' One's never had enough ! With a foot in the grave one'll want something, I shouldn't be surprised ! ' Down here—away from the exigencies of affairs—his grandchildren, and the flowers, trees, birds of his little domain, to say nothing of sun and moon and stars above them, said,' Open, sesame,' to him day and night. And sesame had opened—how much, perhaps, he did not know. He had always been responsive to what they had begun to call ' Nature,' genuinely, almost religiously responsive, though he had never lost his habit of calling a sunset a sunset and a view a view, however deeply they might move him. But nowadays Nature actually made him ache, he appreciated it so. Every one of these calm, bright, lengthening days, with Holly's hand in his, and the dog Balthasar in front looking studiously for what he never found, he would stroll, watching the roses open, fruit budding on the walls, sunlight brightening the oak leaves and saplings in the coppice, watching the water-lily leaves unfold and glisten, and the silvery young corn of the one wheatfield ; listening to the

starlings and skylarks, and the Alderney cows chewing
the cud, flicking slow their tufted tails ; and every one
of these fine days he ached a little from sheer love of
it all, feeling perhaps, deep down, that he had not very
much longer to enjoy it. The thought that some
day—perhaps not ten years hence, perhaps not five—
all this world would be taken away from him, before he
had exhausted his powers of loving it, seemed to him
in the nature of an injustice, brooding over his horizon.
If anything came after this life, it wouldn't be what
he wanted ; not Robin Hill, and flowers and birds
and pretty faces—too few, even now, of those about
him ! With the years his dislike of humbug had
increased ; the orthodoxy he had worn in the 'sixties,
as he had worn side-whiskers out of sheer exuberance,
had long dropped off, leaving him reverent before
three things alone—beauty, upright conduct, and the
sense of property ; and the greatest of these now was
beauty. He had always had wide interests, and, indeed
could still read *The Times*, but he was liable at any
moment to put it down if he heard a blackbird sing.
Upright conduct, property—somehow, they were
tiring ; the blackbirds and the sunsets never tired him,
only gave him an uneasy feeling that he could not get
enough of them. Staring into the stilly radiance of
the early evening and at the little gold and white
flowers on the lawn, a thought came to him : This
weather was like the music of 'Orfeo,' which he had
recently heard at Covent Garden. A beautiful opera,
not like Meyerbeer, nor even quite Mozart, but, in its
way, perhaps even more lovely ; something classical and
of the Golden Age about it, chaste and mellow, and the
Ravogli almost worthy of the old days ' —highest
praise he could bestow. The yearning of Orpheus

for the beauty he was losing, for his love going down to Hades, as in life love and beauty did go—the yearning which sang and throbbed through the golden music, stirred also in the lingering beauty of the world that evening. And with the tip of his cork-soled, elastic-sided boot he involuntarily stirred the ribs of the dog Balthasar, causing the animal to wake and attack his fleas ; for though he was supposed to have none, nothing could persuade him of the fact. When he had finished, he rubbed the place he had been scratching against his master's calf, and settled down again with his chin over the instep of the disturbing boot. And into old Jolyon's mind came a sudden recollection—a face he had seen at that opera three weeks ago—Irene, the wife of his precious nephew Soames, that man of property ! Though he had not met her since the day of the " At Home " in his old house at Stanhope Gate, which celebrated his grand-daughter June's ill-starred engagement to young Bosinney, he had remembered her at once, for he had always admired her—a very pretty creature. After the death of young Bosinney, whose mistress she had so reprehensibly become, he had heard that she had left Soames at once. Goodness only knew what she had been doing since. That sight of her face—a side-view—in the row in front, had been literally the only reminder these three years that she was still alive. No one ever spoke of her. And yet Jo had told him something once—something which had upset him completely. The boy had got it from George Forsyte, he believed, who had seen Bosinney in the fog the day he was run over—something which explained the young fellow's distress—an act of Soames towards his wife— a shocking act. Jo had seen her, too, that afternoon,

after the news was out, seen her for a moment, and
his description had always lingered in old Jolyon's
mind—' wild and lost ' he had called her. And next
day June had gone there—bottled up her feelings and
gone there, and the maid had cried and told her how
her mistress had slipped out in the night and vanished.
A tragic business altogether ! One thing was certain—
Soames had never been able to lay hands on her again.
And he was living at Brighton, and journeying up and
down—a fitting fate, the man of property ! For when
he once took a dislike to anyone—as he had to his
nephew—old Jolyon never got over it. He remembered still the sense of relief with which he had heard the
news of Irene's disappearance. It had been shocking
to think of her a prisoner in that house. to which she
must have wandered back, when Jo saw her, wandered
back for a moment—like a wounded animal to its hole
after seeing that news, ' Tragic death of an Architect,'
in the street. Her face had struck him very much the
other night—more beautiful than he had remembered,
but like a mask, with something going on beneath it.
A young woman still—twenty-eight perhaps. Ah,
well ! Very likely she had another lover by now. But
at this subversive thought—for married women should
never love, once, even, had been too much—his instep
rose, and with it the dog Balthasar's head. The
sagacious animal stood up and looked into old Jolyon's
face. " Walk ? " he seemed to say ; and old Jolyon
answered : " Come on, old chap ! "

Slowly, as was their wont, they crossed among the
constellations of buttercups and daises, and entered the
fernery. This feature, where very little grew as yet,
had been judiciously dropped below the level of the
lawn so that it might come up again on the level of

the other lawn and give the impression of irregularity, so important in horticulture. Its rocks and earth were beloved of the dog Balthasar, who sometimes found a mole there. Old Jolyon made a point of passing through it because, though it was not beautiful, he intended that it should be, some day, and he would think : ' I must get Varr to come down and look at it ; he's better than Beech.' For plants, like houses and human complaints, required the best expert consideration. It was inhabited by snails, and if accompanied by his grandchildren, he would point to one and tell them the story of the little boy who said : ' Have plummers got leggers, Mother ? ' ' No, sonny.' ' Then darned if I haven't been and swallowed a snileybob.' And when they skipped and clutched his hand, thinking of the snileybob going down the little boy's ' red lane,' his eyes would twinkle. Emerging from the fernery, he opened the wicket gate, which just there led into the first field, a large and park-like area, out of which, within brick walls, the vegetable garden had been carved. Old Jolyon avoided this, which did not suit his mood, and made down the hill towards the pond. Balthasar, who knew a water-rat or two, gambolled in front, at the gait which marks an oldish dog who takes the same walk every day. Arrived at the edge, old Jolyon stood, noting another water-lily opened since yesterday ; he would show it to Holly to-morrow, when ' his little sweet ' had got over the upset which had followed on her eating a tomato at lunch—her little arrangements were very delicate. Now that Jolly had gone to school—his first term—Holly was with him nearly all day long, an 1 he missed her badly. ♦ He felt that pain too, which often bothered him now, a little dragging at his left side.

He looked back up the hill. Really, poor young
Bosinney had made an uncommonly good job of the
house; he would have done very well for himself if he
had lived! And where was he now? Perhaps, still
haunting this, the site of his last work, of his tragic
love affair. Or was Philip Bosinney's spirit diffused
in the general? Who could say? That dog was getting
his legs muddy! And he moved towards the coppice.
There had been the most delightful lot of bluebells, and
he knew where some still lingered like little patches of
sky fallen in between the trees, away out of the sun.
He passed the cow- and hen-houses there installed, and
pursued a thin path into the thick of the saplings,
making for one of those bluebell plots. Balthasar,
preceding him once more, uttered a low growl. Old
Jolyon stirred him with his foot, but the dog remained
motionless, just where there was no room to pass, and
the hair rose slowly along the centre of his woolly back.
Whether from the growl and the look of the dog's
stivered hair, or from the sensation which a man feels
in a wood, old Jolyon also felt something move along
his spine. And then the path turned, and there was
an old mossy log, and on it a woman sitting. Her face
was turned away, and he had just time to think:
'She's trespassing—I must have a board put up!'
before she turned. Powers above! The face he had
seen at the opera—the very woman he had just been
thinking of! In that confused moment he saw things
blurred, as if a spirit—queer effect—the slant of
sunlight perhaps on her violet-grey frock! And then
she rose and stood smiling, her head a little to one side.
Old Jolyon thought: 'How pretty she is!' She did
not speak, neither did he; and he realised why with
a certain admiration. She was here no doubt because

of some memory, and did not mean to try and get out of it by vulgar explanation.

"Don't let that dog touch your frock," he said; "he's got wet feet. Come here, you!"

But the dog Balthasar went on towards the visitor, who put her hand down and stroked his head. Old Jolyon said quickly:

"I saw you at the opera the other night; you didn't notice me."

"Oh, yes! I did."

He felt a subtle flattery in that, as though she had added: "Do you think one could miss seeing you?"

"They're all in Spain," he remarked abruptly. "I'm alone; I drove up for the opera. The Ravogli's good. Have you seen the cow-houses?"

In a situation so charged with mystery and something very like emotion he moved instinctively towards that bit of property, and she moved beside him. Her figure swayed faintly, like the best kind of French figures; her dress, too, was a sort of French grey. He noticed two or three silver threads in her amber-coloured hair, strange hair with those dark eyes of hers, and that creamy-pale face. A sudden sidelong look from the velvety brown eyes disturbed him. It seemed to come from deep and far, from another world almost, or at all events from someone not living very much in this. And he said mechanically:

"Where are you living now?"

"I have a little flat in Chelsea."

He did not want to hear what she was doing, did not want to hear anything; but the perverse word came out:

"Alone?"

She nodded. It was a relief to know that. And it

came into his mind that, but for a twist of fate, she would have been mistress of this coppice, showing those cow-houses to him, a visitor.

"All Alderneys," he muttered; "they give the best milk. This one's a pretty creature. Woa, Myrtle!"

The fawn-coloured cow, with eyes as soft and brown as Irene's own, was standing absolutely still, not having long been milked. She looked round at them out of the corner of those lustrous, mild, cynical eyes, and from her grey lips a little dribble of saliva threaded its way towards the straw. The scent of hay and vanilla and ammonia rose in the dim light of the cool cow-house; and old Jolyon said:

"You must come up and have some dinner with me. I'll send you home in the carriage."

He perceived a struggle going on within her; natural, no doubt, with her memories. But he wanted her company; a pretty face, a charming figure, beauty! He had been alone all the afternoon. Perhaps his eyes were wistful, for she answered: "Thank you, Uncle Jolyon. I should like to."

He rubbed his hands, and said:

"Capital! Let's go up, then!" And, preceded by the dog Balthasar, they ascended through the field. The sun was almost level in their faces now, and he could see, not only those silver threads, but little lines, just deep enough to stamp her beauty with a coin-like fineness—the special look of life unshared with others. 'I'll take her in by the terrace,' he thought: 'I won't make a common visitor of her.'

"What do you do all day?" he said.

"Teach music; I have another interest, too."

"Work!" said old Jolyon, picking up the doll from

off the swing, and smoothing its black petticoat.
"Nothing like it, is there? I don't do any now. I'm
getting on. What interest is that?"

"Trying to help women who've come to grief." Old
Jolyon did not quite understand. "To grief?" he
repeated; then realised with a shock that she meant
exactly what he would have meant himself if he had
used that expression. Assisting the Magdalenes of
London! What a weird and terrifying interest!
And, curiosity overcoming his natural shrinking, he
asked:

"Why? What do you do for them?"

"Not much. I've no money to spare. I can only
give sympathy and food sometimes."

Involuntarily old Jolyon's hand sought his purse.
He said hastily: "How d'you get hold of them?"

"I go to a hospital."

"A hospital! Phew!"

"What hurts me most is that once they nearly all
had some sort of beauty."

Old Jolyon straightened the doll. "Beauty!" he
ejaculated: "Ha! Yes! A sad business!" and he
moved towards the house. Through a French window,
under sunblinds not yet drawn up, he preceded her into
the room where he was wont to study *The Times* and
the sheets of an agricultural magazine, with huge
illustrations of mangold wurzels, and the like, which
provided Holly with material for her paint brush.

"Dinner's in half an hour. You'd like to wash your
hands! I'll take you to June's room."

He saw her looking round eagerly; what changes
since she had last visited this house with her husband,
or her lover, or both perhaps—he did not know,
could not say! All that was dark, and he wished

to leave it so. But what changes! And in the hall he said : .

"My boy Jo's a painter, you know. He's got a lot of taste. It isn't mine, of course, but I've let him have his way."

She was standing very still, her eyes roaming through the hall and music room, as it now was—all thrown into one, under the great skylight. Old Jolyon had an odd impression of her. Was she trying to conjure somebody from the shades of that space where the colouring was all pearl-grey and silver ? He would have had gold himself ; more lively and solid. But Jo had French tastes, and it had come out shadowy like that, with an effect as of the fume of cigarettes the chap was always smoking, broken here and there by a little blaze of blue or crimson colour. It was not *his* dream ! Mentally he had hung this space with those gold-framed masterpieces of still and stiller life which he had bought in days when quantity was precious. And now where were they ? Sold for a song ! For that something which made him, alone among Forsytes, move with the times had warned him against the struggle to retain them. But in his study he still had ' Dutch Fishing Boats at Sunset.'

He began to mount the stairs with her, slowly, for he felt his side.

"These are the bathrooms," he said, "and other arrangements. I've had them tiled. The nurseries are along there. And this is Jo's and his wife's. They all communicate. But you remember, I expect."

Irene nodded. They passed on, up the gallery and entered a large room with a small bed, and several windows.

"This is mine," he said. The walls were covered

with the photographs of children, and water-colour sketches, and he added doubtfully :

" These are Jo's. The view's first-rate. You can see the Grand Stand at Epsom in clear weather."

The sun was down now, behind the house, and over the ' prospect ' a luminous haze had settled, emanation of the long and prosperous day. Few houses showed, but fields and trees faintly glistened, away to a loom of downs.

" The country's changing," he said abruptly, " but there it'll be when we're all gone. Look at those thrushes—the birds are sweet here in the mornings. I'm glad to have washed my hands of London."

Her face was close to the window pane, and he was struck by its mournful look. ' Wish I could make her look happy ! ' he thought. ' A pretty face, but sad ! ' And taking up his can of hot water he went out into the gallery.

" This is June's room," he said, opening the next door and putting the can down ; " I think you'll find everything." And closing the door behind her he went back to his own room. Brushing his hair with his great ebony brushes, and dabbing his forehead with eau de Cologne, he mused. She had come so strangely —a sort of visitation, mysterious, even romantic, as if his desire for company, for beauty, had been fulfilled by—whatever it was which fulfilled that sort of thing. And before the mirror he straightened his still upright figure, passed the brushes over his great white moustache, touched up his eyebrows with eau de Cologne, and rang the bell.

" I forgot to let them know that I have a lady to dinner with me. Let cook do something extra, and tell Beacon to have the landau and pair at half-past

ten to drive her back to Town to-night. Is Miss Holly
asleep ? ''

The maid thought not. And old Jolyon, passing
down the gallery, stole on tiptoe towards the nursery,
and opened the door whose hinges he kept specially
oiled that he might slip in and out in the evenings
without being heard.

But Holly *was* asleep, and lay like a miniature
Madonna, of that type which the old painters could
not tell from Venus, when they had completed her.
Her long dark lashes clung to her cheeks ; on her face
was perfect peace—her little arrangements were
evidently all right again. And old Jolyon, in the
twilight of the room, stood adoring her ! It was so
charming, solemn, and loving—that little face. He
had more than his share of the blessed capacity of
living again in the young. They were to him his
future life—all of a future life that his fundamental
pagan sanity perhaps admitted. There she was with
everything before her, and his blood—some of it—in
her tiny veins. There she was, his little companion,
to be made as happy as ever he could make her, so
that she knew nothing but love. His heart swelled,
and he went out, stifling the sound of his patent leather
boots. In the corridor an eccentric notion attacked
him : To think that children should come to that which
Irene had told him she was helping ! Women who were
all, once, little things like this one sleeping there !
' I must give her a cheque ! ' he mused ; ' can't bear
to think of them ! ' They had never borne reflecting
on, those poor outcasts ; wounding too deeply the core
of true refinement hidden under layers of conformity
to the sense of property—wounding too grievously the
deepest thing in him—a love of beauty which could give

him, even now, a flutter of the heart, thinking of his
evening in the society of a pretty woman.   And he
went downstairs, through the swing-doors, to the back
regions.   There, in the wine-cellar, was a hock worth
at least two pounds a bottle, a Steinberg Cabinet,
better than any Johannisberg that ever went down
throat ; a wine of perfect bouquet, sweet as a nectarine
—nectar indeed ! He got a bottle out, handling it like
a baby, and holding it level to the light, to look.
Enshrined in its coat of dust, that mellow-coloured,
slender-necked bottle gave him deep pleasure.   Three
years to settle down again since the move from Town—
ought to be in prime condition ! Thirty-five years ago
he had bought it—thank God he had kept his palate,
and earned the right to drink it.   She would appreciate
this ; not a spice of acidity in a dozen.   He wiped the
bottle, drew the cork with his own hands, put his nose
down, inhaled its perfume, and went back to the
music room.

Irene was standing by the piano ; she had taken off
her hat and a lace scarf she had been wearing, so that
her amber-coloured hair was visible, and the pallor of
her neck.   In her grey frock she made a pretty picture
for old Jolyon, against the rosewood of the piano.

He gave her his arm, and solemnly they went.   The
room, which had been designed to enable twenty-four
people to dine in comfort, held now but a little round
table.   In his present solitude the big dining-table
oppressed old Jolyon ; he had caused it to be removed
till his son came back.   Here in the company of two
really good copies of Raphael Madonnas he was wont to
dine alone.   It was the only disconsolate hour of his
day, this summer weather.   He had never been a large
eater, like that great chap Swithin, or Sylvanus

Heythorp, or Anthony Thornworthy, those cronies of
past times; and to dine alone, overlooked by the
Madonnas, was to him but a sorrowful occupation,
which he got through quickly, that he might come to
the more spiritual enjoyment of his coffee and cigar.
But this evening was a different matter! His eyes
twinkled at her across the little table, and he spoke of
Italy and Switzerland, telling her stories of his travels
there, and other experiences which he could no longer
recount to his son and grand-daughter because they
knew them. This fresh audience was precious to him;
he had never become one of those old men who
ramble round and round the fields of reminiscence.
Himself quickly fatigued by the insensitive, he instinctively avoided fatiguing others, and his natural
flirtatiousness towards beauty guarded him specially
in his relations with a woman. He would have liked
to draw her out, but though she murmured and smiled
and seemed to be enjoying what he told her, he
remained conscious of that mysterious remoteness
which constituted half her fascination. He could not
bear women who threw their shoulders and eyes at
you, and chattered away; or hard-mouthed women
who laid down the law and knew more than you did.
There was only one quality in a woman that appealed
to him—charm; and the quieter it was, the more he
liked it. And this one had charm, shadowy as afternoon sunlight on those Italian hills and valleys he had
loved. The feeling, too, that she was, as it were, apart,
cloistered, made her seem nearer to himself, a strangely
desirable companion. When a man is very old and
quite out of the running, he loves to feel secure from
the rivalries of youth, for he would still be first in the
heart of beauty. And he drank his hock, and watched

her lips, and felt nearly young. But the dog Balthasar lay watching her lips too, and despising in his heart the interruptions of their talk, and the tilting of those greenish glasses full of a golden fluid which was distasteful to him.

The light was just failing when they went back into the music room. And, cigar in mouth, old Jolyon said :

" Play me some Chopin."

By the cigars they smoke, and the composers they love, ye shall know the texture of men souls. Old Jolyon could not bear a strong cigar or Wagner's music. He loved Beethoven and Mozart, Handel and Gluck, and Schumann, and, for some occult reason, the operas of Meyerbeer ; but of late years he had been seduced by Chopin, just as in painting he had succumbed to Botticelli. In yielding to these tastes he had been conscious of divergence from the standard of the Golden Age. Their poetry was not that of Milton and Byron and Tennyson ; of Raphael and Titian ; Mozart and Beethoven. It was, as it were, behind a veil ; their poetry hit no one in the face, but slipped its fingers under the ribs and turned and twisted, and melted up the heart. And, never certain that this was healthy, he did not care a rap so long as he could see the pictures of the one or hear the music of the other.

Irene sat down at the piano under the electric lamp festooned with pearl-grey, and old Jolyon, in an armchair, whence he could see her, crossed his legs and drew slowly at his cigar. She sat a few moments with her hands on the keys, evidently searching her mind for what to give him. Then she began, and within old Jolyon there arose a sorrowful pleasure, not quite like anything else in the world. He fell slowly into a trance, interrupted only by the movement of his hand taking the cigar out of his mouth at long intervals, and replacing it. She was there, and the hock within him, and the scent of tobacco ; but there, too, was a world of sunshine lingering into moonlight, and pools with storks upon them, and bluish trees above, glowing with blurs of wine-red roses, and fields of lavender where milk-white cows were grazing, and a woman all shadowy, with dark eyes and a white neck, smiled, holding out her arms ; and through air which was like music a star dropped, and was caught on a cow's horn. He opened his eyes. Beautiful piece ; she played well —the touch of an angel ! And he closed them again. He felt miraculously sad and happy, as one does, standing under a lime tree in full honey flower. Not live one's own life again, but just stand there and bask in the smile of a woman's eyes, and enjoy the bouquet ! And he jerked his hand ; the dog Balthasar had reached up and licked it.

"Beautiful ! " he said : " Go on—more Chopin ! "

She began to play again. This time the resemblance between her and ' Chopin ' struck him. The swaying he had noticed in her walk was in her playing too, and the Nocturne she had chosen, and the soft darkness of her eyes, the light on her hair, as of moonlight from a golden moon. Seductive, yes ; but nothing of Delilah in her or in that music. A long blue spiral from his cigar ascended and dispersed. ' So we go out ! ' he thought. ' No more beauty ! Nothing ? '

Again Irene stopped.

"Would you like some Gluck ? " she said. " He used to write his music in a sunlit garden, with a bottle of Rhine wine beside him."

" Ah ! yes. Let's have ' Orfeo.' " And off he went
once more. Round about him now were fields of gold
and silver flowers, white forms swaying in the sunlight,
bright birds flying to and fro. It was all summer.
Lingering waves of sweetness and regret flooded his
soul. Some cigar ash dropped, and taking out a silk
handkerchief to brush it off, he inhaled a mingled scent
as of snuff and eau de Cologne. ' Ah ! ' he thought,
' Indian summer—that's all ! ' And he said : " You
haven't played me ' Che faro.' "

She did not answer ; did not move. He was
conscious of something—some strange upset.
Suddenly he saw her rise and turn away, and a pang
of remorse shot through him. What a fool ! What a
clumsy chap ! Like Orpheus, she of course—she too
was looking for her lost one in this hall of memory !
And, disturbed to the heart, he got up from his chair.
She had gone to the great window at the far end.
Gingerly he followed. Her hands were folded over her
breast ; he could just see her cheek, very white. And,
quite emotionalised, he said : " There, there, my
love ! " The words had escaped him mechanically, for
they were those he used to Holly when she had a pain,
but their effect was instantaneously distressing. She
raised her arms, covered her face with them, and wept.

Old Jolyon stood gazing at her with eyes very deep
from age. The passionate shame she seemed feeling
at her abandonment, so unlike the control and quietude
of her whole presence, was as if she had never before
broken down in the presence of another being.

" There, there—there, there ! " he murmured ; and
putting his hand out reverently, touched her. She
turned, and leaned the arms which covered her face
against him. Old Jolyon stood very still, keeping one

thin hand on her shoulder. Poor thing ! Let her cry
her heart out—it would do her good ! And the dog
Balthasar, puzzled, sat down on his stern to examine
them.

The window was still open, the curtains had not been
drawn, the last of daylight from without mingled with
faint intrusion from the lamp within ; there was a
scent of new-mown grass. With the wisdom of a long
life, old Jolyon did not speak. Even grief sobs itself
out in time ; only Time is good for sorrow—Time who
sees the passing of each mood, each emotion in turn ;
Time the layer-to-rest. The old know that. There
came into his mind the words : ' As panteth the hart
after cooling streams '—but they were of no use to
him. Then he was conscious of a scent of violets, and
knew she was drying her eyes. He put his chin forward,
pressed his moustache against her forehead, and felt
her shake with a quivering of her whole body, as of a
tree which shakes itself free of raindrops. She put his
hand to her lips, as if saying : ' All over now ! Forgive
me ! '   .

The kiss filled him with strange comfort ; he led her
back to where she had been so upset. And the dog
Balthasar, following, laid the bone of one of the cutlets
they had eaten at their feet.

Anxious to obliterate the memory of that emotion,
he could think of nothing better than to exhibit china ;
and moving with her slowly from cabinet to cabinet,
he kept taking up bits of Dresden and Lowestoft and
Chelsea, turning them round and round with his thin,
veined hands, whose skin, faintly freckled, had such
an aged look.

" I bought this at Jobson's," he would say ; " cost
me thirty pounds. It's very old. That dog leaves

his bones all over the place. This old 'ship-bowl' I picked up at the sale when that precious rip, the Marquis, came to grief. But you don't remember. Here's a nice piece of Chelsea. Now, what would you say *this* was ? " And he was comforted, feeling that, with her taste, she was taking a real interest in these things ; for, after all, there is nothing more composing to the nerves than a doubtful piece of china.

When the crunch of the carriage wheels was heard at last, he said :

" You must come again ; you must come to lunch, then I can show you these by daylight, and my little sweet—she's a dear little thing. This dog seems to have taken a fancy to you."

For Balthasar, feeling that she was about to leave, was rubbing his side against her leg. Going out under the porch with her, he said :

" He'll get you up in an hour and a quarter. Take this for your *protegées*," and he slipped a cheque for fifty pounds into her hand. He saw her brightened eyes, and heard her murmur : "Oh ! Uncle Jolyon ! " and a real throb of pleasure went through him. That meant one or two poor creatures helped a little, and it meant that she would come again. He put his hand in at the window and grasped hers once more. The carriage rolled away. He stood looking at the moon and the shadows of the trees, and thought : " It's a sweet night ! She——! "

II

Two days of rain, and summer set in bland and sunny. Old Jolyon walked and talked with Holly. At first he felt taller and full of a new vigour ; then he

felt restless. Almost every afternoon they would enter
the coppice, and walk as far as the log. ' Well, she's
not there ! ' he would think, ' of course not ! ' And he
would feel a little shorter, and drag his feet walking
up the hill home, with his hand clapped to his left side.
Now and then the thought would move in him : ' Did
she come—or did I dream it ? ' and he would stare
at space, while the dog Balthasar stared at him. Of
course she would not come again ! He opened the
letters from Spain with less excitement. They were
not returning till July ; he felt, oddly, that he could
bear it. Every day at dinner he screwed up his eyes
and looked at where she had sat. She was not there,
so he unscrewed his eyes again.

On the seventh afternoon he thought : ' I must go
up and get some boots.' He ordered Beacon, and
set out. Passing from Putney towards Hyde Park he
reflected : ' I might as well go to Chelsea and see
her.' And he called out : " Just drive me to where
you took that lady the other night." The coachman
turned his broad red face, and his juicy lips answered :
" The lady in grey, sir ? "

" Yes, the lady in grey." What other ladies were
there ! Stodgy chap !

The carriage stopped before a small three-storied
block of flats, standing a little back from the river.
With a practised eye old Jolyon saw that they were
cheap. ' I should think about sixty pound a year,'
he mused ; and, entering, he looked at the name-board.
The name ' Forsyte ' was not on it, but against
' First Floor, Flat C ' were the words : ' Mrs. Irene
Heron.' Ah ! She had taken her maiden name
again ! And somehow this pleased him. He went
upstairs slowly, feeling his side a little. He stood a

moment, before ringing, to lose the feeling of drag and fluttering there. She would not be in ! And then— Boots ! The thought was black. What did he want with boots at his age ? He could not wear out all those he had.

" Your mistress at home ? "

" Yes, sir."

" Say Mr. Jolyon Forsyte."

" Yes, sir, will you come this way ? "

Old Jolyon followed a very little maid—not more than sixteen one would say—into a still smaller drawing-room where the sunblinds were drawn. It held a cottage piano and little else save a vague fragrance and good taste. He stood in the middle, with his top hat in his hand, and thought : ' I expect she's very badly off ! ' There was a mirror above the fireplace, and he saw himself reflected. An old-looking chap ! He heard a rustle, and turned round. She was so close that his moustache almost brushed her forehead, just under the threads of silver in her hair.

" I was driving up," he said. " Thought I'd look in on you, and ask you how you got up the other night."

And, seeing her smile, he felt suddenly relieved. She was really glad to see him, perhaps.

" Would you like to put on your hat and come for a drive in the Park ? "

But while she was gone to put her hat on, he frowned. The Park ! James and Emily ! Mrs. Nicholas, or some other member of his precious family would be there very likely, prancing up and down. And they would go and wag their tongues about having seen him with her, afterwards. Better not ! He did not wish to revive the echoes of the past on Forsyte 'Change.

He removed a white hair from the lapel of his closely
buttoned-up frock coat, and passed his hand over his
cheeks, moustaches, and square chin. It felt very
hollow there under the cheekbones. He had not been
eating much lately—he had better get that little
whippersnapper who attended Holly to give him a
tonic. But she had come back and when they were
in the carriage, he said :

"Suppose we go and sit in Kensington Gardens
instead ? " and added with a twinkle : " No prancing
up and down there," as if she had been in the secret of
his thoughts.

Leaving the carriage, they entered those select
precincts, and strolled towards the water.

"You've gone back to your maiden name, I see,"
he said : " I'm not sorry."

She slipped her hand under his arm : " Has June
forgiven me, Uncle Jolyon ? "

He answered gently : " Yes—yes ; of course, why
not ? "

"And have you ? "

"I ? I forgave you as soon as I saw how the land
really lay." And perhaps he had ; his instinct had
always been to forgive the beautiful.

She drew a deep breath. " I never regretted—I
couldn't. Did you ever love very deeply, Uncle
Jolyon? "

At that strange question old Jolyon stared before
him. Had he ? He did not seem to remember that
he ever had. But he did not like to say this to the
young woman whose hand was touching his arm, whose
life was suspended, as it were, by memory of a tragic
love. And he thought : ' If I had met *you* when I
was young, I—I might have made a fool of myself,

perhaps.' And a longing to escape in generalities
beset him.

" Love's a queer thing," he said, " fatal thing often.
It was the Greeks, wasn't it ? made love into a
goddess ; they were right, I dare say, but then they
lived in the Golden Age."

" Phil adored them."

Phil ! The word jarred him, for suddenly—with his
power to see all round a thing, he perceived why
she was putting up with him like this. She wanted
to talk about her lover ! Well ! If it was any pleasure
to her ! And he said : " Ah ! There was a bit of the
sculptor in him, I fancy."

" Yes. He loved balance and symmetry ; he loved
the whole-hearted way the Greeks gave themselves to
art."

Balance ! The chap had no balance at all, if he
remembered ; as for symmetry—clean-built enough
he was, no doubt ; but those queer eyes of his, and high
cheek-bones—Symmetry ?

" You're of the Golden Age, too, Uncle Jolyon."

Old Jolyon looked round at her. Was she chaffing
him ? No, her eyes were soft as velvet. Was she
flattering him ? But if so, why ? There was nothing
to be had out of an old chap like him.

" Phil thought so. He used to say : ' But I can
never tell him that I admire him.' "

Ah ! There it was again. Her dead lover ; her
desire to talk of him ! And he pressed her arm, half
resentful of those memories, half grateful, as if he recognised what a link they were between herself and him.

" He was a very talented young fellow," he murmured. " It's hot ; I feel the heat nowadays. Let's
sit down."

They took two chairs beneath a chestnut tree whose broad leaves covered them from the peaceful glory of the afternoon. A pleasure to sit there and watch her, and feel that she liked to be with him. And the wish to increase that liking, if he could, made him go on :

" I expect he showed you a side of him I never saw. He'd be at his best with you. His ideas of art were a little new—to me "—he had stifled the word ' fangled.'

" Yes : but he used to say you had a real sense of beauty." Old Jolyon thought : ' The devil he did ! ' but answered with a twinkle : " Well, I have, or I shouldn't be sitting here with you." She was fascinating when she smiled with her eyes, like that !

" He thought you had one of those hearts that never grow old. Phil had real insight."

He was not taken in by this flattery spoken out of the past, out of a longing to talk of her dead lover—not a bit ; and yet it was precious to hear, because she pleased his eyes and a heart which—quite true !—had never grown old. Was that because—unlike her and her dead lover, he had never loved to desperation, had always kept his balance, his sense of symmetry. Well ! It had left him the power, at eighty-four, to admire beauty. And he thought, ' If I were a painter or a sculptor ! But I'm an old chap. Make hay while the sun shines.'

A couple with arms entwined crossed on the grass before them, at the edge of the shadow from their tree. The sunlight fell cruelly on their pale, squashed, unkempt young faces. " We're an ugly lot ! " said old Jolyon suddenly. " It amazes me to see how—love triumphs over that."

" Love triumphs over everything ! "

" The young think so," he muttered.

" Love has no age, no limit, and no death."

With that glow in her pale face, her breast heaving, her eyes so large and dark and soft, she looked like Venus come to life ! But this extravagance brought instant reaction, and, twinkling, he said : " Well, if it had limits, we shouldn't be born ; for by George ! it's got a lot to put up with."

Then, removing his top-hat, he brushed it round with a cuff. The great clumsy thing heated his forehead ; in these days he often got a rush of blood to the head—his circulation was not what it had been.

She still sat gazing straight out before her, and suddenly she murmured :

" It's strange enough that *I'm* alive."

Those words of Jo's ' Wild and lost ' came back to him.

" Ah ! " he said : " my son saw you for a moment—that day."

" Was it your son ? I heard a voice in the hall ; I thought for a second it was—Phil."

Old Jolyon saw her lips tremble. She put her hand over them, took it away again, and went on calmly : " That night I went to the Embankment ; a woman caught me by the dress. She told me about herself. When one knows what others suffer, one's ashamed."

" One of *those* ? "

She nodded, and horror stirred within old Jolyon, the horror of one who has never known a struggle with desperation. Almost against his will he muttered : " Tell me, won't you ? "

" I didn't care whether I lived or died. When you're like that, Fate ceases to want to kill you. She took care of me three days—she never left me. I had no money. That's why I do what I can for them, now."

But old Jolyon was thinking : ' No money ! '
What fate could compare with that ? Every other
was involved in it.

" I wish you had come to me," he said. " Why
didn't you ? " Irene did not answer.

" Because my name was Forsyte, I suppose ? Or
was it June who kept you away ? How are you getting
on now ? " His eyes involuntarily swept her body.
Perhaps even now she was——! And yet she wasn't
thin—not really !

" Oh ! I make just enough." The answer did not
reassure him ; he had lost confidence. And that fellow
Soames ! But his sense of justice stifled condemnation.
No, she would certainly have died rather than take
another penny from *him*. Soft as she looked, there
must be strength in her somewhere—strength and
fidelity. But what business had young Bosinney to
have got run over and left her stranded like this !

" Well, you must come to me now," he said, " for
anything you want, or I shall be quite cut up." And
putting on his hat, he rose. " Let's go and get some
tea. I told that lazy chap to put the horses up for
an hour, and come for me at your place. We'll take
a cab presently ; I can't walk as I used to."

· He enjoyed that stroll to the Kensington end of the
gardens—the sound of her voice, the glancing of her
eyes, the subtle beauty of a charming form moving
beside him. He enjoyed their tea at Ruffel's in the
High Street, and came out thence with a great box of
chocolates swung on his little finger. He enjoyed the
drive back to Chelsea in a hansom, smoking his cigar.
She had promised to come down next Sunday and play
to him again, and already in thought he was plucking
carnations and early roses for her to carry back to

town. It was a pleasure to give her a little pleasure, if it *were* pleasure from an old chap like him! The carriage was already there when they arrived. Just like that fellow, who was always late when he was wanted! Old Jolyon went in for a minute to say good-bye. The little dark hall of the flat was impregnated with a disagreeable odour of patchouli, and on a bench against the wall—its only furniture—he saw a figure sitting. He heard Irene say softly: "Just one minute." In the little drawing-room when the door was shut, he asked gravely: "One of your *protegées?*"

"Yes. Now, thanks to you, I can do something for her."

He stood, staring, and stroking that chin whose strength had frightened so many in its time. The idea of her thus actually in contact with this outcast, grieved and frightened him. What could she do for them? Nothing. Only soil and make trouble for herself, perhaps. And he said: "Take care, my dear! The world puts the worst construction on everything."

"I know that."

He was abashed by her quiet smile. "Well then—Sunday," he murmured: "Good-bye."

She put her cheek forward for him to kiss.

"Good-bye," he said again; "take care of yourself." And he went out, not looking towards the figure on the bench. He drove home by way of Hammersmith, that he might stop at a place he knew of and tell them to send her in two dozen of their best Burgundy. She must want picking-up sometimes! Only in Richmond Park did he remember that he had gone up to order himself some boots, and was surprised that he could have had so paltry an idea.

III

THE little spirits of the past which throng an old man's days had never pushed their faces up to his so seldom as in the seventy hours elapsing before Sunday came. The spirit of the future, with the charm of the unknown, put up her lips instead. Old Jolyon was not restless now, and paid no visits to the log, because she was *coming to lunch*. There is wonderful finality about a meal ; it removes a world of doubts, for no one misses meals except for reasons beyond control. He played many games with Holly on the lawn, pitching them up to her who was batting so as to be ready to bowl to Jolly in the holidays. For she was not a Forsyte, but Jolly was—and Forsytes always bat, until they have resigned and reached the age of eighty-four. The dog Balthasar, in attendance, lay on the ball as often as he could, and the page-boy fielded, with a face which was like the harvest moon. And because the time was getting shorter, each day was longer and more golden than the last. On Friday night he took a liver pill, his side hurt him rather, and though it was not the liver side, there is no remedy like that. Anyone telling him that he had found a new excitement in life and that excitement was not good for him, would have been met by one of those steady and rather defiant looks of his deep-set iron-grey eyes, which seemed to say : 'I know my own business best.' He always had and always would.

On Sunday morning, when Holly had gone with her governess to church, he visited the strawberry beds. There, accompanied by the dog Balthasar, he examined the plants narrowly and succeeded in finding at least two dozen berries which were really ripe. Stooping was

not good for him, and he became very dizzy and red in
the forehead. Having placed the strawberries in a
dish on the dining-table, he washed his hands and
bathed his forehead with eau de Cologne. There, before
the mirror, it occurred to him that he was thinner.
What a 'threadpaper' he had been when he was
young ! It was nice to be slim—he could not bear a
fat chap ; and yet perhaps his cheeks were *too* thin !
She was to arrive by train at half-past twelve and
walk up, entering from the road past Drage's farm at
the far end of the coppice. And, having looked into
June's room to see that there was hot water ready, he
set forth to meet her, leisurely, for his heart was
beating. The air smelled sweet, larks sang, and the
Grand Stand at Epsom was visible. A perfect day !
On just such a one, no doubt, five years ago, Soames
had brought young Bosinney down with him to look
at the site before they began to build. It was Bosinney
who had pitched on the exact spot for the house—as
June had often told him. In these days he was
thinking much about that young fellow, as if his spirit
were really haunting the field of his last work, on the
chance of seeing—her. Bosinney—the one man who
had possessed her heart, to whom she had given her
whole self with rapture ! At his age one could not, of
course, imagine such things, but there stirred in him
a queer vague aching—as it were the ghost of an
impersonal jealousy ; and a feeling too, more generous,
of pity for that love so early lost. All over in a few
poor months ! Well, well ! He looked at his watch
before entering the coppice—only a quarter past,
twenty-five minutes to wait ! And then, turning the
corner of the path, he saw her exactly where he had
seen her the first time, on the log ; and realised that

she must have come by the earlier train to sit there
alone for a couple of hours at least.   Two hours of her
society—missed ! What memory could make that log
so dear to her ? His face showed what he was thinking,
for she said at once ·

" Forgive me, Uncle Jolyon ; it was here that I first
knew."

" Yes, yes ; there it is for you whenever you like.
You're looking a little Londony ; you're giving too
many lessons."

That she should have to give lessons worried him.
Lessons to a parcel of young girls thumping out scales
with their thick fingers !

" Where do you go to give them ? " he asked.

" They're mostly Jewish families, luckily."

Old Jolyon stared ; to all Forsytes Jews seem
strange, and doubtful.

" They love music, and they're very kind."

" They had better be, by George ! " He took her
arm—his side always hurt him a little going uphill—
and said :

" Did you ever see anything like those buttercups ?
They came like that in a night."

Her eyes seemed really to fly over the field, like
bees after the flowers and the honey.   " I wanted you
to see them—wouldn't let them turn the cows in yet."
Then, remembering that she had come to talk about
Bosinney, he pointed to the clock-tower over the
stables :

" I expect *he* wouldn't have let me put that there—
had no notion of time, if I remember."

But, pressing his arm to her, she talked of flowers
instead, and he knew it was done that he might not
feel she came because of her dead lover.

" The best flower I can show you," he said, with a sort of triumph, " is my little sweet. She'll be back from Church directly. There's something about her which reminds me a little of you," and it did not seem to him peculiar that he had put it thus, instead of saying : ' There's something about you which reminds me a little of her.' Ah ! And here she was !

Holly, followed closely by her elderly French governess, whose digestion had been ruined twenty-two years ago in the siege of Strasburg, came rushing towards them from under the oak tree. She stopped about a dozen yards away, to pat Balthasar and pretend that this was all she had in her mind. Old Jolyon who knew better, said :

" Well, my darling, here's the lady in grey I promised you."

Holly raised herself and looked up. He watched the two of them with a twinkle, Irene smiling, Holly beginning with grave inquiry, passing to a shy smile too, and then to something deeper. She had a sense of beauty, that child—knew what was what ! He enjoyed the sight of the kiss between them.

" Mrs. Heron, Mam'zelle Beauce. Well, Mam'zelle— good sermon ? "

For, now that he had not much more time before him, the only part of the service connected with this world absorbed what interest in church remained to him. Mam'zelle Beauce stretched out a spidery hand clad in a black kid glove—she had been in the best families— and the rather sad eyes of her lean yellowish face seemed to ask : " Are you well-brrred ? " Whenever Holly or Jolly did anything unpleasing to her—a not uncommon occurrence—she would say to them : " The little Tayleurs never did that—they were such well-brrred

little children." Jolly hated the little Tayleurs;
Holly wondered dreadfully how it was she fell so short
of them. 'A thin rum little soul,' old Jolyon thought
her—Mam'zelle Beauce.

Luncheon was a successful meal, the mushrooms
which he himself had picked in the mushroom house,
his chosen strawberries, and another bottle of the
Steinberg cabinet filled him with a certain aromatic
spirituality, and a conviction that he would have a
touch of eczema to-morrow. After lunch they sat
under the oak tree drinking Turkish coffee. It was no
matter of grief to him when Mademoiselle Beauce
withdrew to write her Sunday letter to her sister, whose
future had been endangered in the past by swallowing
a pin—an event held up daily in warning to the children
to eat slowly and digest what they had eaten. At the
foot of the bank, on a carriage rug, Holly and the dog
Balthasar teased and loved each other, and in the shade
old Jolyon with his legs crossed and his cigar luxuriously
savoured, gazed at Irene sitting in the swing. A light,
vaguely swaying, grey figure with a fleck of sunlight
here and there upon it, lips just opened, eyes dark and
soft under lids a little drooped. She looked content;
surely it did her good to come and see him ! The selfish-
ness of age had not set its proper grip on him, for he
could still feel pleasure in the pleasure of others,
realising that what he wanted, though much, was not
quite all that mattered.

"It's quiet here," he said; "you mustn't come
down if you find it dull. But it's a pleasure to see you.
My little sweet's is the only face which gives me any
pleasure, except yours."

From her smile he knew that she was not beyond
liking to be appreciated, and this reassured him.

" That's not humbug," he said.   " I never told a woman I admired her when I didn't.   In fact I don't know when I've told a woman I admired her, except my wife in the old days ; and wives are funny."   He was silent, but resumed abruptly :

" She used to expect me to say it more often than I felt it, and there we were."   Her face looked mysteriously troubled, and, afraid that he had said something painful, he hurried on :

" When my little sweet marries, I hope she'll find someone who knows what women feel.   I shan't be here to see it, but there's too much topsy-turvydom in marriage ; I don't want her to pitch up against that."   And, aware that he had made bad worse, he added :   " That dog *will* scratch."

A silence followed.   Of what was she thinking, this pretty creature whose life was spoiled ; who had done with love, and yet was made for love ?   Some day when he was gone, perhaps, she would find another mate—not so disorderly as that young fellow who had got himself run over.   Ah ! but her husband ?

" Does Soames never trouble you ? " he asked.

She shook her head.   Her face had closed up suddenly.   For all her softness there was something irreconcilable about her.   And a glimpse of light on the inexorable nature of sex antipathies strayed into a brain which, belonging to early Victorian civilisation —so much older than this of his old age—had never thought about such primitive things.

" That's a comfort," he said.   " You can see the Grand Stand to-day.   Shall we take a turn round ? "

Through the flower and fruit garden, against whose high outer walls peach trees and nectarines were trained to the sun, through the stables, the vinery, the

Y 2

mushroom house, the asparagus beds, the rosery, the summer-house, he conducted her—even into the kitchen garden to see the tiny green peas which Holly loved to scoop out of their pods with her finger, and lick up from the palm of her little brown hand. Many delightful things he showed her, while Holly and the dog Balthasar danced ahead, or came to them at intervals for attention. It was one of the happiest afternoons he had ever spent, but it tired him and he was glad to sit down in the music room and let her give him tea. A special little friend of Holly's had come in—a fair child with short hair like a boy's. And the two sported in the distance, under the stairs, on the stairs, and up in the gallery. Old Jolyon begged for Chopin. She played studies, mazurkas, waltzes, till the two children, creeping near, stood at the foot of the piano—their dark and golden heads bent forward, listening. Old Jolyon watched.

"Let's see you dance, you two!"

Shyly, with a false start, they began. Bobbing and circling, earnest, not very adroit, they went past and past his chair to the strains of that waltz. He watched them and the face of her who was playing turned smiling towards those little dancers, thinking: 'Sweetest picture I've seen for ages.' A voice said:

"Hollee! *Mais enfin—qu'est-ce que tu fais la—danser, le dimanche! Viens, donc!*"

But the children came close to old Jolyon, knowing that he would save them, and gazed into a face which was decidedly 'caught out.'

"Better the day, better the deed, Mam'zelle. It's all my doing. Trot along, chicks, and have your tea."

And, when they were gone, followed by the dog Balthasar who took every meal, he looked at Irene with a twinkle and said :

"Well, there we are ! Aren't they sweet ? Have you any little ones among your pupils ? "

" Yes, three—two of them darlings."

" Pretty ? "

" Lovely ! "

Old Jolyon sighed ; he had an insatiable appetite for the very young. " My little sweet," he said, " is devoted to music ; she'll be a musician some day. You wouldn't give me your opinion of her playing, I suppose ? "

" Of course I will."

" You wouldn't like—— " but he stifled the words 'to give her lessons.' The idea that she gave lessons was unpleasant to him ; yet it would mean that he would see her regularly. She left the piano and came over to his chair.

" I would like, very much ; but there is—June. When are they coming back ? "

Old Jolyon frowned. " Not till the middle of next month. What does that matter ? "

" You said June had forgiven me ; but she could never forget, Uncle Jolyon."

Forget ! She *must* forget, if he wanted her to.

But as if answering, Irene shook her head. " You know she couldn't ; one doesn't forget."

Always that wretched past ! And he said with a sort of vexed finality :

" Well, we shall see."

He talked to her an hour or more, of the children, and a hundred little things, till the carriage came round to take her home. And when she had gone he

went back to his chair, and sat there smoothing his
face and chin, dreaming over the day.

That evening after dinner he went to his study and
took a sheet of paper. He stayed for some minutes
without writing, then rose and stood under the master-
piece ' Dutch Fishing Boats at Sunset.' He was not
thinking of that picture, but of his life. He was going
to leave her something in his Will ; nothing could so
have stirred the stilly deeps of thought and memory.
He was going to leave her a portion of his wealth, of
his aspirations, deeds, qualities, work—all that had
made that wealth ; going to leave her, too, a part of all
he had missed in life, by his sane and steady pursuit
of it. Ah ! What had he missed ? ' Dutch Fishing
Boats ' responded blankly ; he crossed to the French
window, and drawing the curtain aside, opened it. A
wind had got up, and one of last year's oak leaves which
had somehow survived the gardeners' brooms, was
dragging itself with a tiny clicking rustle along the
stone terrace in the twilight. Except for that it was
very quiet out there, and he could smell the heliotrope
watered not long since. A bat went by. A bird uttered
its last ' cheep.' And right above the oak tree the
first star shone. Faust, in the opera, had bartered his
soul for some fresh years of youth. Morbid notion !
No such bargain was possible, that was the *real* tragedy !
No making oneself new again for love or life or anything.
Nothing left to do but enjoy beauty from afar off while
you could, and leave it something in your Will. But
how much ? And, as if he could not make that calculation looking out into the mild freedom of the country
night, he turned back and went up to the chimney-
piece. There were his pet bronzes—a Cleopatra with
the asp at her breast ; a Socrates ; a greyhound

playing with her puppy ; a strong man reining in
some horses. ' They last ! ' he thought, and a pang
went through his heart. They had a thousand years
of life before them !

' How much ? ' Well ! enough at all events to save
her getting old before her time, to keep the lines out
of her face as long as possible, and grey from soiling
that bright hair. He might live another five years.
She would be well over thirty by then. ' How
much ? ' She had none of his blood in her ! In loyalty
to the tenor of his life for forty years and more, ever
since he married and founded that mysterious thing,
a family, came this warning thought—None of his
blood, no right to anything ! It was a luxury then,
this notion. An extravagance, a petting of an old
man's whim, one of those things done in dotage. His
real future was vested in those who had his blood, in
whom he would live on when he was gone. He turned
away from the bronzes and stood looking at the old
green leather chair in which he had sat and smoked so
many hundreds of cigars. And suddenly he seemed to
see her sitting there in her grey dress, fragrant, soft,
dark-eyed, graceful, looking up at him. Why ! She
cared nothing for him, really ; all she cared for was
that lost lover of hers. But she was there, whether
she would or no, giving him pleasure with her beauty
and grace. One had no right to inflict an old man's
company, no right to ask her down to play to him and
let him look at her—for no reward ! Pleasure must be
paid for in this world. ' How much ? ' After all,
there was plenty ; his son and his three grandchildren
would never miss that little lump. He had made it
himself, nearly every penny ; he could leave it where
he liked, allow himself this little pleasure. He went

back to the bureau. ' Well, I'm going to,' he thought,
' let them think what they like. I'm going to ! '
And he sat down.

' How much ? ' Ten thousand, twenty thousand—
how much ? If only with his money he could buy one
year, one month of youth. And startled by that
thought, he wrote quickly :

" DEAR HERRING,—Draw me a codicil to this
effect : ' I leave to my niece Irene Forsyte, born Irene
Heron, by which name she now goes, fifteen thousand
pounds free of legacy duty.'

　　　　　　　　" Yours faithfully,

　　　　　　　　　　　" JOLYON FORSYTE."

When he had sealed and stamped the envelope, he
went back to the window and drew in a long breath.
It was dark, but many stars shone now.

IV

HE woke at half-past two, an hour which long
experience had taught him brings panic intensity to
all awkward thoughts. Experience had also taught
him that a further waking at the proper hour of eight
showed the folly of such panic. On this particular morning the thought which gathered rapid
momentum was that if he became ill, at his age not
improbable, he would not see her. From this it was
but a step to realisation that he would be cut off, too,
when his son and June returned from Spain. How
could he justify desire for the company of one who had
stolen—early morning does not mince words—June's
lover ? That lover was dead ; but June was a stubborn
little thing ; warm-hearted, but stubborn as wood,
and—quite true—not one who forgot ! By the middle

of next month they would be back. He had barely
five weeks left to enjoy the new interest which had come
into what remained of his life. Darkness showed up
to him absurdly clear the nature of his feeling. Admiration for beauty — a craving to see that which
delighted his eyes. Preposterous, at his age ! And
yet—what other reason was there for asking June to
undergo such painful reminder, and how prevent his
son and his son's wife from thinking him very queer ?
He would be reduced to sneaking up to London, which
tired him ; and the least indisposition would cut him
off even from that. He lay with eyes open, setting his
jaw against the prospect, and calling himself an old
fool, while his heart beat loudly, and then seemed
to stop beating altogether. He had seen the dawn
lighting the window chinks, heard the birds chirp and
twitter, and the cocks crow, before he fell asleep again,
and awoke tired but sane. Five weeks before he need
bother, at his age an eternity ! But that early morning
panic had left its mark, had slightly fevered the will
of one who had always had his own way. He would
see her as often as he wished ! Why not go up to town
and make that codicil at his solicitor's, instead of
writing about it ; she might like to go to the opera !
But, by train, for he would not have that fat chap
Beacon grinning behind his back. Servants were such
fools ; and, as likely as not, they had known all the
past history of Irene and young Bosinney—servants
knew everything, and suspected the rest. He wrote
to her that morning :
"MY DEAR IRENE,—I have to be up in town to-
morrow. If you would like to have a look in at the
opera, come and dine with me quietly . . ."
But where ? It was decades since he had dined

anywhere in London save at his Club or at a private house. Ah! that new-fangled place close to Covent Garden . . .

"Let me have a line to-morrow morning to the Piedmont Hotel whether to expect you there at 7 o'clock.

"Yours affectionately,

"JOLYON FORSYTE."

She would understand that he just wanted to give her a little pleasure; for the idea that she should guess he had this itch to see her was instinctively unpleasant to him; it was not seemly that one so old should go out of his way to see beauty, especially in a woman.

The journey next day, short though it was, and the visit to his lawyer's, tired him. It was hot too, and after dressing for dinner he lay down on the sofa in his bedroom to rest a little. He must have had a sort of fainting fit, for he came to himself feeling very queer; and with some difficulty rose and rang the bell. Why! it was past seven! And there he was, and she would be waiting. But suddenly the dizziness came on again, and he was obliged to relapse on the sofa. He heard the maid's voice say:

"Did you ring, sir?"

"Yes, come here"; he could not see her clearly, for the cloud in front of his eyes. "I'm not well, I want some sal volatile."

"Yes, sir." Her voice sounded frightened.

Old Jolyon made an effort.

"Don't go. Take this message to my niece—a lady waiting in the hall—a lady in grey. Say Mr. Forsyte is not well—the heat. He is very sorry; if he is not down directly, she is not to wait dinner."

When she was gone, he thought feebly: 'Why did

I say a lady in grey—she may be in anything. Sal volatile !' He did not go off again, yet was not conscious of how Irene came to be standing beside him, holding smelling salts to his nose, and pushing a pillow up behind his head. He heard her say anxiously: " Dear Uncle Jolyon, what is it ? " was dimly conscious of the soft pressure of her lips on his hand ; then drew in a long breath of smelling salts, suddenly discovered strength in them, and sneezed.

" Ha ! " he said : " it's nothing. How did you get here ? Go down and dine—the tickets are on the dressing-table. I shall be all right in a minute."

He felt her cool hand on his forehead, smelled violets, and sat divided between a sort of pleasure and a determination to be all right.

" Why ! You *are* in grey ! " he said : " Help me up." Once on his feet he gave himself a shake.

" What business had I to go off like that ! " And he moved very slowly to the glass. What a cadaverous chap ! Her voice, behind him, murmured :

" You mustn't come down, Uncle ; you must rest."

" Fiddlesticks ! A glass of champagne 'll soon set me to rights. I can't have you missing the opera."

But the journey down the corridor was troublesome. What carpets they had in these new-fangled places, so thick that you tripped up in them at every step ! In the lift he noticed how concerned she looked, and said with the ghost of a twinkle :

" I'm a pretty host."

When the lift stopped he had to hold firmly to the seat to prevent it's slipping under him ; but after soup and a glass of champagne he felt much better, and began to enjoy an infirmity which had brought such solicitude into her manner towards him.

" I should have liked you for a daughter," he said suddenly ; and watching the smile in her eyes, went on :

" You mustn't get wrapped up in the past at your time of life ; plenty of that when you get to my age. That's a nice dress—I like the style."

" I made it myself."

Ah ! A woman who could make herself a pretty frock had not lost her interest in life.

" Make hay while the sun shines," he said ; " and drink that up. I want to see some colour in your cheeks. We mustn't waste life ; it doesn't do. There's a new Marguerite to-night ; let's hope she won't be fat. And Mephisto—anything more dreadful than a fat chap playing the Devil I can't imagine."

But they did not go to the opera after all, for in getting up from dinner the dizziness came over him again, and she insisted on his staying quiet and going to bed early. When he parted from her at the door of the hotel, having paid the cabman to drive her to Chelsea, he sat down again for a moment to enjoy the memory of her words : ' You *are* such a darling to me, Uncle Jolyon ! ' Why ! Who wouldn't be ! He would have liked to stay up another day and take her to the Zoo, but two days running of him would bore her to death ! No, he must wait till next Sunday ; she had promised to come then. They would settle those lessons for Holly, if only for a month. It would be something. That little Mam'zelle Beauce wouldn't like it, but she would have to lump it. And crushing his old opera hat against his chest, he sought the lift.

He drove to Waterloo next morning, struggling with a desire to say : " Drive me to Chelsea." But his sense of proportion was too strong. Besides, he still felt shaky, and did not want to risk another aberration like that of last night, away from home. Holly, too, was expecting him, and what he had in his bag for her. Not that there was any cupboard love in his little sweet—she was a bundle of affection. Then, with the rather bitter cynicism of the old, he wondered for a second whether it was not cupboard love which made Irene put up with him. No, she was not that sort either. She had, if anything, too little notion of how to butter her bread, no sense of property, poor thing ! Besides, he had not breathed a word about that codicil, nor should he—sufficient unto the day was the good thereof.

In the victoria which met him at the station Holly was restraining the dog Balthasar, and their caresses made ' jubey ' his drive home. All the rest of that fine hot day and most of the next he was content and peaceful, reposing in the shade, while the long lingering sunshine showered gold on the lawns and the flowers. But on Thursday evening at his lonely dinner he began to count the hours ; sixty-five till he would go down to meet her again in the little coppice, and walk up through the fields at her side. He had intended to consult the doctor about his fainting fit, but the fellow would be sure to insist on quiet, no excitement and all that ; and he did not mean to be tied by the leg, did not want to be told of an infirmity—if there were one, could not afford to hear it at his time of life, now that this new interest had come. And he carefully avoided making any mention of it in a letter to his son. It would only bring them back with a run ! How far this silence was due to consideration for their pleasure, how far to regard for his own, he did not pause to consider.

That night in his study he had just finished his
cigar and was dozing off, when he heard the rustle of
a gown, and was conscious of a scent of violets.
Opening his eyes he saw her, dressed in grey, standing by
the fireplace, holding out her arms. The odd thing was
that, though those arms seemed to hold nothing, they
were curved as if round someone's neck, and her own
neck was bent back, her lips open, her eyes closed. She
vanished at once, and there were the mantelpiece and
his bronzes. But those bronzes and the mantelpiece
had not been there when she was, only the fireplace
and the wall! Shaken and troubled, he got up. 'I
must take medicine,' he thought; 'I can't be well.'
His heart beat too fast, he had an asthmatic feeling in
the chest; and going to the window, he opened it to
get some air. A dog was barking far away, one of the
dogs at Drage's farm no doubt, beyond the coppice.
A beautiful still night, but dark. 'I dropped off,'
he mused, 'that's it! And yet I'll swear my eyes were
open!' A sound like a sigh seemed to answer.

"What's that?" he said sharply, "who's there?"

Putting his hand to his side to still the beating in his
heart, he stepped out on to the terrace. Something
soft scurried by in the dark. "Shoo!" It was that
great grey cat. 'Young Bosinney was like a great
cat!' he thought. 'It was him in there, that she—
that she was—— He's got her still!' He walked to
the edge of the terrace, and looked down into the
darkness; he could just see the powdering of the
daisies on the unmown lawn. Here to-day and gone
to-morrow! And there came the moon, who saw all,
young and old, alive and dead, and didn't care a dump!
His own turn soon. For a single day of youth he
would give what was left! And he turned again towards

the house. He could see the windows of the night
nursery up there. His little sweet would be asleep.
' Hope that dog won't wake her ! ' he thought.
' What is it makes us love, and makes us die ! I must
go to bed.'

And across the terrace stones, growing grey in the
moonlight, he passed back within.

V

How should an old man live his days if not in
dreaming of his well-spent past ? In that, at all events,
there is no agitating warmth, only pale winter sunshine.
The shell can withstand the gentle beating of the
dynamos of memory. The present he should distrust ;
the future shun. From beneath thick shade he should
watch the sunlight creeping at his toes. If there be
sun of summer, let him not go out into it, mistaking it
for the Indian-summer sun ! Thus peradventure he
shall decline softly, slowly, imperceptibly, until impa-
tient Nature clutches his wind-pipe and he gasps away
to death some early morning before the world is aired,
and they put on his tombstone : ' In the fulness of
years ! ' Yea ! If he preserve his principles in perfect
order, a Forsyte may live on long after he is dead.

Old Jolyon was conscious of all this, and yet there
was in him that which transcended Forsytism. For it
is written that a Forsyte shall not love beauty more
than reason ; nor his own way more than his own
health. And something beat within him in these days
that with each throb fretted at the thinning shell.
His sagacity knew this, but it knew too that he could
not stop that beating, nor would if he could. And yet,
if you had told him he was living on his capital, he

would have stared you down. No, no ; a man did
not live on his capital ; it was not done ! The shib-
boleths of the past are ever more real than the
actualities of the present. And he, to whom living
on one's capital had always been anathema, could not
have borne to have applied so gross a phrase to his
own case. Pleasure is healthful ; beauty good to
see ; to live again in the youth of the young—and
what else on earth was he doing !

Methodically, as had been the way of his whole life,
he now arranged his time. On Tuesdays he journeyed
up to town by train ; Irene came and dined with him,
and they went to the opera. On Thursdays he drove
to town, and, putting that fat chap and his horses up,
met her in Kensington Gardens, picking up the carriage
after he had left her, and driving home again in time
for dinner. He threw out the casual formula that
he had business in London on those two days. On
Wednesdays and Saturdays she came down to give
Holly music lessons. The greater the pleasure he took
in her society, the more scrupulously fastidious he
became, just a matter-of-fact and friendly uncle.
Not even in feeling, really, was he more—for, after
all, there was his age. And yet, if she were late he
fidgeted himself to death. If she missed coming,
which happened twice, his eyes grew sad as an old
dog's, and he failed to sleep.

And so a month went by—a month of summer in
the fields, and in his heart, with summer's heat and
the fatigue thereof. Who could have believed a few
weeks back that he would have looked forward to his
son's and his grand-daughter's return with something
like dread ! There was such delicious freedom, such
recovery of that independence a man enjoys before

he founds a family, about these weeks of lovely weather, and this new companionship with one who demanded nothing, and remained always a little unknown, retaining the fascination of mystery. It was like a draught of wine to him who has been drinking water for so long that he has almost forgotten the stir wine brings to his blood, the narcotic to his brain. The flowers were coloured brighter, scents and music and the sunlight had a living value—were no longer mere reminders of past enjoyment. There was something now to live for which stirred him continually to anticipation. He lived in that, not in retrospection; the difference is considerable to any so old as he. The pleasures of the table, never of much consequence to one naturally abstemious, had lost all value. He ate little, without knowing what he ate; and every day grew thinner and more worn to look at. He was again a 'threadpaper'; and to this thinned form his massive forehead, with hollows at the temples, gave more dignity than ever. He was very well aware that he ought to see the doctor, but liberty was too sweet. He could not afford to pet his frequent shortness of breath and the pain in his side at the expense of liberty. Return to the vegetable existence he had led among the agricultural journals with the life-size mangold wurzels, before this new attraction came into his life—no! He exceeded his allowance of cigars. Two a day had always been his rule. Now he smoked three and sometimes four—a man will when he is filled with the creative spirit. But very often he thought: 'I must give up smoking, and coffee; I must give up rattling up to town.' But he did not; there was no one in any sort of authority to notice him, and this was a priceless boon. The servants perhaps

wondered, but they were, naturally, dumb. Mam'zelle
Beauce was too concerned with her own digestion, and
too 'well-brrred' to make personal allusions. Holly
had not as yet an eye for the relative appearance of
him who was her plaything and her god. It was left
for Irene herself to beg him to eat more, to rest in the
hot part of the day, to take a tonic, and so forth. But
she did not tell him that she was the cause of his thinness
—for one cannot see the havoc oneself is working. A
man of eighty-four has no passions, but the Beauty
which produces passion works on in the old way, till
death closes the eyes which crave the sight of Her.

On the first day of the second week in July he
received a letter from his son in Paris to say that they
would all be back on Friday. This had always been
more sure than Fate ; but, with the pathetic impro-
vidence given to the old, that they may endure to the
end, he had never quite admitted it. Now he did, and
something would have to be done. He had ceased to
be able to imagine life without this new interest, but,
that which is not imagined sometimes exists, as the
English are perpetually finding to their cost. He sat
in his old leather chair, doubling up the letter, and
mumbling with his lips the end of an unlighted cigar.
After to-morrow his Tuesday expeditions to town
would have to be abandoned. He could still drive up,
perhaps, once a week, on the pretext of seeing his man
of business. But even that would be dependent on his
health, for now they would begin to fuss about him.
The lessons ! The lessons must go on ! She must
swallow down her scruples, and June must put her
feelings in her pocket. She had done so once, on the
day after the news of Bosinney's death ; what she had
done then, she could surely do again now. Four years

since that injury was inflicted on her—not Christian
to keep the memory of old sores alive. June's will
was strong, but his was stronger, for his sands were
running out. Irene was soft, surely she would do this
for him, subdue her natural shrinking, sooner than give
him pain ! The lessons must continue ; for if they did,
he was secure. And lighting his cigar at last, he began
trying to shape out how to put it to them all, and
explain this strange intimacy ; how to veil and wrap
it away from the naked truth—that he could not bear
to be deprived of the sight of beauty. Ah ! Holly !
Holly was fond of her, Holly liked her lessons. She
would save him—his little sweet ! And with that
happy thought he became serene, and wondered what
he had been worrying about so fearfully. He must not
worry, it left him always curiously weak, and as if but
half present in his own body.

That evening after dinner he had a return of the
dizziness, though he did not faint. He would not ring
the bell, because he knew it would mean a fuss, and
make his going up on the morrow more conspicuous.
When one grew old, the whole world was in conspiracy
to limit freedom, and for what reason ?—just to keep
the breath in him a little longer. He did not want it
at such cost. Only the dog Balthasar saw his lonely
recovery from that weakness ; anxiously watched him
go to the sideboard and drink some brandy, instead
of giving him a biscuit. When at last he felt able to
tackle the stairs he went up to bed. And, though still
shaky next morning, the thought of the evening
sustained and strengthened him. It was always such
a pleasure to give her a good dinner—he suspected her
of under-eating when she was alone ; and, at the opera
to watch her eyes glow and brighten, the unconscious

smiling of her lips. She hadn't much pleasure, and
this was the last time he would be able to give her that
treat. But when he was packing his bag he caught
himself wishing he had not the fatigue of dressing for
dinner before him, and the exertion, too, of telling her
about June's return.

The opera that evening was ' Carmen,' and he chose
the last *entr'acte* to break the news, instinctively putting
it off till the latest moment. She took it quietly,
queerly ; in fact, he did not know how she had taken
it before the wayward music lifted up again and silence
became necessary. The mask was down over her face,
that mask behind which so much went on that he could
not see. She wanted time to think it over, no doubt !
He would not press her, for she would be coming to
give her lesson to-morrow afternoon, and he should
see her then when she had got used to the idea. In the
cab he talked only of the Carmen ; he had seen
better in the old days, but this one was not bad at all.
When he took her hand to say good-night, she bent
quickly forward and kissed his forehead.

" Good-bye, dear Uncle Jolyon, you have been so
sweet to me."

"To-morrow then," he said. "Good-night. Sleep
well." She echoed softly : " Sleep well ! " and in
the cab window, already moving away, he saw her face
screwed round towards him, and her hand put out in
a gesture which seemed to linger.

He sought his room slowly. They never gave him
the same, and he could not get used to these ' spick-
and-spandy ' bedrooms with new furniture and grey-
green carpets sprinkled all over with pink roses. He
was wakeful and that wretched Habanera kept throbbing in his head. His French had never been equal

to its words, but its sense he knew, if it had any sense,
a gipsy thing—wild and unaccountable. Well, there
was in life something which upset all your care and
plans—something which made men and women dance
to its pipes. And he lay staring from deep-sunk eyes
into the darkness where the unaccountable held sway.
You thought you had hold of life, but it slipped away
behind you, took you by the scruff of the neck, forced
you here and forced you there, and then, likely as not,
squeezed life out of you ! It took the very stars like
that, he shouldn't wonder, rubbed their noses together
and flung them apart ; it had never done playing its
tricks. Five million people in this great blunderbuss
of a town, and all of them at the mercy of that Life-
Force, like a lot of little dried peas hopping about on
a board when you struck your fist on it. Ah, well !
Himself would not hop much longer—a good long
sleep would do him good !

How hot it was up here !—how noisy ! His forehead
burned ; she had kissed it just where he always worried ;
just there—as if she had known the very place and
wanted to kiss it all away for him. But, instead, her
lips left a patch of grievous uneasiness. She had never
spoken in quite that voice, had never before made that
lingering gesture, or looked back at him as she drove
away. He got out of bed and pulled the curtains aside ;
his room faced down over the river. There was little air,
but the sight of that breadth of water flowing by, calm,
eternal, soothed him. 'The great thing,' he thought, 'is
not to make myself a nuisance. I'll think of my little
sweet, and go to sleep.' But it was long before the
heat and throbbing of the London night died out into
the short slumber of the summer morning. And old
Jolyon had but forty winks.

When he reached home next day he went out to the
flower garden, and with the help of Holly, who was very
delicate with flowers, gathered a great bunch of carnations. They were, he told her, for ' the lady in grey '
—a name still bandied between them ; and he put
them in a bowl in his study where he meant to tackle
Irene the moment she came, on the subject of June
and future lessons. Their fragrance and colour would
help. After lunch he lay down, for he felt very tired,
and the carriage would not bring her from the station
till four o'clock. But as the hour approached he grew
restless, and sought the schoolroom, which overlooked
the drive. The sunblinds were down, and Holly was
there with Mademoiselle Beauce, sheltered from the
heat of a stifling July day, attending to their silkworms.
Old Jolyon had a natural antipathy to these methodical
creatures, whose heads and colour reminded him of
elephants ; who nibbled such quantities of holes in
nice green leaves ; and smelled, as he thought, horrid.
He sat down on a chintz-covered window-seat whence
he could see the drive, and get what air there was ;
and the dog Balthasar who appreciated chintz on hot
days, jumped up beside him. Over the cottage piano
a violet dustsheet, faded almost to grey, was spread,
and on it the first lavender, whose scent filled the room.
In spite of the coolness here, perhaps because of that
coolness, the beat of life vehemently impressed his
ebbed-down senses. Each sunbeam which came through
the chinks had annoying brilliance ; that dog smelled
very strong ; the lavender perfume was overpowering ;
those silkworms heaving up their grey-green backs
seemed horribly alive ; and Holly's dark head bent
over them had a wonderfully silky sheen. A marvellous, cruelly strong thing was life when you were

old and weak ; it seemed to mock you with its multitude . of forms and its beating vitality. He had never, till those last few weeks, had this curious feeling of being with one half of him eagerly borne along in the stream of life, and with the other half left on the bank, watching that helpless progress. Only when Irene was with him did he lose this double consciousness.

Holly turned her head, pointed with her little brown fist to the piano—for to point with a finger was not ' well-brrred '—and said slyly :

" Look at the ' lady in grey,' Gran ; isn't she pretty to-day ? "

Old Jolyon's heart gave a flutter, and for a second the room was clouded ; then it cleared, and he said with a twinkle :

" Who's been dressing her up ? "

" Mam'zelle."

" Hollee ! Don't be foolish ! "

That prim little Frenchwoman ! She hadn't yet got over the music lessons being taken away from her. That wouldn't help. His little sweet was the only friend they had. Well, they were her lessons. And he shouldn't budge—shouldn't budge for anything. He stroked the warm wool on Balthasar's head, and heard Holly say :

" When mother's home, there won't be any changes, will there ? She doesn't like strangers, you know."

The child's words seemed to bring the chilly atmosphere of opposition about old Jolyon, and disclose all the menace to his new-found freedom. Ah ! He would have to resign himself to being an old man at the mercy of care and love, or fight to keep this new and prized companionship ; and to fight tired him to death. But his thin, worn face hardened into resolution, till it

appeared all jaw.   This was his house, and his affair;
he should not budge ! He looked at his watch, old and
thin like himself ; he had owned it fifty years.   Past
four already !   And kissing the top of Holly's head
in passing, he went down to the hall.   He wanted
to get hold of her before she went up to give her
lesson.   At the first sound of wheels he stepped out
into the porch, and saw at once that the victoria was
empty.

"The train's in, sir ; but the lady 'asn't come."

Old Jolyon gave him a sharp upward look, his eyes
seemed to push away that fat chap's curiosity, and
defy him to see the bitter disappointment he was
feeling.

"Very well," he said, and turned back into the
house.   He went to his study and sat down, quivering
like a leaf.   What did this mean ? She might have lost
her train, but he knew well enough she hadn't.   'Good-
bye, dear Uncle Jolyon.'   Why 'Good-bye' and not
'Good-night ' ?   And that hand of hers lingering
in the air.   And her kiss.   What did it mean ?
Vehement alarm and irritation took possession of him.
He got up and began to pace the Turkey carpet,
between window and wall.   She was going to give him
up ! He felt it for certain—and he defenceless.   An old
man wanting to look on beauty !   It was ridiculous !
Age closed his mouth, paralysed his power to fight.
He had no right to what was warm and living, no right
to anything but memories and sorrow.   He could not
plead with her ; even an old man has his dignity.
Defenceless ! For an hour, lost to bodily fatigue, he
paced up and down, past the bowl of carnations he
had plucked, which mocked him with its scent.   Of all
things hard to bear, the prostration of will-power is

hardest, for one who has always had his way.   Nature had got him in its net, and like an unhappy fish he turned and swam at the meshes, here and there, found no hole, no breaking point.   They brought him tea at five o'clock, and a letter.   For a moment hope beat up in him.   He cut the envelope with the butter knife, and read :

" DEAREST UNCLE JOLYON,—I can't bear to write anything that may disappoint you, but I was too cowardly to tell you last night.   I feel I can't come down and give Holly any more lessons, now that June is coming back.   Some things go too deep to be forgotten.   It has been such a joy to see you and Holly. Perhaps I shall still see you sometimes when you come up, though I'm sure it's not good for you ; I can see you are tiring yourself too much.   I believe you ought to rest quite quietly all this hot weather, and now you have your son and June coming back you will be so happy.   Thank you a million times for all your sweetness to me.

" Lovingly your
" IRENE."

So, there it was ! Not good for him to have pleasure and what he chiefly cared about ; to try and put off feeling the inevitable end of all things, the approach of death with its stealthy, rustling footsteps.   Not good for him ! Not even she could see how she was his new lease of interest in life, the incarnation of all the beauty he felt slipping from him !

His tea grew cold, his cigar remained unlit ; and up and down he paced, torn between his dignity and his hold on life.   Intolerable to be squeezed out slowly, without a say of your own, to live on when your will was in the hands of others bent on weighing you to the

ground with care and love. Intolerable! He would
see what telling her the truth would do—the truth
that he wanted the sight of her more than just a
lingering on. He sat down at his old bureau and
took a pen. But he could not write. There was something revolting in having to plead like this; plead that
she should warm his eyes with her beauty. It was
tantamount to confessing dotage. He simply could
not. And instead, he wrote:

"I had hoped that the memory of old sores would not
be allowed to stand in the way of what is a pleasure and
a profit to me and my little grand-daughter. But old
men learn to forego their whims; they are obliged to,
even the whim to live must be foregone sooner or later;
and perhaps the sooner the better.

                              "My love to you,
                                   "JOLYON FORSYTE."

'Bitter,' he thought, 'but I can't help it. I'm
tired.' He sealed and dropped it into the box for the
evening post, and hearing it fall to the bottom, thought:
'There goes all I've looked forward to!'

That evening after dinner which he scarcely touched,
after his cigar which he left half-smoked for it made
him feel faint, he went very slowly upstairs and stole
into the night-nursery. He sat down on the window-
seat. A night-light was burning, and he could just
see Holly's face, with one hand underneath the cheek.
An early cockchafer buzzed in the Japanese paper
with which they had filled the grate, and one of the
horses in the stable stamped restlessly. To sleep like
that child! He pressed apart two rungs of the venetian
blind and looked out. The moon was rising, blood-red.
He had never seen so red a moon. The woods and fields
out there were dropping to sleep too, in the last glimmer

of the summer light.   And beauty, like a spirit, walked.
' I've had a long life,' he thought, ' the best of nearly
everything.   I'm an ungrateful chap ; I've seen a lot
of beauty in my time.   Poor young Bosinney said I had
a sense of beauty.   There's a man in the moon to-night ! '
A moth went by, another, another.   ' Ladies in
grey ! ' He closed his eyes.   A feeling that he would
never open them again beset him ; he let it grow, let
himself sink ;   then, with a shiver, dragged the lids
up.   There was something wrong with him, no doubt,
deeply wrong ; he would have to have the doctor after
all.   It didn't much matter now ! Into that coppice
the moonlight would have crept ;   there would be
shadows, and those shadows would be the only things
awake.   No birds, beasts, flowers, insects ;   just the
shadows—moving ;   ' Ladies in grey ! ' Over that log
they would climb ;   would whisper together.   She and
Bosinney ! Funny thought ! And the frogs and little
things would whisper too ! How the clock ticked, in
here ! It was all eerie—out there in the light of that
red moon ;   in here with the little steady night-light
and the ticking clock and the nurse's dressing-gown
hanging from the edge of the screen, tall, like a woman's
figure.   ' Lady in grey ! '   And a very odd thought
beset him :   Did she exist ?   Had she ever come at
all ? Or was she but the emanation of all the beauty
he had loved and must leave so soon ? The violet-grey
spirit with the dark eyes and the crown of amber hair,
who walks the dawn and the moonlight, and at bluebell time ? What was she, who was she, did she exist ?
He rose and stood a moment clutching the window-sill,
to give him a sense of reality again ;   then began
tiptoeing towards the door.   He stopped at the foot
of the bed ;   and Holly, as if conscious of his eyes fixed

on her, stirred, sighed, and curled up closer in defence. He tiptoed on and passed out into the dark passage ; reached his room, undressed at once, and stood before a mirror in his night-shirt. What a scarecrow— with temples fallen in, and thin legs ! His eyes resisted his own image, and a look of pride came on his face. All was in league to pull him down, even his reflection in the glass, but he was not down—yet ! He got into bed, and lay a long time without sleeping, trying to reach resignation, only too well aware that fretting and disappointment were very bad for him.

He woke in the morning so unrefreshed and strength-less that he sent for the doctor. After sounding him, the fellow pulled a face as long as your arm, and ordered him to stay in bed and give up smoking. That was no hardship ; there was nothing to get up for, and when he felt ill, tobacco always lost its savour. He spent the morning languidly with the sunblinds down, turning and re-turning *The Times*, not reading much, the dog Balthasar lying beside his bed. With his lunch they brought him a telegram, running thus : ' Your letter received coming down this afternoon will be with you at four-thirty. Irene.'

Coming down ! After all ! Then she did exist—and he was not deserted. Coming down ! A glow ran through his limbs ; his cheeks and forehead felt hot. He drank his soup, and pushed the tray-table away, lying very quiet until they had removed lunch and left him alone ; but every now and then his eyes twinkled. Coming down ! His heart beat fast, and then did not seem to beat at all. At three o'clock he got up and dressed deliberately, noiselessly. Holly and Mam'zelle would be in the schoolroom, and the servants asleep after their dinner, he shouldn't wonder. He opened

his door cautiously, and went downstairs.   In the hall
the dog Balthasar lay solitary, and, followed by him,
old Jolyon passed into his study and out into the
burning afternoon.   He meant to go down and meet her
in the coppice, but felt at once he could not manage
that in this heat.   He sat down instead under the oak
tree by the swing, and the dog Balthasar who also felt
the heat, lay down beside him.   He sat there smiling.
What a revel of bright minutes !   What a hum of
insects, and cooing of pigeons !   It was the quintessence
of a summer day.   Lovely !   And he was happy—
happy as a sand-boy, whatever that might be.   She
was coming ;   she had not given him up !   He had
everything in life he wanted—except a little more
breath, and less weight—just here !   He would see her
when she emerged from the fernery come, swaying just
a little, a violet-grey figure passing over the daisies
and dandelions and ' soldiers ' on the lawn—the
soldiers with their flowery crowns.   He would not
move, but she would come up to him and say :   ' Dear
Uncle Jolyon, I am sorry ! ' and sit in the swing and
let him look at her and tell her that he had not been very
well but was all right now ;   and that dog would lick
her hand.   That dog knew his master was fond of
her ;   that dog was a good dog.

It was quite shady under the tree ;   the sun could
not get at him, only make the rest of the world bright
so that he could see the Grand Stand at Epsom away
out there, very far, and the cows cropping the clover
in the field and swishing at the flies with their tails.
He smelled the scent of limes, and lavender.   Ah !
that was why there was such a racket of bees.   They
were excited—busy, as his heart was busy and excited.
Drowsy, too, drowsy and drugged on honey and

happiness; as his heart was drugged and drowsy. Summer—summer—they seemed saying; great bees and little bees, and the flies too !

The stable clock struck four; in half an hour she would be here. He would have just one tiny nap, because he had had so little sleep of late; and then he would be fresh for her, fresh for youth and beauty, coming towards him across the sunlit lawn—lady in grey ! And settling back in his chair he closed his eyes. Some thistledown came on what little air there was, and pitched on his moustache more white than itself. He did not know; but his breathing stirred it, caught there. A ray of sunlight struck through and lodged on his boot. A humble-bee alighted and strolled on the crown of his Panama hat. And the delicious surge of slumber reached the brain beneath that hat, and the head swayed forward and rested on his breast. Summer—summer ! So went the hum.

The stable clock struck the quarter past. The dog Balthasar stretched and looked up at his master. The thistledown no longer moved. The dog placed his chin over the sunlit foot. It did not stir. The dog withdrew his chin quickly, rose, and leaped on old Jolyon's lap, looked in his face, whined; then, leaping down, sat on his haunches, gazing up. And suddenly he uttered a long, long howl.

But the thistledown was still as death, and the face of his old master.

Summer—summer—summer ! The soundless foot-steps on the grass !

1917.

THE WHITEFRIARS PRESS, LTD., LONDON AND TONBRIDGE.